FABULOUS TIME

was born in Kuala Belait, British Borneo, and spent her
in Venezuela and Jamaica. She now reviews fiction for
which she also writes on travel. Her second novel, *Undis-*
received the 1999 Encore Award. Both this and her first
cide (1992), are published in Penguin.

Fabulous Time

CHRISTINA KONING

PENGUIN BOOKS

PENGUIN BOOKS

Published by the Penguin Group
Penguin Books Ltd, 80 Strand, London WC2R ORL, England
Penguin Putnam Inc., 375 Hudson Street, New York, New York 10014, USA
Penguin Books Australia Ltd, 250 Camberwell Road, Camberwell,
Victoria 3124, Australia
Penguin Books Canada Ltd, 10 Alcorn Avenue, Toronto, Ontario, Canada M4V 3B2
Penguin Books India (P) Ltd, 11 Community Centre, Panchsheel Park,
New Delhi – 110 017, India
Penguin Books (NZ) Ltd, Cnr Rosedale and Airborne Roads,
Albany, Auckland, New Zealand
Penguin Books (South Africa) (Pty) Ltd, 24 Sturdee Avenue,
Rosebank 2196, South Africa

Penguin Books Ltd, Registered Offices: 80 Strand, London WC2R ORL, England

www.penguin.com

First published by Viking 2000
Published in Penguin Books 2001
1

The moral right of the author has been asserted

'Sunny Afternoon': Words and music by Ray Davies © 1966 Davray Music Ltd and Carlin
Music Corp NW1 8BD. All rights reserved. Used by permission

'I'm a Believer': Words and music by Neil Diamond © 1966 Colgems-EMI Music
Inc./Stonebridge Music USA/Sony/ATV Music Publishing. Reproduced by
permission of Screen-Gems/EMI Music Ltd, London WC2H 0QV

Set in Monotype Dante
Printed in England by Clays Ltd, St Ives plc

For Anna and James

Acknowledgements

I should like to thank the Society of Authors, whose generosity at a critical stage during the writing of this book made finishing it a lot easier; Derek Johns, whose advice was equally invaluable; and Anya Waddington, whose editorial comments were, as ever, finely judged.

Contents

I

Some Quaint Types

It is as she is painting the rose that she knows something is wrong. The realization comes upon her all at once. She has just finished one petal – a sumptuous curving shape, like a shell, or a baby's ear – and is dipping her brush before starting another, when she feels that clutch around the heart that presages disaster. The feeling is so sharp that she wants to cry out, restraining herself just in time because it might disturb Wilfred; although that's silly, she thinks, because Wilfred is dead.

With fingers that tremble only a little she completes the action she has begun, swilling the brush around in the jar until the clear water turns cloudy; the sound it makes as it clinks against the glass seeming to her heightened senses to be the sound her heart is making as it knocks against her ribcage. Only when she has washed the brush and dried it – squeezing out the excess moisture against the rim of the jar and then laying the brush down carefully – does she surrender to the rush of a feeling she finds herself unable to name. Fear, perhaps? Her hands are trembling so badly she has to press the palms together to control the impulse. Fear – but also something else. Exhilaration; excitement; even a kind of joy.

Slowly – because that is the way it has to be these days – she lowers herself into the armchair, her hands still clasped together, feeling the smooth worn upholstered sides close around her, the comforting solidity of things. She sits very still, looking out at the room in which all the objects are familiar to her: the gate-leg table now strewn with her paints; the glass-fronted cabinet with its chipped china ornaments and tarnished silver; the worn Turkey carpet, its colours darkened by age and dirt; the piano, massive and dark as a coffin, with its stained ivory keys. She considers, too, the blackened mirror, the books with their mildewed covers, the portrait of her mother that hangs on the brass chain – as if these objects might hold the key to her unquiet state of mind. Her gaze comes to rest upon the rose. A beautiful thing, creamy white flushed with dull pink, dropping its petals on the table's smeared surface. She will never paint it now.

Connie feels the silence grow around her. The house ticks like a breathing machine: quiet creaks and groans; a footfall overhead. Wilfred, she thinks automatically; remembering, in the same instant. Not Wilfred. A ghost, then? The sound of a mouse gnawing behind the wainscot; the fall of dust; a spider spinning its web. Implacable, invisible – the passage of air across a room as someone closes a door in another part of the house. Voices. Whispers. The shifting of shadows as the sun moves around.

Again the feeling. Her fingers clutch and uncurl in her lap.

'Is it Death?' she wonders aloud (not an unusual thing for one who often goes for days without hearing another voice). But the feeling passes, the clutching in her chest below the breastbone subsides and she thinks quite calmly, no. Not Death. At least, she amends this, again speaking aloud to the listening room – not yet.

The dust falls, and the house is given over to emptiness and silence. Connie sits and dreams, and thinks of everything she has lost. For her, the past is a series of interconnecting chambers through which she walks, picking up objects and setting them down again. Inconsequential things – the smell arising from the opened lid of a sandalwood box; a smear of rose madder on the edge of a plate – provide the key to rooms she hasn't visited in decades.

Just now, she is thinking about Guy Strickland, although it's years since she had reason to revisit *that* particular chamber of horrors. *Be bold, be bold, but not too bold – lest your heart's blood should run cold* . . . Bluebeard, indeed. Not that she'd been unaware of his reputation on that score. Edith Challoner had warned her that he was a bad lot, their first or second day out – just before they'd hit that sticky patch in the Bay of Biscay. 'An artist, my dear – need one say more?' Then, seeing the look on Connie's face – 'Oh, sorry. I was forgetting. You dabble, too, don't you? But you *know* what I mean. These chaps are all the same. Rumour has it –' here Edith had lowered her voice, leaning across the table with a conspiratorial air – 'he's had to leave England in rather a hurry, if you follow me . . .' Edith could always be relied on for that kind of story. 'According to Marjorie – who knows the family quite well, because she was engaged to the younger brother before that unfortunate business with the gamekeeper – he (Guy S., that is, not the brother) has been given an ultimatum to leave the country until all the fuss has died down (the girl's no better than she should be, of course, but still) and so Shanghai's the obvious place for him, don't you see? There's an uncle out there, according to Marjorie (*sweet* girl – did you ever meet her?). Owns half of Shanghai, apparently. The uncle, that is, not Marjorie. The idea is to ship the black sheep out there for a year or two, Marjorie says. Find him a job – and perhaps a wife into the bargain . . . So you see,' Edith had concluded, with her customary air of malicious enjoyment, 'you really don't want to set your sights on *him*.' And Connie, laughing, had replied, 'Oh, don't worry. He's not my type.'

3

What her type *was*, she'd yet to discover. Although the fellow was attractive enough: tall and blond, with a handsome face and the easy, arrogant manners of the well-born. She'd met men like him at the Slade – dilettantes, for the most part; living off family money while they played at being painters. Now she came to think of it, there had been talk of a Strickland. One of John's acolytes, she rather thought – a flamboyant lot *they* were, given to sweeping around in capes and those soft hats that only artists and poseurs wore. She wondered if it could have been the same man; not that she cared. All that sort were the same. Too pleased with themselves by half.

It wasn't until a week after the conversation with Edith that she actually spoke to Strickland. They were through the worst of the storms by then, although it was still pretty choppy. She'd been up on deck with her sketchbook, fiddling with a drawing that wouldn't come right and trying to expel the lingering stench of seasickness from her nostrils, when she became aware that someone was watching her. She was used to this (you couldn't draw and expect not to attract a crowd from time to time) and so paid no attention. Only when he came up to her and, without a by-your-leave, took the book from her hands and leafed through it did she realize who it was. 'Not bad,' he'd said carelessly, handing the sketches back when he'd looked his fill. 'If you like, I'll show you some of mine.' She'd opened her mouth to say no. 'I don't mind,' was what she said.

And so, thrown together in that closed world, they'd become, if not exactly friends, then more than acquaintances.

'Tell me about yourself,' he'd said that first evening, as, escaping the polite society of 'A' deck, with its bejewelled matrons playing piquet and loudly convivial groups of 'China hands', they'd found themselves alone. 'What takes you to Shanghai?'

When she'd started to explain about the Selbys, and their pressing need for a mother's help during Lily's forthcoming confinement, he'd cut her off with a gesture of impatience. 'That isn't what I meant. You must have some other reason. Is it a husband you're after? Some dull young man who'll save you from the worse fate of being left on the shelf? Or is it something else?'

She'd hesitated, wondering how far to trust him. 'I wanted to get away,' she'd said at last.

He'd raised an eyebrow. 'And you think the Police Commissioner's household offers your best chance of escape?'

'There wasn't an awful lot of choice,' Connie'd said.

'I suppose not.' He'd stood silently for a while, smoking his cigarette and looking out at the vastness of the night sea, flecked here and there with the phosphorescence of a breaking wave. 'Well,' he'd said. 'I wish you all the luck in the world. Only don't expect too much . . .'

Of course, she hadn't been entirely straight with Strickland – there had been reasons apart from her own ennui which had prompted her acceptance of Cousin Lily's offer. Her father's threatened withdrawal of her allowance, for a start. She wasn't due to come into the money from Great-Aunt Dolly until her twenty-eighth birthday – which was still four years away. Her father had intimated that he hoped to see her married – 'settled' was how he put it – well before that.

So Strickland's observations about finding a husband weren't so far off the mark – although if Connie herself had any say in the matter, she'd prefer not to marry at all. A stupid business all round, with that ridiculous pretence about being in love, when everyone knew it was all about hard cash. A financial transaction, with herself as the bill of goods. She'd said as much to her father and he'd flown into one of his rages. 'You talk some sense into her,' he'd shouted at her mother (who'd of course been listening at the door of the study and had heard every word). 'I've done with her.'

Then it had been up to Mama to try and smooth things over – although if anything she was keener on the whole idea of marriage than Connie's father. She'd already managed the trick with her youngest daughter (but then Peggy was such a pet) and with Leonora's looks it wouldn't be long before she was settled (although the silly girl had ideas about going on the stage). Getting dear Constance off her hands was proving more of a trial. It had been a mistake to let the girl have her way about the Slade. Three years which could have been spent finding her a suitable husband had been wasted, messing about with paint and charcoal, and picking up a lot of silly ideas. Financial transactions, indeed. Anyone would think they were living in an age of arranged marriages.

Constance had always been difficult, even as a child. Preferring to romp around with Hugh and his friends, bird's-nesting and climbing trees, instead of settling down with her needlework, like dear Peggy and Leonora. So it was a bit of luck, Helen Joliffe thought, that Lily's letter was still awaiting a reply. *I did wonder if one of your girls might like a change of scene. Shanghai is very pretty at this time of year. Freddie knows some very nice people – not all of them stuffy old married types! There's quite a crowd of ambitious young chaps working their way up through the Service, or doing interesting things in Tea . . .*

So it had been decided. As far as Connie herself was concerned, it wasn't such a bad idea to get out of London. The whole Slade thing was becoming a shade incestuous. If you weren't a protégée of Tonks or Brown (and she'd never been able to stomach all the toadying one had to do) your work didn't have a hope of selling. Women painters – the very idea was anathema to some. At least Shanghai might offer fresh perspectives, she thought. Surely people there wouldn't hold such narrow views? She'd been wrong about that, as it happened.

Ray is sulking, because Sandy has snapped at him twice in the past half-hour, and it wasn't his fault they'd taken the wrong turning after Lewes. He hadn't wanted to come on this jaunt in the first place. In fact if things hadn't been getting a bit sticky in Brighton he'd have told Sandy where to put his weekend in the country. It made you laugh the way he said it. *My aunt's place in Sussex.* Very lah-di-dah. We could motor down for lunch if you like, he'd said. Give Auntie a nice surprise.

Sandy, glancing sideways, catches the look of disdain on his passenger's face and feels his heart turn over. How adorable he looked when he was cross. And of course it wasn't fair to blame him for getting them lost. He didn't know the country-side the way Sandy did, growing up in the slums of Deptford or wherever it was, poor love.

'Sorry for being a grumpy old bear,' he says huskily. He wonders if he dare take his hand off the wheel for a moment to give Ray's knee a squeeze, but thinks better of it. Ray could be touchy at times.

Ray's only reply is a shrug. His profile (such a charming one!) fixed on the undistinguished Sussex landscape as if it were the most interesting thing in the world.

'Won't be long now,' Sandy adds, in the falsely bright tone one uses to a recalcitrant child. 'I wonder if Auntie'll have the sherry out . . .'

Ray makes a noncommittal sound, which Sandy takes for encouragement: prattling on into the silence about his beloved auntie, and what a dear she was, and how good she'd been to him when he had that spot of bother with Lily Law, and how much he'd loved spending his hols there as a boy, and how jolly it all was, with the orchard where he'd scraped his knees scrumping for apples and the garden with its hollyhocks – 'taller than I was, when I was a nipper' – and the big black range in the kitchen, where he'd had his bath in a tin tub – 'before they installed the mod-cons' – and the tea tray brought in at four o'clock with scones and plum cake, and the clock in the hall which tick-tick-tocked until the sound of it entered his dreams, and on and on and on until Ray is almost ready to *scream* with boredom.

Sandy himself, although unconscious of the effect his recital is having on his captive audience, is fleetingly troubled by an awareness of certain discrepancies between his rosy memories and the reality. It wasn't that he was making it up, exactly – the orchard and the kitchen range and the grandfather clock were real enough – it was just that a certain amount of embellishment (poetic licence, you could say) has crept in between his version and the truth. A very clear image of that dark chaotic house, overstuffed with old-fashioned furniture and with the relics of every transaction that has ever taken place there, rises in his mind as he speaks, dispelling the bright visions he has conjured.

'You mustn't think . . .' he starts to say, then hesitates. He so wants Ray to enjoy himself. Indeed, the success of all his hopes depends upon it. 'I mean, it's all a bit different now, of course. Auntie's getting old, poor darling. She's become rather forgetful. And of course it's impossible to get the help these days . . .'

'Look at *that*!' Ray, who stopped listening some time ago, suddenly sits bolt upright.

A racing-green Alfa Romeo, this year's model, is approaching from the opposite direction. The lane along which they are driving is narrow, scarcely wide enough for two vehicles to pass. The oncoming car shows no sign of giving way and so Sandy is obliged to move over. The Morris (which, it has to be said, has seen better days) has to go right up on to the verge so that the shiny green monster can get by.

'Beautiful . . .' Ray makes kissing noises at the car and indirectly at its driver, a spivvy sort in a flat cap and string motoring gloves. 'That's my baby.'

They drive the rest of the way in silence.

Connie wakes with a start, a drying snail's trail of saliva at the corner of her mouth. The sun has moved round and the room is dark and cold. She feels suddenly, fiercely hungry. In the kitchen, among a litter of eggshells and empty sardine tins from which Rufus, it appears, has recently breakfasted, she finds a congealing cup of cold tea. She throws the slops down the sink and inexpertly rinses the cup – one of her mother's best Royal Doulton, only slightly chipped – before looking around for the means to make a fresh one. There is tea, she knows, in the caddy with its Diamond Jubilee portraits and curly Twinings lettering. She has seen it somewhere – but where? After a half-hearted search (Under the table? In the china cupboard?) she gives up the attempt, contenting herself with a slurp of water from the tap and a stale crust rescued from the bucket by the door, to which scraps intended for the goats are consigned; although the goats, like Wilfred, have long ceased to exist.

The kitchen where Connie stands, contentedly munching

her breakfast, is not a large one by the standards of the late Victorian rectory where she spent the first ten years of her life. *That* was a kitchen, if you like, with sculleries and wash-houses to match. Stone sinks. An iron range. There'd been a range here, of course, when she and Wilfred first moved in – a nasty thing that smoked. It is still there, somewhere, buried under the pile of old newspapers, empty jars and bottles and ancient savings coupons with which almost every surface in the house is covered. The Baby Belling she'd bought to heat Wilfred's suppers on was much better. It did for her meals now.

The longer she lives alone, the harder it is to remember that it has ever been otherwise. But then Wilfred had always been more of an absence than a presence: a man so quiet one forgot he was in the room. Towards the end, she'd passed whole days in his company without hearing him utter a word. Sounds he disliked, but other people were what he feared. When visitors called – and there were never many – he'd retreat to the top of the stairs, hiding there in the shadows until Connie had dealt with the intruder. Latterly, he preferred not to leave his room at all, even for meals. Then, as she sat downstairs in the evenings, the sound of his footfall overhead or the sudden flushing of the lavatory was a startling and not wholly comforting reminder of his existence.

It wasn't always so bad, of course. When they were first married he'd liked her to sit with him; even liked to hear her read aloud. The *Waverley Novels* and *King Solomon's Mines*. Kipling's poems. Nothing modern. Wilfred hated anything modern. It was one of the reasons (another being the lack of a proper studio) why, after her marriage, she'd taken up painting in watercolours rather than oils. Abandoning portraiture, life drawing and other unsuitable subjects for the safer realms of still life and landscape painting. These, as it happened, were areas where Wilfred felt at home; in art as in literature, he preferred the known to anything too obscure or difficult. Which ruled out Cubism, Vorticism, Futurism, Dadaism and all the other 'isms' which had been bandied about years before, when Connie was an art student. Modern, all far too modern.

How he'd have hated the Stricklands, Connie thinks, wiping a stray crumb from her chin with the back of her hand. A good job, really, that he wasn't around to see them delivered. Such a strange day that was – last year, or was it the one before? Living alone, one tends to lose track . . . She remembers the van drawing up outside with its consignment of large flat squarish objects wrapped in sacking. Two burly chaps manhandling them into the house ('Sign here please, dear . . .'). Then the moment of truth: unwrapping the layers of sackcloth and brown paper covering the first of the six parcels to reveal what lay beneath. Her own face, as it happened – gazing back at her from the canvas where he'd set her, so many years before, when they were young.

How strange it had been to see herself pictured there, so full of that assurance the young all possessed without knowing that they possessed it; not smiling, but holding the viewer's gaze with a kind of challenge. She'd been rather full of herself, at that age. Twenty-four or five. Silly little fool. Thinking the world was her oyster . . . For a moment, as she stood there, she'd been almost angry with Strickland for visiting such memories upon her. Remembering, in the same instant, that he was beyond her reproaches now . . .

Sighing a little at the memory – which, like a Chinese box, conceals another within it – Connie pads into the drawing room in her stockinged feet. She finds her shoes where she has left them – slipped off while she was dozing – and puts them on. She has never flattered herself that she was tidy, but there are certain standards, after all. Her mother, whose winsome image, dressed in the outlandishly flounced and beribboned fashions of the 1880s, gazes down from the wall above Connie's head, was never seen by her children until midday, when she would appear, immaculately turned out, with gloves, hat and umbrella, for her walk to the shops.

Connie puffs and blows a little as she stoops to put on her shoes. Her feet, once so small and pretty her lover had kissed the soles of them, are now swollen like sausages in their pale-pink lisle stockings. Feeling her head swim with the effort, she crams them in. *There!* She rests for a moment, her hands on her knees, until the black swirling spots in front of her eyes have gone.

Hat, she thinks mechanically, wondering where she left it; guiltily recalling a time when she'd retrieved it (only a bit more shapeless than usual) from Rufus's basket. But the hat, for a wonder, is on the hat stand; triumphant, she pops it on, deftly skewering the dun-coloured felt in place with two long pearl-tipped hatpins. Gloves. Her face, as she smooths out the wrinkles in each grey kid finger, as she has seen her mother do a thousand times, is watchful as that of a small nocturnal creature: mouse-like, it peers from the depths of the hall stand's spotted mirror. A delicate, wrinkled face, slightly flushed with its exertions, beneath a frizz of white curls. It always surprises Connie that her hair has grown so white.

'Now where's that dratted purse?' she demands of the silent house. Humming a little under her breath, she goes in search of it. In the basket? Not in the basket. The chair, then? No. She frowns, and at the same moment a snuffling explosion that never quite achieves the resonance of a bark announces the waddling arrival of Rufus, her cocker spaniel. Rufus is nearly blind, but he has retained a sharp canine intuition for the putting on of hats and the finding of purses.

'In a moment, Rufus. Good boy,' murmurs Connie distractedly. 'Purse, purse, purse, purse . . .'

At last she finds it, innocently resting on top of the mantelpiece clock, at which she has had no other occasion to glance, since, like all the other clocks in the house, it stopped some time ago. The purse having been found, there remains only the business of affixing Rufus's lead – which, since both mistress and dog become breathless easily, takes longer than might be supposed. Keys. 'Where did I put them?' muses Connie. But as she seldom locks her doors, theirs is not a serious omission. Umbrella?

Cautiously, Connie unlatches the front door and puts her head out. It doesn't look like rain, but there is a patch of cloud no bigger than a man's hand on the horizon. Satisfied, Connie addresses her companion. 'I think we'll chance it, Rufus, old boy.'

It is a mile and a half from Dunsinane to the village – a distance which would have been nothing to Connie in the old days, but which she now negotiates in the awareness that her reserves of energy are no longer inexhaustible. Ahead of her blunders Rufus, snorting asthmatically, his stumpy tail wagging from side to side as he stops to identify new smells – the only reliable source of pleasure he has left to him. Connie enjoys these excursions, too – but the growling in her stomach cannot be ignored much longer. 'Shake a leg, Rufus,' she murmurs, giving the lead a gentle tug, so that the dog, splay-footed with resistance, is towed reluctantly away from whatever fascinating object – dead vole or owl's dropping – he has been engrossed in. Grumbling, he shuffles after.

Swinging her free arm energetically, Connie strides out, her mud-brown tweed skirt (a riding habit of Mother's altered to fit) flapping about her calves. She breathes deeply, enjoying the fresh, faintly manure-scented air; the warm breeze in her face. Summer, Connie thinks, her heart lifting. Those rambles with Hugh. The day he'd shown her the kingfisher's nest and she'd leaned out over the brook to see and lost her balance and fallen in. How wet and muddy she'd been. How he'd laughed and laughed. Smiling at the memory of her long-dead brother, Connie doesn't hear the car until it is almost upon her. Then it's only because Rufus has chosen that moment to lumber into the ditch in search of frogs that she avoids being knocked flat. She has time for no more than a fleeting impression of hurtling green, a blaring horn, before the thing is past, leaving nothing but a smell of scorched rubber behind it.

Reaching the village without further incident, Connie makes straight for the post office, which is also the general store. Here, as she waits for Mrs Doherty to finish measuring out the sugar, she glances incuriously around at the shelves with their familiar display of Bisto and Smedley's peas and Lifebuoy soap, and at the Dr Barnardo's boy with his callipered leg next to the bacon slicer, and at the bottles of humbugs and pear drops and winter mixture ranged in rows behind Mrs Doherty's head, and at the knitting patterns – *Smart Pullovers for Active Kiddies* – and at the copies of *The Lady* and *Woman's Own* and the *Daily Express*, with its blaring headline: SOVIET SPIES HELD IN BATTERSEA.

'Fine day,' remarks Mrs Doherty pleasantly, as Connie hesitates between pressed tongue and luncheon meat, and Connie agrees that it is. As she is putting the last of her purchases in her string shopping bag, the jangling of the shop's

bell and a pungent smell of tobacco announce the arrival of
Iseult Barrett-Smythe.

In her customary uniform of men's corduroys and blue-
checked shirt, Iseult is lean as a boy. Her dark-brown hair,
now flecked with grey, is worn in two plaits tied up over her
head. Her bright blue eyes, surrounded by a web of crow's-feet,
regard the world from a tanned and wind-burnt face. Iseult's
chief – that is, only – beauty is her teeth, which are square,
white and strong. Since these are seldom revealed (she is not
a ready smiler), beauty is not a word one would tend to
associate with Iseult. Not that this – if it entered her head at
all – would trouble her. Claptrap, she would call it; poppycock.

'Morning, Mrs D.,' Iseult mutters gruffly. 'Morning, Aunt
Constance.' As she speaks she casts her eyes around, looking
at anything but the person she is addressing. At forty-five,
Iseult is bashful as a child; hopelessly awkward in company,
she is only ever at ease with her employees – the farmhands
and Alf Fletcher, the farm manager, with whose assistance she
runs her late father's farm. Years ago, when Iseult was a shy
twenty-year-old, there'd been gossip in the village about her
and Fletcher, a married man. Much had been made of the fact
that he'd given her a lift once or twice on the back of his
motorbike, and that they'd shared fire-watching patrols for a
night or so. Had she been even dimly aware of this scandalous
talk, Iseult would have laughed like a drain. Not that she didn't
like Alf Fletcher well enough – he was a fine figure of a man
if it came to that, albeit nearly twenty years her senior. But
monkeying with another woman's chap just wasn't on. And
there was the small matter of *noblesse oblige*. Iseult isn't a snob
– not a bit of it. But one had to think of the example one was
setting.

'How's old Rufus?' Iseult inquires tenderly, bending down

to scratch the dog's ears. Iseult much prefers dogs to people –
you knew where you were with a dog. Under her hard caress,
Rufus wriggles ecstatically. 'Good old Rufus. Dear old fellow,'
Iseult murmurs. 'And are you keeping well, Aunt Constance?'
she remembers to add, when her order ('Packet of Woodbines
and a box of matches please, Mrs D.') has been delivered.
Wool-gathering as usual, poor old love, she thinks fondly,
noting Connie's air of distraction.

But Connie is only thinking how brown Iseult has become
these last few years: her face as leathery as an old shoe. You
would never have called her a pretty child, of course, but she
could look very nice when she tried. That time on Sandy's
birthday, when Leonora had made her wear the green velvet.
Her face in the flickering light had been almost beautiful –
golden, rapt – as she'd waited for him to blow out all the
candles.

Poor old darling, Iseult thinks, as the shop bell clanks behind
them and they stand once more upon the windy high street.
Getting a bit rickety on her pins.

'Got the Norton with me,' she offers abruptly. 'Give you a
lift, Aunt.'

Before Connie can protest, she finds herself bundled into
the motorbike's capacious sidecar – a monstrous appendage
resembling the cockpit of an aircraft – with Rufus shivering
across her feet and the canvas hood with its brittle yellow
porthole snapped down over her head.

'Get you home in a jiffy,' Iseult shouts cheerily, donning
vast leather gauntlets and goggles. She flings her leg over the
big machine, stamps down with a booted foot. There is a
shuddering roar and Connie's head jerks forward as they start
to move. 'Hold tight!' yells Iseult above the din, although
Connie is no longer able to hear her. Inside the hurtling capsule

her bones feel as if they are coming loose from their sockets; her teeth buzz with the vibration. At her feet, Rufus whimpers as if at a bad dream. The last time Connie travelled in this fashion had been in another world. It was 1910 or thereabouts. Shanghai. The night of the Embassy dance, when Benjy Furnival gave her a lift on his motorbike along Bubbling Well Road. He'd wanted to kiss her but she'd told him not to be an ass. He was two years younger than she was and, besides, she'd finished with all that sort of thing.

With the wind roaring in her ears and the smell of petrol pleasantly filling her nostrils, Iseult can spare no more than a passing thought for her passenger, crouched small as a child in the sidecar's bucket-seat, her head bobbing up and down as they bounce over the potholes. All getting too much for her, poor old thing. Even the walk to the shops did her in, you could tell. Getting on a bit now of course. Older than Mummy. And *she* hadn't ventured out on her own in months. A vision of her tiny, delicate mother, exquisite in pink crêpe de Chine, reclining on the sofa as she skimmed a Boots novelette, flashed across Iseult's mind. Before she became a farmer's wife, Leonora had been an actress. In old age, she has reverted to the mannerisms of this earlier incarnation.

'Nearly there, Aunt,' bellows Iseult as, with a practised shifting of her body, she brings them around the corner and into the home stretch. Above the screen of trees at the end of the lane the house comes into view. Not a pretty place, Iseult thinks, with the twinge of unease she always feels at the sight of its tall chimneys with their barley-sugar twists and its pointed windows. Like that house in the fairy-tale she'd hated so much as a kid. *Nibble, nibble little mouse.* A memory surfaces of a white face at the window, a shuffling step on the stair. Uncle Wilfred having one of his bad days, Aunt used to say.

They reach the gate. 'Hello! Looks like you've got company,' Iseult observes. A blue Morris Minor is parked untidily half-way in and half-way out of the drive.

The sound of the motorbike's engine has not passed unnoticed, either. As Iseult dismounts and goes to let her passenger out, two figures emerge from the house.

There is a moment's startled pause.

'Well, I'm damned,' says the first of these interlopers. 'This *is* a surprise . . .'

'Hello, Sandy,' mutters Iseult, her face a vivid scarlet.

Both seem equally at a loss for words.

So that for Ray, coming last upon the scene, the encounter has the look of a bleeding what-d'ya-call-it – *tableau* – with the two of them standing there gawping at one another like that, Sandy as red in the face as she is – if it *is* a she and he had his doubts about *that*, dear – and the mad-looking one, the old bat, with one of those fox-fur things with glass eyes that gave you the creeps just to look at, coming slowly up the path behind them with the dog in her arms like a bleeding baby.

If it has crossed Sandy's mind once or twice in the past that Iseult is in love with him, it is a thought he prefers to dismiss as quickly as possible. Oh, when they were kids – no doubt about it – Izzie'd had a bit of a crush on him. Hero worship, you'd call it. And of course (if he says so himself) he was a good-looking lad in those days. Red-gold hair swept back from a forehead you'd have had to call noble. Eyes a piercing blue. A well-shaped mouth. The nose really quite his best feature: neither too big nor too small, with that fine straight bridge. *Grecian*, he supposed you'd say. And he'd always had a pretty good build. A six-footer, even at sixteen. Broad shoulders. A well-turned leg. Oh, yes. He'd been a handsome youth . . .

And she was such a tomboy, dear old Izzie, with her rough brown curls and dirty knees. Always tearing her frocks – it used to drive Leonora wild. Such a terrible hoyden, my daughter, she used to say with that laugh like a tiny scream. How ever did a daughter of mine turn out this way? And it was certainly true that they weren't a bit alike. Unkind people said Leonora'd got her comeuppance for wanting a boy so badly. Instead she got Izzie. Jolly little chap she'd have made, too, with that round freckled face and a grin she seemed to switch on like a light whenever she looked at you. Plucky little kid.

He remembers the day he and Joe Fairfax (now he *was* a nice boy; killed at Monte Cassino, worst luck) had been messing about in the old stables with a rope they'd rigged up from the rafters, shinning up hand over hand and then climbing out along the beam to swing there for a minute or so before dropping back down to the floor – a good fifteen feet it must have been, silly little fools, they might have broken their necks. Izzie had appeared, as she always did sooner or later – like a blessed shadow, Joe said – wanting to see what they were up to.

Noticing her standing there looking at him so trustingly was enough to put the devil in him. I say, Izz, he'd said, ever so casual, I don't suppose you can do this. The dare was hardly out of his mouth before she had both hands on the rope, hauling herself up like a little monkey. Did all right, too, until she was almost at the top. Then just as she'd let go of the rope to grasp the beam, her legs had kicked out and there'd been a flash of white knickers. Oh, oh, I see daylight, Joe'd howled, the coarse oaf – those village louts were all the same, nothing on their minds except S-E-X (although it could work to one's advantage on occasion).

At any rate, it had been enough to distract her. She'd

faltered, dangling there helplessly for a moment, before crashing back down to the floor. She must have winded herself quite badly, because she went white as a sheet, her freckles standing out against the pallor. He'd felt a beast for egging her on, but it wasn't the first time he'd seen her risk her neck. Bit of a kamikaze merchant, old Izz.

And now here she is again, blushing all over her big plain face with the pleasure of seeing him. He wonders with an idle stirring of cruelty whether she's worked out yet just exactly how much of a lost cause he is, or if she still, in her heart of hearts, cherishes fond hopes that one day her passion might be reciprocated. If so, she'll wait a long time, poor old maid, smirks Sandy to himself. Till hell freezes over, in fact.

'Darling Izzie. It's been . . . what?'

'Three years,' says Iseult.

'Is it really? Good Lord,' exclaims Sandy. 'I hadn't realized it was as long as that. Well, I must say, you haven't changed a bit . . .' He is gratified at the paroxysm of shyness this induces in his cousin, who smiles and stammers something incoherent. 'And you, too, Auntie,' he adds, addressing Connie but turning to wink at Ray, who is hanging back from this happy reunion, shy boy. 'I swear you get younger every year – doesn't she, Izzie?'

At this, Iseult, who has been staring fixedly at the ground, rallies her senses. 'Here, Aunt Constance. Give Rufus to me.' She scoops the dead weight of the old dog out of the old woman's arms as if it weighed no more than a kitten, setting the flea-ridden thing down on the path, where it flops like a great slug, positively inviting one to kick it, Sandy thinks spitefully.

'Thank you, dear,' says Connie – the first words she has spoken. 'Why, Sandy, what a pleasant surprise,' she continues, as if people were in the habit of dropping in unexpectedly every day instead of once in a blue moon – or slightly less often than that, to judge from the state of the house, Sandy sniffs disdainfully. 'Such a bit of luck you found me in.'

'Quite a coincidence,' Sandy agrees, winking at Ray, who regards him stonily. 'Allow me to present a friend of mine,' he adds hastily, realizing that he has neglected to perform this introduction. 'Aunt Constance, this is Raymond . . .'

'Brown,' supplies Ray, before Sandy can say anything more. He smiles. As if butter wouldn't melt in his mouth, the little minx, Sandy thinks fondly.

'Charmed, I'm sure.'

In the end, lunch isn't as bad as Sandy had feared it might be when he first set eyes on Auntie – not to mention the house itself. Gawd help us, what was the old girl thinking of, to let it get into such a state? The dust. The cobwebs. And (not to put too fine a point on it) the smell. It was enough to make one want to *heave*. If one were being charitable, one could put it down to the dog.

Really, it was too bad. He'd had such high hopes of this weekend. Even though Ray (bless him!) was being remarkably good about it – so far, at least. He'd sat through the whole of that interminable meal without a murmur, although there'd been moments – when she'd come staggering in with the soup in that huge, cracked old tureen – when his eyes had met Sandy's and it had been as much as Sandy could do not to burst out laughing at Ray's look of mingled outrage and incredulity. When he'd eventually nerved himself to taste it, the soup hadn't been as bad as all that. In fact, considering where it had been made (that kitchen!), it had been surprisingly good. Not packet, either. But then Auntie had always been a decent cook. Fairy cakes. He could taste them now. Light as a feather and with a nice buttery texture that melted on the tongue. Although sometimes you found the odd dog hair or nameless something which was not part of the recipe.

The soup (which Ray has left untouched, Sandy can't help noticing) had been followed by tinned salmon and boiled potatoes – the metallic taste of the former exacerbated by that of the silver dish on which it had been served, part of Great-Aunt Dolly's dinner service, now almost black with age and infrequent cleaning. This had met with the same treatment from Ray as the first course – although he did spend somewhat longer thinking about it, staring at the dish with its flaky mound of pinkish fish as if he had never seen such a thing before in his life.

'Do eat something,' Sandy had urged him, during one of Auntie's absences from the room. 'You'll waste away otherwise.'

But Ray had only frowned and shaken his head, cross boy, as Auntie returned with a tin of stale water biscuits and the cheese on its big Delft platter.

Not that Auntie noticed anything untoward. Away with the fairies as usual, poor old love. That was the disconcerting thing about Auntie – you never knew which version of her you were getting. There was the aunt of Sandy's childhood recollections – what a good sort she'd been. Almost like a child herself in her enthusiasms. Climbing trees and making paper aeroplanes. He remembers the summer they made the kite – 'a proper Chinese dragon, to bring you luck'; the time he'd had German measles and she'd made him the tiger mask – 'So you can see yourself with stripes instead of spots . . .' Oh, she'd been a dear.

Of late, the place of this youthful, resourceful aunt has been usurped by a vaguer creature. Auntie had always had an impractical streak – it came from being a bohemian, Sandy supposed. She'd leave the washing-up for days – and as for the way she dressed . . . 'Constance always looks as if she's been dragged through a hedge backwards,' Mumsie used to say. Auntie wasn't a great one for talking. Conversation bored her – unless it was about things that mattered, she said. Which meant painting, of course. From an early age, he'd got used to hearing words like *chiaroscuro* and *impasto* bandied about. He was used to her silences – but really, with Ray here, it was too embarrassing . . .

So: 'How are you, Auntie?' he says. 'You're looking well.'

She considers this. 'Am I? I suppose I must be, if you say so. I'm not dead yet, at any rate,' she says.

This *is* a good start, thinks Sandy grimly. Why were old people so obsessed by death? You'd have thought they'd avoid the subject, all things considered. He tries another topic.

'Fine weather we're having . . .'

There is a contemptuous snort from Ray.

'Is it?' says Auntie. 'Do you know, I hadn't noticed? I suppose it is . . .'

'Garden's looking nice.' (A shocking fib, but one had to say *something*.)

'Is it? Oh, good . . .'

After that, Sandy gives it up as a bad job. No one could say he hadn't *tried*.

So for a while there is no sound in the big dark room in which the smell of fallen soot mingles with the riper odour of Cheddar just starting to sweat as well as the faint, ghostly whiff of port and cigars emanating from the massive sideboard with its freight of cutlery canteens, silver trays and empty soda-water siphons. Only the tintinnabulation of knives against

23

plates, the creak of a chair as one or other of them uneasily shifts his weight.

And then, just as Sandy has given up hope of ever hearing either of his companions utter another word, Auntie wakes from her dream.

'Tell me,' she says, addressing Ray with what seems to her nephew like extraordinary animation. 'How is your dear mother these days?'

You have to hand it to him, Sandy thinks – he picks up his cue without missing a beat.

'Mummy?' The drawling inflection is just right. The note of languid hesitation. 'Oh, Mummy's very well. Never better, in fact.' The artless smile with which he ends the performance. '*Dear* Mummy . . .'

A real little pro, thinks Sandy, with the mixture of admiration and faint unease Ray's improvisations always inspire in him. Isn't he laying it on a bit thick – even for Auntie?

The really eerie thing is, she doesn't seem to think so. To judge from the way she is smiling – quite like her old self, in the days before she'd started to go gaga – Ray's remark is no more than she's been expecting. It is as if, Sandy realizes with a twinge of jealousy, they'd known one another for ages, instead of a matter of minutes.

Her face lights up. 'Oh, she *is* such a dear, isn't she?' she smiles. 'Such fun. Dear Poppy.'

And Sandy thinks, of course. She's got it into her head he's Julian.

Even from where he's sitting, it's an understandable confusion. Because with that cut-glass profile and those raven locks, Ray, if he did but know it, is the spitting image of Cousin Julian. Those whom the gods love etcetera. Poor Julian had copped it in '42 when his sub was torpedoed off Iceland. Such a shame. He'd looked so delicious in uniform, too, Sandy thinks, quite misty-eyed for a second. About the age Ray is now when it happened. No wonder the old girl was seeing double.

Ray nods and smiles, but wisely says nothing. His eyes, meeting Sandy's over Auntie's head, are cold as stones.

The silence prolongs itself. Looking at Auntie, Sandy sees that she has fallen into a light doze. Her eyes are open, but their expression is vacant. No one at home, thinks Sandy, resisting the temptation to pass his hand in front of her face. *Asleep*, he mouths at Ray.

Ray's answer is a shrug. 'Got a fag?' he demands abruptly – the first words he's addressed to Sandy since their arrival, Sandy realizes.

'Shh,' he hisses, jerking his head towards the still-unconscious Auntie. 'You'll wake her.'

'Won't make much difference, will it?' sniffs Ray.

Connie isn't asleep in fact; it's just that she sometimes forgets to talk. When you live alone, there isn't the same need – and besides, her thoughts are still occupied with Julian. Her brother's only child – and so like him, she recalls. Such a pretty baby. He'd been quite spoilt by them all. Because after Hugh was killed at Ypres, dear Poppy had come to live with them for a while. A household of women they'd been by then, because as well as Hugh, they'd lost Father in the flu epidemic that year. Even after Poppy'd remarried, the boy had come to them for holidays. It had made up for the times when Sandy wasn't there. An engaging little chap he was by then – as dark as Sandy was fair. So handsome in his navy-blue uniform with the gold braid – although of course that was later. Now she looks a bit closer, she can see this one isn't as like him as she'd thought . . .

As if he senses her scrutiny, Ray makes a big show of yawning and stretching. Carelessly he pushes back his chair, making a scraping sound on the bare floorboards, on which sheets of newspaper (now yellow with age) have at one time been spread in lieu of a carpet, during some long ago, never completed spring-cleaning. The room, like the rest of the house, smells of neglect – its wallpaper blotched here and there with damp, so that its intertwining roses seem to have sprouted monstrous growths. The curtains – once a deep crimson but now faded to brownish pink – are mildewed, their cream silk linings hanging in shreds. Expensive, too – like all Auntie's things, thinks Sandy. That was Great-Aunt Dolly's influence, of course – she'd always had an eye for quality. Pots of money, too, in the old days – but that had gone now. All that was left was what he saw around him: the house and its contents. It would come to him in the end, he supposed. His precious inheritance.

With a proprietorial air he runs his hands over the mahogany table – large enough to lay out a corpse on – observing with distaste the sticky bloom upon it. Nothing a good French-polish couldn't cure, but still. The sideboard, too, where Ray is even now poking about among the empty bottles and decanters in search of something to drink, was another nice piece. A bit on the heavy side for modern tastes, but Victoriana was going to be big. Already the smart set, the Mayfair and Chelsea crowd, were getting rid of their Swedish teak and stainless steel and snapping up all this kind of thing. Oil lamps. *Chaise-longues*. You name it, they'd be panting for it.

'Find anything?' he asks Ray.

'Not a sausage,' Ray says flatly.

'There's a village shop,' Sandy ventures, seeing the mutinous frown on the boy's face. 'Sells everything. I could run us down there later, if you like. Pick up some supplies for Auntie . . .'

'I'll walk,' Ray says curtly. 'Need some fags, anyhow.' He pauses in the doorway, his expression suddenly conciliatory. 'Lend us a coupla quid.'

'Typical,' Sandy grumbles fondly. He fishes out a crumpled note or two. 'There. You've cleaned me out. Don't get lost!' he calls after Ray's retreating back.

The sound of a raised voice startles his aunt back to consciousness. She blinks at him. Smiles. 'Silly of me,' she murmurs. 'I must have dropped off for a moment . . .' She looks around her, all vagueness gone. 'Where's your young friend?'

'Oh, him,' says Sandy. 'He had to go out for a bit. Won't be long.'

'I was just about to make some coffee.' Connie gets to her feet – quite sprightly now, Sandy thinks. A tidy little body, his mother would have said. Compact. That round, childlike face he recalls smiling down at him in childhood days – *Now, Sandy, dear, won't you have some more cake?* – has changed not at all. The agelessness of old age, he thinks, rather pleased with the observation. A second childhood. Sans eyes, sans teeth . . .

'And what exactly does he do, your friend?' inquires Auntie crisply.

It was disconcerting how suddenly the old girl could change tack. One minute bats-in-the-belfry, the next all there.

'Raymond?' Sandy blusters. 'He's an artist. Well, more of an art student, really. Still very young, of course. But talented, you know. He . . . er, helps me out in the shop sometimes . . .'

It is hard to lie with Auntie's eyes upon him, their mild gaze bringing back memories of other inquisitions. The time Izzie'd cut her head open when they were climbing on the roof – that had not been his fault, but he got the blame of course. That business with the chickens. Not that Auntie, on those far-of occasions, had ever been severe. Slight reproach was the worst she'd ever mustered – although somehow that was worse, he recalls, than either Father's rages or Mumsie's tears.

'An artist,' she muses. 'Indeed. A painter, would that be?' Auntie's Scotch forebears surfacing in the dryness of tone she adopts. The hint of a rolled 'r'. Painter-r.

'Something like that,' agrees Sandy. He can hardly admit that what Ray actually does is a specialized form of painting politely described as restoration, more brutally called forgery. A branch of the antiques trade, which is Sandy's own pro-fession. Buying cheap and selling dear is how he thinks of it. Although naturally you had to know what you were buying.

Paintings – Victorian, mostly – were a speciality of the firm. And Ray had a talent for this particular branch of the restorer's art. A genius, you might say.

Sandy thinks of the time he first saw Ray, a month ago, in the big first-floor studio in Roly Fisk's house in Royal Crescent. My *pied-à-terre*, Roly called it, with that oh-so-casual air he liked to affect when referring to his not inconsiderable inheritance. *Pied-à-terre* my foot, Sandy thinks sourly. Place must be worth a cool twenty thousand. Immense light rooms that made you feel as if you were on the deck of an ocean-going liner. And the view. On a clear day you could practically see what they were having for breakfast in Boulogne.

He likes that about Brighton as a whole – that feeling of foreignness. As if a little piece of France had somehow detached itself from the mainland and drifted across. Some-thing about the light – the effect of all those white buildings, he supposes – made the place seem almost Mediterranean at times. A city of dreaming piers. Failed bridges, someone had said – but he rather liked them. Extravagant constructions – follies, really – with no earthly purpose except to prove it could be done. The British genius for engineering harnessed in the cause of pure frivolity. Oh yes, he thoroughly approved of piers.

That day he'd walked into Roly's studio they'd all been standing at the window. As befitted the room's graceful eighteenth-century symmetry, there were two of these, opening out on to wrought-iron balconies overlooking the street and, beyond it, the sea. He remembers the light flooding in, dazzling him momentarily so that he stood there blinking. A large mirror over the fireplace filled the room with marine reflections; this was the room's only furniture, apart from a large easel which stood in the centre of the floor and a trestle table strewn with Roly's paints and brushes. If the rest of the house testified to its owner's fondness for fine things, this room was the ascetic exception. My monastic cell, Roly used to say, with his little laugh.

It was here that Roly played the artist, got up for the purpose in a fisherman's smock artfully stained with oil paint; here he entertained boys – his 'models', he called them – beginning with a healthy dose of flattery (My dear! Such skin! Such hair!) and ending with an hour's vigorous sex on his white sheepskin rug. Meeting Ray for the first time, Sandy had assumed he was merely the latest in the series. One of Roly's beauties. He was certainly lovely. Seeing him turn from the window, where he and Roly and the rest of them had been ogling a bunch of townie boys, had been for Sandy a kind of revelation.

Such skin, such hair. Eyes the colour of a stormy sea. Not especially tall, but with a lithe, muscular build – broad shoulders, a tapering waist, a tight round bottom – which was, in Sandy's view, the epitome of masculine perfection. And his clothes: *white trousers* and a striped matelot jersey. Espadrilles. Sandy almost groans aloud. Lust, clouded by envy (damn Roly!), blurs his vision.

With his customary airy insouciance, Roly performs the introductions. 'You know Nigel, of course. And dear Terry. And this is Ray . . .'

Sandy blinks and smiles, trying to recover his equilibrium, as Roly, chattering as usual, draws him away from the others towards the centre of the room. So absorbed is he in his thoughts that it's a moment before he realizes his opinion is being solicited.

'So what do you think?' Roly hisses in his ear. 'Marvellous, isn't she?'

This is blatant even for Roly. The boy's only standing a few feet away, for heaven's sake – even if he is being monopolized by Nigel and co. Surely Roly isn't proposing to give him a blow-by-blow account of his latest conquest's no doubt versatile talents while the subject of his eulogy is still in the room?

Sandy coughs discreetly, signalling his discomfort at this insensitivity.

But then Roly, impatient for a response, plucks him by the sleeve – and Sandy realizes, with a stab of relief, that it's merely his opinion of a picture that is being asked. He is Roly's dealer, after all. Thanks to him, the downstairs rooms of this far from austere residence are crammed with paintings, valuable furniture, bibelots of all kinds. For Roly, in common with a lot of rich people, has more money than taste. He relies on an army of others – interior decorators, landscape gardeners and antique dealers – to supply his deficiencies. When he does try to branch out on his own, the results are usually calamitous. Sandy thinks of the particularly frightful canvas by a minor

Pre-Raphaelite which hangs in Roly's opulent drawing room. *Mariana in the Moated Grange*. Dear God.

He composes his features to address Roly's latest disaster. And sees at once that he has misjudged him. The thing is a masterpiece. Exquisite. A gem.

There it sits, propped up on Roly's easel. Quite a small thing, really – not more than twelve by twenty. A charcoal sketch of a woman's head. Unmistakable, to anyone who knew what they were looking at. Those voluptuous, Cupid's-bow lips. Those languorous eyes. That Grecian nose. The squiggle denoting the hair.

But *what* a squiggle, Sandy thinks, his heart swelling with a complex mixture of emotions, of which envy of Roly Fisk's good fortune and naked desire were uppermost.

'It's . . . it's very fine,' he says when he can trust himself to speak.

'Isn't it, though?' Roly's smile is one of barely suppressed glee. The cat that got the cream, Sandy thinks.

'What did you pay for it?' he asks, as casually as he dares.

To his astonishment and chagrin, Roly bursts out laughing. 'Oh, I say!' he splutters. 'That's too priceless. I might have known that'd be the first thing you'd ask . . .'

Before Sandy, flushing at the insult, can think of a riposte, Roly is calling the others over. 'You'll never guess what dear Sandy just said. It's too funny for words . . .' Tears of laughter standing in his eyes.

'I merely asked what you gave for it,' Sandy says, affronted. 'I might have been able to get a better price for you, that's all . . .'

'I doubt that very much,' Roly gasps, wiping his eyes. 'What do *you* think, Ray,' he says, addressing the marvellous boy. '*Was* it a reasonable price?'

'A bargain, I'd say,' grins loathsome Nigel. His paramour giggles. At this moment, Sandy would like nothing better than to punch both their heads.

'Ray?' Roly persists.

'S'pose so.'

Even in his confusion, Sandy notices that the boy will not meet his eyes. Because – as Roly has to explain, so that he, Sandy, can share the joke – Ray's in a position to say.

'Considering that he drew the precious thing himself not ten minutes before you came in.'

All that Sandy can do is shake his head and laugh, and admit that they'd had him fooled – and he's no mean judge, when it comes down to it. Even once visited the old maestro's studio in Nice. You wouldn't believe the stuff he had lying around the place. Unfinished paintings and sketches. Most of them not half as fine as this one, he adds gallantly.

But while Roly is chuckling over the trick they've played, and calling for a glass of champagne to celebrate – because he's as thrilled with it as if it were a real Matisse, he insists – Sandy finds himself catching Ray's eye. And what he reads there – the look of pure scorn for Roly and his antics – makes his humiliation seem suddenly worthwhile. Because Ray, he sees, with one of those flashes of insight which occasionally surprise him, is in the same boat as he is. Both are hirelings – court jesters – to be pushed around at the whim of a rich man. And he knows (oh, he knows!) exactly how that makes one feel.

2

Chinese Boxes

Connie's memories are a set of magic-lantern slides, lifted one by one from a dusty cardboard box with a pencilled inscription – *Views of Old Cathay* – slipped into place, then brought into sharper focus by the twist of a lens. Here's a street scene with shops selling baskets and cooking pots, and crowds of people in broad-brimmed straw hats going up and down. A river scene with fisherman and tethered cormorants. A carnival procession with a many-legged dragon, and paper lanterns like little moons. A pagoda. A view of the harbour . . .

A long, grey shelf of land emerging from the miasma. A straggle of low, white buildings with, here and there, a taller brick- or stone-built edifice breaking the monotony. Flat roofs of go-downs along the waterfront. Ships lying at anchor, their masts as finely drawn, against the whitish haze, as strokes of a pen. This had been her first sight of the place, from the deck of the SS *Medea*. She remembers the eagerness with which she'd strained for a better view . . .

'Queer-looking place, don't you think?' said a voice in her ear. Guy Strickland. Very dashing in a slouch hat and black velvet jacket – though perhaps somewhat overdressed for the tropics. 'Not a bit what I expected . . .'

She'd murmured something.

'Your people meeting you, I suppose?' Strickland had drawled as if the matter were of little interest to him.

'Yes.'

'Good show.' His eyes scanned the quayside, as if he

33

expected to find a familiar face among that heterogeneous crowd of Chinese coolies in blue pyjamas, scarlet-turbaned Lascars, English naval officers in white ducks, Japanese in silk kimonos and mandarins in long dark robes resembling those of English clergymen. 'Oh, well, must be toddling along,' said Strickland. 'I expect we'll meet, in the way of things, before long . . .'

It wasn't until several weeks later, in fact – by which time she'd settled in to the life of the place, such as it was. An excruciating round of small talk and dull parties, presided over by the matronly figure of her cousin's wife, the insufferably vivacious Cousin Lily. *Don't stand about moping, Constance, dear. There's a nice young man over there who's dying for someone to talk to* . . . Frankly, it had been a relief to escape to the nursery. Children, at least, didn't expect small talk. They didn't blush and stammer and look at their feet, and ask you how you liked Shanghai.

Those first six weeks had been like some dreadful dream. She had traded what independence she had been able to wrest from her life at home for a kind of domestic servitude. Not that she minded that part of it. After the initial awkwardness (*Leo! Daisy! Come and kiss your cousin. She's come all the way from home to look after you* . . .), they'd accepted her readily enough. Jolly little kids. Another picture fills her mind: a wide green lawn across which children, dressed in white, come running. A hand flings something. A red ball spins towards her through the air, describing a perfect arc. She reaches up for it. *Oh, I say! Well caught!* A circle of laughing faces surrounds her: Leo in his sailor suit; Daisy in her smock; the Simpson twins – Maud and Victor. And little Philip, who was to die of yellow fever the following spring . . .

No, it wasn't the time she'd spent in the nursery she'd

grudged, but all the rest of it. Hours frittered away playing piquet or gin rummy in Cousin Lily's brightly lit drawing room, with its overpowering scent of hothouse flowers. Making conversation with some tongue-tied youth invited for her benefit. Yes, she liked Shanghai – what little she had seen of it. No, she had not yet been to the races. Yes, she was perfectly comfortable where she was. No, she did not want her shawl . . .

Escaping from this claustrophobic atmosphere had required a certain resourcefulness. She'd acquired a map of the city without too much trouble. Evading Lily's vigilant eye proved somewhat harder. But in the end, she'd managed it. A judicious bribe to the servant at the gate and she was free, for a few hours at least. So it was that she came to know Shanghai – not the leafy streets of the French Concession, with its pink Italianate palaces, neo-Gothic castles, Tudor cottages and Chinese pavilions, each surrounded by its own high wall, but the real city . . .

The smooth green lawns of the International Settlement give way, in her mind's eye, to the dustier reaches of the Nanking Road, where young girls with painted faces lounged in the doorways of the silk shops, and street vendors hawked their pungent-smelling wares. She'd stopped to watch a street magician pulling coins out of people's ears and paper flowers from empty shopping bags and hadn't been looking where she was going. Next thing she knew, she'd walked slap-bang into Guy Strickland. Handsomer than ever – if a shade more dishevelled – in his white linen suit. 'Miss Joliffe. Or may I call you Constance? It *is* Constance, isn't it?' And, as she'd stood there, gaping like a fish: 'Playing hooky, are we? Oh, don't look so worried. *I* won't tell on you. I say, d'you fancy a spot of tea? There's a good little place not far from here where the

English don't venture as a rule . . .' Taking her arm in his as they'd strolled along the broad avenue, with its fluttering scarlet banners. 'Colourful, isn't it? I get some of my best ideas just rambling around . . .' Over bowls of green tea, he showed her his sketchbook, with the drawings he'd done that day. A study of coolies, their naked backs gleaming with sweat as they pushed a wooden barrow piled high with crates. An old woman in blue cotton trousers and padded jacket, carrying trays of tea and spices suspended from a yoke slung across her shoulders. A smiling girl holding up a live snake. A group of beggars, dressed in rags so shredded and filthy they resembled the plumage of exotic birds . . .

'They're good,' she said.

He shrugged. 'Do you think so? Sometimes I wonder if I'm wasting my time. My uncle certainly thinks so. *He* won't be happy until I'm settled in one of his many counting houses, adding further lustre – or do I mean lucre? – to the family name . . .'

Ray is angry. He feels he has been misled. Dragged down here under false pretences. Sold.

It's all the fault of that Sandy, with his Auntie this and his Auntie that – and all the time making sheep's eyes, the simpering old queen, as if anyone couldn't see exactly what he was up to.

Ahead of him, on the drearily empty road, a wood pigeon struts like a clockwork toy in the dust. Its air of innocent stupidity fills him with rage. Slowly, so as not to alert it, he stoops and finds a nice sharp stone.

'Fat bastard.' He launches the missile. He used to be good at this once.

But instead of the satisfying thud of stone against flesh,

there is nothing but the feathery whirr of wings. From the safe distance of a nearby tree, the bird regards him with its round eye.

'Bastard,' Ray says, with hatred. 'I'll get you yet.'

He continues his hang-dog slouch towards the distant village, his hands sunk deep in the pockets of his windcheater, his eyes moodily scanning the road ahead in search of some new adventure. Around him the woods are loud with the warning cries of birds. The pungent smell of wild garlic lingers under the trees. The ditches are full of flowers.

Oblivious of all this, Ray marches on, his thoughts circling like sun-dazed flies.

Easy pickings, he'd said. The place was stuffed with things, he'd said. You could be sure she didn't know the value of half of it. Glad to get rid of it, most likely, the way these old girls always were. It all belonged to him anyway – or would, in the fullness of time.

Ray curls his lip – a gesture he often practises, although there is no one to see.

The stupid old fool. Anyone with half an eye could see there was nothing worth having. The house was a wreck; anything half decent in it had already gone to pot. He'd had a sniff around while the old dear was wittering on to Sandy about something. Junk. If there'd ever been anything of value it had been got at by woodworm, or mice, or rust, or rot.

The place gave him the heebie-jeebies, that was the truth. Like Dracula's castle or – what was that film he'd seen once? *The Fall of the House of Usher*. All cobwebs and mouldering draperies. And the stench. You didn't get *that* at the flicks, he was glad to say. Wet dog and bad drains and that terrible old-lady smell.

The old woman was nuts. He hated mad people. Cunning,

37

too, you could tell. For all her jabbering on, she knew exactly what was what. Good at hiding things, as well. Old people were like that.

A brief, disagreeable memory of the woman he'd called Mum for the first fourteen years of his life flickers across his mind.

Mum was old – she'd always been old. She wore corsets that creaked and pink bloomers with elastic at the knees. Her hair was a pepper-and-salt frizzle that smelled of fag ash. There was always a fag in her mouth, clamped tight between puckered lips. Swags of loose skin hung under her chin. Deep lines scoured her forehead and ran down from nose to mouth, giving her a permanently disgruntled look.

He was a child of the Change; a mistake, he'd been given to understand. The others had all left home by the time he came along. His brothers – Stan and Walter – were away doing National Service (he'd missed out on all that – good job, too) and Sal was working in some factory. Dad died the year he was born – he had no recollection of Dad. Heart trouble, Mum said, with the air of someone closing a subject.

Sal was the only one he cared about at all. The boys were so much older, with wives and babies of their own, but with Sal it was different. She'd been fifteen when he was born, she'd told him, laughing – not a day more, no matter what anybody said. Sal had boyfriends, too – lots of 'em – but he was her favourite boy. Sometimes when she was visiting she'd sit beside him on the settee and squeeze up close to him as if they were sweethearts, rumpling his hair with her sharp red nails and planting kisses that left cherry-coloured smears at the corners of his mouth, until Mum told her not to be so disgusting.

It wasn't until after Mum had died he learned the truth. Sal said she was surprised he hadn't worked it out for himself, from the resemblance. And of course they were alike – but he'd always put that down to the fact that they were brother and sister. Except that the relationship turned out to be closer than that.

Not that it made a blind bit of difference, Sal said. She was married now, with a kid who knew who his father was, if he got her meaning. She was sorry, but that was how it was going to stay. He was a big boy now – he'd be leaving school soon. Get a girl of his own, too – with looks like his. Take a tip from me – don't put her up the spout, Sal said, with one of her laughs.

Things might have followed a predictable course if it hadn't been for Mr Cauldwell. Mr Cauldwell was the art teacher. He had a wooden leg, pathetic old cripple. Queer, too. You had to hand it to him, though – he knew about art.

Mr Cauldwell had taken an interest in him. Encouraged him, when all the rest of them – that bastard maths teacher for one – had written him off as a lost cause.

It was through Mr Cauldwell that he'd met Roly and the rest of that Brighton lot. It was at one of those evenings – soirées, he called them – at the Nag's Head in Borough High Street. Old Cauldie had asked him along, to meet some old college chums of his he thought Ray might take a shine to. It'd help Ray's art appreciation no end, he'd said. Mingling with real artists. Not that *he* gave a toss, but it was a night out. Old Cauldie was usually pretty free with his cash. He'd stand drinks all night and expect nothing in return – or he might have expected it, but he didn't get it. *Dear boy*, he'd say when he got squiffy, his eyes filling with tears, the silly old fool. *Has anyone ever told you you have a look of Donatello's* David?

Sentimental, the poor old queen – the way they all were. Too nicely brought up, most of 'em, that was their trouble.

For himself, he liked a nice hard fuck from a rough boy under the railway arches, or behind the wall of the Seamen's Mission on Jamaica Road. A Deptford lad he was, born and bred. He didn't hold with nancys.

That first night they'd been all over him. Couldn't tear their eyes away. *Who's the girlfriend?* That had been Higgs. Henrietta, they called her. Big blond with too much pancake and a five o'clock shadow. Little Ryan was there – the one that'd topped himself a few months after. They were like that, the arty ones. Unstable. Still, it was a shame.

Roly was there that night, too. Sitting in the corner – not saying a word at first, just looking him up and down. Licking his lips, the dirty old bugger. Lovely manners, though. Refined, Sal would have said. You'd never have guessed he could be thinking those thoughts all the time. *Crispin! Do introduce your young friend* . . . Old Cauldie blushing all over his face. *Such a talented boy. One of my best pupils, in fact.* And Roly: *I can believe it, dear heart* . . .

He'd gone back with Roly that night, in Roly's sports car. Poor old Cauldie didn't stand a chance. Not that Roly was up to much in the looks department, but he made up for it where the readies were concerned. One look at that fabulous house, stuffed with real antiques and paintings in big gilt frames, had been all it took to convince Ray he'd made the right choice. And Roly'd been generous enough at first. Buying him things and taking him round his swanky friends' houses. *This is Raymond – my latest model, you know* . . . He was another one who liked to call himself an artist.

It was Roly who'd introduced him to Sandy. *Just your type, dear. I know you like them tall* . . . He'd wanted to get shot of Ray, that's all. Other fish to fry. Types like Roly were all the same. No sooner had they got what they wanted than they wanted something – or someone – else. Ray wasn't stupid. He could take a hint. And if Roly wasn't interested, he'd soon find someone who was. Sandy'd seemed like just the man. With that upper-class air of knowing his way around. Dropping hints about people he knew. *A chum of mine in the Foreign Office . . . Someone I know with a place in Gloucester . . .* He'd seemed like a good proposition. That was before Ray found out what he knows now. Which is that it's all a con. A sell. A swizz. The truth is, poor old Sandy is pretty much stony broke . . .

The village shop stocks nothing but Wincarnis and ginger wine. Try the public house, the postmistress advises him with a disdainful I-know-your-sort kind of sniff. He does so, after pocketing twenty Senior Service and a couple of rolls of Fruit Gums. Serve her right, sarky old cow.

The Feathers is just closing when Ray strolls in, although the door is unlocked and one or two customers – stout, red-faced men in mud-coloured corduroys and weathered tweeds – are finishing their pints in obscure corners. But the landlord has his back turned when his new customer enters and does not seem to see him – intent, it would appear, on the glass he is polishing. Nor does he alter his posture when Ray calls 'Shop,' and clicks his money on the bar.

Eventually, and with extreme deliberateness, the landlord turns. 'We're closed,' he informs Ray, making no effort to disguise his satisfaction at this state of affairs.

'It's not two yet,' protests Ray, thrusting forward his wrist-watch (a smart Ingersoll Roly bought him) to confirm this fact.

But the landlord – stupid bald old git – is adamant. 'It is by my clock . . .' He indicates the dial above his head, on which the hands irrefutably point to the hour. 'What do you make it, Billy?'

This is to one of the red-faced men, who consults his own timepiece, a battered turnip watch. 'Two o'clock it is,' the old fart sings out.

Ray throws him a filthy look. The landlord resumes his polishing. For a minute the only sound in the big dark room with its smells of spilt beer and tobacco is the tick of the offending clock.

'Pity, that,' says Ray to the landlord's impervious back. 'Auntie'll be so disappointed. And with her lumbago playing her up and all . . .'

His enemy gives no sign that he has heard, other than to set down one glass and take up another.

'A martyr to it, she is, poor old soul. Bent double with the pain some days. Only thing that takes it off is a hot gin and water. Never fails, that does.' Leaning on the bar, with one boot on the brass rail, as if settling himself in for a good long session, Ray warms to his improvisation. 'Sandy, she says to me – I'm her favourite, if I say so myself – Sandy, just pop down to the Feathers like a good boy and ask the landlord to fetch us up a bottle of his best Gordon's. And be sure and say the lady at Dunsinane sent you, because we wouldn't want no mistakes about a thing like that, would we . . .'

The landlord half-turns his head. 'Dunsinane, did you say?'

'That's right. Big old place about a mile up the road there. Left it to me, she has, in her will. I'm her nephew, see, and as I was visiting she says to me . . .'

'You're Mrs Reason's nephew?' The man stares at him with barely concealed dislike.

'Dear old Auntie,' says Ray. 'Getting a bit forgetful now, of course. Maybe you know her . . .'

'Mrs Reason? Course I know 'er,' growls the landlord, producing from somewhere beneath the counter a bottle of

Gordon's gin. 'That'll be ten an' six,' he mutters, glaring at Ray, who favours him with an expression of asinine goodwill.

'Oh, put it on the slate, would you, my good man,' warbles Ray, seizing the bottle before the man has a chance to wrap it up. 'Ta very much,' he calls over his shoulder, grinning fit to burst at the success of his adventure.

All the same, he takes the time to double back behind the pub, in order to relieve himself copiously against the wall. The look on that bald bastard's face, Ray thinks with savage enjoyment, as he shakes the last drops from his cock and zips up his fly. As if he'd lost a fiver and found a farthing.

Still laughing, Ray retraces his steps through the village, pausing once to inspect his reflection in the window of the wool shop, and again to lob a stone over the churchyard wall at the nose of a mourning angel.

Sandy's first thought when the telephone rang – a shocking sound in that profound quiet – was that it must be Ray, to say he'd got lost and needed picking up from somewhere. Because it had been long enough since he'd set out and it was only supposed to have been a quick trip down to the shops, which, by Sandy's reckoning, oughtn't to have taken more than half an hour. And it was gone three o' clock. So that when he went to answer it, because Auntie, poor love, was still flat out, his lips were already forming a wry response to the anticipated distress call. *Stopped off for a quick one, did we? Forgot the time?* Oh, he'd quite looked forward to the prospect of teasing Ray.

Only it wasn't Ray at all, but Izzie – as indeed he might have expected, after the sheep's eyes she'd been making at him when they'd first met. Now she was trying to get him on to home territory, as if that would make a blind bit of difference. Couldn't she *tell* he was a lost cause, as far as she was concerned? You'd have thought Leonora would have set her straight on *that* one all those years ago. God knows he'd tried a couple of times himself. An excruciatingly awkward conversation he'd had with his young cousin about Greek love, a year or so after he'd come down from college, sprang to mind.

His first impulse had been to fob her off. *Such* a lovely idea – and *what* a pity he and Ray had to get away so soon. But then it had occurred to him that Ray was the one who deserved to be taught a lesson. Let him come back (no doubt the worse for wear) and find them out. Let him see that Sandy, too, could act the independent.

His righteous indignation had lasted up until the moment of leaving the house, which was quite a long time, because Auntie needed to be got going and it seemed an absolute age before she had powdered her nose and put on her hat and done all the things that women felt it necessary to do before they could face the world. So that it had been a quarter to by the time they were ready to toddle off and Ray *still* hadn't appeared – and Sandy's crossness had been starting to turn into anxiety. Supposing something had happened, he'd fretfully thought. The poor darling might have wandered off and had no idea how to get back. Perhaps he'd hurt himself and was lying unconscious somewhere. Or he might have accepted a lift from someone – one read such *hideous* stories in the papers – and be lying dead in a ditch . . .

Leaving Connie in the car, he'd run back to write a note.

To say they'd just popped out for tea might sound a bit heartless, he'd thought, to someone who'd just escaped abduction or worse. *Called out on urgent business*, he'd eventually put. *Will return post-haste. If in a condition to speak* (which covered every eventuality), *ring this number*. He'd underlined it twice

– then thought to add a map of the route from Dunsinane to Yew Tree Farm. It wasn't a very good map, he'd had to admit when it was finished. But at least it would enable Ray to find his way – if he could still walk, of course . . . A brief, horrifying vision of a bloodstained corpse had flashed across Sandy's mind at that point. Squeezing his eyes tight shut, he'd willed it away.

Iseult lifts her large, red hands clear of the bowl, letting the blended flour and fat run through her fingers like a length of fine silk, the way she had been taught all those years ago by Miss Gee, in Domestic Science. When the mixture is like sand or breadcrumbs, she adds a handful of currants (dusted first with flour to stop them sinking), then begins to stir in the milk, thinking, 'In less than an hour he will be here.' As she stands up from putting the scones in the oven, her nostrils are met with a breath of lemon sponge cake, an earlier product of that afternoon's industry, which stands on the wire rack waiting to be iced. A walnut and date loaf (because men sometimes prefer a more robust combination of flavours) sits cooling in its oblong tin. Sandwiches (fish paste, cucumber and Bovril) lie wrapped in a clean, damp tea-cloth to prevent curling.

She casts a critical eye around the big kitchen, whose fittings – the cast-iron stove with its speckled enamel hob, the deep porcelain sink with its wooden draining board – had been the latest thing in 1918, the year of her parents' marriage. Everything is as it should be: the flagstone floor swept and washed, its usual ranks of manure-caked gumboots consigned to an outhouse; the long pine table cleared of its piles of seed catalogues and out-of-date calendars and scoured to perfect whiteness; plates and cups tidied away into cupboards, dog leads untangled from their messy heap beside the back door and every surface – shelves, walls, window-sills – testifying to the power of Vim and elbow grease.

'Not bad, not bad,' says Iseult aloud, receiving by way of acknowledgement a gratified thump from the tail of the supine Labrador under the table. 'Good boy, Nimrod,' she murmurs. 'Oh, Lord,' she adds, catching sight of herself in the chipped bit of mirror which hangs on a nail above the sink – a remnant of the days when her father used to shave there on Sunday mornings, because you could at least be sure of getting the water hot. What a fright she looks. Hair coming loose and frizzing around her face with the heat from the oven. A smudge of flour on her cheek and egg yolk all down her front, hardening to a crust on what had been a clean jumper. And those hands . . . With a howl of dismay, Iseult regards their coarse and weathered backs, the knuckles too prominent, the skin too crazed with lines and pitted with tiny scars to be a lady's hands. Iseult thinks, fleetingly and bitterly, of her mother's hands: small, white and delicate, with pink enamelled nails. Hands which have never done a hand's turn of work in seventy-nine years.

Such thoughts, she knows, are best left unthought. A whole world of recrimination lies behind them. That morning when she had brought Leonora her tea, her mother had sleepily inquired from among the pillows what time lunch was going to be. 'Because I think I might have a quiet day today, dear. After what Dr MacIntyre said the last time, I don't want to risk overdoing things . . .' Iseult had made no reply, but then Leonora's remarks seldom required any. Merely the presence of another person was enough for someone of her solipsistic habits. 'A poached egg on toast is all I really want,' Leonora had called after her daughter's retreating figure, 'or a little bit of steamed fish. Whatever's easiest . . .' It was Leonora's belief that she was one of those people who went out of their way not to be any trouble. 'Rice pudding,' she added, in tones of martyred sweetness, as Iseult lifted the brimming bowl from the commode and set off down the hall to empty it.

Of course, what with all the shenanigans with Aunt Constance and meeting Sandy – and then remembering that in all the excitement she'd forgotten to return Mummy's library books – it was already a quarter to one by the time she got back, and Mummy was thumping her stick on the floor to find out whether by any chance Iseult might have forgotten to bring up her tray. So that it wasn't until she'd settled Mummy down, done her some eggs the way she liked them and then brought her her tea ('Very weak, dear. My heartburn . . .') and was sitting down to her own bit of fodder that she thought of the plan.

It was such a good plan that she wondered why it hadn't occurred to her before. She'd ask him to tea. Aunt Constance, too, of course, and – she supposed – that young friend of his, although she hadn't thought much of him to tell the truth. Bit of a nasty piece of work. But that was Sandy all over, Iseult thought fondly. He was simply too kind-hearted for his own good. A soft touch for any Tom, Dick or Harry who wanted to take advantage.

It had been Sandy who'd answered the telephone when she'd rung with the invitation. Even though she had known this was a possibility when she'd picked up the receiver, the sound of his voice on the end of the line still threw her into a tizzy. 'Aunt Constance?' she'd stammered like a fool, feeling her face go hot with chagrin. He'd laughed, but not unkindly, bless him. 'Auntie's having a little nap, Izzie, dear,' he'd said (and she wondered how on earth she could ever have mistaken those warm, masculine tones for those of an old woman). 'Do

47

you want me to wake her?' And she'd said, with a boldness that, as she recalled it, surprised her anew, 'As a matter of fact, it was you I wanted . . .'

In Iseult's room, the afternoon sun casts a web of shadows across the bed – silhouettes of the full-blown roses and intertwining briars which form the pattern of its yellowing lace curtains. Dust motes dance in long golden beams. The faint smell of Sloane's Liniment mingles with the pervasive odour of Woodbines. A slight air of neglect hangs over the room, in which every surface is cluttered with objects. The furniture is old-fashioned; heavy and unpleasing to look at. Not that Iseult herself ever looks at it. It has simply always been there. In one corner of the room – the darkest – stands a dressing table of the sort fashionable in ladies' boudoirs in the era between the wars. A flounced chintz skirt surrounds a kidney-shaped table with a mirror in which one could see oneself from three different angles simultaneously.

It is hard to decide, thinks Iseult despondently, which of the three is the worst.

She makes a brave attempt to repair the damage wrought by forty-five years' sun and wind with the aid of a chalky spattering of Helena Rubinstein (filched from her mother's drawer) and a dried-up tube of Crimson Rhapsody. Has she time to do her hair? This – a process of unplaiting, brushing out, replaiting and securing with bobby pins – is rather a long job which she generally performs only first and last thing. But today she will make an exception. It isn't often she has company. Humming a little under her breath – a silly song she'd heard that morning on the wireless when she was milking Buttercup – she starts pulling out the long black pins which keep the plaits anchored to her head.

Then I saw her face –
Now I'm a believer.
Not a trace
Of doubt in my mind . . .

A mere matter of hours ago, she'd been blissfully oblivious of all that was to happen – conscious of nothing in fact except the moment and the various elements which gave it its particular coloration: the sun coming in through the cobwebbed window of the byre, with its sweet smells of fresh dung and clean straw, and the languid swish of Buttercup's tail flicking away flies, and the soft puff of breath – so like a human sigh – she made as she exhaled. For Iseult, crouched on her three-legged stool, with her cheek resting against Buttercup's flank and the slippery resistant feel of the teats between her fingers as the warm white milk hissed into the bucket, it had been a day like any other. Now it was lost, that mood of pleasant lassitude – swallowed up in a fever of longing.

I'm in love –
Ooh –
I'm a believer
I couldn't leave her
If I tried . . .

Iseult sees herself in the dusty glass of the triple-mirror, her hair hanging loose and shiny after her efforts with the brush. 'A woman's hair is her crowning glory,' Daddy had said. He'd been wild when Leonora'd had hers shingled. A mixture of deference to her father's ideas and the desire to be as different as possible from her mother had prevented Iseult from following suit. Having long hair is a bore, she sometimes thinks; but she's kept it like this for so many years it hardly seems worth the bother of changing. Besides (she barely allows herself to think), Sandy had admired it once, hadn't he?

The night of the Hendersons' dance. Her first and, as it turned out, her last – because then the war had intervened and afterwards she'd been too old to bother about such things. She was seventeen. An awful age, she thinks now, recalling with a shiver the misery of getting dressed, knowing the frock Mummy had insisted should be cut down for her from one of Mummy's own did nothing to conceal her plainness and in fact only drew attention to her embarrassing deficiency in the bosom department, and hating the way her palms kept sweating, and feeling a headache beginning to start because her hair was twisted up much too tight under the stupid headband Mummy had made her wear, and wanting to call the whole thing off – only she knew the car would arrive any minute.

And then Sandy had said something which had made it all right.

He'd been staying at Aunt Constance's that summer because Aunt Peggy and Uncle Harold were visiting friends in Scotland and the London house was shut up – everything shrouded in dustsheets, Sandy said. Too depressingly sepulchral. He'd been between jobs, she remembers: the little gallery in Bayswater which sold handpainted furniture and conversation pieces (most of it frightfully bad, Sandy said) had folded, and the job cataloguing Lord Somebody's library wasn't due to start until September . . . Anyway, he must have stopped by to see her father about something – she can't think of any other reason why he should have been there. But he was certainly there, that night. She'd descended the stairs in a fog of self-consciousness, the hateful dress billowing around her (it was turquoise, she recalls – an unflattering colour which turned her complexion to mud), and he'd been there, dashing in his blazer and Oxford bags. Smiling at her. She'd wanted the ground to open and swallow her up.

'Gosh, Izz,' she'd heard him say, in the moment of utmost humiliation. 'You look awfully nice. I do like your hair like that . . .'

Dear Sandy. A faint smile playing around her lips, Iseult toys with her hair, drawing its kinked and greying strands down across her shoulders. *You have lovely hair, Izzie. Really thick.* She savours the memory, hearing all over again the way his voice had sounded.

Her fingers encounter a crusted scab of egg-stain above her left breast. Horrors. She'll have to change.

In the wardrobe hang the half-dozen or so checked shirts she'd inherited from her father, with his favourite corduroys and a couple of scratchy tweed jackets. Well suited as these are for farm work, they hardly seem appropriate wear for a tea party. There's a skirt somewhere, she knows. A hasty rummage discloses nothing but more shirts. Damn. Then she remembers. She'd worn the skirt for church last Sunday. She'd caught the hem on a stile when she was walking back over the fields. Now a good six inches hangs down at the back – and Sandy is always so particular about such things.

Shoving the ranks of padded hangers back along the rail in an access of irritation, Iseult uncovers the dress. For a second or two she stares at it, trying to account for its presence in that otherwise masculine preserve. Gingerly, she fingers its alien fabric, slippery to the touch. It must be all of fifteen years since she last wore it. The vicarage garden party. She'd run the cake stall. Alf Fletcher had bought a whole tray of her coconut fancies.

Almost before she knows what she is doing, she's sloughed off her trousers and jumper, and is sliding the dress over her head. It still fits, of course. Whatever else about her has altered, her weight hasn't varied by so much as an ounce in twenty years. All the same, she is unprepared for the apparition which meets her gaze in the wardrobe mirror. With her hair loose and the frock with its pattern of scarlet poppies, she looks a vision of her former self: a younger, less determined Iseult. Frowning slightly, she surveys herself from various angles. It isn't really as bad as she'd feared. But the grey woollen socks and stout brogues she is wearing look wrong. She knows a further search is unlikely to turn up the necessary appurtenances – suspender belt and flesh-coloured stockings – she needs to complete the ensemble. Perhaps Mummy . . .

Iseult freezes in horror as a thought strikes her. The scones.

The acrid stench of burning is already seeping into the hall as she tears downstairs, barking her shins on the elephant's-foot umbrella stand.

'Damn and blast.'

The kitchen is full of blue smoke. Grabbing a tea-cloth, Iseult wrenches the oven door open. In her haste to rescue the by now ruined scones, she catches her bare arm on the hot shelf. Tears spring to her eyes.

'Oh, blast it *all*,' cries Iseult.

And so it is that Sandy, arriving, as is his custom, by the back door, finds his cousin – *dear* old Izzie – looking the most extraordinary sight, with her hair all over her face like a madwoman, and in that dress (which was surely far too young for her), weeping into the sink over a pile of blackened scones, from which she is trying – without much success, it has to be said – to scrape the burnt bits.

★

Ray'd meant to have only a nip of the gin to keep him going on the homeward slog, but – as these things do – it had all got a bit out of hand. He'd been heading back the way he'd come – or as far as he could tell, when every field looked just like another – and was starting to feel just a tiny bit thirsty, considering he'd walked all this way without so much as a half of shandy to sustain him. It was hot, too – hotter even than when he'd set out. What he needed was a drink. The gin was to hand. It wasn't the most refreshing thing you could think of, but it certainly pepped him up. Only trouble was, it left him feeling thirstier than before.

Absent-mindedly, he takes another swig. This time it doesn't taste quite so bad. Before him stretches the dusty white road, flat green fields on either side. Surely it's further than it was before? Come to think of it, he doesn't remember this bit at all. What Ray *does* remember is how much he hates the country. The reason he hates it is that it all looks the same. Bloody trees. Bloody fields with cows. Bloody fields without cows.

'Bloody hell,' mutters Ray, consoling himself with a drink.

A field of billowy grass, softly waving in the light breeze, invites him. A quick nap is what he needs, Ray decides. Getting over the stile is a poser, but he manages it after a couple of goes. Finds a nice, comfy spot not too close to any cowpats. Stretches out and closes his eyes.

Which is a mistake. Because everything that has been going on around him, more or less minding its own business, thank you very much, suddenly rushes in on top of him, whirling round and round until his tired brain feels like the Big Dipper. Hastily, Ray opens his eyes. A forest of grass stalks rises all around him, a green tunnel, at the far end of which is the sky. Something loud buzzes in his ear. He brushes it away with a shiver of disgust. Creepy-crawly. If there's one thing he can't stand it's creepy-crawlies. He sits up – too quickly, as it happens. The Big Dipper starts again, only this time there's no stopping it. Down and down and down, hurtling faster and faster, until you feel your stomach rise up to meet it and you know that if it doesn't stop soon you're going to chuck . . .

Heaving himself up on to his hands and knees just in time, Ray vomits copiously on to a patch of meadow-sweet. At once he feels better. Much. He swipes his hand across his streaming eyes and clears his nostrils of the watery phlegm which clogs them. There. Right as rain.

It's then he becomes aware that someone is laughing.

At once he's on his feet. Because nobody laughs at Ray. People have tried, but those are only the ones to whom this fact has not yet been explained. He doesn't waste time, either. Just launches himself at the place the laugh has come from. It's a skill he learned early: get your enemy on the floor, then hit him wherever you like. In the face, in the goolies, in the soft underbelly. Which actually turns out to be harder than expected. His fists collide with firm young muscle. A hard hand claps him, none too gently, around the ear.

'Steady on,' says a voice with a good deal too much laughter in it. 'Or you might get yourself hurt . . .'

A pair of bright-blue eyes regard him smilingly, from beneath a quiff of startling red hair. A pair of strong arms clasp him around the waist.

'Fucking let go,' Ray tells the stranger sternly.

'Language,' retorts Carrot-top. 'Good job there's no ladies here.'

His teeth set in a vixen's snarl, Ray lashes out with his foot.

He feels the satisfying crunch of steel-capped toe on bone, hears the still more gratifying yelp of pain.

'Ow!' His red-haired tormentor releases him; hops on one leg. Ray seizes his chance.

A second, well-aimed kick brings down his enemy. A blow to the gut knocks the stuffing out of him. Less burly than the country-bred boy, Ray knows a trick or two about fighting. Nor is he hampered by namby-pamby concerns about fair play. Straddling his winded opponent, he brings his head down hard on the bridge of the other's nose. At once it starts to bleed, in copious streams.

'All right, all *right!*' cries Carrots, his face now milky white beneath his freckles, as Ray is about to deliver the *coup de grâce* of a chop to the windpipe. 'You win. Let me go . . .'

As a general rule, Ray tends to pay no attention to such pleas for mercy. You asked for it, so you're fucking going to get it, is his motto. But something about the way the lad is looking at him with those baby-blues all wide-eyed like, and the sour-sweet tang of sweat that is pouring off him, and the slight, but unmistakable, bulge Ray can feel between the other's spread legs, pressing against his own by now hard John Thomas, makes him stay his hand.

'You dirty little sod,' Ray says softly. 'You liked that, did you?'

The boy's freckled face is now suffused with blood; angrily he twists and turns, but the bulge in his trousers can no longer be denied.

'Ooh,' groans Ray, reaching down to free his own swollen prick. 'You would, would you?'

In the meadow's long grass they roll over and over, their scuffles turned to a different kind of fighting, each thrust and parry a continuation, merely, of that earlier contest; so that when one or the other cries out it is impossible to tell whether pain or pleasure is uppermost, or which, in the end, is the victor and which the vanquished.

3
Tea Ceremony

The afternoon, it seems to Iseult, is going very well – much better than might have been expected, after the débâcle of the scones. First of all, Sandy had been so sweet, saying it didn't matter a bit, and why on earth was she boo-hooing over a few old scones that had gone a bit dry around the edges, but were otherwise perfectly edible, when there was all this other lovely stuff, cakes and sandwiches – and, goodness me, was that bloater paste, his absolute favourite? – that she'd ended up feeling the day might not turn out to be such a complete washout after all. Then there was the fact that he'd turned up on his own – or, at least, with Aunt Constance, which amounted to the same thing – instead of with that horrid young man in tow. Sandy had made some excuse for him, of course (he was always the soul of politeness), but you could tell he was embarrassed by his friend's bad manners – which was what it came down to, really. Iseult believes in calling a spade a spade.

She'd done her best to make Sandy feel better about being let down, without allowing her own delight at what was for her an unlooked-for stroke of good luck appear too obvious. And Sandy, bless him, had entered into the spirit of things in quite his old way, fetching rugs and deck-chairs when, on a whim, she'd decided they'd have tea in the garden; settling Aunt Constance down in the shade and then sitting himself down beside Iseult on the grass with such a lovely, confiding smile that she'd felt, for a moment, as if they were the only two people left in the world.

'So how's my dear old Izzie?' he'd said, and she'd mumbled something, blushing like a fool. And then he'd said, with such a sweet look, 'We were always the best of *chums*, Izz, weren't we?' And there'd been such a lump in her throat that she couldn't speak.

It's been so lovely sitting here, with the only sounds the lazy hum of the bees going in and out of the delphiniums and the breeze gently stirring the branches of the willow, that it seems to her as if the past twenty years or so have fallen away. Looking at Sandy, it is hard to believe that so much time has passed. Apart from a touch of grey at the temples (which suits him, she thinks), and one or two (very becoming) lines, he is the same young man whose charm so bewitched her all those years ago. Such a very *English* kind of handsomeness, thinks Iseult. Boyish, yet by no means gauche. Distinguished. Like Leslie Howard in *Intermezzo*, she sometimes thinks, with that same mixture of sensitive good looks and old-fashioned masculine elegance. He'd always dressed so beautifully, too, dear Sandy. But then people did, in those days. You'd never see a man without a hat – at least not in town; gloves, too, as often as not. Such style they had. Though there was never anything the slightest bit *showy* about it. Good-quality clothes that were made to last for years and years. You could always tell a gentleman by his shoes, Mummy said . . . Suddenly conscious of her own somewhat eccentric appearance, Iseult tugs her skirt down over her knees.

'Sandy . . .' she begins timidly.

'Mm-hm?' replies Sandy cautiously. He hopes old Izz isn't going all moony on him. He knows that earnest, impassioned look of old.

'Oh. Nothing. Just thinking,' she says.

This is his cue to ask her what she's thinking about. Three

guesses, groans Sandy to himself, clenching his teeth. How *nice* it is to be sitting there, just the two of them. How *long* it is since they last saw one another like this. How *much* she's missed their lovely long chats. And has he been terribly busy these past few years, and doesn't he ever get lonely, and is there anyone *special* in his life?

'That's nice,' he says. 'Gosh, aren't those lupins splendid?'

'Yes.' She seems comically at a loss. For a moment, he almost feels sorry for her.

'I do love lupins, don't you? Such . . . *ebullient* flowers.'

'They attract the slugs,' says Iseult, in a small, bleak voice.

Having exhausted this horticultural topic, both are silent for a while: Sandy feigning interest in the sleeve of his jacket (an attractive lightweight model in pale-blue Terylene); Iseult gazing tragically out across the burnt grass of the lawn, with its borders of sprawling Canterbury bells and nasturtiums, its network of metal hoops set up for a game of croquet which seems to have been in progress for as long as Sandy can remember, even though it must be years – decades, even – since the long pine box, the size of a child's coffin, which holds the mallets and balls and the rest of the paraphernalia was last opened.

'So,' Sandy says, clearing his throat, 'how's the farm doing these days?'

There is a longish pause before Iseult replies.

'The farm's all right,' she says flatly. 'At least, it could be worse. Might have to sell another bit of the Long Meadow, if things don't pick up soon, though . . .'

'Oh dear,' says Sandy.

'Actually,' says Iseult, with what Sandy takes to be a 'brave' smile, 'since Daddy died, the farm hasn't exactly been what you'd call a going concern . . .'

'Ah,' says Sandy.

'In fact,' Iseult says, sounding more and more cheerful – a sure sign that she is being deadly serious – 'even *before* Daddy died things were looking a bit ropy, if you want the truth of the matter . . .'

Sandy is not sure he does. 'I see,' he murmurs. 'Jolly difficult for you.'

The solicitous tone in which this is said brings Iseult to her senses. Because complaining about one's lot simply isn't done. One's made one's bed, after all. No use crying over spilt milk . . .

'But enough about me,' she says briskly. 'Let's talk about you. Tell me everything you've been up to.'

'Everything?' He can't resist a teasing look.

'Oh, you know . . .' She smiles at him encouragingly. 'Parties and so on. You always used to go to lots of parties . . .'

'Did I? I suppose I did . . .' Sandy likes this account of himself as a gay young blade. He arches an eyebrow at her. 'They *were* parties in those days, I can tell you!'

Visions of sophisticated goings-on, encompassed in a single phrase, 'The Smart Set', are briefly conjured up in Iseult's mind. She nods eagerly.

'Not like the poor affairs you have nowadays,' Sandy goes on, thinking of one such occasion – the *only* occasion in recent memory in fact, although he does not say so to Iseult – at which there had been nothing to drink but warm beer and some very iffy-looking punch, and no one he knew except Roly, who had waved at him once and then ignored him. '*Very* poor affairs,' he sniffs, reaching for the last sandwich.

'But you're having fun?' The 'brave' smile is back, Sandy notices. His mouth full, he can only nod, eyes popping, to indicate whole-hearted endorsement of this view.

'That's good,' sighs Iseult, winding a straggling curl around her forefinger – a gesture of girlish wistfulness which would be absurd, Sandy thinks, if it were not so sad. 'Because I like to think of you having fun . . .'

'You know me,' says Sandy, swallowing hard to dispose of a glutinous lump of partially masticated bread and fish paste, 'life and soul of the party.' Where *has* that boy got to? he wonders, with a sudden stab of alarm. It's been hours. 'Can one hear the telephone from out here?' he asks Iseult. 'If it *were* to ring, I mean . . .'

'With the French windows open – quite easily,' she replies stiffly. 'More tea, Sandy? Or would you prefer a slice of walnut loaf?'

'Not for me, thanks,' he says hastily. 'Watching the old waistline, you know . . .'

'Just as you like,' says Iseult.

Strange how, as one grows older, people tend more and more to ignore one, Connie thinks. It's like being invisible; a part of the furniture. One hears and sees everything, and no one remembers one's there at all. Now, for instance, as she sits here, in this pleasant garden (and how pretty it's looking, with the roses climbing over the pergola), letting her thoughts wander where they will, it's just as if she didn't exist for the others. Images of other gardens – the vicarage garden in Lymington, where she'd grown up; the shady lawns of the Police Commissioner's residence in Shanghai – click in and out of focus, while, with her sharp and very present sense of hearing, she tunes into Iseult and Sandy's conversation.

And what a wretched time they seem to be having – especially poor dear Iseult. Because Sandy (much as Connie loves him) isn't ever going to be the answer to a maiden's prayer. Knowing what she knows, she sometimes feels it incumbent upon her to say something to set the poor girl straight. Although, of course, it wouldn't be the slightest use. If Connie's learned one thing in a long and not always happy life, it's that people only ever hear what they want to hear.

– *Would you care for a stroll in the garden, Miss Joliffe? The flowers are awfully pretty just now . . .*

– *Thank you. But I don't care for flowers.*

– *Oh, come now! Surely all young ladies like flowers?*

Which one had that been? Benjy Furnival or Lionel Jenkins or any one of the other hapless suitors who'd tried their luck with her. She can't remember now. Just that all the time she'd been thinking only of *him* – and wondering how long it'd be before she saw him again. What a fool she was – no better than poor Iseult, when all's said and done . . .

'Aunt Constance?' Iseult's voice breaks into these reflections. 'Can I get you anything?'

'Why, no thank you, dear,' says Connie, turning her mild blue gaze on her niece. 'I believe I've everything I need. Why look,' she adds. 'Here's dear Leonora. How nice that she's going to join us . . .'

Leonora is in pink – her Ascot frock, Iseult sees, with the dull horror her mother's appearances in company so often inspire. She stands, coquettishly poised on one foot, in the open French windows, the pose that of a startled wood nymph about to take flight, or a society beauty making an entrance. When she sees that she has been noticed, she gives a tinkling laugh.

'Coo-ee,' she simpers, fluttering her fingers. 'It's only little me . . .'

After a moment's startled pause, Sandy jumps up, with becoming athleticism, and goes to embrace her.

'Leonora,' he exclaims. Long ago, when he was a schoolboy, Leonora forbade the use of the honorific: it made her feel 'too dreadfully ancient', she said. 'What a lovely surprise!'

'Sandy, dear . . .' She offers him her cheek to kiss, and for the second time that day he flinches, performing this duty, at the powdery touch of aged skin. In Leonora's case, the sensation is made still more unpleasant by the textures and scents of the cosmetics with which she is plastered – so thickly, in fact, that her eyes seem to peer from behind a crazed porcelain mask, her yellowing false teeth flashing a death's-head grimace from between scarlet Cupid's-bow lips. Close to, she is repellent; at a distance – say, a hundred yards – she would just about pass muster, Sandy thinks. In her strawberry crêpe de Chine and with those (surely artificial?) golden curls, she looks like the flapper she once was forty-odd years ago.

'My, you do look well,' Sandy tells her. 'Radiant, in fact . . .'

'Flatterer,' laughs Leonora, wagging a finger at him.

Iseult comes up, exuding disapproval from every pore. 'I thought you were staying in bed,' she says sulkily to her mother.

An expression of gleeful cunning flashes across Leonora's face. 'I felt better,' she replies, with a petulant shrug. 'I was just getting dressed, when I happened to look out of the window and saw you all sitting out here. You didn't *mention* we were having visitors,' she says accusingly to Iseult.

'I didn't think you'd be up to seeing anybody,' Iseult blusters. 'You know how much it always overtires you . . .'

'Such a killjoy, my dear daughter,' says Leonora sweetly, with a naughty look at Sandy. 'Always trying to stop me having fun . . .'

'Well, *I'm* jolly glad you're here,' says Sandy diplomatically, with a wink at Iseult. He takes Leonora's arm. 'Come and say hello to Auntie Connie. She's dying for a good old chinwag . . .'

And indeed the poor old girl does seem to have perked up a bit at the sight of her sibling. Even though they've always been chalk and cheese, if the truth were told.

'Hello, Lolly,' she calls, as Sandy, having negotiated the tricky bit with the steps and the croquet lawn, now pilots his elderly charge over the home stretch. Beside him, Leonora puffs and blows. In spite of her seeming youthfulness, she isn't much of a walker. Her scrawny, child-sized body – so insubstantial under the floating chiffon that Sandy is disagreeably reminded of the apophthegm about a rag, a bone and a hank of hair – advances precariously along the path. She ignores her sister's greeting until she is settled in the relative security of the deck-chair.

'Hiya, Con,' she says at last. 'Long time no see.' A devotee of *Perry Mason* and *Wagon Train*, which she watches on the television set she has had Iseult bring up from downstairs, Leonora is fond of slipping into Americanese. 'Howdy pardners' and 'Hot dogs!' pepper her conversation, to more or less incongruous effect, and she prides herself on her familiarity with the finer points of American jurisprudence.

'Gracious, it's hot!' she exclaims, more Scarlett O'Hara than cowpoke for the moment. She fans herself with a wrinkled paw. 'How can you *bear* tweed in this weather?' Her pitying look is meant for Sandy to see, establishing a complicity between them. Leonora is always like this where stray men are concerned, ganging up with them, where possible, against her daughter or (when he was still alive) her husband. 'Scratchy, I'd have thought,' she continues, with a wink at Sandy.

Connie looks down, surprised, at the offending skirt – which she hadn't thought to change, because in general she didn't bother much about such things and it *was* only afternoon tea, although dear Iseult had obviously gone to a lot of trouble. Lolly was always one for making a fuss about clothes – such a worry to poor Cyril when he was alive; those dressmaker's bills had nearly put him in Queer Street, he'd said once, with that funny little smile that was meant to make you think it was only a joke.

'You're well, I take it?' she says, deciding to ignore the earlier remark. The hint of frost in her sister's tone wipes the supercilious smile off Leonora's face.

'So-so,' says Leonora, patting her lips to conceal a non-existent yawn. 'We're none of us getting any younger. Except Sandy, of course. Ah declare,' tinkles Scarlett, with a sly look at her nephew, 'he's the same handsome feller he was when he came down from Oxford, putting all the young things in a flutter with those matinée-idol looks . . .'

'I made a fresh pot of tea,' interrupts Iseult loudly, plonking the tray down so abruptly that the cups rattle in their saucers. 'Would you care for another cup, Aunt Constance?'

'Very weak for me, dear, and just a *sprinkling* of sugar,' says Leonora. 'Sit down by me, Sandy,' she commands, patting the grass beside her chair. 'I want to hear about all the exciting things you've been doing since we last met . . .'

It seems that Sandy is fated, that afternoon, to be quizzed about his social life by his female relations. He only wishes it lived up to their collective illusion.

'Oh, you know,' he says modestly. 'There's not much to tell, really. One goes to the odd party, of course. The occasional first night. You know what Brighton's like. Always something going on . . .'

'Oh, I do so love Brighton!' enthuses Leonora. 'Before the war, we had such marvellous times there. Such a wonderful crowd. Bunty Crawford and Jimbo, and – what was the feller's name, Con, that friend of Cyril's who had the house at Rottingdean? Bobby something. Such a scream. And Reggie Cunliffe – the one who married Bubbles – he was sweet on me, of course, silly boy. Surely you remember Reggie?' Leonora pouts.

'You forget I was married by then,' says Connie. 'Wilfred didn't much like parties.'

'Nor did Cyril – but I used to make him go,' chuckles Leonora in fond reminiscence. 'Used to sit in the corner and sulk. Such an awful old stick, my dear husband . . .' Leonora laughs her 'musical' laugh, which, half a century before, had reminded one besotted theatre critic of silver bells.

Iseult's cheeks have grown very red. 'Daddy wasn't a stick,' she says hotly.

Her mother makes a wry mouth, her eyes very big, like a naughty child after a scolding. 'You weren't married to him,' is her retort – after which Iseult says nothing, only puts her head down, as if she were suddenly very interested in the pattern on her dress.

'Gosh, that sponge looks awfully good,' remarks Sandy into the silence. 'Maybe I'll change my mind and have something else after all.'

At once Iseult's head comes up and she shoots him a look of such fervent gratitude – her eyes very bright, as if she has blinked away tears – that he is quite taken aback. She cuts him a large slice, trowels it tenderly on to his plate. Then, the knife in her hand, she looks sternly at the sisters.

'Anyone else?'

Connie has shaken her head, with that vague smile which suggests her thoughts are already elsewhere after their brief engagement with the here-and-now, and Leonora has muttered something in martyred tones about not wanting to overload her stomach with too much rich food, when there is a low sound – midway between a laugh and a jeer – behind them.

Sauntering across the grass, his hands in the pockets of his by now somewhat stained and crumpled white trousers, comes Ray.

'Wotcher,' he says cheerily, with a nod at the rest of them. 'In time for a cuppa, am I?'

Leonora is the first to recover the power of speech.

'And who is this?' she demands, with thrilling sweetness. 'One of Sandy's young friends, I take it?' Sharp as a bird, she looks to her daughter for confirmation. But Iseult can only stare at the interloper, blank dismay written all over her face.

'You're awfully late,' snaps Sandy, forgetting, in the heat of the moment, his earlier alarms. 'I thought you weren't coming . . .'

'Got held up, didn't I?' Ray replies with a shrug. He notices Connie. 'Auntie's looking perky,' he remarks to Sandy. 'Must be the tea.'

Reluctantly, Iseult gets to her feet. 'I'll get you a cup,' she says hollowly. 'Do make yourself at home, Mr . . . er . . .'

'Do call me Raymond,' he says with a smirk.

There is something insufferably smug about his manner, to Sandy's eye. 'What have you been up to?' he mutters.

'Wouldn't you like to know?' Maddeningly enigmatic, Ray flashes his pearly-whites. 'Charming place you have here,' he drawls, addressing the old horror in pink.

Leonora is enchanted. 'I don't believe we've been introduced, Mr . . . er . . .'

'Brown,' says Ray. 'But no need to get formal.'

'*So* nice to see a fresh face,' coos Leonora. 'Are you staying in the neighbourhood long, Mr Brown – I mean Raymond?'

'That depends . . .' Ray begins, but Sandy cuts across him.

'*Raymond* and I have to get back tonight, *unfortunately* . . .'

'What a pity,' sighs Leonora. 'Although of course the country must seem awfully dull to a young person . . .'

'*Au contraire*,' says Ray, with a smile which strikes Sandy as decidedly sinister. 'It gets more and more interesting . . .'

Iseult returns with fresh supplies of tea and crockery. There is a pinkness about her eyes and a redness about her nose which suggest that her sojourn in the kitchen has not been entirely untroubled. Attempts have clearly been made, with cold water and face powder, to conceal the worst effects of this agitation.

'Your tea,' she says coldly to Ray, handing him a cup.

'Ta,' he says with a grin.

'Sugar?'

'I'm sweet enough, thanks,' says Ray, with a wink at Leonora.

There is definitely something *different* about Ray, Sandy thinks – something altogether more relaxed and confident. The sullen youth of a few hours before has been replaced by this lordly young buck, lolling around on the grass in his dirty white slacks as if he hadn't a care in the world. On the pretext of shooing away a marauding wasp, Sandy edges closer.

One sniff and his worst fears are confirmed. 'You're drunk!' he hisses.

Ray smiles. 'What's it to you?'

'That's it. We're leaving,' Sandy tells him furiously. He gets up, but Ray makes no attempt to follow him.

'Not going already, Sandy, dear?' says Leonora. 'I was just about to suggest a glass of sherry . . .'

'Mummy,' says Iseult in a warning voice.

'Sounds like a good idea to me,' says Ray.

And of course from then on things go from bad to worse. Because until then Ray has been behaving himself as well as can be expected from one of his sort, and Sandy had been hoping that the afternoon might pass off without fuss after all. But that was before good old Leonora came out with her famous suggestion. As if *she* needed any more pepping up. The woman was irrepressible as it was. And the way she got herself up, at her age. That dress. That hair. Not to mention enough slap for a chorus line. The worst thing was the disgusting way she was making up towards Ray. Positively *fawning* over him, the silly old trollop – as if he were one of her precious admirers, instead of young enough to be her grandson. Some people had no shame.

Just listen to her: 'Raymond,' she warbles, in that ridiculously actressy way, as if anyone could believe all that stuff about giving up a West End career to marry poor old Uncle Cyril, when everyone knew it had never amounted to more than a few years in provincial rep. 'Raymond, sit by me, do. There's something I want to show you . . .' Brazen old trout, thinks Sandy. And Ray – dear *Raymond* – is lapping it up, naturally. Loves being the centre of attention, the hussy. Now they're looking at the photograph album . . . Oh, *surely* not the one of her as Little Bo Peep? 'My first appearance on the public stage, at the tender age of four . . .' Simpering old fright.

'Charming,' says Ray. Drawing the word out as if silver spoons wouldn't melt in his mouth.

Leonora: 'And this is me aged, oh, sixteen, I think . . .'

Sandy (*sotto voce*): 'Thirty-five if she's a day.'

Leonora (sharply): 'Did you speak, Sandy?'

Sandy: 'Just clearing my throat, Leonora . . .'

Leonora: 'Well, don't.' To Ray: 'This is me as Cecily. My first speaking role.'

A red glare of late-afternoon sun gives a melodramatic aspect to the big drawing room, to which they decamped some time ago, to avoid the dangerous miasmas of evening. It's an ugly room, Sandy thinks, casting a professional eye over the massive, boxy settee and matching chairs (all the rage thirty years ago but now hopelessly out of date) and the what-not with the barley-sugar legs, and the dreadful standard lamp with the waxy shade, and the ghastly cross-stitched firescreen with the crinolined lady – all quite, quite hideous. Add to this the appalling clutter of knick-knacks and photographs with which Leonora has filled every surface – china dogs and Benares brass elephants and winsome shepherdesses – and you ended up with a sort of museum of bad taste.

Sandy eyes with particular loathing the flat painted figure of a Negro in footman's uniform holding out a salver for visiting cards – an 'amusing' purchase sometime in the 1920s. He wonders idly if this room – the newest part of the house, tacked on by Cyril during one of his periodic bursts of 'improvements' – is especially awful or if the rest of the house is just as bad. There must be some good stuff somewhere, surely? They're not a family for throwing things away.

Probably *cupboards* full of lovely things, he decides – Victorian bibelots and the like. People never knew what they'd got; some of his best 'finds' had been things put out for the dustcart. Sandy stifles a yawn. Sitting in the sun has made him sleepy. The sherry hasn't helped. And with all the tea he's drunk . . . He blunders to his feet, a half-strangled apology on his lips.

70

'Ah . . . hmm . . .'

Iseult's eyes, which have instantly turned towards him, look away demurely, as he makes his escape, under the mantle of invisibility conferred by his supposed need to answer a call of nature. He does, in fact, pay a swift visit to the WC, luxuriating, as he unbuttons, in the blessed hush of that echoing tiled space, with its bracing medicinal smells of Sanilav and Bronco toilet paper, each sheet of which bears the printed admonition *Now Wash Your Hands*. After drying his on the seat of his trousers, because he can't face the horror of the roller-towel, he is out on the landing, checking to see that he is not observed, before making his way, step by creaking step, along the corridor to the master bedroom.

This, while not quite the Aladdin's Cave of treasures he had hoped for, offers enough in the way of satisfactions to make it worth the visit. Execrable as Leonora's taste undoubtedly is, it does not entirely obscure the solid workmanship of what remains, in essence, a mid-Victorian bedchamber. Sandy's gaze roams hungrily over the contours of serpentine chest and tallboy, dwelling with a lover's obsessiveness on details of beading and inlay and linen-pleat carving. The bed is a beauty, too: 1850s, at a guess. Mahogany. Even half-smothered as it is in mauve satin furbelows, it is still a splendid piece. Pride of the Great Exhibition, Sandy thinks.

Something else catches his eye. Holding his breath against the fusty smell emanating from the bed's tossed and wrinkled sheets, he edges towards the chest of drawers on which, among a battalion of Elizabeth Arden's jars and bottles, lies Granny's silver dressing-table set, with its hairbrushes (hard and soft), its clothes-brushes and trinket box. Lovely things. He runs an appreciative finger over their intricate chased backs. Regards his face in the matching oval hand-mirror, now somewhat spotted and blurred. More elegant days, he sighs, replacing it gently.

The door to what he takes to be Iseult's room stands open, as if flung wide in haste. He sticks his head in, takes a dekko. But nothing here seems worthy of his attention. Then he spots the really rather nice early Victorian rosewood card table, doing duty as a bedside table. It needs a bit of touching up, of course – there are a few chips in the veneer, and a scratch or two on the surface – but nothing he couldn't handle. He wonders whether Izz might consider an offer, or if she'd be insulted . . . Running his hands over the pretty little piece, his fingers encounter an obstruction in an otherwise smooth surface. Aha. A secret drawer. Handy place to stow cards and those mother-of-pearl 'fish' they used instead of money. Chips. That's the word. Under his practised fingers, the drawer slides open. The chips are down, he thinks. Quaint phrase.

It's quite a shock to see his own face staring up at him, from a curled and faded studio portrait taken about thirty years before. He is holding it, lost in admiration for the sheer glamour of his youthful appearance (That tie! That artfully tousled hair!), when he hears a slight sound behind him.

'Oh, *Sandy*,' breathes Iseult, red as a rose. 'I hoped I'd find you here . . .'

For what seems a long moment Sandy stares at her.

'Hello, Izz,' he croaks at last. He is still holding the photograph, he realizes; it seems rather late in the day to try to conceal it now. Both watch as he returns it to its hiding place and slides the drawer shut.

'Do you remember,' Iseult says huskily, 'the day you gave that to me?'

He doesn't, of course – but he has the feeling she is about to remind him.

'You met me off the train at Euston,' she says. 'Because I was on my way home from school and you were motoring down, and so you said to Mummy and Daddy you'd give me a lift . . .' She pauses, arrested by the memory of her younger self, all elbows and knees in the sack-like gymslip, with the greasy brown-paper parcel of sandwiches she'd been given for the journey in one hand and her lacrosse stick in the other, catching sight of the elegantly turned-out figure of her grown-up cousin in the station's milling crowd. Her voice is not quite steady as she goes on. 'We went for tea first – to an ABC, I think it was . . .' Iseult smiles, thinking how sophisticated she'd felt, alone for the first time in a public place with a man who was not her father. 'And you'd just picked up the photographs from that place in the Strand, and you showed them to me and said that you didn't think much of them, but that Aunt Peggy would be pleased, because she'd wanted a snap of her darling boy for absolutely ages . . .' She pauses again, perhaps to allow him to contribute his own recollections of the occasion. He says nothing, however. 'And then you took up one of the studies from the table where they were all spread out among the tea things, and you said, "There you are, Izz – there's one for you." It was the nicest present I'd ever had,' says Iseult, her eyes very bright.

'Ah,' says Sandy. 'Well.' He gives a weak smile.

'So now you know,' says Iseult. 'After all these years . . .'

'Not interrupting, am I?' says a voice. Ray's. Praise the Lord, thinks Sandy. 'Only I was looking for the little boys' room . . .'

There is a moment's frozen silence and then Iseult makes a bolt for the door, brushing past the grinning little guttersnipe who has once again, it seems, come between her and her hopes.

They hear her footsteps pounding along the corridor.

'Oh dear,' remarks Ray. 'I seem to have broken up your cosy little tête-à-tête . . .'

'Don't,' says Sandy wearily.

'Don't what?' Ray moves closer, so that Sandy can smell his gin-scented breath. 'You're not *cwoss* with me, Sandy-poos, are you?' he wheedles, curling the tip of his tongue over his teeth.

For the second time in the space of the past half-hour, Sandy finds himself at a loss for words. He can only stare, mesmerized, at the flickering pink tongue, and at the dark down, now lightly beaded with sweat, which outlines the lovely contours of the boy's upper lip. And he knows that, in spite of the way Ray's behaved this afternoon (and indeed throughout most of their previous encounters), he forgives him everything: his spite, his petulance, his selfishness. These, in fact, have become reasons to love him more.

There is no hope for him now, Sandy dimly realizes.

When they go downstairs, Iseult is nowhere to be found, Leonora is asleep on the sofa and Connie . . . Connie seems unusually restless, pacing up and down the big sitting room as if impatient to be up and doing.

'You see,' she says, without preamble, as Sandy enters the room with Ray at his heels. 'It's Rufus. He'll be fretting.'

Rufus? Who the hell is Rufus? Sandy thinks at first that Auntie must be referring to some long-dead swain, or family member perhaps – but then he realizes she's talking about the dog.

'Don't worry, Auntie,' he says soothingly. 'We'll be off in a sec. Just as soon as we've made our farewells . . .'

Where has Izzie got to? he wonders, a touch impatiently. Really, it is too bad of her to choose this precise moment to do her disappearing act. Sandy coughs, pointedly. 'Izzie, dear,' he calls.

But the answering silence is broken only by the sonorous ticking of the long-case clock in the hall, and by a wheezing snore from the occupant of the sofa.

Ray gives a rude snigger. 'Pissed as a newt, the old dear,' he says.

Sandy ignores him. 'Izzie?' he calls again.

He runs her to earth in the kitchen, where she stands at the big table, her nose redder than before, her hands plunged wrist-deep in the carcass of a freshly plucked chicken.

'We're just off,' says Sandy cheerily.

'Oh,' says Iseult, not raising her eyes from her task. Holding the bird steady with one hand, she gives a sharp tug with the other and withdraws a glistening tangle of entrails. 'I thought you might be staying for supper,' she adds. There is blood on her hands – a pale red slime – he notices. She notices it, too, all of a sudden, and wipes it away on her apron.

'Auntie's worrying about Rufus,' he says.

Iseult nods, evidently satisfied with this excuse. 'Well,' she says, still not meeting his eyes. 'It's been lovely to see you.'

'Hasn't it, though?' he hastens to agree. 'I mean – it's been lovely to see you, too.'

'You know,' Iseult says, with the air of someone choosing her words carefully. 'We're always here.'

'I know.'

'Don't leave it so long next time, will you?' she murmurs.

'I won't.' Against his better judgement, he takes a step towards her, holding out his hands. 'So long, old thing.' He hesitates a moment longer, wondering whether to kiss her. After that scene upstairs . . . He compromises with a quick pat on the shoulder – which seems to do the trick, because Iseult lifts her head at last and gives him her bravest smile.

Then it's just a matter of bundling Auntie into the car, dragging young Raymond away from his new-found friend (in the course of which *adieux* Leonora becomes quite sentimental, calling Ray darling boy and covering him with magenta-lipstick kisses) and getting the car to start (which she does, after a bit of choke), and they're off at last, bumping away down the weed-infested gravel drive and into the lane, with its towering hedges casting a strange green underwater light. He's almost tempted to switch on the headlamps, although really it shouldn't be necessary for at least another hour at this time of year. Almost the longest day, thinks Sandy.

'Comfy, Auntie?' he calls back over his shoulder – receiving by way of reply only a vague smile and a bob of the white head in his rear-view mirror.

Ray, sprawled beside him, seems to have fallen asleep. Honestly, thinks Sandy crossly, it's as well *some* of us still have our wits about us. He wonders whether he's got enough petrol. With thirty miles to drive after he's dropped off Auntie, he'll be pushing it a bit. Had they passed a petrol pump on the way, he tries to remember. The local garage should have one – that is, if it's still open . . . Preoccupied with this worry, he almost doesn't see the turning and has to slam on the brakes to stop from overshooting. Whoops-a-daisy.

The lane seems longer than he remembers; darker, too. Objects – a dead tree, a roofless barn – emerge with eerie suddenness from the twilight. Something – a rabbit, perhaps – scuttles across their path into the ditch. Another few hundred yards and the twisting chimneys of Dunsinane are visible through the trees. Then the house itself looms into view. No lights on, of course. The thought of living alone in such a place is enough to make him shiver.

'Here we are, Auntie,' he cries.

It's then that it happens. A white shape fills the windscreen: noiseless, terrifying. Enormous yellow eyes glare at him. His blood turns to water. There's a scream – his or Ray's, he can't tell – and then a sickening thump as the car leaves the road. It's all over so quickly he can't believe it's really happened. If it weren't for the smell of burning rubber and the nasty crick in his neck, he'd think it had all been a dream – or nightmare, rather.

From the floor behind him comes a small voice: 'Oh dear. We seem to have had an upset . . .'

There's a stifled snort from the passenger seat. To Sandy's horror, he sees that Ray is covered in blood.

'Ray – darling,' he cries, distraught. 'You're hurt. Oh, God. Can you ever forgive me?'

Through a mouthful of blood, Ray gargles something. A bloody hand is thrust towards Sandy.

'Dose bleed,' gasps Ray. 'Hadky.'

With a surge of relief – his beloved is unscathed – Sandy finds the handkerchief and offers it. It is rudely snatched.

'Whad the fug was thad?' demands Ray, with the blood-soaked wad pressed to his nose.

'An owl,' replies Sandy, still trembling with the shock of it. 'You get them around here . . .'

'For fug's sake,' says Ray, shaking his head in disbelief.

With a guilty start, Sandy remembers his other charge. 'Auntie,' he says, 'are you all right?'

'Perfectly,' comes the surprisingly cool reply. 'Except that I seem to be upside-down, you know . . .'

In the time it takes to disentangle Auntie and to clean up a by now thoroughly disgruntled Ray, darkness has fallen and the likelihood of rescuing the Morris before morning seems increasingly unlikely. The car, Sandy observes glumly, is resting nose-first in the ditch, with its back wheels off the ground. It'll need a tractor to drag it out. When he explains this to Ray, the latter goes into one of his monumental sulks.

'If that isn't the *limit*,' he says witheringly. 'If that isn't the flipping *limit* . . .'

Auntie, despite having had the worst of it in some respects, is remarkably chipper. Her main concern, once she's back on her feet, is still the wretched dog. The beastly thing is lying in wait for them by the front door – puffing and wheezing like some demented steam engine and slobbering all over the place, disgusting smelly object – so that Sandy is tempted to shut the creature out, except that he doesn't want to upset Auntie.

'Poor boy,' she croons. 'Did you miss me, then? Did you think I wasn't coming back? Poor old fellow . . .'

At least the dog keeps her busy, leaving Sandy to deal with Ray, who is in a terrible mood. First he refuses to enter the house at all – the dump gives him the horrors, he says; he'd rather wait by the car until help can be fetched. When it is explained to him that – at this time of night and in so remote a spot – help will not be forthcoming until the next day, he is at first shrilly furious, then ominously silent. Through a mixture of cajolery and the promise of hot, sweet tea, Sandy succeeds in enticing him inside. Ray's nose has stopped bleeding but it is still a mite swollen; this, together with his sulky demeanour, makes him look more than ever like an adorable – if undoubtedly *spoilt* – little boy, thinks Sandy.

'You'll just have to call a cab, won't you?' he says irritably,

78

his accent growing commoner by the minute, Sandy can't help noticing. 'Because if you think I'm spending the night here . . .' He shudders prettily. 'You'll have to think again.'

Exasperated as he is by his companion's intransigence, Sandy has to admit he has a point. At night the house's eccentricities are magnified; it seems larger, emptier and yet, at the same time, peculiarly inhabited. Rooms whose vacancy is obvious by daylight now have the look of having only just been quitted. Floorboards creak, a pipe bangs loudly and, in the chimney, something flutters. There's a lingering dampness, too – the smell of rooms infrequently aired, of things decaying.

In the kitchen, Sandy fumbles with the gas ring, trying not to see the mess which surrounds him. Old bottles, some half-full of nameless, viscous substances, are ranged along every surface; blackened rinds of food, chewed bones and rusting tin cans are strewn beneath the table. On the draining board, an evil-smelling cloth sprouts various species of mould. The string bag containing the shopping Auntie purchased that morning still sits on the chair where she has left it, its waxed paper packages of ham, cheese and softening butter an open invitation to passing dogs and marauding flies. He moves these to the relative security of the meat safe, since there is, of course, no refrigerator. Supper, thinks Sandy glumly, regretting all the more his thoughtless refusal of Iseult's plump roast chicken. But supper will have to wait; for the moment, tea is the priority. As the whistling kettle splutters to its crisis, he extracts a trio of cups from the china cupboard, then, from a toppling pile, three mismatched saucers. The tea caddy proves more elusive; at last he locates it, on a shelf filled with empty Kilner jars. Milk is on its usual shelf in the pantry, in a blue-and-white striped jug veiled with a muslin cover, weighted with coloured beads. Sugar . . . He is about to give up on the sugar, when a tin marked Spiller's Dog Biscuits catches his eye. Sure enough, it proves to be half-full of sugar lumps – Rufus's particular weakness. With a feeling of triumph, Sandy fills the tarnished silver bowl to the brim, adding with a flourish the pretty, matching tongs.

Carrying the tray back along the cobweb-festooned passage towards the drawing room, he is disconcerted to hear conversation. When he had left them, the mistress of the house was ensconced in her favourite chair, with the pestilent dog at her feet. Ray was slumped on the sofa, a sulky look on his face. Now there's the sound of laughter, and what he recognizes as Ray's fake-posh voice expressing the opinion that someone or something is 'ev-ah so int'restin''. Pushing open the door with his shoulder, Sandy finds quite a cosy little scene: Ray perched on the arm of Auntie's chair, in the circle of light thrown by the lamp which stands on the table beside her, peering at something – a photograph, evidently – from which he presently glances up.

'Why, Sandy,' he remarks, with a mischievous smirk that makes Sandy's heart skip a beat. 'Haven't you changed?'

And for the second time that day, Sandy is confronted with an image of his younger self: a very much younger self, this time – a mere child, in fact. He is flanked in this instance by three smiling women: his mother and aunts. He stares straight at the camera, his freckled face open and trusting beneath his tousled fringe. Unexpectedly, Sandy feels a lump in his throat – an access of tenderness and pity towards his eight-year-old self. Dear, sweet-faced little chap, he thinks. If only you knew what I know now. He flips the photograph over. 'Broadstairs, 1920,' he reads.

'So who's this, then?' Ray's finger rests first on one cloche-hatted figure, then the next.

'That's Mumsie,' Sandy tells him. 'And that's Auntie, of course. And Leonora. She's the one on the left, in the striped frock . . .' It had been Leonora who'd driven them all down in the Lagonda. They'd gone bathing and after their picnic they'd had a game of rounders. He'd scored six runs and then Auntie had bought them all ices. Later, they'd watched the Punch and Judy show. He'd laughed at the Crocodile, but the Hangman had made him cry.

'Sweet,' says Ray archly, pursing his lips in an appreciative *moue*. The look he gives Sandy, sidelong through long lashes, sends a frisson of desire along the latter's spine.

'How's the head?' he inquires, his hand not quite steady as he pours the tea.

'Throbbing something cruel,' says Ray.

There is a brief, charged pause.

'Auntie,' says Sandy, 'it looks as if we might have to trespass upon your hospitality for a tiny bit longer than we'd thought . . .'

Connie seems not a whit perturbed. She smiles and waves her hand with magnificent insouciance. 'Soap,' she says. 'Towels. I'm sure there are soap and towels somewhere . . .'

'Don't worry about that, Auntie,' he reassures her hastily. 'I'm sure Raymond and I don't mind roughing it for one night . . .'

'Speak for yourself, dear,' says Ray.

Connie is brushing her hair before getting into bed, when, in the mirror behind her, she sees Wilfred, sitting in the Lloyd Loom chair. She's so surprised that she nearly drops the brush – but manages not to, although her hands are shaking so badly she has to hold them still in her lap. For what seems like a long time – but is perhaps no more than a minute – the eyes of her late husband meet hers in the glass with a steady, mournful stare. She wonders briefly if she should turn around to face him, but finds she is quite incapable of moving; she continues, therefore, to gaze at his reflection, which is certainly enough to be going on with, she decides.

It strikes her as strange that, of all the ways he might have come back to her, he has chosen the one she's never seen: himself in uniform, just before he was discharged from active service, in 1917. Over a year before they met. He's wearing a small moustache (she recalls him as clean-shaven), but the face above the khaki tunic is otherwise as she remembers it from that first meeting, in the tea-room of the Grand Hotel. He'd been with his mother, as she'd been with hers (it must have been not long after Hugh was killed, because they were both in mourning; she remembers fidgeting with her black gloves, and wishing she could have worn a less ugly hat).

At the time, she'd taken his silence for embarrassment at the nature of the meeting, and the obviousness with which it had been contrived. Because, of course, it was understood by all concerned – the two matriarchs and their respective off-spring – that a marriage was being arranged. At over thirty (her mother had said) she was lucky to be getting an offer at all – even if the bridegroom in question wasn't exactly what you'd call an ideal match, with his nerves all in pieces (although he couldn't help that, poor boy) and no money to speak of. Still, any husband was better than no husband at all, said Mama. There were many worse off. At least he still had all his limbs intact . . . With her mother's remarks still unpleasantly fresh in her mind, Connie'd been too shy to say more than a few words to her suitor. A request for a clean cup, she seems to remember. He'd said nothing at all. Sitting there very pale and still, his eyes moving restlessly around the room, meeting her gaze only once in the . . .

'Mirror,' breathes Connie, her lips barely shaping the word, her gaze fixed on that of the figure slightly to the left of her own reflection in the dressing-table glass.

Then, as now, his eyes had flinched away – like those of a frightened animal, she remembers thinking. As if he saw not the mundane scene before him, with its stiff linen tablecloths and its flimsy gilt chairs, and its ladies in absurd feathered hats the size of cartwheels, but something else entirely: a vision of horrors too terrible to mention.

That was the look his eyes held now. Such sadness, such pain – she'd thought the dead were beyond all that. Unable to bear it a moment longer, she turns, and finds herself staring at an empty chair.

Sandy is having trouble sleeping. With Ray in the next room – the two of them separated by only the thickness of a wall – it's as much as he can do to keep his hands to himself. Little tease. As they'd been getting Ray's room ready (it is much the nicer of the two, but Sandy doesn't mind) there'd been a moment when things might have taken a different turn. Sandy was straightening up from making the bed (he'd found some sheets which weren't too damp once they'd been aired a bit, and if the blankets were a shade musty – well, they were probably a lot better than Ray was used to) when Ray'd caught his eye.

That would have been the moment, if it was going to happen, for something to have happened. Sandy'd held his breath. But all Ray had actually said was could he have another blanket, because this house was as cold as a morgue – however did she stand it, the old girl? If Sandy had thought to say it then (instead of now, when it was too late) he'd have said something sweetly daring about Ray not needing any blankets when he had Sandy to keep him warm . . . But the moment had passed. Ray'd given one of his exaggerated yawns.

'I'm shagged out,' he'd said.

And the next thing Sandy knew, he was all on his own, in a room he thinks must once have been a dressing room, to judge by the meanness of its proportions, lying flat on his back with his eyes wide open to the darkness, with the sound of Ray's gentle snores through the wall a provoking reminder of his own timidity. Although really he's quite prepared to wait, if that's what Ray wants. Because Ray is special. Worth waiting for, in Sandy's opinion. Dear boy. A little thoughtless at times, it was true, but so charming when he wanted to be, sighs Sandy. Oh, but he so wants things to work out this time!

He's in that fitful state between sleeping and waking – has, in fact, embarked on a dream, in which he somehow finds himself back at school, about to sit his exams in the big hall, with the stink of chalk dust, boiled cabbage and boys' undershorts all about him – when he hears the cry. At once he's wide awake, although a second before he was unpleasantly aware that if he didn't turn over soon or pinch himself, he'd be stuck for the duration in the gloomy vaults of his *alma mater*, with the shade of Old Beaky in his long black gown hovering at his shoulder and no earthly chance of escape until the bell went for rec.

His first thought is that Ray must have had a nightmare; poor lamb, it'd hardly be surprising, given that this is a strange house (stranger than most, thinks Sandy). In no more than the time it takes to slip on Uncle Wilfred's dressing gown (a fetching number in spotted silk which, he rather thinks, gives

84

him a look of the Master), he's out on the landing, ready to offer words of comfort, and more besides.

But it isn't Ray he sees; in fact, he isn't sure quite who or what it is that rushes by him – really, just as you'd push past someone in a crowded street if you were in a tearing hurry and that someone were in your way. There's a definite sensation of being not *shoved* exactly, but shouldered aside. Barged. He opens his mouth to protest.

Only the queer thing is, there's no one there; or at least, not until a heartbeat later, when he sees the white glimmer of Auntie's nightgown as she emerges from her room and realizes that it's her voice he's heard crying out, *No, Wait. Don't go.*

'It's only me, Auntie,' Sandy calls softly, to reassure her – even though he's trembling like a leaf himself at the shock of what has just passed. Had she felt it, too? There's a smell of something: cordite, is it? His nostrils twitch.

'Did you have a bad dream?' he asks kindly, taking a step forward so that she can see it's only him and not some intruder after her life savings, poor old duck.

Auntie stares at him. 'Why didn't you stop him?' she demands. 'He might have waited for you . . .'

A sensation like a cold finger sends gooseflesh up Sandy's spine. 'What do you mean?' he blurts out, knowing as he asks the question that he doesn't want to hear the answer.

'If he'd waited for anyone, it would have been you,' is all Connie will say, adding with a sad little smile, 'He was always so fond of you.'

4
A Turn-up for the Books

Alone in the fusty-smelling morning room, where the toast crumbs from a succession of breakfasts have left their crunchy residue on the carpet, Connie idly stirs her cooling tea and thinks about a party she attended nearly sixty years before. A reception at the British Consulate. Not her sort of thing at all, of course – but Lily had insisted. It was the highlight of the season, she said. The whole of Shanghai would be there. Connie remembers a room packed with people, all talking at the tops of their voices. The heat from their bodies combined with that of the chandeliers was overpowering; the atmosphere a cloying mixture of powdered female flesh, bear's grease and cigar smoke. Hardly surprising that she'd felt in need of air. Making for the French windows on the far side of the ballroom, she'd heard her name spoken; turned to find him there.

In evening dress Strickland looked, if anything, even more louche than at their first meeting. 'What a crush,' he'd said. 'Worse than the Royal Academy's Summer Exhibition and almost as much of a bore . . .' From an inside pocket he'd taken out a flat silver case, clicked it open and offered it to her. 'No? They're Russian. Quite good. But I agree it's a filthy habit. Not as filthy as smoking opium, but every bit as addictive.' He'd tapped the cigarette on the lid of the case and transferred it to his lips. Clicked his fingers to summon the hovering boy with his tray of wax-tipped Lucifers. 'So tell me,' said Strickland, inhaling the Sobranie's perfumed smoke. 'What have you been up to since we last met?'

What had she said? She can't recall. Absent-mindedly, she swallows a mouthful of cold tea. How handsome he'd been. Quite the most handsome man there. How cross Lily'd been when she'd found them together . . .

– *You silly girl. Have you any idea what you're getting yourself into?*

– *I only talked to him for a minute . . .*

– *Don't be pert, Miss. Half of Shanghai must have seen you with that . . . that man.*

– *I don't see what's so bad about him . . .*

– *Then you don't see very much. Guy Strickland isn't a suitable friend for a girl like you . . .*

Poor Lily. She'd meant so well. But really there was nothing she could have said or done which would have made any difference, thinks Connie, dreamily buttering toast. She takes a bite, then puts it down. These days, she doesn't have much of an appetite.

When had she seen him again? It must have been that time at the museum. She'd been given permission to go, because the children were out at a party – and even Lily couldn't see the harm in looking at a few Ming vases and a roomful of dusty old silk paintings. Had she arranged to meet him there or had it been mere chance that brought him? She can't recall. Although after the first time – deliberate or otherwise – there were further meetings. She'd developed quite a taste for Chinese art.

'The calligraphic style,' murmurs Connie, sketching landscapes in the air with a half-eaten slice of toast. 'Mountains. Clouds. Bamboo groves in spring rain . . .'

What's she wittering about now, daft old bat? wonders Ray, hearing a voice from the morning room. Making no more sound than a stalking cat, he edges closer.

It must have been around that time he'd taken her to hear the Chinese opera. 'With your passion for all things Oriental you might just enjoy it,' he'd said. She can't think how she'd managed to evade Lily's vigilant eye on *that* occasion. Some fib about needing to visit the dentist, perhaps. Strickland had been waiting at the corner of Avenue Joffre and Rue Lafayette. They'd travelled by rickshaw. In that confined space, thrown together as the contraption rattled over the potholes, it had been impossible not to touch. To his credit, he hadn't tried to kiss her.

Even now, if she shuts her eyes, she can re-enter the moment: feeling again the rocking movement of the car, the slight pressure of his leg against hers, as they hurtled along through a warren of narrow streets packed with people whose faces she'd only glimpsed in passing. Old men playing Go in the open door of a tea-shop. Babies asleep in hammocks, slung in doorways. A man cutting the legs off frogs with a pair of scissors before tossing them into a smoking pan of oil. A woman with her dress torn down the front and her hair disordered, holding up what seems to be a dead child . . . ('You mustn't mind,' he'd said, when he'd seen her looking. 'That kind of thing's all too common here. They're used to it, one imagines . . .')

They'd arrived at the theatre only moments before the performance was due to start. Strickland had helped her down, then turned to shout at the rickshaw boy. 'These people always try and cheat one,' he'd remarked to Connie with a shrug. 'It's almost a point of honour with them.' Inside, the flaring gas lamps made it unbearably hot. Men sat in front of the stage cracking nuts and throwing the shells on the floor. The opera itself was unlike any piece of theatre she had ever seen, although admittedly her experience had not been wide. But if her visits to Sadler's Wells to see Miss Marian Fay in *Peter Pan*, to the Royal Court to see Mr Casson in *Macbeth* and to Covent Garden to hear Miss Melba sing Mimi in *La Bohème* had prepared her for anything, it had not been for this.

The Spirit of the Green Carp Pond was a tale of thwarted love ('like *Tristan and Isolde*,' said Strickland) but with a good deal of fairy-tale and pantomime thrown in; perhaps, after all, *Peter Pan* was not so wide of the mark. From what she'd been able to gather there was a fairy, of sorts, who was also a fish – the eponymous Carp. The fish fell in love with a man, and then turned itself into a beautiful young girl, the better to catch the eye of the beloved. Like the Little Mermaid, in Mr Andersen's tale, she remembers thinking. But the girl had a father who disapproved of the match. He'd enlisted the support of the gods to prevent what was evidently a highly irregular affair.

Despite these idiosyncrasies of plot, it wasn't the story itself which presented the problem, but rather the mode of its execution. For from the moment that the Spirit of the Green Carp Pond – disguised as the beautiful Golden Peony – first opened her mouth to declare her love for the modest Scholar Zhang, Connie found herself fighting a strong desire to laugh. The curious mewing sound that issued from Peony's painted lips as she vowed her undying devotion was disconcerting enough, bearing little or no relation to the kind of singing with which Connie was familiar. But it was when her lover – poor but honest Zhang – started to sing, in a high falsetto like a parody of female intonation, that the utter strangeness of the performance became apparent.

'Do I sense that you don't admire the native style?' said Strickland, seeing her face. 'It is, I grant you, a touch strident . . .'

'It's very fine,' she'd said hastily. 'It just takes a bit of getting used to.'

'Like cats being strangled, one unkind critic has said. I myself think it's rather worse than that. If you like,' he'd added carelessly, 'I could introduce you to the cast . . .'

Which had been rather fascinating, she recalls. Seeing them with their masks off. Such elaborate masks, too. Although that was mainly the demons and other supernatural types. The strangest thing was that all the parts were played by men, even that of the beautiful princess. Just the same as in Shakespeare's day, of course – but still, it had given her a bit of a turn when he'd taken his wig off . . .

Connie's eyelids droop; snap open. She must have dropped off for a minute there, she thinks. She remembers what she has to do now. The letter, the letter . . . 'Now, where did I put it?' she murmurs. Chest of drawers? Linen cupboard? Desk? 'Ah, yes . . .' Third drawer from the bottom. She remembers putting it there only last week . . . She makes a move to rise, but the attempt is ill-judged; instead of doing what she expects of them, her feet slide out from under her. She flails her arms as if about to execute a comic pratfall, teeters for an excruciating second on the brink of saving herself – hands grasping at thin air – before toppling slowly backwards, and ending in a heap on the floor.

'Confound it,' mutters Connie, when she has got her breath back. 'Sandy,' she calls, in a voice that trembles slightly, before remembering that Sandy has gone to see about getting Bert to fix the car. Hadn't he just been in to tell her he was off?

Thinking of Sandy reminds her of what's got her into this pickle in the first place, because if it hadn't been for Sandy's showing up so unexpectedly, she'd have forgotten all about the letter . . . Now it seems imperative that she should find it. To Ray, watching from the doorway, she seems galvanized, all of a sudden, into action. What *is* the old dear up to? he wonders, grinning to himself at the ridiculous sight of her as, determination written on every feature, she shuffles across the floor on her beam-end, arriving, with no small effort, at the foot of the big black desk. Oh ho, thinks Ray. What have we here?

He watches greedily as the old bat gets a purchase on the thing, then, with an audible grunt, hauls open the drawer. Which proves, as far as Ray (craning his neck) can tell, to be stuffed with a litter of crumbling old papers, used envelopes and bills long ago paid or forgotten. But Auntie's clearly got her mind set on something. Calmly sifting through the rubbish, discarding what doesn't interest her upon the floor, she unearths at length a long brown envelope, which Ray (with a good deal of previous in such matters) recognizes as belonging to that category of official documents – summonses, affidavits and the like – which inspires respect. And as Auntie withdraws the folded article from the envelope and, with some difficulty on account of the stiffness of the paper, smooths it flat, he sees that it is a very interesting document indeed. Even with his restricted viewpoint, he is able to identify its arrangement of sub-clauses and scarlet seals as those pertaining to financial agreements: contracts, deeds and, of course, wills.

Hardly daring to breathe, Ray watches as she reads over what is written there in the fine copperplate hand of the lawyer's clerk, clucking every now and then as she negotiates a tricky clause, nodding her head – *'Mmhmf, mmhmf'* – as if approving the choices she has made. Apparently satisfied that everything is in order, she replaces the document in its envelope and the envelope in its drawer.

Something else attracts her attention. 'There you are!' she mutters. 'Knew I'd put you somewhere . . .' 'You' turns out to be a stiff white envelope with two sheets folded inside it. A letter of some sort, Ray sees, squinting from his corner. Again, this elicits an approving response from Auntie. 'Mmhmf, mmhmf,' she grunts. 'Just so . . .' When she has read it through, she stuffs the letter back in its envelope and returns it to its hiding place. Only when it is safely stowed, beneath an artfully disordered pile of paper, does Ray make his move. With a gentle cough, he steps out of the shadows. 'I say,' he murmurs, all bashful *politesse*. 'You seem to have had a bit of a tumble. *Do* let me help you up . . .' Holding out his hand as he speaks and smiling so brightly that Connie, looking up, startled at the sound of his voice, is momentarily dazzled. Julian, she thinks, before remembering that of course it can't be Julian. Julian's at the bottom of the sea.

Sandy is kicking himself, because he should have known something of this sort was going to happen – what could you expect in a hole-in-corner place like this, where the motorcar was still regarded as a new-fangled invention and no one had even heard of the RAC? From the way the chap looked at him when he'd asked for the local rep's number, you'd have thought he'd made an improper suggestion. 'It's Sunday,' Bert or Fred or whatever his name was had said. 'You won't get nobody coming out on a Sunday.'

Living so long in the metropolis, he'd forgotten how religiously they observed their sabbath, these yokels. You'd have more chance of getting pigs to fly than of getting Bert or Fred to shed his Sunday collar and roll up his shirtsleeves for a bit of honest work – paid at overtime rates, too! 'I'd make it worth your while, naturally,' Sandy'd told him, straight out.

Showing him the ten-bob note, just to make it plain as daylight.

But no amount of affable, man-to-man stuff had had any effect on the bumpkin. He'd shaken his head, with a slowness that made Sandy want to shake him. 'Can't do it, Oi'm afraid. We're closed, Sundys. Se'en o'clock Mundy mornin's the best Oi can do you.'

Routed, Sandy'd been reduced to muttering imprecations ('Call this a service? If this were Brighton or London you'd be out of business in a week!') before, reluctantly, retracing his steps Dunsinane-wards.

To add insult to injury, hadn't the bloody church bells started up just as he was passing, adding their clangour to the usual rustic din of crowing cocks and barking dogs which always started up so hideously early in these parts? Bing*bong*-bing*bong*bing*bong*bing*bong*. The whole ghastly sequence bringing back memories of bell-ringing practice on frosty mornings before school (which he'd only got into in the first place to impress Perkins Minor, who'd repaid his devotion by taking up with Piers de Winter, little tart). Getting up at six to chip the ice off the water in the washstand jug, because the dean was a stickler about boys washing their necks, then tumbling downstairs and across the quad still half asleep to the belfry steps. Taking the winding stairs at a stumbling run ('Come along, Foulkes, get a move on, do!') with barely time to draw breath before the horror of the thing itself . . .

Absorbed in these thoughts, he doesn't at first hear his name being called.

'Why, Sandy!' Iseult attracts his attention at last by the simple expedient of blocking his path. 'Fancy your still being here! I thought you were motoring back last night . . .'

'Hello, Izzie.' Of course he was bound to meet her, he thinks bitterly. In a place this size the biggest social event of the week was church – and here they are. 'Slight change of plan, I'm afraid.'

He explains what has happened. Iseult makes sympathetic noises. But when he starts to describe the uncooperativeness of Bert the garage man over hauling the car out of the ditch, she interrupts him.

'Bert's a good sort, really. He'd have done it any day but Sunday . . .'

'So I gathered,' says Sandy, with a dryness which is perhaps lost on his cousin, who merely frowns.

'Not to worry,' she says briskly. 'Soon as I've dropped Mother off from church, I'll bring the tractor over. Have you back on the road in two shakes . . .'

'That's awfully good of you,' he tells her.

'Don't mention it,' says Iseult gruffly. Self-consciousness makes her unable to meet his eyes. Instead, she scans the crowd of communicants presently emerging from the church porch for the figure of her mother.

'You're not a member of the vicar's fanclub, then?' remarks Sandy, following her gaze.

She gives him a startled look. 'What? Oh, I see. No, it's not that. He's not a bad sort, actually – the Reverend Allbright, I mean. It's just that Mummy likes to take communion –' and having an excuse to wear her best hat, she might have said – 'whereas Aunt and I prefer Evensong. It's not so . . . *churchy*, somehow, if you know what I mean . . .'

Sandy nods vaguely, although it's years since he set foot inside a church – not since Mumsie's funeral, in fact. Something about the atmosphere makes him uncomfortable – the odour of sanctity, perhaps. All it takes is a whiff of that smell – a peculiar compound of incense, floor wax and stale flower-water – for him to feel eight years old again. Buttoned into his navy-blue worsted coat with the velvet collar to sit through hour upon hour of long words whose meanings were, to him, opaque.

To be carnally minded is death.

What did it mean, he'd asked Mumsie afterwards, recalling the way the priest's eye had paused in its restless perusal of his parishioners' faces, to linger on Sandy, as if the words were meant for him alone. But she, shrugging off her furs with that careless motion he loved, wasn't listening, as usual. 'Don't bother me now, sweet,' she'd merely replied. 'It makes my poor head ache so . . .'

Thinking about his mother – that enchanting air of helplessness she had, and those eyes (like rain-drenched violets, one of her admirers had said) – makes him come over a bit tearful. Dearest Mumsie. Such good chums they'd been, the two of them – more like sister and brother, people said, than mother and son. She'd been the youngest of the three sisters, of course; the first of them to marry ('barely out of the schoolroom') and the first to die. Poor darling, she'd always been delicate. It was her heart, they said. That was the reason there'd only ever been Sandy. Her special boy, she called him.

'Coo-ee!' Leonora is bearing down on them, her Sunday-go-to-meeting hat at a rakish angle. She, of course, is certain to live to be a hundred, Sandy thinks sourly. Tough as old boots. Auntie was the one he worried about. She was definitely well on the way to losing her marbles, poor old duck.

'Well, I never!' gasps Leonora, waddling up on the arm of a red-faced young curate. 'Fancy seeing *you* at church, Sandy, dear . . .'

'Sandy's had a prang,' explains Iseult.

'Oh, hard luck!' Leonora gives a rendition of her silver bells. 'Mr Dixon here,' she says, with a coy look at the blushing curate, 'has undertaken to escort me to the car. So gallant. Such a credit to Mrs Dixon . . .'

'As a matter of fact,' splutters the curate, 'there isn't a Mrs Dixon . . .'

'I was referring to Mrs Dixon *Senior*. Your revered mother. So wonderful for her age,' dimples Leonora prettily. 'Did you hear that?' she hisses to her daughter, as the clergyman makes his escape. 'He's available. He practically said so . . .'

'*Mother!*' begs Iseult, overcome with mortification.

But Leonora only laughs. 'Don't "Mother" me,' she says, with a wicked look at Sandy.

She allows herself to be settled into the front seat of the Armstrong Sidley, giving Iseult a momentary respite from this embarrassing topic.

'You'll be needing a lift,' Iseult says to Sandy. 'I'll drop you off first, shall I?'

'No need,' says Sandy, now ensconced in the back seat. 'I can hitch a ride back on the tractor. What fun,' he adds. 'I don't think I've been on a tractor since I was a lad . . .'

'Haven't you really?' Iseult throws him a melting glance over her shoulder.

'I believe the last time was with *you*, Izzie. Haymaking. Such larks!'

By the time Izzie has returned with the tractor and hitched the whole thing up, made a couple of false starts, then really put her foot down and given the most almighty heave and got the whole thing out of the ditch, it's past lunchtime, and Sandy isn't the only one who's starting to feel a bit peckish. So that when Izzie (very hot and sweaty, with a fetching smear of oil on her cheek) delivers her verdict – *No can do, Sandy old thing. Axle's broken, I'm afraid* – it's almost a relief to know they're done with all that for the rest of the day. Because thanks to Bert and his Lord's Day Observance scruples, there's not a snowball's chance in hell of getting the Morris repaired before Monday morning; and knowing the way these people work, it'll be teatime before they get away.

Sandy's first thought is how he's going to break the news to Ray, after the way he'd carried on yesterday. So that it's a nice surprise when the dear boy doesn't seem in the least bit put out. It's almost as if he's been hoping something like this would happen. And then Izzie, bless her, rises to the occasion in the way she can be relied upon to do, saying, 'Well, if that's the case, why don't you all come back to the farm for a spot of lunch, and I'll run you to the station in time for the four o'clock?' 'What about the car?' objects Ray (unusual for him to take such an interest in practical matters), and Izz says, 'Oh, don't worry about that. As soon as it's ready, Sandy can pop down on the train and collect it, can't you, Sandy? Just give me a ring and I'll pick you up at the station.'

Sandy's ready to fall in with this plan, which sounds pretty foolproof to him, but Ray doesn't seem convinced. 'It seems a long way to go, just to come all the way back,' he says, in that whining voice Sandy wishes he wouldn't use quite so often. Izz stops herself from saying Stuff and Nonsense, but you can see it's on the tip of her tongue from the way her eyebrows shoot up. 'It's only half an hour on the train,' she observes mildly.

Then it's just a matter of breaking the good news to Auntie (who takes it very well, all things considered) and of getting themselves spruced up as far as possible, given that they've only one shaving kit between them and no change of shirt. And then Izzie, who's driven back with the tractor in the meantime and changed out of her working togs and back into her best skirt (or what passes for it, poor love), returns to collect them in the Armstrong Sidley. Which, apart from being about a hundred years old, smells horribly of dog and those dreadful gaspers the dear girl will insist on smoking. Uncomfortable as the journey is, at least there's the prospect of Izzie's roast beef at the end of it. Wonderful cook, old Izz, thinks Sandy warmly.

They arrive at the farm, to be greeted by the usual flurry of muddy dogs, so that Sandy's once-presentable Daks end up even more mauled about and slobbered on than they were from the attentions of Rufus. As they enter the dark hall, a rich smell of roasting meat assails their nostrils and Iseult, muttering something about needing to see to the potatoes, scuttles into the kitchen. 'Iseult!' bawls Leonora from the sitting room, where she has been lying at her ease, tucked up on the sofa with the *Sunday Post* and a glass of Amontillado to hand. 'My cushions have slipped . . .'

Sandy thinks regretfully of his own lost Sunday morning, with its leisurely rituals of warm bath (a *soupçon* of Penhaligon's Vervain swished into the water), wet shave (followed by a splash of Trumper's Gentleman's Cologne) and other niceties of grooming. A fleeting image of his dressing table, with its ivory-backed hairbrushes (nothing like a good stiff brush to keep the scalp in tip-top condition), its elegant manicure set and silver-stoppered bottles of hair-wash and aftershave, flashes across his mind. He sighs appreciatively.

'Sandy, do stop gawking there and get us all some drinks, there's a good boy,' comes Leonora's voice, dashing these pleasant reflections to smithereens.

How he'd like to brain the old boot. Who does she think she is, talking to him like that? As if he were twelve years old, thinks Sandy disgustedly. 'So what'll everyone have?' he says, between gritted teeth.

'Ooh, a nice sherry for me, I think,' says Leonora, quick off the mark as usual.

'A nice strychnine, more like,' mutters Sandy under his breath, as he hunts out the bottle, which, after the punishment it had yesterday (not to mention the couple of glasses the old soak had before they arrived), turns out to be practically empty. 'We're almost out of sherry, I'm afraid,' he says innocently.

'If I've told Iseult once, I've told her a thousand times,' grumbles Leonora. 'You don't waste a good sherry by putting it in trifle. Oh, well,' she adds resignedly, 'I suppose it'll have to be a G and T . . .'

Which is a bore, thinks Sandy, because then of course Ray pipes up that *he* rather fancies one, too; and even Auntie looks brighter at the thought of a fizzy pick-me-up. And then there's all the palaver of digging out the Schweppes (which hasn't gone flat, for a wonder) and finding a lemon – which means a trip to the kitchen, because there's nothing in the fruit bowl except some wizened apples and a black banana – so that by the time he's sorted out glasses and looked in vain for some ice and dished out the old mother's ruin, he's more than ready for a stiff one himself.

Even when he's successfully completed his mission and returned to base, the old trout won't give him a moment's peace, with her 'Oh, Sandy – could you hand round the nuts?' and her 'Sandy, be a love and fetch some coasters. If there's one thing I can't *bear*, it's rings on the veneer . . .' What did your last servant die of? he's tempted to retort, but escapes, instead, back to the kitchen, where Izzie, steam plastering wisps of hair to her forehead, at least asks him nicely if he'll give her a hand with the veg.

What with one thing and another – the gravy going lumpy,

and then Izzie remembering that she'd forgotten to make the custard – it's past two by the time they're sitting down at table and by now some of them are more than a little squiffy. Leonora's the worst, giggling and telling off-colour stories to which she keeps forgetting the punch-line, and poking her food around like a naughty child, complaining that the meat's tough and the cabbage is watery and the roast potatoes are too hard, while Izzie just sits there, getting quieter and quieter. And Ray's almost as bad. Letting out a loud belch just as Izzie is about to say grace, and then making it worse by saying, 'Pardon'.

Even Auntie seems affected by the general hilarity, launching at one point into an incomprehensible and rambling story about something her governess once told her when she was six to do with putting salt on birds' tails to stop them flying away. And how she'd waited all morning in the garden with the salt cellar, but no birds had come. 'Because they're not daft, you know, birds. They knew perfectly well what I was up to . . .'

'Are you sure they was birds and not bats?' mutters Ray, not quite softly enough.

Sandy frowns at him. But really he's relieved that Ray seems to be in such good form. His earlier crossness about the trains has vanished, superseded by a blatant flirtatiousness. Every time Sandy catches his eye, Ray flashes him a wink, and once, as he leans over to pick up his napkin, Sandy is astonished to feel a sly pinch on his bottom.

Well! Things *are* starting to look up. Sandy can hardly wait for the moment when they'll be alone at last. He must make sure they get an empty compartment on the train . . .

'*Do* let me help,' says Little-Ray-of-Sunshine to their hostess, as she starts to clear the table. He wrests the pile of dirty plates she has been collecting from her grasp. 'It's the least I can do, when you've put on such a lovely spread . . .'

Deaf to her protests ('Please don't bother. I can do all that later . . .'), he starts for the door, staggering a little under his burden. He's only gone a few paces (just time enough, in fact, for Sandy to admire the firm globes of his buttocks in their by now distinctly off-white trousers) when something – a loose thread in the carpet, perhaps – trips him up. There's nothing any of them can do except watch as, with the graceful inevitability of a slow-motion film, the plates fly up in the air, and Ray falls down.

The sound of the bump with which he hits the floor seems, in their collective perception of the event, to occur a second or so after the moment of impact; the crash of the plates, as they smash one by one, seems to come even later. The silence which follows both sounds seems to go on for ever. Ray is the first to break it.

'Oh dear,' he says. 'Clumsy me.' And then, as he tries to sit up. 'Ouch. I seem to have twisted my ankle . . .'

Well, after the shock of what happened, and clearing up the mess and having to see to that wretched boy with cold compresses and the like (although in Iseult's opinion he wasn't hurt at all, just shamming), they hadn't a hope of catching the 4.03. By that time, it was obvious they wouldn't be leaving at all, and that there'd be three more guests for supper that night. Not that Iseult minded a bit; if you were making sandwiches for two, you might just as well make 'em for five, was how she looked at it. And Sandy was always such a help – look at the way he'd pitched in at lunchtime, lending a hand with the potatoes when others were putting their feet up.

No, of course it wasn't Sandy she minded about; and even

if he wasn't always a perfect dear, well – blood was thicker than water, wasn't it? She did wonder, though, whether he knew what he was getting into where that young man was concerned. Devious wasn't too strong a word for it, in her opinion. That business at lunch, for instance. She'd had her eye on him, even before it happened, worrying about her poor china, because he hadn't seemed exactly *steady* on his feet, when he'd made such a fuss about helping. Even so, she could have sworn there was something not quite right about the accident. As if he'd staged the whole thing on purpose. He *said* he'd caught his foot on the edge of the carpet – but she'd nailed it down herself not the week before.

As for spraining his ankle or whatever it was he claimed to have done – well, this wasn't like any sprain she'd ever seen. Not the slightest bit of swelling or redness anywhere. And it certainly wasn't broken, because he could wiggle his toes. Claiming he felt faint when he stood up, so that Sandy practically had to carry him to a chair. Little fraud.

The worst of it was, poor Sandy seemed quite taken in by the performance.

Look at him now, thinks Iseult gloomily. Running hither and thither with cups of tea for the poor sufferer and cushions for his precious foot. He'd even offered to pay for the broken crockery, dear thing, saying he'd take the whole lot off her hands if she liked, and replace it with a brand-new service. Sweet of him, really – although she thought, on the whole, that she'd stick with the Rockingham, chipped and battered as it was. It'd been in the family for donkey's years, and she was rather attached to it.

It was kind, too, thinks Iseult fondly, the way Sandy'd offered to help with the cows. Jumping up when he saw her putting on her boots, as if it were the most natural thing in the world. After the day she'd had, with Mummy being so difficult at lunch, and then that disaster with the plates, it felt like a kind of reward. Getting out of the house was always a relief, she found; a brisk walk across the fields with the dogs was all it took to blow the cobwebs away. She didn't mind the rest of it, either – even the rough work had its soothing side, so that mucking out the cows or feeding the pigs often left her feeling as near to content as she got these days.

'It's a hard old life, Izz,' Sandy'd said, as they finished shutting the cows up for the night. 'Don't know how you stand it.'

'It's not so bad,' she'd told him – and, just at that moment, leaning on the gate to light a Woodbine, with the pleasant reek of the byre in her nostrils and the evening light gilding the old brick farm buildings so that they looked like something out of an Old Master, she'd meant it, too.

'You've never wanted anything else?' he'd asked her then, wrinkling up his brow in that funny way he had that reminded her of Nimrod after a rabbit. 'Away from all this?' His gesture took in the fields across which they had come, which had once marked the boundary of the farm, before she'd had to sell the water-meadow.

She'd hesitated no more than a second. 'No. Not really.'

It wasn't quite a fib. She'd always known the farm would be her destiny. If she'd married of course . . . If there'd been children . . . But she hadn't married and there'd be no children now. You had the life you had. No sense in moping after what could never be.

'You're lucky,' he'd said, with a sad little smile. 'Sometimes I wish . . .' He broke off, with a sigh.

'Yes?' said Iseult.

But Sandy only shook his head. 'Nothing,' he said.

'But surely . . .' She frowned a moment. 'You're perfectly content? I mean, with the business going so well and everything . . .'

'Oh yes,' he agreed heartily. 'Never been better.'

Of course it wasn't quite the truth. Things were far from rosy. The paltry amount he'd got from Mumsie's estate (after the death duties had been paid and the funeral expenses settled) had been sunk into the business. Now it was nearly all gone. *Alexander Foulkes. Antiquarian. Restoration a Speciality*, the cards he'd had printed read. *Very* high-falutin'. Although the reality was rather more mundane. A mental picture of the dingy shop in a less-than-fashionable side street off the Lanes surfaces briefly. The glass door with its skewed sign. The jangling bell. The moth-eaten bear (a rash purchase at an out-of-town auction). The worm-eaten spinet. Then there was the mirror whose silver was flaking off, so that one saw oneself only in patches. The Chinese silk rug (but that was stained with damp). The (really quite good) walnut lady's writing desk – now sadly warped – and the silver tea service (missing its sugar basin). The broken-backed prayer chair and the cracked Sèvres chocolate pot and the (slightly foxed) first edition of *Sonnets from the Portuguese*. All junk – all of it – junk, thinks Sandy glumly.

Not that there weren't compensations for the precariousness of this existence. In spite of the headaches and the endless bills, he was still his own master. For every day spent poring over the accounts, or cataloguing stock (had he really paid good money for that gimcrack pair of candlesticks, that treacly Victorian study of Highland cattle?), there was another when he'd swing the sign round to Closed, put the key in his pocket and wander down to the beach. On a fine spring day, with the clouds scudding across a sky right out of a Philip Wilson Steer, one could think oneself, if not actually in France or Italy, then at least not in England.

Somewhere away from this mean, cold, *savage* little country, with its pettifogging rules and its withering glances. Somewhere open, free, untrammelled by dreary convention; where you could wear your trousers rolled to your knees if you felt like it, without some grubby brat pointing. *Ooh, er! Look at the funny man!* Where you could enjoy a simple lunch (a loaf of bread, a jug of wine) with your friends in the open air, with no disapproving looks from old fogeys with dogs who thought they owned the beach. On days like these (playing ducks and drakes off the end of the breakwater), he could forget about his money worries and everything else that oppressed him. Losing himself in the sky-blue infinite . . .

'I say, Sandy, old thing,' Iseult's voice says timidly, breaking the thread of these reflections. 'Oughtn't we to be getting back?'

She'd wanted to kick herself afterwards. Hadn't he been on the verge of confiding in her? Things might have taken such a different turn if he had . . . If only (she thought later) she could have the time again! But that was the way life went. One never knew until the moment was past how important the moment had been . . .

So (after settling Mummy down in front of *Songs of Praise*) she'd got them all into the car – which wasn't easy, with that frightful little beast taking up most of the room in the back – and then they'd set off. Aunt Constance beside her, of course, because Sandy is in the back, too, having offered to hold the invalid's leg going over the bumps. And as they're going along, Aunt suddenly says, in that odd way she has of seeming to pick up a conversation from where she's left off (only you never knew quite when that was: five minutes ago or fifty years) –

'Can you believe that all the time it was going on, I never had the slightest idea what he was up to?'

Battily inconsequential as it is, her remark creates a silence in the back of the car.

But Iseult is used to her aunt's gnomic utterances. 'You don't say?' she replies encouragingly.

'Oh, I know it sounds absurd *now*,' says Connie. 'But it never occurred to me not to trust him. I was awfully green in those days . . .'

Funny how easily they slip into the past, thinks Iseult, reminded of Leonora's predilection for describing the finer points of frocks she'd worn to cocktail parties before the war, and hats she'd worn to lunch with long-dead suitors. Only with Aunt it wasn't just silly stuff about clothes, but whole conversations she came out with. As if it were all, somehow, still going on inside her head.

The last rays of the setting sun cast a bloody glare on the old house, which seems, to Sandy's nervous fancy, almost to be lying in wait for them behind the trees, like a large animal poised to spring. He stifles a yawn – another symptom of the ennui which has possessed him since the conversation with Izz. Why had he avoided her question? The truth was, there was nothing all right with his life. In fact it was a sham, a washout, a complete farce. His business was failing, his friends had drifted away (all except those he owed money to, who were all too embarrassingly in evidence). Then there was Ray. His gaze rests a moment on the youth's exquisite profile, savouring its chiselled Italianate beauty, its expression of bored hauteur. If Ray would only let him be something more than just a friend! But Ray, although he had hinted he might be willing to change his status – for the right price – had so far remained aloof, rebuffing Sandy's timid caresses ('Lay off, can't you? You know I can't stand that slop . . .') and muttering darkly about needing to think of the future. Which meant money, of course. Not that one could blame the poor lad for being that way. Mercenary. It was an ugly word. But poverty (which meant the kind of real poverty Ray'd known at first hand, not being merely a bit strapped for cash) was an uglier one.

'Here we are,' Iseult was saying, bringing the car to a halt outside the gates. 'Home sweet home.'

For a moment nobody moves. Then Ray says, in the patient, sweet sufferer's voice he's been using all afternoon, 'If it's not too much trouble, maybe someone could help me up the path. Only I think if I sit here much longer I might start getting cramp . . .'

And then Iseult, acting as if she hasn't heard this, leans across Auntie to open the door on the passenger side, which sticks. 'Come on, Aunt,' she says gruffly. 'Let's see what old Rufus is up to, shall we?'

'I suppose it's having torn the ligaments or twisted them or whatever it is I've done that's making it so painful,' Ray continues, allowing Sandy to help him out of the car.

Slowly, they hobble up the steeply sloping drive towards the house, each pair with its incapacitated partner and its able-bodied. On the way, they have to skirt around the hulk of the wrecked Morris, left where it had been abandoned that morning, after Iseult's efforts with the tractor. Seeing it there, so forlorn and useless, Sandy feels a stab of pity as if for a sick friend, or a shipwrecked vessel come to grief on a foreign shore. But then Ray clutches his arm, leaning heavily on Sandy as if he has missed his footing, and Sandy's heart swells with the pleasure of being so close to the object of his desire; of being there, and of being needed. 'Gently does it,' he murmurs in Ray's ear. 'Don't want to make that poor ankle any worse, do we?'

And Ray, clinging to Sandy like a trusting child to his nurse's hand, says, 'Do you know, I can feel it getting better already . . .'

This sweet, shy boy is a new phenomenon; a promising one, thinks Sandy, suddenly impatient to get rid of Izzie (who does have a tendency to hang around when she's not wanted, poor old love) and pack Auntie off to bed so that he and Ray can be alone. Maybe there's hope for him yet . . . But even after Iseult has taken her leave, with much shuffling of feet and many muttered promises to lend a hand with the car tomorrow morning, it's still an age before they see the last of Auntie. First there's the blasted dog to feed, then the bedtime cup of tea to make.

Even after she's had her 'cuppa', Auntie seems in no hurry to move, Sandy sees with irritation, settling herself down for another session with the photograph album as if she'd all the time in the world. It didn't help to have Ray egging her on, picking out one stiff portrait after another: the hourglass-shaped women in their white frocks; the stern-jawed, musta-chioed men.

'That's Veenie. She died of a broken heart,' Auntie murmurs of one frizzle-haired 1880s beauty; or of some dull-looking chap in the uniform of a Guards officer, 'That's Cousin Reggie. He was at Mafeking . . .'

Ray laps it up – or pretends to. 'Really?' he coos, nodding and smiling as each long-dead family member is dragged into the limelight to do a 'turn'. 'How interesting. You don't say?'

'You must be tired, Auntie,' Sandy interjects at one point, when this calvacade of fish-eyed clergymen and battle-axes in black bombazine shows no sign of abating. 'Why don't I make you a nice hot-water bottle to take up to bed?'

'Oh, don't go yet,' begs Ray (to tease him, Sandy suspects). 'I want to see the ones of Sandy-poos . . .'

Before Sandy can protest, there they all are: the photographs that constitute his life to date. Not so very many of them, when you came to think of it – a couple of studio portraits of him as a baby aged about two in a smock and with his hair in ringlets ('Sweet,' Ray pronounces them); another of a seven-year-old Sandy, in his prep school uniform; then the one of the three of them on the beach; then one of him in cricket whites ('Handsome boy,' says Ray); then Oxford. Himself at the centre of a group of laughing freshers, in blazers and college scarves. He picks out Teddy Wilson – hadn't he ended up in Singapore? Running the family rubber business, or some such. And Jonty Mullins. He'd surprised them all by getting engaged right after his Finals. Some strapping girl picked out by his mother, they said. Then there was little Swinburne. That'd been a dreadful business. They'd hushed it up, of course, because the other chap was married, but everyone knew the truth of it . . . There's a snap of himself in uniform ('Ooh, look at the soldier-boy,' says Ray), followed by a couple of nondescript passport photos. After that, nothing.

Except that, tucked in behind one of the more formal studies (himself looking winsome in gown and mortarboard), Sandy sees with a start, is a snap taken much more recently – just a year or two ago, in fact. It's of the two of them together – himself and Mumsie – standing in front of what must be Brighton Pavilion. He remembers the occasion (how could he not?): the last time she came to see him. 'Uncle' Algy – that ghastly old roué – had brought her down (was it he who had taken the photograph, perhaps?). They'd had lunch at the Grand. He'd taken her to see the new shop. It was after this they'd visited the Pavilion, because she'd always wanted to see it and never had. They'd had such a lovely couple of hours, wandering from room to room of that outlandish monument to an imagined China. How she'd adored it all: the pink and gold parlours with their faux-bamboo pillars, the nodding mandarins and simpering ladies, the yellow satin day beds with lion's feet. What she'd liked best was the music room, with its flying dragons and ceiling like the inside of a great pearl. 'How splendidly vulgar,' she'd cried, clapping her tiny white hands.

'Not a bit like you, your mum, is she?' says Ray, shattering these happy reminiscences. 'Being so little and dark, and you so tall and fair. S'pose you must take after your dad . . .'

'As a matter of fact I'm nothing like my father,' replies Sandy coldly.

Ray says nothing, only raises his eyebrows. It's Connie who speaks first.

'I think, if you don't mind, I'll wander away,' she says, with a bright, vague smile. 'It's been delightful, but I really must love you and leave you . . .' She hauls herself to her feet and stumps towards the door. A minute later, they hear her ascending the stairs.

'Off to Dreamland,' says Ray. 'Not that she ever leaves it, poor old dear. Sad, isn't it, the way some people end up? Better for everyone, really, when the Happy Release comes . . .'

Something about the way he says this arrests Sandy's attention.

'Auntie's fighting fit,' he says. 'She'll go on for a long while yet.'

'I wouldn't be too sure about that,' says Ray softly. 'She looks awful shaky to me. Once people start to go, you know, they go awful fast. One minute, right as a trivet, the next . . .' He snaps his fingers. '*Kaput*.'

'You shouldn't say such things,' Sandy says, with a nervous glance over his shoulder. But they are quite alone. 'It isn't nice, with the poor old thing only upstairs. She might hear . . .'

'She won't,' says Ray. 'Anyhow,' he adds, examining his fingernails with a critical air, '*you* shouldn't worry. When the time comes, *you'll* be laughing . . .'

'What do you mean?'

Ray smiles. 'I mean,' he says deliberately, 'that when Auntie *goes*, you'll be left a very rich boy.'

Sandy looks startled; then his face clears. 'Oh, you mean the house. I suppose it must be worth quite a bit – although who'd want to buy an old-fashioned place like this is another matter . . .'

'It's not the house,' Ray says, with the patient air of someone explaining calculus to a small child. 'Leastways – it *is* the house, but it's a lot more than *just* the house, if you get me. Have you had a dekko at what's *in* the house – on the walls, f'rinstance? Take a look, then, go on . . .'

Sandy casts no more than a cursory glance around. His eye comes to rest on the wall opposite. A portrait, he supposes you'd call it. The sort of thing a rich husband wanting something to remember his wife by might conceivably shell out for. Although what wife would choose to be remembered like this, with a hatchet face and one eye somewhat higher than its fellow – even if the poor lady had been born that way (which he rather doubted)? Great calves like tree trunks under the too short skirt. The hair – or was it some kind of turban?

– a virulent shade of green, contrasting nicely with the lilac tones of the skin.

'I suppose you mean the Stricklands,' he says in a bored tone. 'Frightful daubs, if you ask me. But I imagine they might fetch a bob or two. Although he's terribly out of fashion. Can't think what possessed the old love to pay good money for the things . . .'

'She didn't,' says Ray flatly. 'He gave them to her, didn't he? That's to say – he *left* them to her, when he popped his clogs.'

Sandy's head is beginning to ache from all these explanations. 'I do wish you wouldn't use such coarse expressions,' he says peevishly.

'Ay'm sorray, deah boy,' drawls Ray, slipping easily into a parody of Sandy's own well-modulated vowel sounds. 'You'll hev to forgive my rough, street-arab ways. Only I thought you'd be interested, that's all . . .'

'Interested in what?' says Sandy, still thoroughly ruffled. 'In the fact that some minor Bloomsburyite friend of Auntie's saw fit to leave her half a dozen mediocre canvases in his will? I fail to see why I should get excited about *that* . . .'

'I see,' says Ray. 'Then it won't interest you to know that Auntie's old chum also "saw fit" to drop her a load of loot. A cool hundred thousand, to be exact. No, it wouldn't interest you at all . . .'

There is a silence.

'What are you talking about?' says Sandy.

'Got your attention at last, have I?' grins Ray. He saunters over to the desk and hauls open the drawer. 'Here. Take a look at that if you don't believe me. And then look me in the eye and tell me you won't be jumping for joy when the old girl snuffs it.'

'It's a letter. Boodle and Boodle, solicitors. A Doughty Street address. Dated May 1966. *Dear Madam*, Sandy reads.

He breaks off, casts a reproachful glance at Ray. 'Don't tell me you've been going through Auntie's private papers?'

'Just read it,' says Ray.

Dear Madam
* re: the late Guy Perceval Strickland Esquire*
As sole executors of the estate of the above-named we are
instructed to inform you that the following monies, together with
the properties specified in the attached (see Appendix i), have been
left to you under the terms of our late client's will (see Appendix ii
paragraph a). To wit: one hundred thousand pounds in
Government bonds and cash . . .

'A hundred *thousand*!' gasps Sandy.

'Told you,' says Ray.

. . . plus a further thirty thousand pounds being the estimated
value of paintings and other properties willed to you under the
terms of the same bequest.

'Lumme,' breathes Sandy, feeling suddenly as if he might faint.

'Couldn't've put it better myself,' grins Ray. 'And you know the best part of all?' He fishes a second document, thicker than the first, out of the drawer and waves it under Sandy's nose. Despite his agitated state, Sandy is *compos mentis* enough to recognize the thing for what it is. Auntie's will. He'd always assumed he'd do quite handsomely out of it, when the time came. Although quite how handsomely has never crossed his mind till now. 'According to this, you're her sole beneficiary,'

says Ray. He gives a disdainful sniff. 'Apart from some jewel-
lery and other rubbish she wants that old frump cousin of
yours to have. But all the rest – the house, the paintings and
the luverly lolly – is all yours, Sandy boy . . .'

'Well,' says Sandy, a little too brightly. 'This *is* a turn-up for
the books . . .'

'My exact thought,' says Ray.

There's something in the air which Sandy can't quite pin
down, but which gives him a distinctly uncomfortable
feeling. It's on the tip of his tongue to ask Ray what on earth
he's driving at, but he's more than a little afraid of what the
answer might be. That young man, in any case, seems in no
hurry to pursue the conversational hare he's started. Hopping
up with alacrity (no hint of a limp now!), he helps himself to
a generous slug of Auntie's sherry from the decanter on the
sideboard and then settles himself back down in the comfiest
chair.

'I've been thinking,' he says in a ruminating tone. 'About
you and me. Know what? We could make a good
team . . .'

Sandy's heart is in his mouth. He doesn't trust himself to
speak.

'Yeah,' Ray goes on, putting his feet up on the fender. 'I
reckon we could be really good together, you and me . . .'

'Ray, *dearest* . . .'

'But,' says Ray sharply, 'it won't work, see, the way things
are at present. Not with you in that poky flat and me on my
uppers. *Modelling* for Roly –' here his voice assumes an accent
of bitterest scorn – 'or some such tripe. I can't *live* like that,'
Ray cries passionately, turning his beautiful, limpid gaze full
on Sandy. 'It isn't right and it isn't fair to expect it . . .'

'Of course not, Boysie, dear,' stammers Sandy.

'Because I've had it up to *here*,' says Ray, ignoring this interruption, 'with all that rubbish. Peddling my arse around all the sad old queens of the south coast – it's no way to make a living . . .'

'You poor, poor love,' breathes Sandy.

'Not that Roly wasn't always very *generous*,' Ray says pointedly, flicking imaginary dust off his sleeve. 'Only trouble is, he gets *bored* rather quickly. Very *fickle*, is Roly. I suppose rich types like him can afford to be . . .'

Sandy is silent, thinking of all the times he has been made to suffer – deliberately or otherwise – by the irrepressibly good-humoured and frankly unbearable Roly.

'Of course,' adds Ray casually, '*he'll* be nothing to you, once you come into your own. Piddling little nobody, that's who *he'll* be, compared to you . . .'

'Ray – darling,' says Sandy hoarsely. 'You know I'd do anything for you . . .'

'Would you really?' interrupts Ray. 'Anything at all?'

'. . . but I don't see . . . I mean, you talk as if Auntie's money (and I must say, it *does* sound an awfully nice lot!) were, well, *mine* for the taking . . .'

'It is, though,' says Ray softly. 'Yours. For. The. Taking.'

'. . . whereas the fact of the matter is, Auntie's still very much of this world . . .'

'Not as much as all that,' says Ray.

There is a short, charged silence.

With his pointed pink tongue, Ray slowly licks the sticky residue of the sherry from the bottom of his glass, looking at Sandy over the rim as he does so. When the glass is empty, he sets it down and gets to his feet.

'Well,' he says, fluttering his eyelashes and pouting in provocative parody of a swooning *fin-de-siècle* stunner, 'I don't know about *you*, but *I* could do with a nice, hot bath. If you're a *very* good boy, I might let you scrub my back . . .'

5
Unquiet Spirits

The minute she opens the door, she knows she's not alone. His presence fills up every corner of the room. It's so sharp she can almost smell it – the sour reek of fear and . . . something else, she thinks. Anger. As she lets the door fall to, she sees that the bedclothes have been disarranged – torn up by the roots and flung higgledy-piggledy across the bed. The clothes she is almost certain were on the chair this morning now lie scattered around the room, as if caught up by a whirlwind. On the dressing table, a box of ancient face powder has been upset. In the spilled peach-coloured dust a word has been scrawled: *NO*.

Connie sits down abruptly on the stool, her heart beating like a frightened bird against a window. 'Wilfred?' she whispers. 'Is that you, Wilfred?'

The silence is so intense it seems almost like a sound; but nothing stirs.

'Wilfred?' says Connie again. 'I know you're there . . .'

What could have brought this on? she wonders. Maybe it was the presence of other people. When he was alive he'd hated unexpected visitors. Although he'd had his good days and bad days, like everyone else. So that there were times, even in the early years of their marriage, when he'd be as right as rain, pottering around the house with his oil can and screwdriver (he'd liked taking things apart and putting them back together again – not always with complete success), or muttering over the crossword. On the odd occasion, he'd felt well enough to accompany her to church – although he'd preferred to wait until the very last moment before going in, in case someone – that dreadful woman from the rectory, for instance – waylaid them on some pretext or other . . . Oh, there were lots of days like that. When really he could be as sane as you or I. Not that he was ever mad, as such. Only more than usually nervous, and distraught, at times. It came from sleeping so badly, of course. The nights were his particular terror. Because it was then that everything he'd heard and seen in those terrible years came back to him. 'Blood will have blood,' he'd shouted out once, in the grip of one such nightmare. Sitting bolt upright in bed, his eyes wild and staring, his pyjamas drenched in sweat. *Blood will have blood.* So that for weeks afterwards she'd been frightened to leave him alone in the house, and had hidden the kitchen knives and his service revolver.

'What is it?' she says softly. 'Has something upset you? Wilfred?'

She doesn't afterwards know quite what it was that happened, but in that moment there is a rending crash, and when she looks again, the mirror has cracked right across.

Sandy doesn't go as far as admitting to himself the implications of his conversation with Ray, but something about it troubles him obscurely: a consciousness of having behaved in a somewhat reprehensible fashion; a feeling of guilt – which he puts down to the fact that (at Ray's insistence) he's been privy to Auntie's secrets without her consent. Not the act of a gentleman, he's the first to concede – although presumably, since the secret in question concerns him, Auntie'd want him to know about it eventually. And my word, as secrets go, it was a corker. A hundred thousand pounds! It was nothing less than a fortune.

As he lies there, wakeful and sweating, in the small hours of the morning, the words go round and round in his head, like a maddening jingle from a television quiz show. *A hundred thousand pounds, a hundred thousand pounds, who's-a-lucky-boy-then? A hundred thousand pounds* . . . Bright visions of clinking coins tumbling out of the sky. Winning the jackpot. Roly's beautiful house. You could buy him, lock, stock and barrel, hadn't Ray said? How lovely he'd looked, disporting himself in Dunsinane's immense sarcophagus of a bath, his long, tawny back emerging from a cloud of steam. ('Pass me the towel, would you, there's a love?') A heartbreaking glimpse of perfectly shaped buttocks.

'Oh, Ray,' moans Sandy. 'How could you do this to me?'

That night Ray'd let him go further than he'd ever done before – asking Sandy to scrub his back (oh, the slippery gleam of him, the springy-smooth muscular feel!) and allowing him a tantalizing glimpse of bobbing pink cock ('Naughty, naughty!') as he sat, in a froth of lavender-scented bubbles. When he was dry (and what a delicious age he'd taken to dry himself; such delightfully heroic attitudes he'd struck, as he stretched and towelled himself: a veritable Michelangelo), Sandy'd helped him into his dressing gown – Uncle Wilfred's, that is – which of course suited him down to the ground. Such an alluring combination of Dionysiac beauty (those damp tousled curls! that pouting nether lip!) and elegant *déshabillé* had brought tears to Sandy's eyes. 'Darling. It's you. Keep it,' he'd said quickly, with only the smallest pang (it *was* Simpson's of Piccadilly, after all) and Ray'd said, 'Ta. Don't mind if I do . . .' Dark blue was his colour.

But any hopes Sandy'd had of gaining some advantage from this coup were swiftly scotched. Adjusting the set of the garment across Ray's shoulders, he'd let his hands linger there a moment, his lips lightly brushing the ever-so-slightly rough edge of the boy's perfect jawline. 'Don't. That tickles,' Ray (still admiring himself in the steamed-up bathroom mirror) had said. 'You know it's no good getting yourself all het up when it's not going to happen,' he'd added, twitching his shoulders out from under Sandy's hands. 'Because the thing is, it can't happen, can it? Not with things being the way they are *at present*. I mean – I've got myself to think of, haven't I? And despite the fact that you're sitting on a tidy little fortune, you're not in a position *at present* to take me on. Not *at present* you're not. So there's no sense in being a silly-billy, Sandy-poos, because it'll only end in tears . . .'

Of course, he's right, thinks Sandy morosely. The whole situation's hopeless. What's all the more galling is that, after what he's learned that night, he now knows that one day he'll have the means to make things different. He could be Ray's *bona fide* protector. The vision is a delightful one. Himself and his darling – together at last. And all because of the money . . . But how long, thinks Sandy fretfully, how long am I going to have to *wait* for the money? And will Ray lose interest in the meantime? He thinks he already knows the answer to *that* one . . .

He'd never felt like this before. It was Oscar and Bosie and Verlaine and Rimbaud all rolled into one – only, of course, Ray was more beautiful than either insipid Lord Alfred (blonds had never really been Sandy's thing) or cross-faced Arthur with his prison haircut. Not that it was just about looks – that was what was so marvellous. Oh, he wouldn't deny it had been what attracted him in the first place – Ray's heavenly body and his angel's face – but it had long ceased to be the only thing. Pretty faces were two a penny – if one knew where to look for them. And Ray's more than just a pretty face, of that Sandy is convinced. Underneath it all, he's sensitive. Vulnerable, even. When he'd spoken that evening about the dreadful way he lived his life, it had brought tears to Sandy's eyes. Forced to sell himself to the highest bidder, poor lamb – no wonder he was bitter. That sort of existence coarsened anybody. He needed looking after, that was all. Oh, Ray, darling, thinks Sandy. If you'd only let me look after you. 'We could be a good team,' he'd said, hadn't he? But would he be willing to throw in his lot with a pauper?

Because what, after all, does Sandy have to offer? What looks he once had are fading fast. As to money, fast cars, a nice flat, smart clothes and all the other appurtenances of wealth which might conceivably attract a boy like Ray – these, too, are conspicuous by their absence. Already he senses that Ray is restive, casting his eye around for pastures new – and who can blame him? A young man in Ray's position has to look after number one. Oh, Ray, thinks Sandy, I simply couldn't bear to lose you to someone else. Someone who can give you everything I can't in the way of material rewards, but who'll never, never love you the way I do. This is the real thing – of that he is certain. The real moonlight-and-roses, eyes-meeting-across-a-crowded-room, summer-with-a-thousand-Julys sort of thing. Oh, there've been flings before – but nothing like this. My last chance, thinks Sandy.

In a few years he'd be past it. Washed up. Old. Ray would have moved on long since. You couldn't expect a boy with Ray's looks to hang on for ever, on the off-chance that some miracle might happen. And the fact is, one *had* – it was just he couldn't take advantage of it. Or not yet. That was the maddening thing. All that money going to waste. Why, it could be *years*, thinks Sandy miserably. Years and years . . .

There was the shop, of course. But even that was a bloody mess. Debts up to here and the bank making noises about foreclosure. Horrible, shudders Sandy – remembering in the same moment that he still owes three months' rent. That ghastly little bully Moynihan would be showing his face before too long. *Top o' the mornin' to ye, Mr Foulkes. Got anything to give me?* There was the down payment on the car. That last consignment from Scotland. It had seemed like such a good idea at the time – a job lot of stag's heads and stuffed fish, from some baronial castle; now he was not so sure. He'd had to borrow from Roly to pay the driver . . . 'Oh, God. Oh, God,' mutters Sandy.

It's not as if I'm a bad person, he thinks glumly, it's just that I've been unlucky. Everything I've ever touched has turned to dust – like the Midas touch, only in reverse. Other people did all right. Me, I've never had a lucky break in my life. After Oxford, everything had gone downhill. There'd been the war, of course – but lots of chaps had done all right out of that (those that hadn't bought it). Shardelow with his partnership in that tobacco business, Hoggart working for the FO. *He* was the only one still scraping a living. It didn't seem right. It isn't as if he hasn't had to put up with his fair share of misery, in the time since Mumsie died. That awful, poky flat, with its smells of boiled cabbage and mice and its communal lavatory on the landing. Having to make do with last year's jacket, when vulgar types like that Roly flaunted their latest acquisitions in one's face. *What do you think of the gear? Awfully smart, don't you think? Quentin persuaded me to buy the tie, didn't you, ducks?* Why, with *his* eye for quality, he could dress ten times as well on half the money.

How *lowering* it all was to the spirits! He, with his love of Beauty, and his taste for fine things, surrounded by nothing but sordidness and mediocrity. It's a crime, that's what it is, thinks Sandy passionately. But what is he to *do*?

Falling asleep at last, he dreams, as he not infrequently does, about the war. But where other dreams have tended to return him to the labyrinthine corridors of the War Office, to which, after Aldershot, he'd been seconded, this has a more bucolic setting. Ploughed fields and a distant wood. The suggestion of a bonfire nearby. He himself is in uniform, he knows even without glancing down. Merely the weight and the scratchy feel of the damp-smelling wool are enough to tell him he's back where he least wants to be. He can feel the weight of the mud on his boots, too, as he trudges on across the enormous field . . .

Beside him, other figures are advancing. He can't see their faces, but he guesses they must be men from his platoon: McPherson, Johnson, Wright and little Smedley – although surely he was dead? Silently, they move towards the wood – because in this kind of exercise there was always something you had to take, or something to keep hold of. So that when they eventually showed their hand, it was strange that there was no answering gunfire. By now, you'd have expected those defending the wood to have made some attempt to repel the attacking party.

It's a trick, Sandy wants to shout, but somehow his voice won't work. He's getting deeper and deeper in among the trees, and still there's nothing but a horrid silence, and the dreadful sense of something about to happen. It's very dark in the wood; twigs and brambles snatch at his clothes and hair. He looks for the others, but they seem to have fallen behind. Then, in front of him, he sees someone moving: the figure of a man in uniform. In the half-light, it's hard to tell what rank he is, or whether he is friend or foe . . .

But as the figure turns, Sandy sees that the soldier is definitely one of theirs – even though there's something odd about the uniform he's wearing. Instead of regulation battledress, it's the old-fashioned tunic and puttees worn by the previous generation of combatants; instead of a tin helmet, he's sporting a peaked cap. A fellow officer, then, Sandy surmises, relieved to have found an explanation for the eccentricity of dress. Wait, he cries breathlessly, but the other's step never falters. Wait, damn you – but the soldier only quickens his pace still further, slashing at the branches with his swagger stick in a fury of impatience.

It strikes Sandy all at once that maybe the other man can't see him – because this is a dream, and in dreams, as often as not, one finds oneself invisible. But then the other stops in his tracks and turns, with terrible slowness. And Sandy realizes that he knows him, after all . . .

Sandy goes down to breakfast – or what passes for it in this establishment. Mealtimes at Dunsinane seem to be catch-as-catch-can. Not that it was ever the Ritz, even when Auntie still had all her marbles. When she was painting, she'd often forget to eat for days, except for cups of tea and such. At least the milkman's been, Sandy observes. He picks up the bottle with its thick crust of cream from the doorstep. Noticing as he does so that Auntie's coat is gone from the hall stand. Probably walking the dog, he guesses. He feels an obscure sense of relief that he won't have to face her just yet. In the morning room he finds Ray, helping himself to the last of the toast.

'Well,' says this young man archly. 'And how are *we*, this morning? Sleep well, did we?'

'Not particularly,' says Sandy. 'In fact, not very well at all.'

' 'Spect it was the excitement,' says Ray. 'Finding out you'd got all that lovely loot coming your way. I know *I'd* be excited if it was me. I'd be spending it already, *I* would . . .'

'Damn the money,' says Sandy crossly.

'Temper, temper,' says Ray.

'You know that's not the reason I couldn't sleep,' Sandy says in an impassioned whisper. 'It's cruel of you to pretend you don't know how I feel about you . . .'

'So I'm cruel, am I?' says Ray, licking the jam spoon with an air of deliberation. 'That's *very* nice . . .'

'I didn't mean it like that,' says Sandy.

'It's not me that's the cruel one, if you want my opinion,' says Ray. 'I mean – take you, for instance. Sitting on all that money and not caring if I starve – or worse. That's cruel, that is.'

'But I only found out about the money last night!' cries Sandy.

'So you say,' chips in Ray. 'I've only got your word for it, haven't I?'

'Besides which, you know perfectly well I can't get my hands on the wretched stuff for ages and ages . . .'

'Can't you?' says Ray, opening his eyes very wide. 'Why's that, then?'

'It's a legacy,' says Sandy, exasperated at this seeming obtuseness on Ray's part. 'One doesn't get money from a legacy until somebody dies. I should have thought it was obvious . . .'

'It is,' says Ray coldly. 'Completely obvious. It's you that's refusing to see the way things are . . .'

'You're not suggesting that . . . I should . . . well, *hurry things along*?' Sandy's voice sinks to an appalled whisper.

'I'm not suggesting it. I'm *saying* it. That is, if you want the money . . .'

'But . . .' Sandy is speechless for a minute. 'That's immoral. I mean to say – it's *wrong*.'

''Course it is,' replies Ray. 'Lots of things is wrong, when you come to think about it. Like you having to live in that horrible little shoebox of a rented room, 'stead of in a nice sea-front pad like Roly's. Like me having to suck old men's cocks for a living. *That's* wrong, that is . . .'

'Oh, I know,' breathes Sandy.

'What I'm saying is, it doesn't have to be like that . . .'

'Dearest boy, of *course* not,' says Sandy fervently. 'But you see, it's not as simple as all that. I mean,' he stammers, with Ray's basilisk glare upon him, 'you must see . . . One can't just . . . *do* it, like that . . .'

'*Can't* one?' asks Ray, all icy *politesse*. 'I can't imagine why. What's so difficult about it, after all? You can take it from me,' says Ray, taking a step closer to Sandy so that Sandy can feel his warm, vanilla-scented breath against his cheek. 'There's lots of ways. It's not hard. Especially not when someone's half-way to heaven already . . .'

The door opens: Auntie stands there, smiling her most beatific smile.

'Good morning, dears,' she says. 'I hope you both slept well. Do you know – I think I could fancy a nice boiled egg for breakfast.'

'*What* a good idea,' Ray says smoothly. 'Tell you what – why don't you sit yourself down like a good girl, and Sandy and me'll see to it, *tout suite* . . .'

Gripping the by now foolishly gaping Sandy by the elbow, Ray steers him towards the evil-smelling kitchen, where a colony of bluebottles are already feasting on the remains of yesterday's lunch, thoughtlessly left in the sink. 'Pull yourself together, do,' he hisses in Sandy's ear. 'Standing there gawking as if you'd seen a bleeding ghost . . .'

'But don't you *see*?' moans Sandy, collapsing all of a sudden on to a kitchen chair. 'What you're suggesting. It's out of the question . . .'

'Oh, I *see* all right,' says Ray, with a quiet venom which is perhaps more alarming than shrill anger. 'Yes, I *see* perfectly well . . .' He lifts a battered tin saucepan from the stove and half-fills it with water, before banging it back on the ring. 'Matches,' he says, clicking his fingers.

'In the toast rack,' replies Sandy dully.

'Mustn't forget to light the cooker, must we?' Ray mutters, as if to himself. 'Wouldn't want to *gas* anyone, would we? Now then,' he adds, with horrible jocularity, 'where's the jolly old eggy-weggies? Fancy an egg, Sandy-poos? I know *I* do. Nice soft-boiled one, with soldiers . . .'

'Not for me,' breathes Sandy faintly. He is feeling rather sick.

'Lost your appetite, have you?' says Ray. He finds the eggs – in the egg rack, for a wonder – and perches two of them on the speckled enamel rim of the stove, ready for when the water starts to boil. A third he tosses lightly up and down in the palm of his hand. Coming closer, with each toss, to the reluctant Sandy. 'Lost your appetite for all *kinds* of things, I shouldn't wonder,' he muses, throwing the egg up and catching it again, right under Sandy's nose. 'Lily-livered, that's your trouble. Like all your sort.' He throws the egg up again; catches it as before. 'No real guts. When push comes to shove, you're nothing but a weak-willed, spineless, pathetic old *queen* . . .'

With this last word, the egg, which he has been squeezing

progressively harder, explodes in his hand. 'Oops,' says Ray, dropping the sticky mess on to the floor. 'Silly billy. But never mind, eh? Accidents do happen. They do happen,' he croons, turning back towards the stove, where the pan of water is now bubbling like a witch's cauldron. 'All kinds of accidents. Every day.' He drops first one egg, then the other into the swirling steam. 'You'd be surprised at just how many things can – and do – go amiss. F'rinstance,' he adds, shaving two slices off a stale heel of bread and popping them under the grill, 'that loose stair-rod at the top of the stairs – have you noticed? Very nasty fall someone could have, if they didn't watch out for *that* one. Or slipping on the soap. Another all too common occurrence. One crack on the head and you're a goner – 'specially if the bath's already nice and full. Then there's the gas. Leaks, see? Very popular cause of death, that one. Forgetful, some people. Turn on the taps for a nice cuppa and nod off before they manage to find the matches. Don't hardly know nothing about it, so they say. 'Lectric's dangerous, too. Faulty switches. Bare wires. To say nothing of losing your footing on the cellar stairs when the bulb goes dead, sudden like. Nasty. There,' he says, abruptly, snapping out of his reverie. 'Three and a half minutes. Just the way I like 'em.' With an exclamation, he snatches the toast from beneath the grill, just as it is starting to blacken. 'Whoops-a-daisy. Nearly had another accident there. *Cahm* on, Sandy-poos – chuck us the butter, there's a good boy. Auntie'll be wondering what's happened to her brekker . . .'

They are still breakfasting when the surly parping of a car horn announces the arrival of Bert, the garage man.

'About time, too!' says Sandy hotly, making a great play of his indignation, by way of distracting himself – and Ray – from further homicidal speculations. The thought does cross his mind, as he marches out to do battle with Bolshy Bert, that he's taking a risk leaving the two of them together – Ray and Auntie. But then he reassures himself that if Ray were serious about wanting to do the old girl in, he'd hardly choose to do it then and there. The whole point was surely to make it look like an accident – wasn't that what he'd been saying? Bashing her over the head with the silver teapot or carving her up with the butter knife could hardly be seen in *that* light, giggles Sandy nervously.

With luck, he thinks, nodding a curt good-morning to the utterly charmless Bert, the car'll be fixed by lunchtime and they can be on their way. Any ideas Ray might have about translating his sinister thoughts into deeds will be forestalled. Once away from the malign influence of the house – and that damned will – he'll probably forget all about it, Sandy tells himself, knowing as he does so that nothing could be further from the truth.

While he's occupied with these melancholy reflections, Laughing Boy Bert has been taking a look at the car. Now he clears his throat with a phlegmy rattle, as the prelude to delivering the bad news. 'Don't know as how I'm going to be able to mend her in a hurry,' he says, with a lugubrious head-shake. 'Axle's bent for a start. To say nothing of the rest of the gubbins. Spare parts, that's what her'll need . . .'

'Really?' says Sandy. 'You astound me. Spare parts. Correct me if I'm wrong, but . . . isn't that rather your stock-in-trade?'

'Depends what kind,' retorts sullen Bert. 'Might not have 'em for this here model. Being as how it's one of the older sort,' he sneers.

'Well, I suggest you telephone your place of work as soon as possible and find out,' says Sandy, witheringly polite. 'Because I need this car back on the road by lunchtime at the latest. I've important business in Brighton, d'you see . . .'

A hollow laugh from Bert cuts short these explanations. 'Won't be lunchtime by the time her's mended. Won't be teatime, neither,' he says with a smirk at his own doltish wit. 'Might have to send off to Eastbourne for the parts. Could take a week . . .'

'A week!' explodes Sandy.

'Maybe two. Older models like this one here,' Bert says with satisfaction, 'you got to order the parts for. Don't keep 'em in stock, see?'

'Yes, yes. So you keep saying,' snaps Sandy, by now thoroughly put out. 'But it's not as simple as all that. I have a business to run.'

Bert shrugs, as if to say that this is not his problem. 'Do you want me to hitch her up or not?' he demands rudely, jerking his thumb towards the wreck.

'You don't leave me much choice,' replies Sandy huffily. 'Although how on earth I shall manage for a whole week without a car I really can't imagine . . .'

As Bert is hooking the chain from the breakdown van on to the Morris's mangled bumper, Ray comes sauntering out of the house.

'What's the matter with you?' he asks. 'You got a face like a week's wet washing . . .'

'Oh, nothing, nothing,' replies Sandy airily. 'These fellows can't resist making mountains out of molehills . . .'

'Looks like a total write-off,' remarks Ray, with a nod at the Morris. 'Fit for the scrap heap, if you ask me.'

'Oh, you are a pessimistic boy!' says Sandy, with a nervous titter. 'Always looking on the black side . . .'

'Give us a ring tomorrow,' Bert calls by way of a parting

shot. 'I'll have heard from Eastbourne by then. Let you know what's what. If her *can* be fixed, Eastbourne'll fix her . . .'

'Tomorrow,' says Ray, with a gloating look in his eye Sandy doesn't quite like. 'Couldn't be better. *Lots* of time between now and tomorrow, eh, Sand?'

Of course when Izzie heard about it, she reacted just as one would have expected, with a sympathetic cluck – *Oh, I say. Hard cheese* – and some brisk advice. Hire a car, was her idea. 'It'll only be for a couple of days, after all. There's a place in Uckfield that does 'em. Quite reasonable rates, I'm told. I'd lend you our car, only I need it myself this week to run Mother to the chiropodist's . . .'

Sandy hasn't the heart to tell her that, in his present straitened circumstances, hiring a car is out of the question – reasonable rates or no. He'd barely been able to afford the petrol for the trip up. But then Izzie has another idea. 'Tell you what – why don't I run you down to Brighton this afternoon, after lunch? Do the Armstrong good to stretch her legs a bit. If you like, we can take a run along the coast. Have a bit of a blow on the cliffs. A spot of tea. Then I can whisk you back to town in time for the evening news. You can pop up in a day or two to collect the motor, when Bert gives you the go-ahead . . .'

Ray is sulky when told of this plan. 'What does *she* think she's up to, sticking her oar in? Wouldn't have thought she wanted to get rid of you so bleeding quick . . . Ay say, Sandy, deah,' he continues, in cruelly accurate mimicry of Iseult's mannish tones. '*Would* you mind *awfully* just giving me a hand with the potatoes? It's just such an awfully beastly frightfully ghastly dreary job if one has to do it *alane* . . .'

*

It had been terribly sweet and somehow awfully *touching*, the look on Sandy's face when she'd come up with her suggestion (and it wasn't such a bad idea, if she said so herself). 'Oh, Izz, you are a *brick*,' he'd said, with such gratitude in his voice that she'd been quite overwhelmed. He was so *appreciative*, that was the thing about Sandy. Making one feel, when one had offered something really quite small, that one had positively saved his bacon. The picnic idea *was* an inspiration, though. It had come to her out of the blue. Because otherwise it would have been nothing but a dull drive back, with that awful boy whining non-stop and only time for a quick cup of tea before turning around to come home. This way, she'd have almost the whole day in his company, with the chance of a nice walk and a chat and some jolly good sea air to blow the cobwebs away. They'd pack a flask of tea, and some sandwiches and apples and a packet of Bourbons (his favourites), and walk as far as the headland, the way they used to when they were kids. She couldn't think of anything nicer.

In real life, things never turned out as you'd imagined. Because when Mummy heard (and there was no way one could have avoided telling her, worst luck), she wanted to come, too, of course. Mummy adored picnics. Then there was Aunt Con. Not to mention the dog. And that wretched boy. So what had started off in her vision of it as just her and Sandy ended up with the whole bang-shoot of 'em, as Mummy would say.

Still, it's good to get going – when they eventually *do* get going, and heaven knows, that takes long enough, what with getting Mummy dressed in her outdoor things and persuading her not to wear her furs, because it is June, after all, and even though it'll be blowy on the cliff tops, it isn't likely to be thirty below, and then collecting the others. It's such a joy to be bowling along the open road, with the wind in one's face, the tang of salt in one's nostrils and the promise of adventure beckoning one with its siren's call. With Sandy beside her as map-reader and the rest of them stowed in the back, it's almost possible to recapture the delightful sense of its just being the two of them, setting off like a couple of kids on a day trip to Bexhill, with the promise of sea-bathing and a stroll along the prom, followed by tea and potted shrimps, to the strains of a Palm Court orchestra . . .

Yes, for that all too brief half-hour which lies between them and their destination, Iseult tastes the bliss of anticipation – the purest kind of happiness. Nothing – not Mummy's complaining, or the frightful smells emitted by poor old Rufus, or that horrid little oik's incessant simpering – can mar her contentment, her feeling of utter *rightness*. So that when, beyond Alfriston, they crest the brow of the hill and suddenly there it is before them, that immense and shimmering blue, and the sky above it as clear as if it had been created that instant, there isn't one of them who can suppress an *Oh* of delight, a feeling that here, where the land falls away into that pure marine emptiness, the possibility might still exist of making oneself anew.

After that first rapturous glimpse, they dip down into the hollow again and follow the winding lane which leads to the cliff path. Iseult is afraid for a minute that the place will be packed with trippers, because generally the least *sniff* of fine weather brings them rushing to the sea in their hordes, with their transistor radios and their Kiss-Me-Quick hats; but in fact the parking place seems relatively deserted, with only one elderly couple in a van sharing a Thermos, and one of those flashy open-topped sports jobs taking up more that its fair share of space – the latter, predictably, exciting the admiration of the oik.

Iseult suggests that the older generation should stay in the car, while the rest of them stretch their legs – those of them who aren't incapacitated by injured ankles, of course. There's a perfectly good view of the sea from here and they'll not be gone long, she and Sandy. An hour at the most.

But Mummy won't hear of it, of course. 'Oh, Con and I want a walk – don't we, pardner?' she brays, brandishing her stick like a weapon. 'We used to be great walkers in our day, didn't we, Connie, old gal? Why, we'd have walked these here young whippersnappers off their legs in *them* thar days,' she continues to insist, as, leaning heavily on Sandy, she totters the few paces from the car to the sheltered nook where Iseult, resignedly, is spreading out the rug. '*Oh*, yess,' Leonora wheezes, lowering herself gingerly on to a pile of cushions. 'Twenty miles was nothing to us in those days – eh, Con?'

Encumbered as she is with the by now wildly excited Rufus, Aunt Constance does not reply – although she *isn't* a bad walker for her age, Iseult thinks. She offers to take charge of the dog, thinking Aunt might prefer to put her feet up for a change, but the old girl seems quite put out by the idea. 'Kind of you, dear – but poor old Rufus will be so disappointed if I don't take him,' she says firmly. 'I've never missed a day yet – and I think dogs notice these things . . .'

Which leaves Mummy on her lonely-ownsome, as she herself would say. She's already looking a mite peeved when the boy – of all people – saves the day. 'My silly old ankle's playing up again,' he says, with an ingratiating look at Sandy. 'You go without me. I'll stay and keep Mum company . . .'

So it's settled: he'll entertain Leonora (a proposal she clearly finds entirely to her satisfaction), while the rest of them go for a tramp; then they'll have tea.

Of course, like most plans, it bears little relation to what actually happens. At that precise moment, however, everything is just as it should be, with the sky a clear blue, dotted here and there with baby clouds, and the lightest of breezes stirring the clumps of sea-pinks at the cliff's edge. So that to Iseult, striding along with the wind in her face and the long, coarse grass at the edge of the path catching at her skirt, it feels as if she could ask for nothing more than just this combination of place, time and company. Herself and the man she loves; a dog; the sea.

To one side of them lie the rolling curves of the South Downs, a prospect of rural England which has remained unchanged since the Romans arrived with their longboats – or was it the Vikings? Iseult wonders, a little muddled. History has never been her strong point. Anyway. The other side was the sea – whose flat expanse, furrowed here and there with white, seemed only another kind of field, just blue not green. Elysian fields, thinks Iseult, rather pleased with the allusion. Such a pity she'd never had a proper classical education. She'd have enjoyed all that. Homer and so forth. The wine-dark sea . . . Although surely wine was red, not blue? Literature could be so muddling.

Ahead of her, Sandy lopes glumly along, with his hands sunk deep in his pockets. She wonders whether something that horrible boy said has put him in a bad mood. 'Don't be long,' the little brute had trilled, as they were setting off. 'Otherwise I might start to think you'd had an *accident* or something . . .'

Ever since then, Sandy's seemed preoccupied, responding to her remarks about the beauty of the weather and the splendour of the view with the distracted air of a man who has just received bad news. Maybe the business wasn't going as well as hinted. Or perhaps his dyspepsia was troubling him; unfortunately, the provisions in Aunt Constance's larder weren't always of the freshest . . . Well, whatever the reason for Sandy's present air of abstraction, it doesn't bother her. He'll snap out of it eventually. Nothing like some good sea air to make one feel on top of the world again.

Sure enough, they've only been going for a few minutes – just long enough to get out of sight of the others – when Sandy lets out a great breath, as if expelling all the poisonous thoughts that have been making him look so sick, and draws in another, with an appreciative 'Ahh'. Then, to Iseult's delight, he begins to sing, roaring out the first verse of 'One Man Went to Mow' with a gusto she hasn't seen him display in ages. She picks up the refrain – and soon the one man and his dog are joined by two, three, four, five and six of his fellow artisans, all marching along, in Iseult's mental picture of them, towards some vast but as yet unconquered savannah.

Ahead of them, the clouds go scudding, the grass sways and seagulls drift like snowflakes on the wind, while from far below the sound of waves crashing on the rocks can be heard between their shouted choruses. Even Aunt Con joins in the spirit of things, humming along in her quavery soprano and beating time with her finger. It makes Iseult smile to see how pluckily the dear old thing keeps up, swinging her arms like a little soldier, and whistling Rufus out of trouble (a gorse bush; a dead stoat) with a good deal of her old vim.

'Enjoying your walk, Aunt?' she inquires.

'Oh, yes,' says Connie. 'But your mother's right, you know. I always was a great one for walks. I once walked the Great Wall of China . . .'

'Goodness,' says Iseult. 'I imagine that was a pretty stiff hike.'

'Oh, it was,' says Connie. 'It's three thousand miles long,

you know. Not that I walked the whole of it. But one certainly needed stout boots . . .'

'I suppose one would,' murmurs Iseult, a bit distracted because Sandy has just stopped to admire the view – which *is* spectacular – and she, talking to Aunt, has all but walked into him. 'Oops. Sorry,' she mutters, conscious, as she often is in his presence, of the unmanageable size of her feet and the clumsiness of her gestures. Trying to right herself, she makes matters worse, missing her footing altogether and saving herself only by grabbing hold of Sandy's sleeve.

'For God's sake – look out!' he snaps.

His alarm seems excessive, since it was merely a momentary loss of equilibrium and they are nowhere near the edge. But Sandy's face is as white as if the consequences of Iseult's mishap had been far more serious – as, indeed, so many along this very path so often were, with a single false step making all the difference, in bad light or treacherous weather, between continuing on one's way unscathed and not.

It is gratifying, Iseult has to admit, to be the object of such solicitude. She tries to reassure him. 'Don't worry. The path's quite safe here. It's only nearer the edge it starts to crumble . . .'

'Yes, yes. I can see that,' he says, so crossly that Iseult is quite taken aback. It occurs to her that maybe Sandy is scared of heights. Funny. It's not a weakness he's ever betrayed before.

Just now he seems decidedly twitchy.

'Where's Auntie?' he cries suddenly, looking wildly around, so that in spite of herself Iseult feels a surge of alarm – which, of course, turns out to be quite unfounded, because they've no sooner missed her than Aunt Con pops up safe and sound, lugging a recalcitrant Rufus by the collar from whatever interesting rabbit hole or decaying corpse he's found.

Evidently still very much rattled, Sandy mutters something about its being time to turn back – even though they've barely been walking half an hour and haven't even reached the headland. But in some indefinable way, the mood is spoilt. Casting one last look at the prospect which lies in front – the white path disappearing over the next ridge; the incandescent bay – Iseult turns her face resolutely away. 'Fancy a spot of tea, Aunt?' she says, trying to make the best of it.

They are still some way off from the place where they have left the others when Sandy, who has been stumping along morosely with his head down, suddenly comes to an abrupt halt. Iseult, following the direction of his gaze, sees that what appears at first glance to be a flock of brilliantly coloured butterflies has alighted upon the cliff top. Bright wings (or are they merely scarves?) flutter against the sky, rendering it quite insipid by contrast. Splashes of shocking pink, purple and lime green bring a touch of *The Yellow Book* to the South Downs' chalky terrain.

'Hello,' says Sandy, frowning. 'Looks as if we've got company. A pretty rum bunch, by the look of 'em.'

6

Band of Gypsies

And indeed they are a motley crew, the people who have joined their party – having sprung, it appears, from nowhere, like some roving band of gypsies. There's a decidedly bohemian look to the way they're dressed, which puts Iseult in mind of Mummy's theatrical friends, incorporating as it does an abundance of velvet and satin, a predilection for kohl eyeliner and a fondness for large-brimmed hats and feather boas. All these elements are in evidence, she sees, as they advance towards the newcomers. If anything, the males are more flamboyantly attired than the females of the group (although that could also be said of the theatre crowd). That chap with the long blond curls (she assumes it must be a chap) is surely wearing a *dress* – albeit over skin-tight trousers tucked into snakeskin boots – but even *so*. As for the one in black with the lace ruffles which give him rather a look of Lord Byron, isn't he wearing . . . well, *lipstick*? Iseult is rather afraid that he is.

'What kept you so long?' cries Leonora in high excitement. 'We were just about to send out search parties, weren't we, Nick?'

The dissolute-looking chap in the ruffles gives an enigmatic smile.

'Nick's a pop singer,' confides Leonora in a stage whisper.

'*Rock* singer,' corrects Ray, who is lolling on a pile of cushions at the centre of the group. 'How many times do I have to tell you, Leonora? He's a bleeding rock singer, not some poncy pop star . . .'

'Oops,' giggles Leonora. 'Silly me. *Anyway.* Nick and his charming young friends are having their picture taken for the cover of their new LP – isn't that exciting?'

'Sort of a conceptual idea,' says an epicene type in a lilac paisley shirt, with an expensive-looking camera slung around his neck. 'Nick and the boys against a backdrop of rugged cliffs. Stormy seas. The whole bit. Sort of untamed Nature kinda thing . . .'

'This is Jocelyn, by the way,' says Leonora. The chap with the camera flutters his fingers at them. 'Jocelyn manages the group. And this is Brian, who plays the electric guitar or something equally clever, and . . .' She waves her hand helplessly to indicate the remaining members of the group.

'Keith,' supplies Ray, with a nod at a surly-looking type with tattooed forearms and a Zapata moustache. 'Keith's the drummer, aren't you, dear?'

'And these are their, er, young ladies . . .'

'Chicks,' says Ray with barely disguised contempt. 'Sam.' He stabs a finger at the pretty blonde beside Nick, who blushes furiously. 'Mandy.' The brunette next to Brian gives a small, cool smile.

'Nick and his friends are going to join us for a picnic,' says Leonora grandly. 'Iseult – oh, this is my daughter, everyone. Not a bit alike, are we? Iseult, *do* see if you can find some more cups and plates and things. These poor young people must be gasping for their tea . . .'

'Cups. Plates. Righto,' says Iseult.

'Don't put yourselves out on our account,' interjects Jocelyn, with a smirk. 'We've brought our own refreshments with us, haven't we, Nicky?'

The Byronic youth shrugs. 'S'pose so.'

Jocelyn clicks his fingers. 'Mandy, love. Sam. Be good little girlies and fetch us the hamper, would you?' He tosses his car keys to the blonde girl, who fumbles the catch. 'Butterfingers! Off you go, now. And don't forget the champagne . . .'

'Champers. Ooh, lovely,' coos Leonora.

'Plenty to go round,' says Jocelyn airily. 'Ray here was telling me,' he adds, addressing Sandy, 'that you've got a weekend place in Sussex. *Very* nice . . .'

'Yes. Well . . . no, actually,' says Sandy, rather flustered. 'I mean, yes, it is nice and no, it's not mine, exactly. It belongs to my aunt . . .'

'That her?' interjects the blond youth in the frock, with a nod at Connie, who has wandered into view, with Rufus trailing in her wake.

'Yes.'

'Old people,' says the youth, pulling a disgusted face. 'Can't stand 'em meself.'

'Brian! That's not *very nice*,' protests Jocelyn, flapping a hand at him.

'Brian couldn't be nice if he tried,' drawls Nick.

Brian sticks out his tongue at his friend and waggles it suggestively.

'Boys, boys,' murmurs Jocelyn reprovingly. 'So tell me,' he goes on, picking up the thread of his conversation with Sandy, 'is it far from here, your place?'

'Half an hour's drive. Less, I shouldn't wonder, in your motor,' Ray answers for him. 'Did you see it, Sandy? Lovely thing, it is. Powder-blue Jag. E-type. Goes like a bomb, I'd imagine . . .'

'It has its moments,' admits Jocelyn modestly.

'Tell you what,' says Ray. 'If you've nothing better to do

this afternoon, why don't you pop down and take a look at the old place? Plenty of room for visitors . . .'

The *cheek* of the lad, thinks Sandy. 'Ray, dear, I hardly think . . .' he starts to say.

'What?' says Ray, opening his eyes very wide. A look of injured innocence, which contrives at the same time to be faintly menacing.

'I mean,' says Sandy, in a strangulated undertone. 'It's not fair to Auntie. Inviting people to her home, without so much as a by-your-leave . . .'

'Oh, *she* won't mind,' Ray says airily. 'Prob'ly won't even notice.'

'We wouldn't want to put anyone out,' says Jocelyn. 'But it *would* be a treat, wouldn't it, Nicky, love?'

'Yeah,' murmurs the dark boy. 'Far out.'

'That's settled, then,' says Ray, with a triumphant look at Sandy.

'But . . .' Too late, Sandy remembers the original purpose of their trip. The proposed return to Brighton. How perfectly *typical* of Ray to throw a spanner in the works. You'd almost think he'd done it on purpose . . .

'I thought we were supposed to be on our way home,' he hisses to Ray. 'At this rate, it'll be midnight before we reach Brighton . . .'

'Silly old Sandy-poos,' says Ray indulgently. 'Always fussing about something. Jocelyn here'll give us a lift back, later – won't you, Joss?'

'Happy to oblige,' says Jocelyn. 'Oh, goody. Here's the food at last . . .'

A flurry of girlish shrieks heralds the return of Mandy and Sam, staggering under the weight of a large wicker basket, filled with provisions of various kinds. Several sticks of French bread, a large round object in a blue-and-white-checked cloth, which, unwrapped, proves to be a whole Brie, a bunch of grapes, a brown pottery crock of something which looks exotic and is probably *fois gras*, half a dozen bottles of champagne and a chocolate cake are tumbled out on to the grass.

'Golly,' breathes Leonora. 'What a ripping spread . . .'

'Smashing,' agrees Ray. 'I do love a nice drop of bubbly.'

'Dig in, everybody,' says Jocelyn, with a lordly wave of the hand. 'Girls, you forgot the glasses. How are we supposed to drink this lovely fizz if we don't have any glasses?'

The glasses are eventually found (Sandy nobly makes do with a teacup) and the food – augmented by the embarrassingly scrappy provisions Iseult has brought – is distributed. For a while there are no sounds apart from contented swilling and guzzling, and the popping of champagne corks.

'Well,' says Jocelyn, raising his brimming flute. 'Bottoms up, if I say so myself . . .'

He is looking, as he speaks, at Ray, Sandy notes with mounting indignation. And Ray, sprawled at full length between the cadaverous dark boy, Nick, and the pretty blond with the Liverpudlian twang, is looking straight back at him. Surely he can't find that pigeon-chested type attractive? That absurd frilly shirt – like a *girl*, thinks Sandy. And as for that dreadful, faux-Cockney voice . . .

'Cheers, Joss, me old mate,' says Ray, knocking back his bubbly as if it was going out of fashion. He's getting more and more *in* with these types, Sandy observes jealously. Acting as if he's known them all for years (*me old mate*, indeed!), instead of a mere five minutes. Look at him now, little flirt – his head practically lying in that creep's *lap* as he lolls at his ease, holding out his glass for a refill ('Don't mind if I do!') and whispering sweet nothings in the dark boy's ear. Sick with misery, Sandy sips his champagne, whose acid taste is that of all the one-night stands and headachy mornings-after of his unedifying amorous history . . .

'What sort of music do you play?'

It's an astonishing intervention, coming as it does from so unexpected a quarter – so that for a moment the others are startled into silence, glancing around as if uncertain where the small, clear voice has come from.

For it's Connie who's spoken, perched on a large rock a few feet from the rest of them like a diminutive Oracle, with her champagne glass held daintily between finger and thumb and an expression of polite interest animating her features, for all the world as if she were at a Bloomsbury dinner party between the wars, and someone had just said something clever about Stravinsky. The question is addressed to Nick, it seems; certainly he appears to think so, tossing his long dark locks back from his face with a languid air.

'Rock music,' he says. 'Know what I mean? Loud. R&B. Kind of. Blues. You know blues?'

Connie nods seriously, appearing to consider this.

''Slike that. Only louder, like I said . . .'

'Nick's had three singles in the Top Twenty,' says Jocelyn fondly. 'Very talented boy, is our Nicky . . .'

''Scuse *me*.' Brian is loudly indignant. 'You're talking as if Nick was the only one who's ever made a hit record around here . . .'

'Nick and the band was what I meant,' Jocelyn murmurs soothingly.

'Nick de Vil and the Vampyres,' says Ray, as if this means something.

'Never heard of them,' mutters Sandy.

'You've *never heard* of the Vampyres?' Jocelyn is shrill with incredulity. I mean, I know this is the *sticks*, but even so . . .'

' "Vampire Love",' prompts Ray. 'Top of the hit parade for, ooh, ever so long, wasn't it, Joss?'

'Six weeks,' confirms Jocelyn. 'You *must* have heard "Vampire Love" . . .'

As if on cue, the two girls, silent up till now, burst into song.

> 'Gimme some of your
> VAMPIRE LOVE
> Ooh yeah, baby
> You know I'm dyin' for your
> VAMPIRE KISS
> Don't mean maybe . . .'

Sandy shakes his head, tight-lipped. 'Not my kind of music, I'm afraid,' he says, attempting a laugh.

'I met a Chinese vampire once,' pipes up the Oracle from her rock. 'At least, that was the rumour about her. She'd had three husbands, you see – or was it four? Very pretty girl, needless to say. Unkind people said she kept her looks by drinking the blood of her suitors . . . All rot, in my opinion.'

'Groovy chick,' murmurs Nick, with his melancholy smile.

And now the girls are cutting the cake and passing out slabs of the moist dark stuff, whose sweetness overlays a rather more bitter taste – something earthy, herbal, vaguely medicinal. Sandy nibbles dubiously at his slice, leaving most of it on the plate. Iseult, too, he notices, has left hers untouched.

Ray gobbles his in a couple of bites. 'Eat up,' he says to Sandy, giving the latter's knee a squeeze. 'Don't want to hurt the lickle girlies' feelings, do we?'

Numb with desire, Sandy does as he is told. Oh, Ray, he

thinks fervently. If we could only be alone together for once. Away from all these people . . .

'That's the stuff,' Ray says softly. 'Yum, yum.' His hand tightens its grip on Sandy's knee. 'Enjoy our walk, did we?'

A crumb sticks in Sandy's throat. 'I . . .' he splutters. The rest is lost in a fit of coughing.

'Good job I'm here,' mutters Ray, bashing the gasping and empurpled Sandy savagely on the back. 'A person could *choke* to death just like that . . .'

'Happened to a mate of mine, 'smatter of fact,' mumbles Brian, who has finished his cake and is now rolling a cigarette. 'Blue in the face when they found him. Chocolate Digestive was what did for him, they reckoned. 'Course, the smack didn't help,' he adds, firing up the cigarette.

He has an exaggerated way of smoking, Sandy notices, wiping his streaming eyes. Like a little boy sneaking his first puff. Inhaling so fiercely it makes sparks fly out of the cigarette's end. Holding the smoke in for what strikes Sandy as a ridiculously long time. It's years since he gave up the evil weed, of course, but his hand still remembers the right way to hold the thing. *Not* between thumb and forefinger – the way this nancy with the golden curls is holding it – but firmly clamped between the second and third joints of middle and index fingers: a man's grip, strong and elegant. As for the way the poor lad is actually smoking . . . It's all Sandy can do not to burst out laughing at the sight. Anyone would think he was *swallowing* the stuff. The way his eyes are nearly popping out of his head as he does so is just too *killing*, in Sandy's view. Try as he might, he just can't stop the laugh from rising in his throat, so that he's in danger of choking for the second time.

'Got the giggles?' says Ray.

Before Sandy can reply, there's a cry from Auntie.

'Has anyone seen Rufus? He was here a minute ago. *Roo-fuss!*'

'Who the hell's Rufus?' says Jocelyn.

But Connie has already scrambled down from her rock and is trotting off along the path up which they climbed earlier, calling, 'Rufus! Where are you, you bad boy?' as she goes.

Ray, too, is on his feet. 'Hang on, Auntie,' he calls. 'I'll help you look. Wouldn't want poor old Rufus wandering over a cliff, would we?'

'Will someone please tell me who this Rufus cat is?' shrieks Jocelyn, losing patience.

'Oh, it's only Constance's horrid old dog,' sniffs Leonora. 'She's completely besotted with the creature. I suppose it's because she's never had a child to love,' she adds lugubriously. 'Terribly important, to have a child to love . . .'

Two fat tears roll down Leonora's cheeks, leaving sooty tracks in the bright-pink powder.

'Dogs have souls, you know,' says Brian, passing the half-smoked cigarette to Nick. 'I read it in this book.'

'Sounds like a load of bollocks to me,' opines Nick, taking a puff.

Now *there's* a smoker, thinks Sandy admiringly. Handsome boy, too – if a shade on the thin side. He prefers a bit more meat on the bones. The Italian look. Well muscled. Sculptural. That was Ray's style, of course . . .

Ray . . . Suddenly the fact of Ray's absence – the *implications* of Ray's absence – pierce the fog of Sandy's consciousness. *What if something were to happen to Auntie?* She and Ray are still within sight on the cliff path, but getting smaller and smaller . . .

With what seems a colossal effort of will, Sandy gets to his feet. 'I'll just go and help them look,' he wants to say, but the words tumble out all wrong somehow, so that they make no sense at all.

Not that anyone else is paying the slightest attention.

Leonora is still weeping loudly, tears flowing unchecked down her rouged and wrinkled cheeks. Iseult watches from a distance, her face like stone. Brian and the dark girl are feeding cake to one another. Jocelyn is rolling another cigarette with an air of extreme concentration. The blonde girl is meekly stacking plates in the now half-empty and despoiled hamper.

Sandy's limbs feel terribly heavy. He seems to have forgotten how to walk. Experimentally, he swings one foot out in front of the other and follows through with the corresponding foot. It feels all wrong, somehow – but it seems to do the trick. Around him, something is happening; in fact, a great deal is happening – far more than he can deal with all at once. Grass is blowing in the wind. Clouds are racing overhead with astonishing swiftness, their swirling baroque shapes like nothing he has ever seen before. Indeed, it occurs to him, as he advances along the track, whose white stones gleam with an almost phosphorescent light, like the pebbles dropped by resourceful Hansel to guide him back from the middle of the dark wood, that he has never really seen *anything* before.

And what is that *sound*? A vast sighing, as of a thousand hearts breaking, a moaning as of souls in torment, a wailing of sirens, a murmur of distant thunder . . . Far below, the ink-black waves churn around the rocks, throwing up gusts of spume. Sandy is transfixed by this spectacle: the great and timeless sea, whose depths hide who knows what terrible Leviathans? *Here Be Monsters*. He acknowledges the thought with a shudder, although it is not one he recognizes as his. Just now his mind is an empty room, into which all kinds of strange ideas are entering, like a troupe of uninvited visitors.

What's even stranger is the way ideas, up to now kept within their proper limits, seem to have acquired the disconcerting facility of materializing in the real world – so that the very thought of a sea monster is enough to conjure the hideous vision he now confronts from its resting place on the ocean bed.

'I'm seeing things,' gasps Sandy, wrenching his gaze away from the dreadful thing, with its rearing inky coils, its snaky head and terrible, human eyes. When he looks again there is nothing there; just rocks, a swirl of sea foam, a clump of seaweed. 'All stuff and nonsense,' he reassures himself, wondering if there was something funny about the cake.

He blunders on, impeded in his progress by a sense that the air has been changed to a more solid medium through which he swims rather than walks, like an astronaut in deep space. Beneath his feet the chalky stones sparkle like diamonds, shooting out iridescent fragments which adhere to everything around: the grass, the rocks – even Sandy's shoes, which now glitter as bright as Dorothy's ruby slippers. But then he sees something which brings him up short.

For on the cliff's edge, just where, with shocking abruptness, the green breaks off into a bone-white wall of rock plunging a hundred feet into the sea, stands Auntie, facing Ray. They are quite close together, Sandy sees with alarm – so close that their heads are almost touching. Of the two, Auntie is nearer the edge: a bare yard from perdition. One step, thinks Sandy, his heart in his mouth, one step and she'd be over . . . He slows his pace to a cautious crawl. *Don't make any sudden moves*.

What happens next isn't entirely clear – given that Sandy has come to distrust the evidence of his own eyes rather more than before during the past few minutes – but it seems to him that Connie has grown suddenly taller and straighter, casting off her stooped and withered carapace to emerge, transformed, into a figure in shining white. The golden locks of this splendid creature flow past its shoulders, and its naked feet barely seem to touch the ground, buoyed up as it is by the gently waving pinions of a magnificent pair of . . . *wings*.

A line from a poem he once read in college pops into Sandy's head:

> Wer, wenn ich schriee, hörte mich denn aus der Engel
> Ordnungen?

Either he's going mad or there's something very wrong with his eyes. He looks from the hovering angelic being which was once his aunt to the cowering shape opposite. Ray, too, it appears, has undergone a transmogrification of sorts. He seems smaller – shrivelled – his skin blushed a fiery red. And isn't he sporting horns and a tail? His beautiful Ray – really quite hideously *ugly* . . . Sandy closes his eyes in horror at the sight.

When he opens them again, it's to hear his name being called.

'Sandy! Penny for them, dear. *So* sweet of you to help. But don't worry – we've found dear old Rufus. Chasing rabbits again, the naughty boy . . .'

Returned to her more familiar shape, Auntie stands before him, her rosy, wrinkled face wearing an apologetic smile. Beside her, the old dog thumps its tail. A good few paces behind comes Ray, with a face like thunder.

'Don't ask. Don't fucking *ask*,' he snarls, drawing level with Sandy. 'It was all going according to plan. Got her up there – right to the edge – as easy as pie. Then she starts her fucking *mind games*, man. Tell you what, it fucking *freaked* me out.

She's a fucking *witch*, man. Tell you that for *nothing* . . .'

Gibbering and shaking, Ray continues to mutter in Sandy's ear all the way back to where they left the others. Who are much as they were when Sandy set out (only five minutes has elapsed, after all – even though it seems like a hundred years to Sandy), with the exception of Leonora, who is busy removing her clothes.

'So delightful to feel the air on one's skin,' she babbles, flinging scarves and petticoats to the wind.

'Mummy, *please*. You're making a spectacle of yourself,' pleads Iseult, gathering up these articles as fast as they are discarded – although no one else pays Leonora the slightest bit of attention, absorbed as they all are in their separate delusions. Humming happily under her breath, Leonora unbuttons her blouse, exposing her shrunken white chest.

'Air-bathing,' she says dreamily. 'The best thing for one's complexion . . .'

'Sandy! Thank goodness,' cries Iseult, as he comes into view. 'You've got to help me with Mummy. She's having one of her funny turns . . .'

Sandy isn't sure, in the end, how they manage the journey back, because it's clear that, apart from Izz, who's thankfully *compos mentis*, the rest of them – himself included – are in a bad way. Even when Leonora has been dissuaded from carrying out her alfresco strip-tease, it's still an effort to get her into the car. She seems to have taken against it.

'Nasty black *coffin*,' she shrieks. 'Don't want to go in the nasty black coffin . . .'

Then there's the problem of Ray. Ever since his encounter with Auntie on the cliffs, he's been twitchy as hell, muttering darkly under his breath about the evil eye, and jumping a mile if anyone so much as looks at him. Auntie herself seems more or less as usual – that's to say, at a tangent from reality. But since Sandy is no longer sure what that is, this seems, for the first time, an entirely reasonable position to take. Just now, she is doing her best to persuade Leonora to abandon her prejudice against the Armstrong Sidley. 'Don't be silly, Lolly,' she says brightly. 'It's the Ambassador's car – he's sent it round especially. If you don't hurry up, we'll miss the dancing. And you know how you love dancing . . .'

But Leonora is adamant. 'Nasty black coffin,' she sobs.

'Plenty of room in the Jag,' calls Jocelyn from behind the wheel of this vehicle. 'She can sit in the front with me, if she likes . . .'

'Just as long as the old bag doesn't want to sit in the back with *me*,' chortles Brian, from the depths of the baby-blue motor. 'Sam's the one I want sitting next to me. Because Sam wants to get her head down, doncha, darling?'

'Well, for fuck's sake keep it quiet,' murmurs Nick, closing his eyes.

The drive back is as weird as anything Sandy has ever experienced. Sea monsters, angels . . . even Drag Night at the Pussy Galore hadn't prepared him for this. Because dotty old Leonora turns out to be right – the car *is* a kind of coffin, in which, like the heroine of a horrible story by Edgar Allan Poe he'd once had the misfortune to read as a child, Sandy finds himself buried alive, while all the phantoms of his past rush towards him in a headlong stream, gibbering and squeaking like bats.

Pressing his face against the windscreen is Neville Corcoran – with whom Sandy had shared a Latin primer and the occasional cigarette behind the cricket pavilion – who'd been found hanging from the hot-water pipe in the janitor's cupboard one dreadful day after chapel. No sooner has he been whirled away in the semblance of a dead leaf than Louis de Beers takes his place – still the horrid greenish colour he was when they pulled him out of the Serpentine. They'd recorded an open verdict. Then it's the turn of David Fisher. Sleeping pills washed down with a bottle of whisky. Nervous strain, they'd said. Now he waves cheerily at Sandy over the hedge of a cottage garden, dressed in a long white garment which might, from a different angle, turn out to be nothing but a suit of woollen combinations pinned to a clothes-line.

Recoiling from this disturbing sight (those big dark eyes, that cyanose-blue face), Sandy finds himself confronting another spook. What really gives him the willies about this one is that it's *actually inside the car*. Sitting beside him, large as life, is sweet-faced Jeremy Tremayne – looking just as he did the last time Sandy saw him, in the bar of the Coach and Horses, the night before the accident. If it *was* an accident. Cleaning a shotgun. 'How *are* you, dear?' he says, with a ghastly smile, squeezing Sandy's knee with a hand as cold as ice. 'You're looking a bit pale, I must say. Seen a ghost?' Winking at Sandy in quite his old mischievous way, so that it takes Sandy a minute to realize that his eyes have been playing him tricks again and that the only other person in the back seat with him is Ray.

'Got the colly-wobbles?' Ray hisses in Sandy's ear (and he wonders how he could ever have mistaken that vicious proletarian whine for Jeremy's dulcet tones). 'Don't worry. You leave it to me. *I'll* fix her good and proper . . .'

This last remark is delivered with a savage jerk of the chin towards Auntie, sitting placidly beside Iseult in the front seat of the boxy black Armstrong Sidley, in which, all unknowingly, she hurtles towards her date with destiny.

★

Lulled by the engine's throaty purr, and by the blurred images – fields, trees, hedges – flashing past the window, Connie slips once more into the past. The muggy weather of an English June dissolves, without much effort of imagination, into the sticky heat of Shanghai in 1911. The black-and-white-marble entrance hall of the Police Commissioner's house. She'd been putting on her hat in front of the mirror when she heard Lily calling from the morning room.

'Constance, a word with you, if you please . . .'

Lily had been resting on the sofa on which, nearing the end of her confinement, she spent much of her time. 'Going out?' she'd said pointedly.

'Yes. That is, I . . .'

'Anywhere nice?' said Lily.

'Just the museum.'

'I see.'

Lily was silent for such a long time that Connie started to feel fidgety. That day Strickland had promised to take her to the Jade Buddha Temple. She hadn't been able to stop herself glancing at the clock.

Lily'd intercepted the glance.

'Are you in a hurry?' she'd said sharply.

'No. Not really. I . . .'

'Good,' says Lily. 'Because we've got a lot to talk about . . .'

She'd been seen, of course – Lily did not say by whom. But someone – one of Lily's intimates, presumably – had observed Connie and Strickland entering the tea-house on the zig-zag bridge. They'd gone there after visiting the Yu gardens. So charming, with their pavilions and ornamental lakes. Bridges, like the one they'd crossed to reach the tea-house, which were crooked not straight, to deter devils. Now it seemed as if one had caught up with them after all . . .

'Oh, don't deny it!' Lily cries, seeing that Connie is about to speak. 'Guilt's written all over your face. You silly, *silly* girl!'

As Lily railed, Connie could think only of Strickland, waiting in vain in front of the museum; would he understand that something had happened to delay her? She'd write him a note, she'd decided; or, better still, go in person . . .

'I don't think you fully appreciate the seriousness of this,' Cousin Lily was saying. Her freckled face was patched with red – a sure sign that she was working herself up. 'Going about with a man like that. And in public, too!' she'd groaned.

'I'm sorry,' said Connie.

'Sorry!' Lily emitted a small scream of laughter. '"Sorry",' she'd echoed, shaking her head from side to side. A new and terrible thought seemed to strike her. 'Has he . . . *touched* you?' she said.

'No.'

'Well, that's something at least. Although *what* I'm going to say to your poor dear mother I can't think . . .'

'What do you mean?' said Connie.

Lily'd looked at her then: a long, considering look. 'You silly little goose,' she'd said, almost gently. 'You don't imagine, after this, that you can possibly stay?'

It hadn't been easy to escape the surveillance under which, after that day, she had been kept. Her time was monitored; her careless hours of wandering curtailed. Now, every time she left the room – to fetch a handkerchief or see to one of the children – she sensed their eyes upon her. Lily's, and Cousin Freddie's; the servants, too, had been instructed to watch her.

A week went by before an opportunity presented itself. An invitation came, from the Patterson girls. To refuse might have given offence to Lady Patterson, whose favour was something Lily thought worth having.

'You'll have to go,' she said to Connie, with the peremptory tone she had lately adopted in all exchanges with the girl. 'John will take you.' This was the Chinese servant. 'I'll send the car to collect you after tea.'

At the Patterson house – a large mock-Tudor mansion in Avenue du Roi Albert – she'd made conversation for an hour with Susie Patterson, then pleaded a headache. 'What a shame,' yawned the girls' mother, ringing for the driver. 'You'll miss the charades.' The driver was young, with a smooth, impassive face under his peaked chauffeur's cap. When they reached the crossroads, Connie tapped on the glass.

'Not that way,' she told him. 'This way. I want to go to Rue Lafayette . . .'

Strickland's flat was on the third floor of a Beaux Arts mansion block. He hadn't seemed surprised to see her. 'Come in,' he'd merely said, looking her up and down. 'I'll make you some tea – unless you'd like something stronger?'

The room smelled strongly of turpentine, reminding her of other rooms – in Camberwell, or Chelsea – where she and her friends from the Slade had rented accommodation. Cosy, cluttered, down-at-heel rooms, smelling of burnt toast and Rowney's, where a rust-coloured chenille shawl was always to be found draped over an ugly chair, and a postcard of *Primavera* or *The Anatomy Lesson* tacked to the mantelpiece. This was grander than any of these. High-ceilinged, with tall curtainless windows at the far end and a big gilt mirror over the fireplace. An altogether superior kind of artist's *atelier*. Chairs had been pushed against the wall to accommodate an easel, next to which stood a table, covered with jars of brushes and dry pigments. Stacks of canvases leaned their faces to the wall.

At the nearer end of the room was what she took to be her host's living quarters. A divan, covered in a striped blanket, and a rattan chair. A low table, of black and gold lacquer, on which the remains of an earlier meal could be seen: a blue and white bowl, containing some greasy scraps of meat and rice; a pair of skewed chopsticks; an empty bottle of Tiger beer.

'Sit down,' said Strickland, clearing a space for her on the divan, which was strewn with clothes, she noticed vaguely. Soiled shirts and a pair of paint-smeared corduroys. A scarlet silk dressing gown embroidered with dragons and lotus flowers. One black silk stocking.

'So tell me,' he said, sitting down opposite her. 'To what do I owe the pleasure of this visit?'

'I had to come,' she told him. 'To explain. The fact is . . . I'm not allowed to see you any more . . .'

'Ah.' He hadn't seemed unduly put out. 'Your cousin doesn't approve of me.'

'It isn't that . . .' But she'd hesitated rather too long.

'Oh, but it *is* that. In her place, I'd doubtless feel the same. I'm a man with a certain reputation where women are concerned. That is to say, I like them.' He looked at her quizzically. 'Can I help it if they like me?'

She hadn't known how to answer this. Fortunately, he was used to doing most of the talking. 'I suppose I ought to send you home,' he'd said. 'Although it does seem a pity, after you've come all this way . . .'

'I don't want to go,' she'd said.

'You Slade girls. Always so headstrong . . .' But he'd been smiling as he said it.

He'd been surprised, nonetheless, to find that she wasn't a

virgin. Although the single encounter she'd had on the life-room divan with her drawing tutor – a married man much older than herself – hardly counted as extensive experience. The best thing about the whole sorry affair was being able to hold her head up among the others – Sybil Vane, Dora de Quincy and the rest of that set – all of whom, to judge from their whispered asides and significant looks, had already crossed that Rubicon. Sex. It wasn't something one talked about in polite company; certainly not something one admitted to having *done*. The Slade was different, however. There it was almost a point of honour to have slept with at least one man – 'apart from one's brother, of course,' as Olive Sidwell put it, with a sidelong look from under kohl-darkened lids. They were bohemians, after all.

How they'd have laughed – Sybil and the others – if they could have seen her at that moment, sharing Guy Strickland's bed. He was so much the sort of man with whom, at the Slade, she'd preferred to have nothing to do. Arrogant. A poseur. A preening lady-killer. Watching him as, naked, he stretched himself luxuriously in front of the mirror which hung at the end of the bed ('Very bad Feng Shui, the Chinese would say, but I say that's all rot . . .'), she could almost hear her friends' amused remarks. *My word, you have got yourself a catch . . . One of the Old Man's protégés, no less . . . Watch out. He'll be getting you to sit for him, next. Once he's turned you into his muse, you can never go back to being an artist, you know . . .*

Perhaps sensing her scrutiny, he'd turned to face her, narrowing his gaze as he took in the picture she made – an arrangement of limbs among sheets; white flesh against whiter linen. His expression was one she recognized as the measuring look an artist brings to bear upon his subject. A look of assessment – cold, entirely detached.

'You know – I should paint you like that,' he'd said, yawning and scratching his balls.

Exactly what he'd said to the Selbys to make it all right she never dared ask, but there was no more talk of her being sent home. All Strickland would say on the subject was that he'd squared it with Bella Patterson – 'She owes me a favour or two'; and so that would have made it all right where Lily was concerned. Certainly, the supper party invitation from Lady Patterson Lily'd been hoping for all season ('Just a simple little affair, Mrs Selby. A few of our *closest* friends, you know') had followed shortly after that.

As Strickland observed one afternoon when they were in bed, it's an ill wind that blows nobody any good. Because if Cousin Lily'd decided to turn a blind eye for a while to Connie's comings and goings, that was really no bad thing for all concerned. 'Even if you've lost your taste for Oriental art,' he'd said, with that infuriatingly self-satisfied smile, 'it doesn't mean I can't give you a bit of extra tuition in life drawing . . .'

'Cool pad,' is Nick's verdict on Dunsinane. 'Sort of, like, Gothic, y'know?'

'Good place for a cover shoot,' murmurs Jocelyn thoughtfully. 'I can see it now. Decaying mansion. Cobwebs. Chicks in nighties. The whole vampire bit . . .'

'Pongs, dunnit?' grumbles Brian. 'Old people's houses always pong . . .'

'I'm surprised you notice, the amount of patchouli you're wearing,' sniffs Keith.

Bickering among themselves, they wander inside.

Evening sunshine floods the big drawing room with unearthly light. Wraiths of past guests dance in a haze of dust motes. The overmantel mirror flings out rainbow splinters which form themselves, as Sandy watches, into kaleidoscopic patterns. Curiouser and curiouser, he thinks dreamily. Since his encounter with the ghosts, he's been feeling distinctly odd – as if there were a distance between him and the rest of the world. Granted, the rest of the world seems to have calmed down a bit, and there've been no more supernatural visitations, thank God. But there is a *texture* to everything – a kind of insistent *glow* – which wasn't there before, he's almost certain.

For the past few minutes he's been entirely lost in contemplation of the drawing-room curtains, whose dusty plum-coloured folds seem to pulsate with a wondrous life of their own. When he drags his gaze away at last, it is to encounter yet more richness: the gleaming filigree of a spider's web, stretched across a windowpane; the voluptuous velvet of mould on a rotten skirting board. As for the dog – why hasn't he ever noticed the beauty of the dog? Entranced, he admires the waviness of its gorgeously coloured coat – a dirty Titian red – the glistening of its sorrowful amber eyes.

He holds out a hand to the beast – 'Here, doggie. Nice doggie' – and is rewarded with a slobbery kiss from its rough wet tongue, a sensation which he finds at once repugnant and arousing.

A shape cut out of darkness falls between Sandy and the dog, bringing with it a certain chill.

'Enjoying yourself, Sandy-poos?' says a voice.

After the horror of Ray's demonic metamorphosis on the cliffs, Sandy's hardly dared to do more than glance at him, in case the same thing happens again. Even now, as he raises his eyes to where Ray is standing, silhouetted against the light, he is half afraid of what he might see. But Ray is as lovely as ever, his hyacinthine curls framing his exquisite face in quite the old way. There is a sudden displacement of atoms as he plonks himself down beside Sandy on the sofa, and a squeal from the dog as Ray's foot connects with its rump.

'Useless git,' he says savagely, as the beast takes cover under the nearest chair. 'Doesn't even do what it's meant to. Keep the vermin down. Place is infested,' he hisses in Sandy's ear. 'Rats. Mice. Nasty, creeping things . . .'

His gesture takes in the room, which is empty of rodents as far as Sandy can see – its only other occupant apart from themselves being Connie, who is asleep in her chair. Iseult is off seeing to Leonora, whose earlier fit of hysteria has reduced her to a state of near-catatonia. Jocelyn and the others have wandered out of the French windows into the garden, 'to look at the flowers', Jocelyn says airily, from the centre of a cloud of pungent cigarette smoke. Unusual brand, thinks Sandy drowsily. Turkish, maybe.

'. . . drastic measures,' Ray is muttering. 'Only way to get rid of 'em. Poison. Lots of it.' His mouth is so close that Sandy can feel his moist breath, smell its faint, sweet scent of corruption. 'Potting shed's full of it,' he whispers. 'I just had a gander. All it'd take'd be a couple of pellets in her tea. Easy as winking . . .'

Horribly, he suits the action to the word, screwing up one eye and bulging out the other, in a ghastly imitation of Long John Silver.

The door opens to admit a weary-looking Iseult. 'Mummy's asleep,' she tells Sandy. ''Fraid I might have to leave her here for a bit. Don't want to risk her going off the deep end again . . .'

'Touch of the sun, was it?' inquires Ray sweetly.

Iseult ignores this. 'So, if you don't mind,' she says stiffly to Sandy, 'I'll be toddling along. Cows to see to, you know. In an hour or so I'll drop by and pick up the aged parent. If she wakes before then, perhaps you'd give her a cup of tea . . .'

For some reason, this last remark provokes an explosion of mirth from Ray. 'Tea! Ooh, I like it!' he splutters. 'A nice hot cuppa. Do us all a power of good, *that* would . . .'

'I'll be orf, then,' says Iseult coldly.

'Ah. Oh. Of course.' Belatedly, Sandy remembers his manners. Heaving himself up from the sofa, where Ray is still cackling to himself, he makes a superhuman effort to pull himself together. 'I'll see you out,' he says.

'No need,' says Iseult, but she does not protest when he escorts her to the car, which is parked in the drive, displaced from its usual spot by the blue Jaguar.

'Look,' Sandy starts to say. 'About today. What happened. I mean . . . I'm sorry . . .'

The words die in his throat.

'Oh, I say,' says Iseult. *'That's* a bit much . . .'

Both stand amazed at the sight which meets their eyes.

For on the lawn in front of the house a naked and (Sandy can't help noticing) rather well-hung satyr is dancing with two slender nymphs, one dark, one fair – both also minus their clothes. Music (flutes, a Spanish guitar) fills the air with haunting melodies of love and abandonment.

'Those girls ought to get something on their chests,' Iseult says, after a brief pause. 'These evenings can be awfully damp, you know . . .'

'Yes,' Sandy agrees hoarsely, still transfixed by the golden pelt covering the pale chest and belly of the dancing youth, and the gaily swinging appendage beneath it. Does he imagine it, or are those cloven hooves which twinkle so merrily through the grass, and horns which peep from among the dancer's shaggy curls? 'Good gracious,' he murmurs. 'I've never seen anything like it . . .'

With a snort of impatience, Iseult turns on her heel and walks away. For a stretched-out minute, Sandy thinks about going after her, but his thoughts are so scrambled up (can this really be happening, or is it just some weird dream?) that the words won't shape themselves. *Stop. Don't go.* Mutely, he watches as the big black car, with Iseult at the wheel, backs down the drive and, after making a smart half-turn to the right, disappears off down the road, leaving nothing but a white dust-cloud behind. *I'm sorry, old thing,* he almost calls after her. *This really isn't the way things should have turned out at all . . .*

Sighing at his own ineptitude where Iseult is concerned, he turns back towards the Bacchanalian scene. The golden lads and lasses. Who are no longer to be seen, he notices – the only visible traces of their passing a gauzy scarf tangled in a rose bush, a fallen sandal left upon the grass. From the shrubbery beside the house comes the faint sound of laughter. A strummed chord from an invisible guitar.

'Wait for me,' calls Sandy shyly, already stripping off his jacket, by way of entering into the spirit of things. He hasn't indulged in larks like this since Eights Week.

But then he remembers. Ray. A cold finger of dread tickles Sandy's spine. *Rat poison.* He couldn't have meant it, could he? One never knew with Ray.

Reluctantly, he stops his ears to the voices in the foliage. *Catch me if you can.* Retraces his steps towards the house, which watches him with its blind eyes. Reaches the sitting room – where Ray is no longer to be found, it seems. Nor is there any trace of Auntie . . .

A big tank full of sunshine, the room vibrates with murderous intentions.

7

Weird Scenes

Upstairs, in one of the seldom-used spare bedrooms, Ray is having a poke around. He's retreated up here, as a matter of fact, to get out of the old woman's way. Truth is, she makes him nervous. Witch. Sitting in her corner, quiet as a mouse, just thinking her thoughts. Worse than that, he has a nasty suspicion she may be able to read his. 'I know who you are,' she'd said to him calmly, as the sea roared beneath them around the dangerous rocks. It would have taken so little to have had her over the edge – one shove would have done it. Yet he'd funked it. Something about her steady gaze had unnerved him. The little smile with which she'd turned to confront him. *I know who you are.* He wasn't sure, now, why the words had filled him with such terror. As if her blue eyes saw right into his soul – or the writhing thing that passed for it.

This time'll be different, Ray promises himself, as he yanks out drawers and rifles through the rows of musty-smelling clothes in the wardrobe, in the not very likely hope of finding something of value. *This* time it'll all go according to plan. Drop o' strychnine in the bedtime cocoa and . . . Night-night, Auntie. Careless, some of these old folk. Wrong tin, see. Rat poison next to the Horlicks. Easily done. Sniggering, Ray rips clothes off hangers, glances at them and throws them down. Nothing worth having. Old rags. Old ladies' stuff. Roughly, he casts out tea-gowns, crêpe-de-Chine evening frocks, pin-tucked voile blouses. A fine haze of old talcum powder and eau-de-

Cologne tickles his nostrils, making him want to sneeze. What he wouldn't give now for some matches. One touch and the whole lot'd go up in a trice . . .

A new idea insinuates itself into Ray's catalogue of violent solutions. Maybe *that'd* be the way to do it. Less tricky than the poison. Carelessness with a candle . . . Not a bad thought at all. Only trouble is, they might end up throwing out the baby with the bathwater, as it were. Fires were hard to control (he'd personal experience of that one). Perhaps, after all, a quick shove down the stairs would be the best. Simple, but effective. No mess, no fuss – and, best of all, no evidence . . .

From outside comes the sound of voices. Girls giggling. A whoop of laddish laughter. Ray goes to the window and looks down. Disdainfully, he observes the carryings-on. Not his scene at all, that caper. Too many wobbly tits for a start. The boy had a nice bum, though. Firm. Rounded. Not too big. He knew it, too, the hussy. Flaunting himself. Maybe he liked it up the arse. Lots of 'em did. Always happy to oblige, snickers Ray.

Behind a stack of old clothes at the back of the wardrobe, a flash of scarlet silk catches his eye. It's some sort of dressing gown. Chinesy. Embroidered with flowers – chrysanths, they look like – and a dragony kind of thing with claws and a long tail. Nice, thinks Ray, shaking out the heavy, bright folds. He likes nice things, does Ray. In his twenty-two years, Ray has known a good deal of ugliness. Which has made him – if not sensitive, exactly, then at least *partial* to certain kinds of beauty. In another life, and with his mimetic skills, he might have made an artist. Now, slipping the red robe on, he catches sight of himself in the mirror. A romantic vision stares back at him: part dandy, part courtesan. It raises an ironical eyebrow at itself. I'm wasted, thinks Ray – sucking his cheeks in, the better to enhance his handsome cheekbones – *wasted* in this dump. I need someone who'll appreciate me. Take me out. Buy me things.

He'd like a car, for starters, and some proper clothes – not the rubbish he usually has to settle for. A flat of his own would be nice. Somewhere classy. He knows just how it's going to look, too. None of your cheap and nasty tat. Gilt and flock wallpaper and other tart's-boudoir stuff. In his mind's eye he sees a room – an echoing white space, filled with . . . nothing *but* space. Because poverty is cluttered. Noisy, too. He will have silence. Concentrating on this vision, he scrunches his eyes tight shut. Conjuring exquisite emptiness, with perhaps a few beautiful things (a mirror, a lamp, a white marble statue) to point the contrast – the sheer, arrogant *wantonness* of all that absence . . .

The voices from outside are louder now, chanting a monotonous refrain. Cheated of his epiphany, Ray frowns.

'Shut up,' he mutters, though there is no one to hear him. 'Fucking shut *up*, will you?'

But it's no good. The beautiful room is shattered, the vision fled. Ray's expression turns murderous – he becomes the spitting image (had he been there to see it) of Sandy's cliff-top hallucination.

Ooh yeah, VAMPIRE LOVE
Sweet, sweet VAMPIRE LOVE . . .

Shut up shut up shut up . . . Ray's gaze falls on the mirror. At once his features clear. 'Wasted,' he murmurs, smoothing back his hair.

★

A thundery, midsummer heat lies over the garden, where Connie, in a crushed straw hat and dirty white gardening gloves, wanders among her flowers. She is thinking, as she dreamily snips the tall stems of greenfly-encrusted aquilegia, past-their-best irises and drooping love-lies-bleeding (laying them carefully in her trug), of when it was she last had a summer party. Sandy's graduation, was it? Years ago, at any rate. What fun it's going to be. A spray of Malmaison roses, half strangled by the Russian vine which grows along the garden wall, takes her fancy. She reaches up and gets hold of it, incurring a few scratches in the process and showering petals everywhere, before the thing is safely captured. *Now sleeps the crimson petal, now the white* . . . A favourite of Wilfred's, that. She has a vision of him standing on the hearthrug declaiming the verse, his head flung back in a kind of poetic trance. There was nothing to beat Tennyson, he always said. Now she comes to think of it, the rambler had been one he'd planted (Wilfred, that is, not Lord Alfred) soon after they were married. If there ever was a white rose, she can see no sign of it now. How he'd loved the garden, dear old Wilfred. Pottering about all day in his funny old Panama, with rake or pruning shears at the ready . . .

'Good to have a little tidy-up,' murmurs Connie, spotting another promising bloom – a crimson peony, lolling on to the weed-choked path. The garden, she guiltily admits, is not looking its best – its once carefully tended grass now knee-high, its borders gone to seed; although here and there, in their wild profusion of weeds, the bright flame of tiger-lily or poppy can be seen. The slight pang Connie feels as each flower is sacrificed is alleviated by the thought of how beautiful it is all going to look, once the vases are filled and the candles lit. There will be champagne. There is always champagne. And quail's eggs, she rather thinks. A cold collation. Perhaps a whole salmon, with artfully arranged scales of thinly sliced cucumber . . .

Thinking about the food makes her feel anxious. How did one go about arranging such a feast? Then a happy thought strikes her: she will telephone Iseult. Iseult is always so good at that kind of thing . . .

On a bench in what was once the rose garden, where she has gone in search of a fine specimen she remembers seeing a day or two ago (Souvenir du Docteur Jamain – such a lovely scent), she finds the blonde girl, Sam, wearing nothing but a man's shirt. By the look of her red eyes, the poor child has been crying. There are grass seeds in her hair, and grass stains on her plump white legs. At Connie's approach, she looks up, with a hopeful expression. Then her face falls. 'Oh, hello,' she says. 'For a minute I thought . . . oh, never mind.' Becoming conscious all of a sudden of her flushed and dishevelled state, she does up a stray button. 'Doing a bit of sunbathing,' she explains with a watery smile, although the sun has long since shifted from this part of the garden.

'I wonder,' says Connie diffidently, 'if you'd mind awfully giving me a hand with these flowers?' Without waiting for an answer, she loads the girl with fragrant armful upon armful, until she resembles nothing so much as a figure in a classical frieze, garlanded with roses and crowned with ivy. 'I don't suppose,' she inquires casually as, thus encumbered, the two of them set off towards the house, 'you could lay your hands on some quail's eggs? And perhaps a few dozen bottles of champagne?'

Evidently used to having unreasonable demands made of her, the girl hesitates only a second. Frowns slightly. 'I think there's still some bubbly left over from teatime. Not sure about the other stuff, though . . .'

'Never mind,' says Connie. She heaves the trug up the crumbling stone steps to the weed-infested terrace. 'We'll manage. Come on,' she urges the girl, who still stands at the bottom of the steps, her arms full of flowers (and very pretty she looks, too, thinks Connie – if a shade underdressed), 'you can help me arrange these. After that, I'll give Iseult a ring about the refreshments. Such a *practical* person, Iseult. Then, if you like,' says Connie airily (not wanting to hurt the poor girl's feelings, but really, dressed like that, she wasn't making the best of herself), 'we'll find you something to wear. I've heaps of things that might fit you . . . and your friends, too, of course,' she adds, as, from the overgrown shrubbery, emerge the rest of the Vampyres and their acolytes.

Of the urban sophisticates first glimpsed on the cliff top, little trace remains. Clothes have been discarded, make-up smudged and personal effects exchanged, so that the result is a strange blurring of identities. Nick has cast off his trademark black for one of the girls' long dresses – which is far too short for him, revealing a flash of hairy calf as he walks. Keith, in borrowed velvet, is an altogether more epicene vision than the rough youth of some hours before. Brian, naked except for a silk scarf tied sarong-style around his hips, resembles a Stone Age necromancer, his body daubed with mud and grass stains as if in some arcane rite. Sultry Mandy is a pretty eighteenth-century cabin-boy in a ruffled shirt several sizes too big for her. As for Jocelyn . . .

'Jossy went for a swim,' grins Brian, as they draw nearer.

And indeed he is soaked to the skin. Green pond slime adheres to his face and dripping hair. His smart clothes are a sodden mess.

'It's n-not f-funny,' he complains, his teeth chattering. 'I'm f-fucking f-freezing . . .'

'Should've looked where you was going,' says matter-of-fact Keith.

'How was I to know there was *water* underneath that green stuff? It looked solid enough . . .'

'Oh dear,' says Connie. 'Did you fall in the pond? I'm afraid it needs cleaning out rather badly. What a shame. Your lovely shirt . . .'

'Ossie Clark,' moans Jocelyn, vainly trying to wring water from the sleeves.

'Don't worry. I'm sure we can find you something else to wear. I was just saying to your young lady here . . .'

'I like it!' guffaws the irrepressible Brian. 'Young lady! That's a laff, that is . . .'

'Oh, do shut up,' snaps Jocelyn. 'I'm g-getting *pneumonia* here, while you're s-standing about sniggering . . .'

'What you need,' says Connie firmly, 'is a nice hot bath.'

She leads the way through the open French windows into the drawing room, where she deposits her burden of flowers, scattering petals across the threadbare carpet. 'See to those later,' she murmurs vaguely, marshalling her muddy crew through into the hall and up the stairs to the bathroom. 'Plenty of hot water to go round,' she says. 'Find you some towels, shall I?'

'What about my clothes?' wails Jocelyn. 'It's all very well talking about baths, but what about afterwards? I can't get back into *these* . . .' His gesture takes in the smelly green ruins of his Carnaby Street clobber. 'Well, can I?'

'I don't see why,' snickers Brian. 'Start a new fashion, like. The slimy look. Dead trendy, that . . .'

'Just put a sock in it, will you?' says Jocelyn wearily. 'Now, if you don't mind, I'd like some privacy . . .'

He slams the door in their faces. A moment later, there is the sound of taps being turned on full blast.

'Some people got no sense of humour,' says Brian sorrowfully.

But the others have already lost interest in Jocelyn and his moods. Giggling like a flock of overexcited children, they are racing off along the corridor, opening doors into rooms long shut, and pulling things out of cupboards and drawers placed there years before and since forgotten.

'Fur coats!' cries the dark girl, Mandy, from the recesses of a wardrobe. She emerges, clad in a floor-length Persian lamb, acquired by Connie's mother on one of her Paris trips. 'Fabulous,' she sighs.

'Stinks of mothballs,' says Brian, buttoning up a scarlet guardsman's tunic which had last seen service at Rourke's Drift.

Sam is trying on hats: extravagant confections of feathers and tulle with enormous brims; vampish pillboxes and demure cloches of Leghorn straw. She settles at last for a leopard-skin-patterned toque with a spotted veil – one of Leonora's cast-offs, Connie seems to recall. She was always buying hats and then deciding they didn't suit her. Or she'd fall out of love with the man the hat was bought to impress . . .

Thinking of Leonora reminds her that she still has to telephone Iseult. Time's getting on and she has yet to solve the problem of comestibles. Leaving the young people to their charades, she wanders back along the corridor, descending the broad staircase – built around the middle of the previous century to resemble that of a Jacobean manor house – which is lit at this hour by a roseate glow from the stained-glass window on the half-landing. At the bottom of the stairs she finds Sandy, looking as if he's seen a ghost.

'Auntie?' he stammers. 'Are you all right?'

Always fussing, silly boy.

'Of course, dear. I'm perfectly fine. Why on earth shouldn't I be?' Connie asks, with a shade of her old briskness.

He opens his mouth to say something, but before he can do so the air is rent by a terrible scream. A moment later, Leonora appears at the top of the stairs, quite breathless with indignation.

'A man!' she cries, when at last she is able to speak. 'A man! A naked man!' She points a quivering finger towards the bathroom. 'I opened the door and *there he was*! Without a stitch!'

'Well, I like that!' comes the voice of Jocelyn, a little hollowly, from behind the bathroom door. 'I mean, look who's talking! At least I wasn't prancing around on the cliffs in my birthday suit, like some people I could mention . . .'

Sandy makes an effort to collect himself. Since the tea party on the cliffs (since he'd eaten that awful *cake*, in fact), he's felt as if he were caught up in some ghastly dream. Things keep happening over which he has no control. This recent outbreak of wilful nudity is one of them. 'Now then,' he says manfully. 'No need to get personal . . .'

'Who's getting personal?' Jocelyn's head appears around the edge of the door. 'I was merely stating a few home truths. But since you're here, Sandy love, maybe you could find me something to wear. Twenty-eight waist, thirty inside leg. Any colour but brown. I refuse to wear brown, under any circumstances . . .'

'Never fear,' Sandy assures him. 'We'll find you some togs . . .' He feels ridiculously light-hearted. Auntie's safe. That's the main thing. And Ray . . . He can worry about Ray later. 'There's bound to be something to fit you. Auntie never

172

throws anything away,' he adds with a conspiratorial wink at Jocelyn, who has emerged from the bathroom, wearing a small towel.

'Glad to hear it, dear heart,' sniffs Jocelyn. 'I must say, the idea of wandering around all night completely starkers doesn't appeal. Whatever *some* people might think . . .'

Leonora's mouth works furiously, as if she is about to make a crushing retort, but no sound emerges. Disordered by sleep, her hair has lost its cheerful curl and now sticks up in odd tufts. She looks suddenly reduced – old and foolish.

'Come, Lolly, dear,' says Connie gently. 'Let's make you a nice cup of tea. And then you can give me your advice about the party . . .'

At this, Leonora's expression brightens. 'Of course, dear,' she agrees graciously, descending the stairs with something of her old flamboyant style. 'You know I'm always happy to be of service. Now. First things first. Where are you going to put the band? In the conservatory, I'd have thought. Then you haven't all the bother of taking up carpets . . .'

The house seems much *bigger* than Sandy recalls. Surely it used not to have quite as many rooms as this? Intent on his quest to find suitable attire for Jocelyn ('any colour but brown' indeed!), he pops his head into one dust-sheeted room after another, noticing as he does so that certain *changes* are in progress. The proportions of some rooms seem distorted – their ceilings vertiginously high, their floor space enormous, as if reflected in a convex mirror or a witch's ball. And the wallpaper . . . Regency stripes ripple and quake with unnerving energy, William Morris honeysuckle twists and twines with a life of its own. It makes Sandy feel a mite queasy. In a blind panic, he blunders up a narrow staircase leading to the attic floor. It's a part of the house he hasn't set foot in since he was a lad. Servants' quarters, it must have been once. Not that there've ever been servants, in his recollection. Only old Mrs Pike, who 'did' for Auntie years ago. When she'd left – done in by sciatica or some such ailment – Auntie hadn't troubled to replace her. It unsettled Uncle Wilfred too much, having people about he wasn't used to . . .

It's here, in one of the slope-ceilinged attic bedrooms, that he finds Ray. The relief almost knocks him flat. 'You're here,' he gasps. 'Darling boy. If you *knew* the hell I've been through, trying to find you . . .'

'I was wondering when you'd turn up,' Ray replies.

'Yes. Well. Here I am,' says Sandy, rather too brightly. 'Having fun?' he adds, taking in the sight of Ray in his finery. And really the dear boy does look awfully fetching in that get-up (one of Auntie's Oriental souvenirs, presumably), with his hair combed flat against his scalp like a wartime spiv and rather too much kohl around his eyes. *Very* Rudolph Valentino.

'I'm on the hunt for some *trousers* for your little friend Jocelyn,' Sandy goes on, when Ray says nothing. 'Silly fellow went for a swim in the fish pond, would you believe? Forgot to remove his clothes first, unfortunately . . .'

'I hope *you* haven't forgotten what we was talking about just now,' interrupts Ray. 'Because I haven't. I've been thinking about it a lot . . .'

'Ah,' gulps Sandy. 'Yes. Now you mention it, I hadn't, in fact, forgotten about it.' He gives a nervous laugh. 'Not much chance of *that*! The thing is, Ray – dear one – I wonder if perhaps we ought to think it over a bit. No sense in, ah, *rushing* into things, is there?'

'No sense in hanging about, neither,' says Ray. Yawning, he flings himself back across the bed, heedless of the piles of fragile lace and crushable linen with which it is strewn. Under the scarlet robe he is naked, Sandy notices with a stirring of lust. Ray catches him looking, and smiles. 'I do love the feel of silk against my skin, don't you, Sandy-poos?' he says softly. His eyes, ringed with black like a geisha's, have the cold glitter of precious stones. Propping himself on an elbow, he allows one silken sleeve to slip. 'But I can never decide which is smoother,' he murmurs, running his hands slowly down his body, as if stroking a cat. 'The silk, or . . . me. What do *you* think, Sandy-poos?'

'Oh, Ray,' breathes Sandy, throwing caution to the winds. 'If you knew how much I adore you . . .'

Ray smiles. 'Then prove it,' he says.

The telephone rings as Iseult is about to leave and for a minute she's tempted to ignore it. What with one thing and another, it's later than she intended, and she's afraid that Mummy will be getting in a bit of a tizzy. Mummy hates to be kept waiting. But it's been so lovely having those few hours to herself: an unaccustomed treat. She's milked the cows, fed the chickens, walked the dogs, read the paper and had a smoke – all without a single interruption. Guiltily, she thinks that she could get quite used to being alone all the time, if this is what it would be like (no pointless summonses to the bedroom to change the channel on the television set or plump up pillows; no martyred complaints about the food, or the slowness of the service); but then reprimands herself. Poor Mummy. It isn't her fault that she's so difficult. Brought up the way she was, with servants and so on, and no money worries (at least, none she was privy to), she'd never had a chance to learn about give and take. Even marrying Daddy hadn't changed things all that much. He'd doted on her so. Spoiled her, when all's said and done (ruining himself into the bargain). It was funny, really, when you thought about it – the idea of Leonora as a farmer's wife. A shocking piece of miscasting, if ever there was one . . .

The telephone's peremptory note ruptures the stillness. One ring. Two rings. Three . . . Its squat black shape on the hall table quivers like an unexploded bomb.

'Uckfield 253 . . .'

It's Aunt. Babbling something about quail's eggs. Poor old darling gets battier every day, thinks Iseult fondly.

'Sorry, Aunt Con. I didn't quite catch that,' she says.

It transpires that Aunt's visitors have yet to take their leave (talk about overstaying one's welcome, Iseult thinks). Worse than that, they're apparently having some kind of party. I mean, *really*, thinks Iseult. If that doesn't take the biscuit. That was the trouble with bohemian types – they thought life was just endless fun and games.

'All right, Aunt. I'll see what I can do,' Iseult says, at the end of a long list of demands for items she knows will be quite impossible to get, at this time of night, in this neck of the woods. Caviare, for goodness' sake. *Foie gras.* (Although, come to think of it, she does have a tin of the stuff somewhere – left over from last Christmas.) 'Tell Mummy I'll be as quick as I can. How *is* Mummy, by the way? Not feeling too shaky, I hope?'

The receiver emits a peal of insect laughter. 'Oh, no,' the insect voice assures her. 'Dear Lolly's on splendid form . . .'

'That's rather what I was afraid of,' mutters Iseult, replacing the receiver in its cradle with a clunk. Conscious of a certain unease she cannot quite account for, she goes to see what she can rake up from the depths of the larder; deciding, as a concession to the spirit of frivolity which seems to have possessed her elders, to put on a clean blouse before she sets out . . .

By the time Iseult arrives, a subtle transformation has overtaken Dunsinane. A restoration of sorts. All the lights are on, and all the doors stand open. Voices and laughter can be heard coming from rooms which have long stood empty. From a distance, as she approaches, it is as if she is seeing the house in some earlier incarnation, when it was filled with people and resonated to the sound of their civilized amusements. If one were given to flights of fancy (and Iseult is not, as a general rule), one could almost believe one heard the click of croquet balls on the lawn – the ghostly echo of some long ago match – or smelt a whiff of smoke on the night air, residue of a leisurely *fin-de-siècle* Havana.

And parties, of course. She supposes there must have been parties. With ladies in pastel dresses and long gloves and chaps in evening dress with their hair all slicked down like patent leather. Dancing. There'd have been dancing. Cards. Backgammon. They were great ones for all that sort of thing, her grandparents' generation . . . Although of course it was never like this when Uncle Wilfred was alive, Iseult reminds herself. Uncle Wilfred hated any kind of fuss. (After that little sherry party Aunt Con had given for Sandy to mark the end of his Finals, the old boy had taken to his bed for a week. Nerves, of course. Passchendaele had done him in. After *that* particular show it was hard for him to bear too much noise, or too many people.) No, for as long as she can recall, the house has been a shell. Shuttered. Closed up. Like a house where someone has recently died.

Rather nice to see it come to life for once, thinks Iseult.

As she steps inside the open front door, a low fat shape launches itself at her legs. A rough wet tongue finds her hand.

'Good boy, Rufus. Good *boy*,' she says, cheered by the appearance of an ally.

But as she stoops to pat him, the animal bristles and cowers, emitting a low growl.

'Rufus?' She can't think what has spooked him. Then a figure moves in the shadows. 'Gracious,' says Iseult. 'You gave me quite a turn.'

It's the blonde girl (Sally? Sandra?), last seen wearing considerably less than she is now, Iseult blushes to recall. Now she's much more substantially dressed, in a long white lacy confection with a high neck and leg-o'-mutton sleeves. One of Granny's afternoon frocks, thinks Iseult. A bit too frilly for her liking. Not wholly unsuitable for a young person, though . . . The girl's gaze falls on the basket Iseult is carrying. 'Ooh, good. You've brought some more eats. I'll take that, shall I?' Before Iseult can protest, the girl relieves her of the basket and shimmers off down the corridor towards the kitchen.

Deprived of her one practical excuse for being there, Iseult feels somewhat at a loss. Then she remembers Mummy. The poor thing must be wondering where she's got to. By this time of night, she's usually tucked up in bed with her Horlicks and *Perry Mason*. Iseult hopes Mummy isn't going to make a scene. She gets awfully cross when she misses her favourite programme. Oh, well. Better get it over with, thinks Iseult resignedly. With some trepidation, she follows the sound of voices to the drawing room.

'Oh, I say,' she murmurs. 'How pretty!'

And certainly the room is a picture. Lit only by candles and by the glimmer of twilight which falls through the French windows at the far end, it seems a fairy's bower. Rambling roses twine around the big mirror over the fireplace; scarlet poppies nod from the mantelpiece, scattering their soporific dust. Among the clouded lustres of the chandelier, a passion-flower wreathes its tendrils. Pale fingers of foxglove and monkshood tremble in the light breeze from the open door. It's as if, Iseult thinks, the garden has come inside the house; she half expects to see grass growing up through the floorboards. There's an *atmosphere* in the room – a pervasive aroma of something spicy and herbal which enhances the pastoral feel. The smell of bonfires on an autumn day; of fallen chrysanthemum petals. Quite pleasant, really, thinks Iseult, inhaling – if a bit on the musty side. Through this blue haze, she makes out the figure of her mother, reclining on the sofa. On the floor at Leonora's feet some of the others – that pop singer chap and his friends – are sharing a cigarette. At the sound of her approach, he (Nick, isn't it?) looks up.

'Hey, babe,' he says affably.

Not quite sure what to make of this greeting, Iseult merely smiles.

'Ready to go?' she says to Leonora. With any luck, she'll have forgotten all about *Perry Mason*.

Her mother doesn't reply. Instead, she rolls her eyes heavenward, in what Iseult recognizes as her best 'thespian' manner. 'You see what I have to put up with?' the look implies.

'Are *you* ready to go?' says Nick (who is looking quite extraordinary, Iseult can't help noticing, in a velvet opera cloak, worn over what is surely a woman's blouse – some filmy, lacy thing – and striped trousers like a jester's). He winks at Iseult, thoughtfully offering her a puff on his cigarette.

'*I'm* always ready to go,' leers the blond youth (good job *he's* put some clothes on at last, thinks Iseult). 'All night, if you want . . .'

'Go? Who's going anywhere? I'm quite happy here,' says the dark girl, Mandy, with a soulful glance at Nick. She's also been at the dressing-up box, it seems. A full-skirted ballgown in crimson taffeta makes the most of her generous *décolletage*.

'Think about it,' says Nick, rolling another cigarette (terribly economical with their smokes, these young people, thinks Iseult). 'Should I stay or should I go? It's the existential question . . .'

'Existential bollocks,' says the blond boy. He lurches sideways until his face is level with Mandy's pretty breasts. 'Fancy a shag?'

'Oh, grow *up*,' snaps the girl. 'I'm going outside for a bit. Coming, Nick?'

'In a while, crocodile,' he tells her coolly. 'I want to talk to Iseult here . . .'

'But . . .' Iseult makes one last valiant effort to rally the troops. 'I can't stay long. Mummy . . .'

'Don't worry about Mummy.' He takes a quick drag on the roll-up, then passes it to Iseult. 'She's happy where she is.'

'But it's past her bedtime,' Iseult says, conscious, as she utters the words, of their complete irrelevance. Strange taste, this stuff. A bit too sweet. Give her Golden Virginia any day. How dark his eyes are, she thinks dreamily. She isn't sure she's ever seen eyes so dark before.

'You know something, Iseult?' remarks her companion, taking the smouldering butt from between her fingers. 'You worry too much about time. Time's an illusion. Like all of this . . .' His gesture takes in the room and everything in it: the crushed petals and guttering candleflames; the rickety sofa with its still more fragile human cargo.

'All of this,' she echoes, unable to tear her eyes away from his. So dark. Like falling into a vortex.

Around them, the room hums like a top. Its walls seem

suddenly very far away; its ceiling impossibly high. Like being at the bottom of a well, thinks Iseult.

'Perhaps it's a treacle well,' she murmurs.

Nick exhales smoke in a spiralling cloud, which winds itself among the waving strands of his long dark hair, so that for a moment it seems as if he is wearing a crown of ivy. 'You're a funny girl, Iseult . . .'

She considers this. Is it a good or bad kind of funniness? She hopes the former. She's always thought of herself as a pretty straightforward sort. A good sport. Not one to make a song and dance about things. She knows the kind of life she leads wouldn't be everybody's cup of tea – but it's not been a bad life, has it? Only now does it occur to her that she might have expected more.

Across the room one of the boys – the blond one – has picked up a guitar and is moodily picking out a tune. Some bluesy, staccato ditty which puts Iseult in mind of a field in late summer, with nothing but bare stubble stretching in all directions, and the sound of a train's whistle fading into the distance . .

'I suppose we must seem rather . . . *odd*, to someone like you,' she ventures. 'I mean, holed up in the country like this. Miles away from the bright lights and so on . . .'

Nick stares at her for what seems a long time, his face expressionless. Then he smiles.

'Do you know how I live, Iseult?' he says. 'I live in a big house, by myself, with the walls painted black and thick curtains over the windows so that you can't tell if it's day or night. Except that it's quieter at night. The room where I sleep is all black, like the rest of the house, with nothing in it but a big bed with black sheets. There's a mirror in front of the bed – the kind that stands in a frame on its own – and sometimes when I'm there by myself in the middle of the night, or it might be the middle of the day, I light the candles and pour myself a glass of wine and look in the mirror and what do you think I see? Nothing. A void. An empty space, where a person ought to be. Now tell me, Iseult, don't you think that's strange?'

'It does sound a bit . . . well, *lonely.*' For some reason the thought of him, all alone in the big, empty house, makes her eyes fill with tears. The song winds to its mournful conclusion.

'There are worse things than being lonely,' says Nick.

From the sofa, Leonora emits a loud snore. Her eyelids flutter open, then close again. Asleep, her face wears a guileless expression; her mouth hangs slightly agape.

'Poor Mummy,' Iseult says softly.

'She's a vampire,' says Nick. 'Believe me. It takes one to know one. You should get out before it's too late,' he tells her.

Iseult laughs at that. 'Where would I go?'

'Come and stay with me. I've got plenty of room . . .'

He is perfectly serious, she realizes with some astonishment. It's the first time a man has made such an offer to her.

'You're terribly kind. But I couldn't possibly. I have responsibilities, you know. There's the farm to run. I can't just up sticks and . . . *go.*'

He says nothing to this, but goes on looking at her with his big dark eyes. His face looms closer, swims out of focus. The kiss which follows is so fleeting she wonders for a minute if she has imagined it. But then he gets up, holding out his hand to her. 'Come on,' he says.

In a kind of dream, she follows him upstairs. *Up the airy mountain, down the rushy glen, we daren't go a-hunting, for fear of little men* . . . What will become of me? wonders Iseult. I may never come back. Realizing, as she has the thought (and where are these thoughts coming from? They're most unlike the kind of thoughts she usually has), that she doesn't care. *Good folk, wee folk, trooping all together . . .*

'Green jacket, red cap and white owl's feather,' she says aloud, remembering the childhood terror the verses had once inspired.

'Come again?' says Nick.

'Nothing,' she says. 'Just a poem.'

'You're some weird chick, y'know?'

On the landing, they meet Aunt Con, dressed as if for a pre-war garden party, in a floaty dress and a straw hat ornamented with a tattered silk rose.

'There you are, dears!' she exclaims happily. 'Are you changing, too?'

'We're all changing,' murmurs Nick. 'All the time . . .'

'Do help yourselves to anything you like of mine,' says Connie, wafting past in a cloud of pale-green tulle. 'There's heaps of stuff. Dear Mother always said it might come in handy one day . . .'

Then she is gone, leaving only the subtlest hint of Arpège behind her.

Bereft of this familiar presence, Iseult is suddenly unsure of her ground. 'I don't think . . .' she starts to say.

But he is already opening a door. 'In here,' he says. The memory of a game of hide-and-seek played long ago with Sandy returns to Iseult. (*In here. You first. No, you . . .*) 'Come on,' says Nick.

She obeys, uncertain as to the rules of this new game. For a long moment they stand facing one another, in the room's milky twilight, surrounded by the wreckage of someone's earlier game of dressing-up. Then Nick reaches out a finger, lifts one of her heavy plaits. 'Undo it,' he tells her.

Quite enjoying the novelty of it all – this being alone with a man in a ransacked bedroom; this feeling of risk and strangeness – she does as she is told.

'Now the other one.'

Of course, thinks Iseult, surveying their twin silhouettes in the long mirror of the open wardrobe, he wants us to be the same. For indeed they are of a height; with her hair now tumbling loose, like his, they might be brothers – or sisters, she reflects.

'You have beautiful hair,' he says, drawing his fingers through it – a slow caress that sends electric shivers of pleasure and alarm across her scalp and down her spine. 'Beautiful . . .'

It is so much an echo of something Sandy once said that tears spring to her eyes. 'Gosh,' she murmurs. 'Thanks.'

But then she can't speak any more, because his face has come very close, swimming out of focus in that disconcerting way faces have, and his mouth is against her mouth, and his tongue . . . (Good Lord, thinks Iseult, what is he trying to do?) . . . his tongue is inside her mouth – an *extraordinary* sensation, and not one she is entirely sure she likes – winding itself around her tongue, and withdrawing, and flicking across her lips, and then slipping inside again . . .

'Just relax,' he murmurs, his mouth so close that it is almost as if she herself has spoken. No one has ever stood this close to her before. No one has ever taken such astonishing liberties with her person.

Relax. She does her best to comply with the instruction, but it isn't easy.

For now his fingers have moved from her hair to her waist. To just below her waist. He is unbuttoning her cardigan. One button. Two buttons. Three . . . She feels each button as a small, but distinct, undoing. 'Oh, I say,' she faintly protests. He starts to unbutton her blouse. 'Oh, my goodness.'

'It's OK.' Again the voice, next to her ear. 'Nothing's going to happen unless you want it to . . .'

'Oh,' she breathes – less reassured than she might be, because her blouse is now open at the front, so that only her (happily, clean) white brassière lies between her and . . . 'Stop,' says Iseult.

'You want me to stop?' His words are muffled, somewhat, by the fact that he has her nipple in his mouth. The feeling – oh, my God, the *feeling* – is unlike anything she has ever felt.

'Oh, yes,' says Iseult. 'Oh yes – I mean, no. Don't stop . . .'

Sandy, returning from the kitchen with two brimming glasses for himself and Ray, finds to his chagrin that his place on the sofa has been usurped by the atrocious Jocelyn – now very *à la mode* in one of Uncle Wilfred's dress shirts (dug out for him by Sandy), worn with the bottom half of a pinstriped suit.

'With your bone structure, love, you ought to be in modelling,' he is saying to Ray – who is lapping it up of course, little flirt.

'Here's your drink,' Sandy says, by way of distracting Ray from this shameless flattery.

'Ooh, good,' coos Jocelyn, taking the glass meant for Sandy out of Sandy's hand. '*So* glad the champagne's holding up . . .'

'Wouldn't have been much of a party without it,' says Ray, ungrateful boy. Forgetting that without Sandy there wouldn't be a party at all.

'Jossy was just telling me about his contacts in the music biz,' says Ray, greedily slurping his champers. 'He's got ever so many contacts, has Jossy. Record producers. Famous rock stars. The lot.'

'Well, *one or two* famous rock stars, certainly,' says Jocelyn, with an unconvincing stab at modesty. 'It's a question of moving in the right circles, really . . .'

'Jossy's going to introduce me to this photographer he knows,' says Ray. 'Reckons my face could be my fortune. Can't think how *else* I'm going to get hold of one,' he adds, with a meaning look at Sandy.

Sandy feels himself turn hot, then cold. What has the little idiot been *saying*? 'I'd like a word,' he says to Ray. 'In private.'

'Well, really!' says the maddening youth, rolling his eyes. 'That's not very polite to poor Jossy . . .'

'Oh, don't mind me,' says Jocelyn airily. 'I was just going. Need a refill anyway. Catch you later, sweetie,' he simpers, blowing a kiss at Ray.

'I've been thinking,' Ray says. 'If things don't work out the way we talked about, I might get a lift back to town with Jocelyn. He's *ever* so nice, is Jocelyn. *Lovely* car. His old man's a lord, did you know? Knocking on a bit, too. Jossy-boy's going to end up with quite a nice pile of loot, if he plays his cards right. Not that he's short of a bob or two now . . .' Encircled by sooty rings of make-up, his eyes are enormous, glittering. He's *on* something, Sandy thinks with alarm. *Hassassin.* ''Course, if you was to change your mind about our little agreement, I might have to make other plans,' murmurs Ray sadly. 'Jossy's folks have a place in Monte Carlo, don't y'know. Lovely at this time of year, so they say . . .'

'Boysie – please,' begs Sandy. 'Don't be like that . . .'

'Seems to me I don't have much choice,' retorts Ray. 'Seeing as how you only think of yourself. Selfish, I call it. So,' he says, abruptly changing tack. 'Have you decided yet?'

'Decided what?' says Sandy, rather afraid he already knows the answer.

'When. Where. And how,' says Ray, with a terrifying little smile that Sandy knows means he means business.

Sandy feels himself turn pale. He glances nervously towards where Jocelyn and the others are sitting (out of earshot, he sincerely hopes), on the far side of the room. 'Boysie, please. I hardly think this is the right time . . .'

But Ray is on his high horse.

'Don't tell me,' he sneers, 'you've got cold feet already?'

'Look here,' Sandy protests.

'No, *you* look here,' hisses Ray. 'It's all very well for *you* – with your tidy little nest egg just *sitting* there, waiting to fall into your lap when the old girl turns up her toes – but *what about me*? How d'you think I'm going to manage, for the years and years it'll be before you get your *rightful* inheritance, getting more and more shagged out with the *work* I have to do, so that by the time *you* get your money it'll be "Ta very much, Ray, but I've got other fish to fry."? Off to the Riviera, *you'll* be . . .'

'No,' breathes Sandy, horror-struck at this vision of moral turpitude.

'I mean, look at it from *my* point of view,' says Ray. 'Not much in it for *me*, is there?'

'No,' agrees Sandy brokenly. 'All right. You win.'

'*Now* you're talking,' says Ray, in a voice as sweet as honey. 'Tell you what – why don't we go for a little walk in the garden? There's one of them gazebo-type thingies. We'll be nice and private there. Don't want anybody overhearing our little chat, do we? Might give somebody the wrong idea . . .'

*

So nice to see the young people getting on so well, thinks Connie. Her party is a great success so far. She'll just take a little stroll, she decides, before going to join the others. The garden's looking so pretty. Flowers glimmer like moths in the midsummer dusk, casting their faint perfume on the air. June's always been her favourite month. It makes her think of long walks in the twilight. Of string quartets and *billet doux*. Summer 1911. The last time she'd been entirely happy . . .

She remembers the day Edith Challoner came to tea. That had been June, or early July (although every day was like midsummer there). They'd both been in their white dresses – those dreadful pin-tucked muslin things that creased if you so much as looked at them. She'd asked for tea to be brought to them on the veranda. Which was an unusual thing in itself – most social calls to the Police Commissioner's residence were for Lily.

'So lovely to see you,' Edith had said. 'Such ages since we met. Do you remember our chats on the dear old *Medea*? Such fun. And how,' she'd asked, almost too casually, 'are you enjoying Shanghai? Been to the races yet? Or are you too busy for all that sort of thing?'

At the time, she'd assumed Edith was referring to her duties with the children. Now she wonders if perhaps it had been a leading question.

Tea had arrived. They'd talked of this and that. Parties Edith had been to. Their mutual acquaintances. Various people were getting engaged. 'Lizzie Jenkins. *Dear* girl. You know her brother, don't you? And, of course, the Roper girl. Horrid little thing she is, too, by all accounts. Terribly spoilt. And no beauty, either. I suppose it must be her money he's interested in . . .'

Even then, she hadn't known. More out of politeness than genuine interest, she'd asked whom Edith meant.

'Why – Guy Strickland, of course. You mean you haven't heard? My dear, it's the talk of Shanghai. His people haven't a bean, of course. But then *she's* rich enough for both of them. When her uncle dies, she'll inherit the lot. Lucky for some . . . Oh dear,' Edith had murmured. 'Have I spoken out of turn? I was sure you'd have been the first to know . . .'

In retrospect, it wasn't as much of a surprise as all that, knowing the kind of man he was. It was the timing that was so cruel. Because of course they'd still been lovers. She'd been going to meet him that night, in fact. Some people's capacity for dissimulation was endless . . . The low murmur of voices, coming from the direction of the summer-house, interrupts this melancholy train of thought. For a moment Connie stands transfixed. A long time since it was used for *that* purpose. Courting. Although, of course, it isn't called that now. She catches a glimpse of scarlet silk – doubtless some young thing and her sweetheart, taking advantage of the moonlight.

'Leave them to it,' murmurs Connie, stealing noiselessly away across the grass.

'Hey, babe,' says Nick, through a meditative cloud of smoke. 'Sorry it wasn't, y'know, up to much . . .'

'It's all right, really,' says Iseult.

'I mean, I was really into it, y'know? The *idea* of it. It's just, y'know, I've got this sort of problem . . .'

'You really don't have to apologize,' says Iseult. 'I'm sure I was every bit as much to blame . . .'

The room where they are lying, side by side, on a bed piled high with discarded clothes, is filled with a strange light. A crepuscular blue, which intensifies the sepulchral pallor of their naked flesh. Like Madame Tussaud's, thinks Iseult. The

Sleeping Beauty, was it? With the bicycle pump that made her chest go up and down, as if she were breathing.

'No, I mean it,' says Nick. 'It's not your fault. It's the Horse.'

'Ah.' Iseult nods sympathetically. A riding accident.

'Fucks up your head,' Nick goes on. 'Or your cock. Or both . . .'

'What rotten luck,' says Iseult. 'But honestly, it couldn't matter less. Not that it wasn't very nice while it lasted,' she adds, afraid she might have hurt his feelings.

Which is true enough, she thinks, reaching for her clothes. It's certainly the nearest she's ever come to doing the thing people made such a fuss about doing. On this showing, she can't imagine why – although the kissing part was nice enough. And the business with her bosoms. But the act itself had been a touch disappointing: the shock of feeling oneself invaded, followed by a spasm of movement leading – all too soon, it seemed – to a creeping sensation of dampness in the nether regions. If *that's* what she's been missing all these years, she isn't sure she's missed very much.

'I should go down,' she says, addressing the still-recumbent figure on the bed. 'I mean, it's been fun and all that, but . . .' How *did* one extricate oneself from this kind of situation? she wonders. She hasn't had much practice.

'I meant what I said, y'know,' comes his voice from the shadows. 'If it ever gets too much. You can always doss at my place . . .'

'It's really most awfully sweet of you,' she replies. 'But under the circumstances, I hardly think . . .'

From below comes a resonant crash – as if all the keys on a grand piano have been depressed simultaneously.

'Good Lord,' exclaims Iseult. 'What on earth's *that*?'

'Sounds like something just got broken,' Nick says calmly.

But Iseult has already left the room and is striding to the head of the stairs, drawn by the ear-splitting screams now emanating from the drawing room.

'Mummy!' she gasps, descending the stairs at a run.

Leonora is standing in the middle of the floor, surrounded by what looks like a glittering mountain of ice. 'Murder!' she cries. 'Police!'

'What the fuck's going on?' says Jocelyn, next on the scene.

'There's a maniac loose in here!' shrieks Leonora. 'Not two minutes ago, he tried to brain me with the chandelier . . .'

'Didn't make a very good job of it, did he?' mutters Jocelyn. 'Christ, what a mess. I mean, I'm all for a bit of fun – but did you boys have to trash the place *quite* so comprehensively?'

'Don't blame *me*,' says Keith indignantly. 'I was upstairs – with Mandy – wasn't I, Mand?'

The girl nods.

'Likewise,' says Brian. 'Only Sam not Mandy. Get a load of that!' He whistles admiringly. 'Someone really had a go in here . . .'

Certainly the room is now in a more advanced state of chaos than it has ever been. Apart from the fallen chandelier, whose crystal lozenges have been scattered in a wide radius around the sizeable crater left by its impact, furniture – a small table, chairs, a bookcase – has been overturned and vases scattered, their contents strewn across the carpet.

'Poor flowers,' murmurs Sam, stooping to gather up the trampled remnants of a flung bouquet.

'Careful,' warns Iseult. 'You'll cut yourself. There's glass. It's all right, Mummy . . .'

Because Leonora's sobs, having temporarily subsided at the arrival of her rescuers, now redouble their volume. 'He almost *had me over*. Another minute and he'd have *finished me off*,' she wails. 'One minute I was asleep, the next I heard him rushing about. Throwing things. It was horrible. I thought I'd die of fright . . .'

'What's going on?' It is Sandy, entering through the French windows.

Iseult's heart gives a thump. A slow flush steals up her neck and over her face. Her fingers fly to the (now safely fastened) buttons of her blouse. Apart from her hair, which she has not had time to replait, there is nothing to give her away – yet she is glad of the room's near-darkness. Sandy knows her too well, that's the trouble. One look at her and he'll *know* . . .

'Looks like you've had burglars,' Jocelyn says offhandedly. 'Either that or someone's been having a *very* vivid dream . . .'

'It wasn't a dream,' snaps Leonora.

'Of course it wasn't,' says her daughter soothingly.

Ray's next to appear, a little way behind Sandy. In his mandarin's robe, his eyes very large and bright, he looks like a man in the throes of an opium dream.

'Did I miss something?' he says innocently.

Because in spite of her repeated insistence that it *wasn't* an accident, and that she can *swear* she heard someone creeping about beforehand, Leonora is completely unable to identify the culprit. Which is a relief, in one respect, thinks Iseult. Rather worrying in another. Because if none of *them* caused the chandelier to fall – who *did*?

As if in answer to her question, she hears Aunt Con, wandering in from the garden in her wispy green frock, murmur something that makes the hairs on the back of Iseult's neck stand on end. 'Oh, Wilfred, what have you done?' says Aunt reproachfully. 'You silly, silly boy. What *have* you been up to?' While on the mirror over the fireplace, where a smear of candle-smoke has blurred the glass, Iseult sees, with mounting horror, someone has written *DEATH*.

8

Horrible Imaginings

'Let's split,' says Jocelyn, clapping his hands. 'Sandy, dear, we're going to love you and leave you. Early start at the studios, you know . . .'

Because after this, the party mood deflates like a pricked balloon. Disconsolate Vampyres stand around, bickering like overexcited children who have stayed up past their bedtime.

'That's my shirt you've got on . . .'

'No, it isn't. I bought this shirt in Granny Takes a Trip . . .'

'I tell you, it fucking *is* mine. There's a cigarette burn on the sleeve from that time I passed out in Annabel's and nearly set fire to myself . . .'

'Since when have they let *you* into Annabel's?'

'Boys, *please*,' pleads Jocelyn weakly.

But at last they're on their way.

'*Super* party,' says the dark girl, flashing her teeth at Sandy.

'Glad you could make it,' he replies automatically, unable to tear his eyes away from Ray, who's being terribly pally with Jocelyn – hugging and kissing and exchanging telephone numbers – and looking as if, given half a chance, he might decide to carry out his threat and go with him. Although there'd hardly be room in the car, Sandy reassures himself. Not with all those girls and guitars and whatnot.

Then there's Izz. What *is* the matter with Izz? Ever since that business with the chandelier, she's been nervous as a cat, blushing and stammering and jumping out of her skin whenever anyone addresses her. Just now, for instance, when that pretty dark boy, Nick, came downstairs. The way she'd looked at him, it was as if she'd never *seen* a man before. Of course, he *was* looking rather a dish with those come-to-bed eyes and his shirt all undone – but there was no need to go to pieces, was there? Babbling like an idiot when the boy was just trying to be polite. Asking her to look him up if she was ever in Ladbroke Grove . . . Not that *that* was very likely. Even if she wanted to, poor old Izz couldn't leave the farm.

Still, it was a bit of a hoot, the idea of funny old Izzie shacking up with a rock star . . . She was much too old for him, of course.

Then it all goes quiet. The Vampyres have piled into Jocelyn's car (leaving Ray behind, Sandy sees with relief) and Jocelyn's started up the engine, spun the wheels a couple of times in the gravel and rolled off down the drive and out into the road and away into the night. Gone. Departed. *Disparu*.

A long pause, like an indrawn breath, ensues.

This is broken, at last, by Izz. 'We should go, too,' she says flatly. 'Sorry to leave you with the mess. But Mummy's tired . . .'

'Tired' is putting it mildly, Sandy thinks, observing Leonora's zombie-like state. Since her earlier fit of hysterics, she's been docile as a child. A distinct improvement, thinks Sandy. Dreadful old boot. Now, if it were a question of finishing *her* off, he wouldn't think twice about it . . . Sandy feels a bubble of hysterical laughter rise in his throat. What's got into me? he thinks. This isn't the time or the place. Still, he has to admit there's something dreadfully comic about the whole affair. *Finish her off.* Finish them *all* off, while he's about it. Make room for new blood. They did that in some tribes, didn't they? Culling the weak. Once you got too old to work, they made short work of you. Left you to die on the bare hillside . . . or was that babies? Same principle, anyhow. Not sentimental about these things. Pragmatic, really. Survival of the fittest . . .

'I'll ring you in the morning, shall I?' Izz is saying. Avoiding his eyes, Sandy notices. What *has* she been up to? 'You'll need some help with clearing up. Come on, Mummy. 'Night, Aunt. 'Night, Sandy.'

She doesn't even look at Ray.

'Bitch,' Ray hisses, as the door swings shut behind the two women. 'Well,' he remarks. 'Here we all are. Happy as can be.' He winks at Sandy. 'Some of us, anyway . . .'

'My God,' says Sandy hollowly. 'What a night.'

Auntie has wandered back into the drawing room, where she stands, surveying the devastation. She looks very small and forlorn, and for a treacherous moment Sandy's heart goes out to her, poor old thing, seeing her home reduced to rubble like this – but then he remembers . . . That conversation with Ray in the summer-house. Just before they'd heard the crash. 'If you're serious about wanting us to be *more than friends*, you've got to prove it,' Ray'd said. 'And it's really not hard, what I'm asking you to do. Like taking candy from a baby . . .' Sandy's stomach gives a sickening lurch, like that horrid feeling you get between floors in a moving lift. Blind panic overwhelms him. I can't go through with it, he thinks.

But then Auntie turns, with that fey half-smile which means she's wool-gathering again. 'Wilfred never could bear that chandelier,' she says. 'Always said it was too large for the room. Still, I do feel it was rather an extreme way of getting rid of it, don't you? Such a mess he's made, naughty boy . . .'

What's she on about now? wonders Sandy. She's off her rocker. Completely ga-ga. Perhaps Ray's right, after all. It *would* be the kindest thing . . . Just like going to sleep, really. The best kind of death. 'Doing her a favour, in the long run,'

Ray'd said, hadn't he? 'Saving her from something worse . . .' Because if you thought about it, Sandy thinks feverishly, there were so many hideous alternatives. That dreadful phrase 'a long illness, bravely borne', which cropped up all the time in the obits. An agonizing, drawn-out death, it meant. He'd be saving her from *that*, at least. Peaceful, Ray'd said. Natural causes, almost. Just drifting off, into a beautiful dream, from which she'd never wake . . .

The cocoa, thinks Sandy.

Pasting a smile upon his face (a death's-head grin, it feels like), he turns to his aged relative, who is still standing in the middle of the wrecked room, gazing about her with a bemused look, as if she can't quite work out what she's doing there.

'Beddy-byes, I think, Auntie,' he says cheerily. 'I'll make you some cocoa, shall I? Help you sleep . . .'

There's a slight hiccup when she refuses the cocoa, saying she'd rather have a glass of water if it's all the same to him. But he persuades her. After the long day she's had and all the excitement of the party, a milky drink will be just the ticket . . .

'Well, if you're sure it's no trouble,' she says.

Sandy hastens to reassure her. 'Oh, it's no trouble, Auntie, dear. No trouble at all . . .'

Then it's just a matter of packing her off upstairs while he and Ray do the necessary. Watching her go, he feels a pang of something like envy. Because it's over for her, isn't it? he thinks, his gaze following the diminutive, white-haired figure as it stumps slowly up the stairs and disappears into the cavernous shadows at the top. No more going through the motions. Over. Finished. *Finito*. No more heartache, no more sorrow, no more disappointed hopes. An end to physical decline and mental deterioration. The best way out, really. He'd considered it himself from time to time.

Only . . . this was kinder, somehow. Not knowing what was going to happen. You'd be fast asleep and then – *faster* asleep.

Obscurely comforted by these thoughts, he wanders back into the drawing room. He doesn't see the message on the mirror, because Iseult has wiped it away – but something about the room's atmosphere makes him uneasy, nonetheless. It's cold in here, he realizes. Odd for such a balmy night. Perhaps it's the damp; old houses often were damp. He goes to shut the French windows.

The garden is bright with what seems at first like moonlight, but which is in fact the lingering afterglow of the sunset – or the first intimations of dawn. The grass is shiny with dew. A few sleepy birds are calling: fluting, tremulous notes. The statue by the yew hedge glimmers whitely. *The statue* . . .

'There's someone on the lawn,' breathes Sandy hoarsely.

'Where?' Ray has appeared beside him, in that noiseless uncanny way he has.

'Out there. Look.' Sandy raises a trembling finger.

'I don't see anything. You're dreaming, Sandy-poos. Spooking yourself, again, aren't you?'

When he looks again, the figure by the hedge has vanished – translated itself into an innocent patch of moonlight. But it *was* there, Sandy thinks, I saw it distinctly. Saw the cap, and the boots, and the cane; the familiar silent watchfulness of the face. The way the paler tone of the khaki uniform was thrown into high relief by the yew's dark mass.

'I tell you, I saw . . .'

'What a Nervous Nora you are,' laughs Ray. 'Anyone'd think you'd been smoking those funny cigarettes . . .'

Ray is in a playful mood, it seems. Amorous, too – to judge

by the way he keeps nibbling Sandy's ear as they stand together in the kitchen, making cocoa.

'Ooh, you *are* a one,' he breathlessly shrieks. 'Trying to scare me, were you? Saying you'd seen a nasty man in the garden. A cheap trick, I call it. And that's one thing I'm not . . .'

'What?' says Sandy, rising to the bait.

'Cheap, dear,' says Ray. 'Oh, no, I'm not cheap at all. I'm very, very expensive.' Casually, he unscrews the top of the brown glass bottle he's been holding and shakes out a couple of pills. Drops them into the steaming cocoa. Throws in a couple more. 'That ought to do it,' he says. Then, as the other stands there, frozen to the spot, it seems, he adds, in a voice whose tone seems poised between threat and seduction, 'Come *on*, Sandy, love. Cocoa's getting cold. Haven't got all night, have we?'

But still Sandy hangs back, as rooted to the spot as a man on a high diving board for whom the world has diminished to the narrow plank on which he stands and that immensely distant rectangle of blue towards which he must presently hurl himself.

'Ray. Dearest . . .' he falters.

'What?'

'You do love me, don't you?'

Ray smiles. Prolonging the suspense. He raises an eyebrow. Purses his lips in a lovely simulacrum of a kiss.

'Silly old Sandy-poos. Do you really have to ask? You *know* how I feel about you,' he says.

It's after two by the time Iseult has managed to get Leonora to bed, and let the dogs out, and riddled the boiler, and done all the other things one had to do before one could turn in safely – by which time, sleep is out of the question. So she sits on the back step and has a quiet smoke to calm herself down, because the night's events have proved more than usually upsetting. Quite apart from everything else, she feels guilty about leaving Aunt with the house in such a state. Not that *she'll* notice, bless her; she could live quite happily in a pigsty. But it's the principle of the thing. At least Sandy's there . . .

Iseult can't face thinking about Sandy just now. The way he'd *looked* at her . . . Had he guessed? she wonders. She feels as if her secret must be written across her brow, in scarlet letters: HARLOT.

All these years, thinks Iseult sadly, all these years I've waited. Because that was what true love was – never being prepared to settle for second best. It wasn't much of a love, she sees now – but there was something rather fine about such absolute devotion. Expecting nothing; desiring nothing, except to be close to the beloved. Now it was all wasted. What a fool I've been, thinks Iseult, chucking the stub of her cigarette out into the darkness.

It had been kind of Sandy to bring her the cocoa, but really, she didn't want it. The weather was much too hot, for one thing, and she'd never cared much for the stuff. Too sickly, thinks Connie. But she'd been touched by his thoughtfulness. 'Sleep tight, Auntie,' he'd said, setting the cup by her bed, and looking, as he spoke, so much the way he'd looked as a small child, when he'd been plucking up courage to apologize for something, that she was quite tickled. Of course, she'd thought, he's sorry about the mess – although that was hardly his fault, nor that of the other young people. Quite a jolly crowd, she'd thought them – if a little uninhibited in their behaviour. Although it was nothing she hadn't seen at the Chelsea Arts Ball.

Still, it was a pity about the chandelier. She wonders what could have got into Wilfred to make him so wild. 'It won't *do*, you know,' she tells the empty room. 'I'm sorry, but it's got to stop . . .'

At the open window, a gust of wind, springing up from nowhere, blows the curtains inward; a moment later, the sash falls down with a bang.

Maybe it was having Sandy here which had upset him? Although there'd never been this kind of trouble before. He'd been so good, too, when Sandy was a boy. Never minded having him to stay – even though boys, as a general rule, alarmed him, with their constant chatter and fondness for guns and slingshots. Not that Sandy had ever been that sort of boy.

Or maybe it was the fact that she'd been thinking about Guy Strickland such a lot? But that was only because of the money. Who'd have thought he'd have remembered her, after all these years? She supposes it must have been guilt about what happened – that, and the fact that his marriage had been childless. Odd, the things people did, when posterity was at stake . . .

The silly thing was, she'd already resolved never to see him again. And the likelihood was, she need never have done so, if she hadn't agreed to accompany the Selbys to Peking. It had been Freddie's idea – he and Lily had noticed, he'd said to Connie one evening, that she'd been looking, well, a bit down in the mouth these past few weeks. What she needed to buck her up was a change of scene. He'd some business in Peking – nothing which need concern her. Rogue elements getting out of hand. The usual thing. Lily was going to go with him

– would Connie like to come too? 'See a bit of the countryside, while you're here,' said Freddie. 'It's quite pretty around Peking. And with the new railway – built by our chaps, you know – it's no more than a day and a half's journey . . .'

So in a way, Connie thinks, what had happened afterwards was partly his fault – although he'd only meant it as a kindness.

They'd been to the Great Wall, and the Ming tombs, and the Temple of Heaven, and were spending their last day visiting the Forbidden City. Fortunately, the Emperor wasn't in residence at the time – because otherwise wangling the official permission might have taken weeks. A terribly bureaucratic race, said Freddie. Connie remembers vast courtyards stretching between groups of buildings with extraordinary names. The Palace of Heavenly Purity and the Hall of Supreme Harmony. Red and gold pavilions crowned with roofs that turned up at the edges. Walking in astounding heat across one immense space – some kind of parade ground, she remembers Freddie explaining – and seeing another group coming towards them . . .

Even at that distance, she'd recognized him at once. His height, and his way of walking. Swaggering a little in his light summer suit, as he'd pointed out something or other to his companions. Of which there were two: an elderly gentleman in a solar topee, whom Strickland introduced as his uncle, and a girl in white. 'My fiancée, Miss Roper,' he'd said coolly.

How she'd got through the next few minutes without giving the game away Connie never knew. Luckily the Selbys had been much too busy improving their acquaintance with old Mr Farquharson and his ward to pay much attention to *her*. Strickland himself had been as cool as a cucumber, of course. ('How d'you do, Miss Joliffe? Enjoying the sights?') It occurred to her that it probably wasn't the first time he'd had to deal with a situation of this kind.

Only when – conversation about mutual friends in Shanghai having been exhausted – it was proposed that the two parties should continue their excursion together did she find herself being addressed by her former lover.

'Why haven't you answered my letters?'

'I didn't see what good it could do.'

'I meant what I said, though – I do want to see you . . .'

'I can't imagine why,' she'd said.

'What are you two muttering about over there?' had come the voice – a little peevish on account of the heat – of Amelia Roper.

'We're discussing art. Not a subject which interests *you*, my dear. Miss Joliffe is a painter, however . . .'

'You don't say,' said the girl, with a little toss of her head. 'What kind of painting do you do, Miss Joliffe? Something frightfully clever and modern, I suppose . . . Uncle, can't we get your man to bring the motor round? If I have to walk another step I'll *die* . . .'

She'd thought that encounter would be the end of it, but later the same evening there'd been a note delivered to her room at the hotel. *I must see you. Tonight. I'll come to your room at eight. Tell them you've got a headache. Ever yours, Guy S.* Her first impulse had been to tear it up. What good could it do, to start all that business again? But then she'd decided to hear what he had to say . . . Of course she'd been taking a risk. She'd known that at the time. But what is life without risk? thinks Connie drowsily. Why, nothing at all . . .

He'd waited so long for this night with Ray that when it came to the moment, he couldn't believe it was actually happening.

He and Boysie – together at last. He'd wanted to pinch himself, to make sure he wasn't dreaming. But there was no doubt about it. Here he was, in Sandy's bed. Quite naked. Every bit of him – his well-shaped legs, his firm golden stomach, his muscular arms, his lolling cock – mine, all mine, Sandy'd thought, in a kind of delirium.

The sex had been marvellous, of course – if a teensy bit perfunctory. Not that he was complaining. Even the briefest encounter with Ray was better than hours of passion with someone else. But he'd so looked forward to this moment – not the act itself, but the leading up to it. The tenderness of that first kiss. The ecstasy of touching that glorious body. Gazing into those beautiful eyes. It was that he'd longed for. Knowing that of all the people in the world he could have chosen to be with at that moment, Ray'd chosen to be with him. And then there was the delicious intimacy of falling asleep together – or rather, since he himself was beyond sleep, of watching his beloved sleep. All that was bliss. Worth selling one's soul for.

Because the die is cast, thinks Sandy. There's no going back now. He and Ray are in this together, come fair or foul. What they've planned is quite simple – appallingly so. 'What could go wrong?' says Ray. With Auntie sound asleep (and she'll be sleeping like the dead, after the tablets they've given her), the rest should go like clockwork. 'Nothing to it,' says Ray.

As Sandy lies there, bathed in a cold sweat, feverish thoughts crowd in on him; seductive voices mutter. On her last legs, poor old darling . . . Nothing but a dog's life, really . . . All alone in this great big old house . . . Something could happen and no one'd know for days . . . On the edge of sleep, he feels himself falling from a great height, as if an abyss had opened up beneath his feet. Waking with a start, to find himself tangled in the sheets, while around him the room closes in as narrow and dark as a coffin.

She'd seen Strickland only once more after that. It wasn't the sort of meeting you'd forget. The things he'd said . . . Even now, she can hardly bear to remember them. When he'd offered to write her a cheque she'd almost spat in his face.

'But my dear girl, what will you do?' he'd said.

And she'd said, 'I think that's my affair, don't you?'

'But how will you live? What will become of you?' he'd persisted; then, in the face of her stubborn silence, 'You're still young. You could still marry. If you'd only do the sensible thing . . .'

The following day they were setting sail on the SS *Osiris* – she and Lily, and the children. Bound for Port Said, where they were to wait for Freddie to join them, which he'd do as soon as he could get away. It was a bad business all round – but there was no need for panic, he'd told them. All those wild reports which had been circulating in the weeks since the revolution of Westerners being ill-treated were a gross exaggeration. There'd been a few cases, it was true, of Christian missionaries being roughly handled. Railway tracks had been torn up (a case of cutting off one's nose to spite one's face, if ever there was one, Freddie said); a few churches had been burned and factory windows smashed. Yet, despite this evidence of a definite *cooling* in relations between East and West, one ought not to get these things out of proportion, in Freddie's opinion. There'd been sticky patches before now. Take that Boxer business in '99. Still, one never *knew*, with the Oriental mind. Unpredictable. Dignified retreat seemed the most sensible option.

Strickland certainly hadn't seemed unduly concerned about

the rumours. 'Oh, they're not interested in me,' he'd said with a shrug. 'A mere artist. I'm no threat to *them*. They've better things with which to occupy their time than persecuting effete types who don't even know one end of a gun from the other. As a matter of fact,' he'd added, 'I might see if I can't hang on here a bit longer. Shanghai's awfully interesting at present – now all the ghastly English have gone . . .'

'What about your wife?' she'd asked him.

'Oh, Amelia's already left. You don't suppose she'd want to risk her pretty neck a moment longer in this godforsaken spot, now that she's got what she wants. Me, that is,' said Strickland. 'I don't imagine,' he went on, 'that I'll see a great deal of my wife. A civilized arrangement, don't you agree? Which I must say rather suits me. Such a pity,' he'd added carelessly, 'that you're so determined to make things difficult for yourself. Otherwise you and I could have had such an *amusing* time . . .'

Murder. It had a heavy sound, like that of a door slamming shut. Once you went through with it, nothing would ever be the same – which was as true for the murderer, as for the murderee . . . well, maybe not *quite* as true, thinks Sandy. Still, it was an alteration of a profound kind: to pass from a state of innocence to one of such damnable culpability. *Red-handed*. There was a horrid realism to the phrase. Although, in this instance, no actual blood would be shed . . . He averts his mind from the thought of what he has to do. It was too awful. Even thinking about it is more than Sandy can bear. *Pity and terror*. Another phrase he's never understood till now. Pity for his intended victim (and how *could* he, even for a second, contemplate snuffing out his own dear auntie?) struggles with baser self-pity. This *cursed* imagination! Why couldn't he have been born without one, like most people? It was too unfair.

To commit a crime was nothing. Thousands did so, every day, without a qualm. But to commit a crime in the full knowledge of its enormity – *that* required nerve. Even now that the shadow of the hangman's noose no longer fell across the scene . . .

Although it might have been better if it *had*, argues Sandy, tossing and turning on his bed of nails. A death for a death. Now the worst he can expect is life. And *what* a life, thinks Sandy. Because without Ray, he might as well be banged up in chokey for the rest of his days . . . A bleak and terrible vision of Ray-less days and nights fills his mind. Himself, alone in the Brighton flat, with nothing to look forward to but emptiness. Shuffling from bed to table and back to bed again, with only the gurgling of the slowly filling cistern and the mournful, incessant cry of the scavenging gulls outside his window to drown the quiet. Feeling himself grow steadily older and greyer, so that even the roughest trade will no longer spare him a second glance. Eking out an aimless existence, until the day when, overwhelmed by thoughts of his own folly in passing up the only chance of happiness he'd ever had, he decides to end it all. Setting out the whisky and the sleeping pills, or stuffing newspaper into the cracks around the window and turning on the gas . . .

Either way there's no hope for me, thinks Sandy, taking some perverse consolation from the finality of the thought.

Connie is in that half-alert state into which she increasingly finds herself slipping these days. Neither sleeping nor waking. A twilight zone. At one level, she's conscious of being here, in this room, with all its familiar objects around her; at another, she's somewhere else entirely. Because the excitement of the party has stirred memories of other parties – of one party, in particular. The last one, as it turned out, although they hadn't known that then. As far as she or any of the rest of them knew, it was just another of Lily's soirées. Dancing to the wind-up gramophone for the young people, a rubber or two of bridge for their elders, followed by a cold buffet supper. A perfectly normal evening.

Of course, there were some who'd cried off – the Rawlinsons, for instance. Swept up in the general panic about the revolution. Some people had no backbone, Lily'd said. Naturally, they'd heard the stories about what was going on in the Chinese quarter. People being butchered and hung from lampposts. But it was surely a native quarrel? Nothing that need concern *them*.

So that it had been disconcerting, to say the least, when the man had burst in with his news, while they were at supper. One of Freddie's officers: flushed with the importance of what he had to tell, his face above the too tight collar of his khaki uniform perspiring in the glare of the candelabra. *Beg pardon for breaking in on you like this, sir, but I thought it best to give you the news in person . . .* And Freddie, very grand in evening dress: *You did the right thing, Sergeant.* Then, as he turned to follow the man to the waiting car, remembering his manners: *Excuse me, my dear. Ladies. There's been an incident. It's a bore but it can't be helped, I'm afraid. Do carry on without me . . .*

After that the mood of the party had fallen a bit flat, of course. Because with such things happening in the world outside, it had seemed a bit, well, *callous* to be enjoying oneself like this. Which was a shame, after all the hard work Lily'd put into making the evening a success. They hadn't known the extent of it then, but there was a lot of nervous laughter and speculation about who was behind the outrage.

Much later, after all the guests had gone, Freddie'd returned and they heard what had happened. An explosion in a news-paper office. One man blown to bits and another badly wounded. The worst of it was, Freddie said, that this was only the beginning. Now the rebels had the smell of blood in their nostrils there'd be no stopping them. Were they all going to be murdered in their beds? Lily'd cried, and Freddie'd told her, quite sharply, not to be absurd. All the same, he said, it might be a good idea if what weapons they had were to hand, in case of a surprise attack . . .

Sandy wakes from a dream of labyrinthine tunnels, in which, it seems, he is condemned to wander for ever, with nothing but flaring gas lamps to light the way, and a dreadful wailing in his ears, like a train approaching . . . Ray is standing over him, saying his name, in a low urgent voice. Sandy's first sensation is one of enormous relief – *it was only a dream*; his second is one of dread. Before he can utter a sound, he feels Ray's hand across his mouth.

'Shh,' whispers Ray. 'Come on. Get up. It's time . . .'

And though his mind flinches at the thought of what he has to do, he finds himself compelled into action by the strangeness of it all: the lateness – or earliness – of the hour; the weird excitement of his mission. And Ray – Ray is there with him, soothing his qualms and helping him on with his dressing gown (not Uncle Wilfred's, but the Chinese robe), like a young squire robing his lord on the eve of battle. Spurring him on, at the last, with a kiss full on the mouth and a whispered promise of future rewards, before sending him off along the dark corridor . . .

Connie sleeps so lightly these days that the smallest sound – the creaking of a floorboard, a footstep outside the door – can wake her. She's awake now, although a moment ago she was dreaming. There's someone there. She can hear breathing. Hardly daring to breathe herself, she reaches for what she knows is lying on the bedside table. Wilfred's service revolver. She doesn't remember putting it there, but of course she must have done. Guns don't just appear out of thin air. With hands that barely tremble at all, she releases the safety catch. The door opens slowly.

'Who's there?' she cries, as the shadowy figure enters the room. A sinister shape in a long dark robe, she sees. As it comes towards her, a shaft of moonlight falling through a chink in the curtain shows her a flash of scarlet, embroidered with scales and claws. One of the Small Sword Gang, she surmises. The most feared and ruthless killers in Shanghai. As befitted their name, daggers were their weapon of choice, but they had been known to employ other methods of dispatch – notably strangulation with a silk cord or smothering with a satin pillow. The last of these, she sees, is to be her particular fate . . . Well, she won't go without a fight. 'One step further and I'll shoot!' she cries, levelling the weapon. When there is no reply, she squeezes the trigger, as she had been shown all those years ago by Cousin Freddie, half a world away.

Sandy's world explodes in a whirling mass of feathers. A pillow fight, he thinks, knocked back by the blow. *Steady on*, you chaps, he tries to say, but the words are a meaningless gurgle. With the ruined pillow clutched to his chest, he staggers back across the landing.

There is no pain yet – only a tremendous sense of outrage. Because he'd known as soon as he'd opened the door and seen her sitting up in bed that he couldn't go through with it. If she'd been asleep, as he'd been expecting, after the knock-out pills he'd slipped her, it might have been a different story. All he had to do was put the pillow over her face, Ray'd said. She wouldn't know a thing. Like going to sleep, he'd said. Only, as it turned out, it wasn't.

There's a moment at the top of the stairs when he hangs in the balance, with one foot on firm ground, the other in mid-air. Something feels warm between his fingers. It's the pillow – now transformed to a red satin cushion, he sees with some surprise. Matches the dressing gown, he thinks drowsily. Then he topples forward – only dimly aware that this is happening. Like one of those dreams of falling when you dread, but never feel, the final impact . . .

Sandy is in his swing, going up and down, up and down. And every time he comes down he claps his hands and says, 'Again.' And when he comes down for the last time, the person he loves best lifts him out of the swing and holds him close, close to her. And she whispers, 'You know, Mumsie loves you more than anyone else in the world.' And he looks up into the beloved face, with the round blue eyes and the red, red mouth he knows so well . . . Only something's different. It isn't the face he thinks he knows, but another – so like it that, at first glance, one might think they were the same. But he isn't fooled. Oh, no. The smell is all wrong. And he opens his mouth in a terrible cry of rage and anguish and loss. Because it isn't Mumsie, it isn't Mumsie, it isn't Mumsie at all . . .

9

Fancy Footwork

When Ray hears the shot – and the scream – his first impulse is to run for it. Scarper. No point in hanging around where you weren't wanted, was there? Because if the old witch had a gun, it wasn't a fair contest. Ray has an aversion to guns. Nasty, tricky things. Give a bloke a gun and, like as not, he'll end up blowing someone's head off.

But then he reconsiders. Ray's nothing if not quick-thinking. Maybe there's another way out of what looks at the minute like a right old mess. Trust Sandy. I mean to say – I *ask* you, mutters Ray, shaking his head. Couldn't get him to do even the simplest thing without it turns into an almighty cock-up. It was bloody typical. The more he thinks about it, the angrier Ray gets: That Sandy. Couldn't he do *something* right for a change? But no. Has to go and get himself killed, didn't he? Stupid git.

Well, thinks Ray, the ever-pragmatic. No use crying over split milk. Or blood, in this case, he smirks, pleased with this *bon mot*. First things first, thinks Ray, whose heartbeat has slowed to its normal rate. See how the land lies. He puts his ear to the door, but there's nothing to hear. A deathly quiet hangs over the house. Ray opens the door a crack. What he sees gives him quite a turn. It's the old woman, in a long white nightdress thing that puts Ray in mind of a horror film he once saw. *Bride of Frankenstein*. The bird in that had worn a similar outfit. Frills and a high neck. But it's what the old girl's got in her hand that most concerns him. An old service revolver, by the look of it – not a gun with which Ray is familiar (he's a knife man, himself). It still did the business, though, that much was certain. And Ray has no desire to have this proved to him a second time.

He'd been hoping to make a break for it, but with the old bat on guard outside he doesn't fancy his chances. She's standing now at the top of the stairs, staring down at what lies beneath, with a look in her eyes that makes Ray's blood run cold. Startle her and like as not she'll blow his head off too, without batting an eyelid. Dodgy situation, this, thinks Ray, closing the door. It occurs to him that he's left it a bit late to rush out and say he's just heard the shot. It's a good five minutes since the gun went off. If he were to pop up now, when she isn't expecting it, who knows what she might do? He can just see the headline in the *News of the World*: GRAN SLAYS TWO WITH HERO HUBBY'S GUN. He's no wish to get his name in the papers *that* way, ta very much.

Which leaves the softly, softly approach – always Ray's preferred option. He considers ways of escape. There's the window, of course. A quick shimmy down the drainpipe and – then what? Ray doesn't at this moment have a plan, but he's working on it. Reluctantly, he decides on the window route as being the safest way (though he's not overfond of heights). Quickly, he pulls on shirt and trousers (no time for a wash and brush-up this morning!) and, as noiselessly as he can, edges the window up. He already has one leg over the sill when he hears it. The sound of a motorbike's engine. Ten to one it's that toffy-nosed cow from the farm, thinks Ray. Hadn't she said she'd be round to help with the clearing-up?

He brings his leg back inside the window-frame and eases the sash down. This is the sign he's been waiting for. He knows now what he has to do.

With as much force as he can muster, Ray punches himself in the face. His nose – still tender after the knock it'd had from the Morris's windscreen – immediately starts to bleed. He's always been a bleeder, has Ray. He keeps his head well down, so that by the time the motorbike pulls into the drive he's ready, his shirt now satisfactorily spattered with round red drops. A swift gander out the window confirms it's her. What *does* she look like, in that get-up? giggles Ray. Leathers. I mean to say. *Goggles!* The bloody Red Baron, or what?

It's not yet six, but Iseult can't wait to get out of the house. Anything to get away from Mummy. Who's being a complete *pig* this morning – refusing to let Iseult change her sheets (although they're horribly whiffy) and complaining about the tea.

'I suppose you're off again,' she'd snapped, seeing that Iseult was already in her motorbiking gear. 'Running around across half the county because some *man* asks you to. In *my* day,' she'd added spitefully, 'we let the men run around after *us*. You know, you've only yourself to blame if he takes you for granted . . .'

'It's not a question of being taken for granted,' Iseult had protested. 'Sandy and I are old friends . . .'

'I wasn't talking about Sandy,' the old harridan almost spat. 'I saw the way you were carrying on with that *boy*. That Nick. Ridiculous, at your age . . .'

That was the absolute *limit*, thinks Iseult indignantly. She'd left before she had to hear any more. *Ridiculous, at your age. Old enough to be his . . .*

Whipped by the fresh breeze, Iseult's cheeks are burning. Sometimes Mummy went too far. And it simply wasn't *true*, the things she'd said. She *hadn't* pursued him; it'd been all the other way around . . .

For a blissful, guilty moment, Iseult permits herself a memory of the night before. That mournful, dark-eyed face, pretty as a girl's, leaning over her; those long limbs wrapped around hers. Those hands. The way he'd touched her. As if she were a precious object: strong and fragile at the same time, like a piece of bone china, or a musical instrument.

It had been nice, for once, to feel what other women feel: that sense of being exclusively desired. And that, thinks Iseult, dashing away a tear (damn these useless goggles!) was surely enough. 'Look me up, if you're ever in Ladbroke Grove,' he'd said. A sweet thought, but not one she had the slightest intention of acting on. Their worlds were too far apart . . .

Through its screen of oaks, Dunsinane has a deserted look. Perhaps they're all still sleeping it off, thinks Iseult, bringing the Norton to a halt in a spray of gravel. The front door's locked. She rattles the knocker.

'Anybody home?' she calls through the letter box.

But hears nothing. Or rather, not quite nothing – for the silence, as ever, is full of minute sounds. The mechanistic cheeping of a robin. The steady dripping of a leaking tap. The heavy buzzing of flies . . .

I'll try the back door, thinks Iseult. That, she knows, is never locked.

But then another sound attracts her attention: a gentle tapping. She looks up and sees a face at the bedroom window. *Uncle Wilfred*, she thinks, for a startled moment. Then she sees it's Aunt.

What's the old girl up to? she wonders. She's acting most peculiar. Still in her nightie, too – which isn't like her. Usually she's up with the lark, to walk the dog.

And now she thinks of it, one of the sounds she's been dimly aware of all this time is a soft whimpering. Rufus.

'Poor old boy. Did they shut you in?' she murmurs. That wasn't like Aunt, either, to be so careless . . . 'I'll go round,' she shouts up at the window, making signals to that effect. At this, Aunt, who up until now has seemed struck by a curious paralysis, is galvanized into action. She opens the window.

'Iseult!' she cries. 'Don't come in! I forbid you. Go away!'

Oh dear, thinks Iseult. Poor old thing. All that fuss and bother last night has turned her wits. You'd have thought Sandy . . . But where on earth *is* Sandy? 'Look here, Aunt,' she says gently. 'Everything's all right now. I'll just pop round to the back and be with you in a tick . . .'

At this, Aunt becomes quite agitated. 'Stay back!' she insists. 'Go and fetch a doctor – or the police. Only – don't come inside . . .'

'But, Aunt, why on earth . . .' Iseult starts to say. Then she sees what Aunt is holding. A coldness runs through her.

'Don't you understand?' says Connie sadly. 'Something terrible's happened. I've killed my darling boy . . .'

What's she talking about? thinks Iseult, already dreading the answer. 'It's all right, Aunt Con,' she manages to say. 'You can put down the gun. There's no danger any more.'

From his vantage point at the window, Ray is party to this conversation. At the mention of the word 'police', he knows he has to act fast. Because once you got Lily Law involved, there'd be no room for manoeuvre. He counts to ten, to give the horse-faced bitch time to get inside, hears her faint cry as she stumbles across the stiff, then seizes his chance.

'Stop!' he cries, rushing out on to the landing in his blood-stained shirt. 'Sandy – for God's sake! Don't *do* it!'

I ought to be in pictures, he congratulates himself. The look on their faces – Horse-Face and the old woman's – is priceless. The look on Sandy's face he likes slightly less.

It's not the first time Ray's seen death, but it never ceases to amaze him how very *dead* the dead always look. And Sandy, sprawled on the half-landing, looks deader than most. Funny colour he is. Sort of a dirty cream. Nasty mess he's made of that lovely dressing gown, too – good job it was red to start with, thinks practical Ray.

'Oh no!' he shrieks. (Give that man an Oscar, do.) 'It's too *late*. Oh, Sandy! I knew something dreadful would happen . . .' He turns his attention to the old woman, who hasn't moved from her post at the top of the stairs. 'Auntie!' he says breathlessly, as if he has just noticed her. 'You're safe! Thank heavens!'

Why doesn't she say something, the old fool, thinks Ray, instead of standing there like a waxwork dummy? And after she's caused all this bother, an' all. Inconsiderate, he calls it.

Because so far, neither of his co-stars in this production have uttered a single line. Something helpful like 'What do you mean?' or 'You don't mean to say . . .' is what Ray has in mind. But it looks as if he's going to have to do all the hard work himself. As per usual, thinks Ray.

'I tried to stop him,' he says, panting a little, as if still winded by the struggle. 'But he was too strong for me. Knocked me out, he did. Made my nose bleed something chronic. Boxing blue, old Sandy,' he adds, gilding the lily a touch.

It seems to do the trick, however.

'What are you suggesting?' snaps Horse-Face. She is on her knees, trying to give Sandy-boy the kiss of life. His blood is all over her blouse, notes Ray, a mite queasily. It soaks the pillow he's still clutching as if his life depended on it, poor sod. 'It was an accident.'

''Course it was,' says Ray. ''Least – *that* was . . .' He gestures towards Sandy's tumbled corpse. 'Ask yourself,' says Ray. 'What he was doing in her bedroom with a *pillow*. Ask yourself *that*.'

'I did challenge him, you know . . .'

Both jump at this unexpected intervention from Auntie.

'I couldn't see who it was in the dark, you see, so I called out to him to show himself. But he didn't reply,' she says in a small voice. 'And you know, with him got up like that . . . I suppose I must have mistaken him for somebody else . . . There are some awfully desperate characters about . . . And the gun was in my hand . . .'

'Oh, *Aunt* . . .' sobs Iseult.

What a mess she looks, thinks Ray disgustedly, with her face all blotchy and red. 'The thing is,' he says – anxious not to let the subject drop – 'you mustn't blame him *too* much. Poor old Sandy. It was his debts, see? Drove him to it. Knowing how much he had coming to him made things worse, didn't it? Thought he saw a way out. Didn't want to have to wait, did he?'

Auntie's gaze, which up to now has been fixed on the scene of carnage below, now focuses itself on Ray. 'How do you know about the money?' she says. 'Even Sandy didn't know . . .'

'That's where you're wrong,' says Ray. 'Found the will, didn't he? Told me all about it. Said he needed the cash a.s.a.p. because his creditors were kicking up a stink. Threatening to take him to court. Foreclose on the business and that . . .'

'It's not true . . .' stammers Iseult, now white as a sheet (though nowhere near as white as poor old Sandy, Ray observes). 'Sandy wouldn't do a thing like that . . .'

But she can't stop her horrified gaze from straying to the pillow.

'Why didn't he come to me? I'd have settled his debts for him,' says Auntie.

'Just what I said to him myself,' says Ray. ' "Sandy," I says. "Why don't you *go* to Auntie? Explain what's happened. *She'll* help you out," I says. Know what he says, old Sandy?' Here Ray's voice briefly assumes the cadences of Stowe and Magdalen College. ' "Ray," he says, "I'd be too ashamed. Couldn't do it, old chap. Out of the question. Because I care too much what Auntie thinks of me, you know," ' goes on this eerie revenant. ' "I'd rather *die* than ask her for money." Which is sort of what happened, when you think about it,' says Ray sententiously. 'Tragic, really.'

There is a silence.

'If you knew what he meant to do,' says Iseult at last, 'why didn't you *say* something?'

'Would *you* have believed me?' says Ray. 'Anyway,' he adds. 'Never thought he'd go through with it, did I?'

He descends the stairs, slowly, step by step, until he reaches the spot where Sandy lies, wedged into the turn of the stairs, his legs bent at an awkward angle under him, his head flung back. Ray notes with satisfaction that the pillow is still in place. They won't be able to dislodge *that* without a struggle. *Rigor mortis*, he guesses. He puts out an exploratory finger.

'Don't touch him,' says Iseult.

Like that is it? thinks Ray. 'Pardon me, I'm sure,' he says. 'I hate to mention it,' he adds, 'but it might be an idea to call the police. It's usual when a crime's been committed,' says Ray. Taking care not to get blood on his shoes, he continues his descent. At the door of the sitting room, he pauses.

'Blimey,' he murmurs. 'What a bleeding mess . . .'

In daylight, the room looks worse, if possible, than it did the night before. Water from up-ended vases has soaked into the carpet, across which the ruined chandelier lies like a shattered iceberg. Candle wax drips from the mantelpiece on to a French-polished table. There are cigarette burns on the sofa and empty bottles in the bookcase. A fall of soot, brought down by a trapped bird in the chimney breast, fills the air with its pungent odour. Metallic. Choking. A smell like no other, unless it's . . .

Blood, thinks Ray. He hadn't realized it smelt so strong.

Behind him, a strange high keening starts up, as Auntie, released from her spellbound state, considers the damage she's done. Ray turns, to see the two women wrapped in one another's arms, sobbing as if their hearts will break.

Ahh. *Sweet*, thinks Ray.

At this sound of wailing, the forgotten dog, still locked in the kitchen, sets up a howl. Place is a bleeding madhouse, mutters Ray. He isn't keen to bring Lil into it, but it's got to be done. And it'll look all the more convincing if he's the one to do it. So he picks up the phone, dials 999. Waits for the call to be connected. It's the local police station, of course. Some cloth-ears answers. 'Yer?' His mouth still full of his bacon sarnie, smirks Ray to himself. Turnip heads. All the better, for his purposes.

'Awfully sorry to trouble you, Inspector,' he says in a not half bad imitation of Sandy's RP tones. 'But would you send one of your officers at once? Dunsinane . . . Yes, the big house on the Wivelsfield Road . . . I'm afraid there's been a nasty accident . . .'

Looking back, Iseult isn't sure how she managed to get through that day. She supposes she must just have switched off. That was what the mind did, wasn't it, when things got too much to bear? Like during the war. It was how people coped, that's all. Mercifully, she's blotted most of it out. Only fractured images remain. The dreadful bone-white pallor of Sandy's face on the blood-soaked pillow. His utter stillness. A stopped machine, she remembers thinking. Blood swirling away down the plughole as she'd washed her hands. The dog whining at her heels – they sensed a death, animals.

Afterwards, she'd sat with him for a while. Talked to him. Recalling the times they'd had when they were young. The day they'd built the tree-house. The night of the Hendersons' dance . . . I always loved you, you know, she'd told him. Silly of me, of course, with our being cousins and all. Quite hopeless – but what choice did I have? It isn't as if one has much control over these things, she'd murmured, stroking his hair (his poor dear face was unhurt, thank heaven). I think we both knew that . . .

Well, there was no one to call her mad. Only Aunt – and she was hardly in a position to judge, poor darling. Oh, and that frightful oik – but she didn't care what *he* thought, odious creature . . .

Even now, she can't believe the things he'd said. Lies. All of it. In spite of what seemed like evidence to the contrary. Most of that was circumstantial, wasn't it? The will, and all that. Sandy'd never given *her* the slightest hint that he knew he was the sole beneficiary. They only had the oik's word for that – in fact, the whole cockamamie story depended on him. He'd concocted it, to divert suspicion from himself. That horrible tale about the pillow had come from him, too. Although she had to admit that *was* hard to explain away. What *had* Sandy been up to, in Aunt's bedroom, in the small hours of the morning? Sleepwalking, perhaps? But you didn't sleepwalk with a pillow. Well, they'd never know for certain, now . . . But *murder*? She can't believe it.

Although that business with the cocoa certainly *looked* suspicious. Aunt hadn't drunk it, of course, so they'd found the residue of the sleeping tablets (again, helpfully pointed out by that treacherous boy). *He'd* claimed it was Sandy who'd put them there. He'd tried to dissuade him, he said. Even tried to switch the mugs when Sandy wasn't looking, so that Sandy, not Auntie, got the doped drink. Only Sandy'd switched them back. *Ha*, thinks Iseult grimly. A likely story if ever there was one. My eye and Sweet Fanny Adams, if you want *my* opinion, mutters Iseult.

She could tell Sergeant Hoskins didn't think much of the little beast's story, either. When he came to fetch her from the morning room, where she was sitting with Aunt, he'd had a very queer look on his face indeed. Had she been struck by anything *particular* about the deceased's behaviour on the night of the alleged offence, he'd asked her, when they'd established her relationship with the deceased and her movements over the past twenty-four hours. Remembering the last time she'd seen Sandy alive – towards the end of that beastly party – had brought tears to her eyes. She'd brushed them away. Stupid to give in to such weakness now. 'What do you mean?' she'd said.

'Was he different in any way?' Sergeant Hoskins said. 'Excited? Overwrought?'

Iseult thought she could see where this was leading.

'Not excited, no,' she said. 'If anything, rather calm . . .'

'Distracted?' prompted the policeman. 'As if his mind were on other things, like?'

'Perhaps,' she'd admitted reluctantly. 'But then, he often was, you know . . .'

Had he talked to her about his financial difficulties at all? Hoskins wanted to know. Not really, she'd replied. Although, of course, he must have had his ups and downs like everyone else . . . At this he was silent such a long time, tapping his pencil against his teeth, that she began to feel uneasy. What other lies had that awful boy been telling, to make him look so grim?

'I don't believe he meant to do it,' she'd burst out. 'Sandy – the deceased – well, he just wasn't *capable* of anything like that . . .'

'You'd be surprised what people is capable of when there's a lot of money at stake,' said Sergeant Hoskins gravely.

What had exercised them most, the police, had been the hours leading up to the shooting. The state of the drawing room. *Bit of a mess in here. Been having a party, have you?* She'd explained about the chandelier – although it hadn't seemed a convincing explanation, even to her. Chandeliers don't just fall down of their own accord. *Somebody swinging on it, was there?* How many people had been at this party, the policeman had wanted to know. Had any of these persons displayed signs of intoxication? Had the deceased himself displayed any such signs? And what about *illicit substances*? Drugs, in a word. Had anyone, to the best of her knowledge, been partaking of something they oughtn't?

Iseult had been conscious that she wasn't being absolutely truthful when she'd said that no, she hadn't seen anything untoward. Because if she was being honest, of course, she'd have mentioned the funny cigarette. But that, in turn, would have necessitated mentioning what it led to . . . She'd been unable to suppress a blush at the memory – a reaction, she was uncomfortably aware, which was not lost on Sergeant Hoskins.

Still, he'd been decent about letting her stay when the other man – Constable Dawson – had brought Aunt in from the next room to give her statement. Because it could be upsetting for an elderly person, having to cope with all the palaver of this kind of thing. Not brought up to it, like some he'd had to deal with in his line of work, the policeman intimated. Hardened to it, they were. Cocky. Mrs Reason was a different matter. A real lady. You didn't get many of *them* these days, observed Sergeant Hoskins darkly. Present company excepted.

It had been while she was being questioned by Sergeant Hoskins that Aunt had dropped her bombshell. There'd been some routine stuff – name, age, address and all the rest of it – and then he'd asked, 'What exactly was the relationship between you and the deceased?' and she'd replied, 'He was my son.'

At the sound of Iseult's gasp, the policeman had looked up sharply. 'Your son, you say?'

'Yes,' said Aunt. 'But I wasn't allowed to keep him, you see. He used to come to me for holidays. Wilfred never objected,' she'd added, with a faint, wistful smile as if recalling lost, golden days.

With hindsight, it explained a lot of things. A remark Leonora had once let slip about Aunt Peggy's weak heart, and how it meant she could never have a child of her own; a pencilled inscription on the back of a photograph, tucked into Aunt's Book of Common Prayer: *My Darling Boy, aged two months and five days* . . . And the time Aunt had said Sandy was 'the spitting image' of his father, when everyone knew Uncle Harold had been short and stocky – all these facts, insignificant in themselves, made sense in the light of this new information.

*

The chat with Lil wasn't such a piece of cake as Ray'd expected. For starters, the Village Plod he'd pictured turned out to be a much younger man – closer in both age and general turn-out to his cousins in the (very much to be taken seriously) Brighton squad. Any hopes he might have had of cosying up to Handsome, in his ever-so-smart blue uniform and his big black boots, are soon quashed, however. No amount of matiness can get a smile out of Sunny Jim. Dead serious about it all, he is, with his nice new notebook and his shiny silver whistle. Anyone'd think he was auditioning for Z Cars.

'Exactly where was you when the, ah, *alleged incident* was taking place?' he'd asked Ray, when Ray had finished what seemed to *him*, at any rate, to be a fairly full description of the fateful night. Adding, as an obvious afterthought, 'Sir'.

And Ray'd had to explain all over again how he'd begged and pleaded with Sandy not to do it, and finally got him to agree, and fallen asleep around two, completely *worn out*, only to be awoken at five by the sound of someone moving around in the next room . . .

'Next room, you say?' interrupts DI Fancy Smith. 'You mean to say you weren't actually in the room *at the time*?'

'Well, of course not. I was asleep, wasn't I?' says Ray, his wide-eyed gaze showing exactly what he thinks of *that* suggestion. 'In my *own room*,' he adds helpfully, as if spelling it out for someone exceptionally slow on the uptake. He's not going to be had *that* way. First thing he did after ringing the station was to revisit the scene of the crime. Muss up the bedclothes in his room; throw things around a bit in Sandy's. Just to give a little extra touch or two to the picture. 'Then, of course, I went into the *next room* – to try and stop him, like I said. There was a struggle, and . . .'

'How did you know what he was up to?' says the surly cunt.

'Might've been getting up for some other purpose entirely . . .'

'What do you *mean*?' Again, Ray opens his eyes very wide. Such dirty minds they had, these Boys in Blue. Must come from mingling with the criminal classes.

'Call of nature,' says Plod, but he has the grace to blush.

'Oh, I *see* . . .' Ray allows a longish pause to ensue. 'I suppose it could have been that. But I just knew it wasn't, somehow. Call it intuition, if you like . . .'

The policeman hesitates, then starts to write something in his notebook.

'That's i, n, t . . .'

'I know how to spell "intuition", thank you.'

That had been naughty, of course. But Ray never could resist a tease.

'So,' goes on Sergeant I-Can-Do-Joined-Up-Writing, 'you went into the deceased's room and – then what?' As if Ray hasn't told him, not five minutes ago. Are you hard of hearing or what? Ray wants to shout.

He restrains himself, however. 'As I believe I told you, *Officer*, there was a struggle . . .'

'What – immediately?'

'Yes. I mean – no.' Careful, thinks Ray, he's trying to catch you out. He frowns. Giving it careful thought. 'I think I shouted something – "Stop!" or something like that – and then I must've got hold of him, because the next thing I knew . . .'

'You shouted "Stop"?' interjects Miss Fussy Pants, still scribbling away in her little black book. Betcha *she* doesn't get asked for her phone number very often, thinks Ray.

'Yes . . . That is, I think so. Maybe it was "No!" or "Wait!" Does it matter?' he says sweetly.

'Only Mrs Reason didn't hear a shout,' says Sherlock, *very* pleased with himself. 'First thing *she* heard was footsteps outside her door . . .'

'It was a quiet kind of shout,' says Ray. 'More like a whisper, in fact. Didn't want to wake her, see?'

Now it's the copper's turn to pantomime surprise. 'You didn't want to *wake* her?' he says. 'Why ever not? Surely that's just what you *did* want to do?' Sarky bastard.

But Ray is equal to this. Although it's an effort to keep his cool. His bloodstained shirt (which he's made sure to bring to Fancy's notice) is drenched in sweat by the end of what's turned out to be a much stickier half-hour than he'd antici-pated. 'It all happened so quick,' he says. 'One minute, I was pleading with him, like I said – the next we was fighting. There wasn't time to think. He was a desperate man, you know, Officer. Strength of ten men, like they say. Half-killed me, he did.' Ray shudders prettily. 'Horrible, it was . . .'

He'd tried, quite casual like, to steer the conversation round to the night of the party. Because it wouldn't hurt, would it, to drop a few hints about *that*. Merely a sniff of drug-crazed orgies and suchlike was usually enough to make Lil wet her knickers. Pop stars. Groupies. Reefer madness. Oh, he'd had some fun putting Miss Prim in the picture.

' 'Course, I'm not saying the accused, I mean the deceased, was *high on drugs* or anything like that,' says Ray, all innocent like. 'But drugs was certainly being consumed on the premises, if you get my meaning . . .'

Prim-and-Proper had said sharply that he got his meaning very well, thanks, and left it at that. But afterwards Ray'd heard him telling young Dawkins to bag up a couple of fag ends for analysis, just in case . . . Won't *that* get them going, Ray'd chortled to himself. Rock and Roll Rave-ups in Rural

Rottingdean. Sordid Sex Sessions in Straitlaced Sussex. *Lovely*, thinks Ray gleefully.

And won't Jocelyn be surprised when the filth turns up on his doorstep, asking all sorts of awkward questions? Because it's not going to do Pretty Boy Nick's career any good at all, if it gets out that he and the boys were at a party where someone got stiffed. Even if they can prove they were long gone by the time the deed was done . . . Yes, it could look very bad, thinks Ray. Maybe a quick call to Jossy-boy wouldn't go amiss. To warn him, like. Jossy'd be ever so grateful, wouldn't he – and gratitude can be an awfully useful thing. If Ray ever needed a bolt hole, Jocelyn might be just the boy to provide it – to say nothing of money, even a job (that modelling contract, for instance). And if things got really nasty with Fancy and his mates, it'd be handy to know someone who could pull a few strings. Good lawyers came expensive . . .

Not that it would come to that, thinks Ray.

Because they can't prove a thing – that's the beauty of it. However much they might *insinuate* this and *infer* that, they'll never get him to admit he had anything to do with it. As far as Auntie's concerned, he's a hero. Hadn't he done his best to put the brakes on poor, misguided Sandy? And there's the evidence of the will – they can't argue with *that*. That's *motive*, that is – the best motive in the world. Hard cash.

But of course the clincher had been when the old girl had let slip the truth of the matter. I mean – who'd have thought it? The artful old witch. Pulling the wool over everybody's eyes like that, when all the time they was mother and son. That accounted for the money – people not uncommonly displayed a (to Ray's mind unfair) bias towards their own flesh and blood.

Which raises interesting possibilities. Because, following

this line of reasoning, the person next in the queue for the dough, now Sandy's snuffed it, has to be Iseult. Who's bound to be less of a pushover than the Dear Departed for the simple reason that – as Ray's well aware – she hates Ray's guts. But, thinks Ray (never a man to let mere detail stand in his way), there's more ways than one to skin a cat . . .

It was Mama who'd come up with the idea. She always knew how to manage awkwardnesses of that sort. Although there'd been nothing *quite* like this to tax her ingenuity until that moment.

They'd been at luncheon – Mama, Leonora and herself (Papa was out on one of his parish visits; Hugh of course was away at school and naturally knew nothing about any of it) – when Mama had said, into the silence, 'Peggy. Of course. Peggy must have him . . .' Because as the only one of them married so far (even though dear Lolly'd already had heaps of offers), she was the obvious choice, Mama said.

And so it was arranged. After some initial resistance, dear Harold had agreed it was the best thing all round. What with darling Peggy being so delicate, it was unlikely she'd ever be up to the whole tiresome business. Harold had known that when he'd taken her on. It was much better this way, Mama said. A case of killing two birds with one stone. All that was needed was a bit of forward thinking. Peggy would have to wear looser clothes for a while – but there were *such* pretty things to be had these days. The tricky part would be nearer the time (there were still six months to play with). Constance would have to be got out of the way for a month or two, that was all. By a happy coincidence, Great-Aunt Dolly in Aberdeen had expressed a wish to see her . . .

Her pains had come in the night. By the time they'd roused

the doctor, she'd done most of the hard work by herself. He hadn't cried at first, because the cord was around his neck. She'd feared he was dead – but then he'd screamed with all his might. 'A fine boy,' said Dr McKay.

The strangest part of the whole strange adventure had been the journey home, Connie recalls. Changing trains at Edinburgh in the dark and cold, she'd entertained a wild notion of flight. But where could she go, and who would take her in, encumbered as she was by the softly breathing bundle in her arms? Nearing Berwick upon Tweed, he'd cried to be fed. Fortunately, it had been a sleeping car. At Newcastle, she'd watched the sun come up on a day whose end would bring her only grief. All the way down across the map of England – as the North Yorkshire moors gave way to the Black Country, and the Midlands merged in turn into the bleak, flat wastes of the Fenlands – she'd pondered ways of escape. But at King's Cross, Mama had been waiting, in a closed cab. 'Here you are at last,' had been her only greeting. 'Dear Peggy's so excited,' she'd said, taking the child from its mother without further ado. 'He's a fine big chap, I'll say that for him. He's to be called Alexander, Peggy says . . .'

After the police have gone and the body has been taken away in an unmarked van, a strange lassitude descends upon Dunsinane. The doctor has prescribed a sedative for Aunt, but she won't hear of it.

'Something to knock me out?' she says, waving away the glass that Iseult's prepared for her. 'What would be the good of that? I'd have to wake up eventually. And everything would still be the same, you see. No, I shall manage without, dear. You go on home . . .'

Mummy, thinks Iseult remorsefully. She's forgotten all about her.

'I'll just telephone to say I'm on my way,' she falters, remembering with horror that the telephone is in the hall . . . As she stands, dialling the number with fingers that stupidly persist in missing the holes, she cannot stop her fascinated gaze from returning to the dreadful spot where a darker patch of stair carpet is now the only clue to what was there.

As she listens to the ringing tone (picturing, as she does, Mummy stumping her way along the passage to answer it), she looks at her watch and is astonished to see that it's only half past nine. She feels as if days – weeks – have passed since she got here. A lifetime seems to separate her from the person who'd set out that morning, so insanely confident that everything would be just as it had been before, and the one who now stands waiting, no longer sure of anything – not even her own name.

For when the phone is answered at last – 'Hello? Hello? Who is it?' – Iseult finds herself unable to say.

'I . . .' she manages to croak, before her throat closes up.

'Iseult? Is that you?' squawks Leonora indignantly.

'Y-yes. M-mummy . . .' Something terrible's happened, she wants to say. But the only sound she can make is an ugly sobbing, as if someone had her by the throat and were trying to choke her.

Then the receiver is taken out of her hand.

'Lolly, dear? Yes, it's me,' says Aunt gently. 'Iseult's a bit upset at the moment. I'm afraid it's very bad news. Poor Sandy's dead . . . Yes, a terrible shock . . . Quite unexpected . . . Yes, dear. You go back to bed. Iseult's coming as soon as she can . . .'

'But – I can't leave you,' wails Iseult, as soon as she is able. 'You mustn't stay here, all by yourself . . .'

'She won't *be* all by herself,' says Ray, appearing suddenly from the wrecked drawing room.

Iseult ignores this. 'You must come back with me. In the sidecar. Mummy would want it . . .'

'Thank you, dear. But if you don't mind,' says Aunt, with the same unsettling calm she has displayed throughout, 'I'll stay. There are things I have to do. Accounts to be settled . . .'

What can she mean? thinks Iseult. There's nothing to be done now.

'That's right,' says Ray. 'You carry on. Don't mind me. I've got plenty to keep me busy, *I* have. Tidying and that . . .'

It seems to Iseult that there is an insufferable smugness in his voice. The thought of leaving him alone with Auntie troubles her obscurely.

'Look here, Mr, er, Brown,' she says brusquely. 'You don't have to do that. I'll be back this afternoon to set things to rights . . .'

'Oh, it's no trouble,' insists the interloper. 'It'll give me something to do. Take me mind off things,' he adds, with a meaning look at the stain on the carpet.

Head cocked, Ray stands listening until the sound of the Norton's engine has died away. Talk about relieved. Now the interfering old cow is out of the way, he can get down to business. Clearing up the mess from the party (to say nothing of the mess the police have left, with their big boots and fingerprint powder) is only the half of it. What he really wants to do is have a good poke through Auntie's things. See if he can't turn up any more *interesting documents*, har, har.

'All right, Auntie?' he calls, seeing her hovering there (funny how much older and frailer she looks now she's no longer holding the gun). 'You go and rest, there's a good girl, and I'll make you a nice cup of tea . . .'

Then, conscious of her eye upon him, he starts in on the tidying up, setting a fallen chair back on its legs and picking up the pieces of a broken vase.

'So kind,' he hears the old woman say. Or perhaps it's 'so tired', because when he looks round, she's gone.

At once Ray's industriousness ceases. He drops the armful of stuff he's been holding – nothing but a pile of dusty old books; he glances idly at the first page of one of these: *About thirty years ago, Miss Maria Ward of Huntingdon, with only seven thousand pounds, had the good luck to captivate Sir Thomas Bertram, of Mansfield Park* . . . With a snort of disgust, he throws it down with the rest.

He makes for the desk, which has already been turned over by Fancy and his mates. The will and the letter from Strickland's solicitors have been removed for the time being. But there's a chance he might find something no less useful . . . He thumbs through bundles of old letters – including some in a childish hand which he realizes must be from Sandy (*Dear Auntie Constance, I hope you are well. Thank you for the toffee. Mumsie says to tell you I passed my Common Entrance* . . .) – but there's nothing worth bothering about.

Ray's stomach growls, suddenly. He's had nothing to eat or drink since that over-sugared cup of tea they'd had pressed on them by the other copper, Constable Dawkins or Dobbins or whatever his name was. Plain-looking boy.

The kitchen is a worse tip than it was before, with the leftovers from the party still on the table and champagne bottles – all empty, Ray notes disgustedly – lined up on the draining board. He swats away a fat fly which has been getting stuck into the pâté and has a sniff at the (now very runny) Brie. Foreign muck, thinks Ray. You can keep it. Give him proper English food any day. He could murder a nice fry-up, with all the trimmings. Eggs and beans and bacon and fried bread and mushrooms and tomatoes and black pudding, with lashings of HP. His mouth fills at the thought.

Sod this for a game of soldiers. He has to get out of this dump. If I don't get some food, double quick, I'll *die*, thinks Ray, with an access of self-pity.

A minor problem is the absence of the readies (a quick hunt turns up nothing but threepence-farthing and a collar-stud at the bottom of a dusty jug). Casting around for other sources of moolah, he remembers Sandy's wallet. He's half-way up the stairs, sidestepping to avoid the spongy dark splotch on the half-landing, before an awful thought strikes him. *The pigs have got it.* Bagged up neat and tidy with the dead man's clothes and all the rest of it. He'd watched Auntie sign the receipt . . .

'Bastards,' says Ray.

A slight shuffling sound attracts his attention. He looks up and sees Auntie standing at the top of the stairs. She's dressed now, in her baggy brown tweeds, and is staring down at him as if she's never set eyes on him before. Her lips form a word.

'Julian,' she says. 'Thank goodness you've come. I'm going to need a man about the place now that Sandy's gone . . .'

At the inquest they'd mercifully glossed over the irregular aspects of Aunt's family arrangements. They'd been more interested in the business of the will, of course. That dreadful story about the pillow had exercised them quite a bit, too. Some dull forensic chappie with a foreign name had got up on his hind legs and spouted a lot of stuff about sleeping pills.

Some other bird – a firearms expert – had given his opinion about the gun. Iseult hadn't wanted Aunt to go, thinking it might upset her, but Aunt had insisted. She had to know the truth, she said. It was a case of chickens coming home to roost.

In her mourning black, she'd sat very still and upright as the coroner delivered his verdict: Death by Misadventure.

And all the time that ghastly boy was sitting beside her, pouring fresh poison into her ear. 'Cheer up, Auntie,' Iseult heard him mutter (and who was *he* to call her that?). 'Things are looking up, you'll see. With me to look after you, you won't have nothing to worry about . . .' He was obviously up to something, the toad. Hoping to worm his way into Aunt's good books, now that Sandy was gone. Well, she'd nip *that* one in the bud . . .

'I don't think we'll be needing your services any more, Mr Brown,' she'd taken the opportunity of saying. 'You've been extraordinarily . . . *accommodating* during this whole distressing affair, but I really don't feel we should detain you any longer . . .'

She might have known it wasn't going to be as easy as all that to dislodge the tick. He'd merely smiled. A hateful, gloating kind of smile.

'*Aow*, I think I ought to stay as long as Auntie needs me, don't you?' he'd said. 'And somehow I think she's going to need me more than ever from now on . . .'

The look on her face had been a scream. He'd almost laughed out loud. Silly old trout. Telling him where to get off – the *nerve*. The idea, chortles Ray, that he'd be such a fool as to leave now, with everything going just the way he wants it to go . . . *I* should jolly well cocoa, thinks Ray.

Because he's got a plan, has Ray. (He's never been a boy to

let the grass grow under his feet.) The first stage of the plan, as he sees it, is to make himself indispensable to Auntie. To do that, he needs to be here, doesn't he? Stands to reason. Auntie needs a man about the place. Someone to look after her. Who better than himself? Her rock. Her saviour.

That's stage one. Stage two is more tricky – but not, thinks Ray, impossible, given time. It involves the will. The money. Because who else (argues reasonable Ray) is the old dear going to leave it to, if not to the person who really deserves it? The person who's got her best interests at heart. Yours truly, in short, thinks Ray.

They'd got back from the coroner's court to find the blue Morris Minor parked in front of the house. Ray isn't the nervy type, but the sight gives him quite a turn, he doesn't mind admitting. It's only for a second, because it's obvious almost at once that the man behind the wheel isn't Sandy. It's that bald bastard from the garage, come to bring back the car. Which (apart from the odd dent) looks as good as new.

'Why, there's Bert,' says Miss High-and-Mighty, grinding the gears as usual as she turns into the drive. 'Thoughtful of him to bring the car back,' she adds shakily.

Thoughtful – my arse, thinks Ray. Geezer wants his money, is all. Well, he can whistle for it. Seeing the Morris gives him an idea, which is so A1 he almost laughs aloud. Because with a car the world's his oyster. Just what the doctor ordered, thinks Ray. He elbows his way into the discussion which is even now taking place between Horse-Face and Baldie. Civilities and commiserations having been exchanged, it's down to brass tacks, apparently.

'I'm sure Mrs Reason will settle up with you as soon as possible,' the silly cow is saying.

''Scuse me,' cuts in Ray. 'I'll handle this, if you don't mind.'

He turns to the bald bastard, who flaps a docket – his bill, presumably – under Ray's nose. Ray ignores it. 'Sorry, mate,' he says breezily. 'No can do. You'll have to wait your turn, like all Mr Foulkes's creditors.' Taking no chances, he whips the car keys out of the astonished *garagiste*'s hand. 'I'll take those, ta very much. You can send your bill to Mr Foulkes's solicitor. He's handling all that side of things from now on.'

'Now, look here,' blusters Bert, his fat face turning an unholy shade of beetroot. 'Just who do you think you are, Sonny Boy?'

'Less of your lip,' says Ray. 'Tell you what, Auntie,' he adds casually, when the disgruntled Bert, muttering under his breath about blooming liberties, has taken himself off, 'why don't I take the car this afternoon? I could pop down to the shops for you. Get some supplies in. Coupla bottles of sherry, that type of thing. You'll be needing some for Friday,' he reminds her.

'What a good idea,' says Auntie. 'Don't you think so, Iseult, dear?'

And Horse-Face can only shuffle her feet and look glum, and mutter that she hopes Aunt knows what she's doing, that's all.

'Don't think I don't know *exactly* what you're up to,' she hisses to Ray, when Auntie is out of earshot. 'Trying to curry favour. But it won't work, you know. Because I've got my eye on you, Mr Brown. *Oh*, yes,' says the silly moo, working herself up. 'There's something very fishy about all this. And I intend to get to the bottom of it . . .'

He laughs off her threat – because, after all, what can she do? – but it makes him uneasy, nonetheless. He needs something in writing. That way he'll be safe. He's got to pin the old woman down. And the more he thinks about it, the more it seems to him that there's got to be a new will. Stands to reason, doesn't it? With the old one having to be scrapped and that. You could call it an urgent priority. The question is, how to get her to do what he wants – and in the *way* he wants? He'll need to tread carefully . . .

10

A Bit of a Blow

Coming in unannounced from his shopping trip (a swift half down the Hat and Feathers, followed by a leisurely stroll along the high street, picking up essentials – bread, meat, gin – along the way), Ray hears his name taken in vain.

'. . . not sure about him *at all*. I mean – is his name even Brown?'

It's Horse-Face. Sticking her long nose in where it's not wanted, as usual. He flattens himself against the wall. Bares his teeth in a foxy grin. I'll have *you*, darling . . . He's glad now that he left the car in the lane like he did. He'd got to pop out again for fags and it hadn't seemed worth the bother of reversing into the drive. He waits, breathing shallowly, to hear what Auntie has to say.

'But, my dear, he saved my life, you know. Or tried to. You were there. You heard what happened . . .'

'What he *said* happened,' says Horse-Face. 'We've only got his word for it.'

'My dear, the police were very thorough . . .'

'Oh, the *police* . . .' Horse-Face gives a snort, as if to say, 'What do *they* know?' I'm with you there, darling, grins Ray. 'But, honestly, Aunt,' the meddling bitch goes on, 'what do we *know* about him? Only that he's a friend (a rather poor sort of friend, if you ask me) of Sandy's . . .'

'He's an orphan,' says Auntie, a shade reproachfully. 'His father was in a POW camp in the Far East. Health completely broken, you know. Died when the little lad was a baby. Mother only survived him by a year. Ray was brought up by his grandmother. Devoted to her, apparently. She's dead now, too, of course . . .'

'How convenient,' says the suspicious old boot.

'Now, Iseult, dear, that's hardly fair. The poor fellow can't help his family circumstances. And he has been terribly kind during these past few dreadful days. Running errands and so forth . . .'

'Yes,' says Horse-Face, as if it hurt her to admit it. 'Speaking of which, where do you think he's got to? He's been an awfully long time. You don't suppose he's had an accident, do you?'

Don't sound so pleased about it, you miserable tart, thinks Ray. With an expertise borne of long practice in such skills, he walks backwards a few steps along the passage. Reaches the kitchen door, which he opens and lets falls again with a bang. 'Anybody home?' he calls loudly.

'We're in here, dear,' calls Auntie from the lounge.

Ray pops his head round the door. 'Shopping's all done,' he says. 'Anyone else for the cup that cheers?'

'I didn't hear the car,' says H.F. sourly.

'Parked it in the lane, didn't I?' says Ray. 'Might have to nip out again later, see? Spark plugs need looking at, don't they?'

'You don't say,' says Iseult.

No, it's not going to be quite the piece of piss he'd hoped, getting the old girl round to his way of thinking. Not with Little Miss Goody-Two-Shoes sticking her oar in every five minutes. Although from what he'd heard of their conversation, he didn't have too much to worry about on *that* score . . . Still, it was best to be on the safe side. But when he broaches the topic of the will that night over tea (cheese on toast, prepared by his own fair hands), he finds she's already ahead of him.

'Funny you should mention it,' she says, with that loopy

smile of hers. 'Because dear Iseult was saying the very same thing to me only this morning. Sweet of you both to be so concerned. But don't worry – it's all in hand. I telephoned Mr Cowper this afternoon, while you were at the shops. My solicitor, you know. He's coming the day after tomorrow. After the funeral . . .'

'Oh, good,' says Ray, a bit taken aback at such efficiency. 'That's a relief, I must say. It's such a comfort to know you're in *safe hands*, Auntie,' he adds meaningfully. 'Relying on people you can *trust*. After what happened with Sandy, you'll be wanting to make sure your future's, well, a bit more *secure*. You need to know you're going to be well *looked after*,' says Ray. 'It must be nice to feel that,' he sighs.

He waits for her to say something in return – preferably something which will enable him to develop his theme – but she says nothing, the dotty old baggage, gazing off into space the way she does when she's in one of her funny moods. Probably moping about her darling boy again.

'Auntie, dear,' Ray says winsomely, after a few moments of this silence. 'Now that we're on the subject of *wills* and all that . . . I do hope you're not going to do anything *rash*. I mean, I'm not expecting any kind of *reward* for what I did. I mean, *perish* the thought. What I did – saving your life and that – I did because, well, I thought it was the *right* thing to do, know what I mean? I didn't do it for *money* . . .'

'Of course, dear. I know that,' says Auntie.

For a minute Ray wonders if he's gone a bit too far. Maybe a hint that, despite his protestations, he wouldn't actually be *averse* to being given a load of loot would do the trick . . .

''Course, it's your money,' he says. 'To do with as you will. Far be it from me to try and tell you what to do with your money. I mean, who am *I*, after all? Just some poor bloke who happened to be in the right place at the right time – that's *all* . . .'

'Dear boy,' says Auntie. 'Always so considerate. And so modest, too. But don't worry, I won't forget what you've done for me. You'll have your reward, never fear . . .'

Ray has to be content with that. But it was something, wasn't it? His *reward*, she'd said. That meant money, didn't it? 'Course it did. But *how much* – that was the question . . .

'I was wondering, Auntie dear,' he says, never one to pass up the chance of killing two birds with one stone, 'if I could possibly have the car again tomorrow? Only I've nothing to wear to the funeral. And I *do* want to look my best . . .'

'Oh,' says the old bat, looking as if she'd just woken up to find herself somewhere she'd rather not be. 'Of course, dear. Whatever you say . . .'

'And I was *thinking*,' wheedles Ray, in the new, well-modulated, faintly hesitant voice he's been adopting more and more in his conversations with Auntie, 'that it might be a good idea for me to run down to Brighton for the day, while I'm about it. I could look in at Sandy's flat. Make sure the police haven't left too much of a mess. Pick up the post for you. That sort of thing . . .'

'What a splendid idea,' says Auntie, smiling properly now. 'You *are* a kind boy . . .'

'Anything to please *you*, Auntie,' says Ray.

It's such a blessed relief to be out of that stinking dump at last – tooling along the open road with the window rolled down and one hand on the wheel (although he could wish he was driving something with a bit more *poke*, instead of this clapped-out old banger) – that Ray feels like bursting into song. He switches on the radio, gets a snatch of highbrow waffle on the Third Programme and twiddles the knob until he finds Caroline. An insidiously catchy melody fills the car. *That's* more like it, thinks Ray, humming along.

> The taxman's taken all my dough,
> Left me in my stately home,
> Lazing on a sunny afternoon . . .

His plan is to be back before dark. He doesn't want to leave the old girl too long. Not with old Izzy-Whizzy-Let's-Get-Busy sniffing around, spreading mischief, and the lawyer expected next day. Ray's pretty sure of his own abilities when it comes to the art of persuasion, but even he's well aware he's got his work cut out for him with Auntie . . . Frowning and chewing his lip, he meditates on strategies. He's now within five miles of Brighton. He sniffs the air's familiar salty tang. To one side, as he starts to descend, rises the great wall of the Downs; to the other lies the tarnished mirror of the sea. Ray sees neither hills nor sea, his gaze dully fixed on the ribbon of tarmac which leads him down, all the way to the white town at the cliff's foot.

He leaves the Morris in a side street off the Old Steyne and saunters in the direction of the Lanes. Business first; then pleasure. The sun, reflected off the shifting planes of waves, throws a hard white light on everything: the tall houses with their wedding-cake façades; the gleaming bonnets of cars – Jags, Mercs, Bentleys – parked along the front. The very pavement seems to glitter. Paved with gold, thinks Ray.

He goes first to Sammy the Greek's. Not a man to ask questions, Sammy – his only virtue, as it happens. In the dark little shop sandwiched between the Dolls' Hospital and the Lucky Fortune restaurant, he stands, a swarthy, dwarfish figure barely taller than a child, poring over the items Ray has brought. One of these, a necklace, he holds up to the light, twisting it around his fat fingers with a disparaging air. 'Freshwater pearl,' he says at last. 'Not so good – see?' He considers a pair of cufflinks. 'Engrave,' he says. 'Initial. Who wants to buy with initial?'

'They're gold,' says Ray, already bored with the ritual. 'Do you want 'em or not? Because I can always go somewhere else . . .'

When the transaction has been concluded – not entirely to his satisfaction, but he hasn't time for further argy-bargy – Ray heads for his next port of call. It isn't far. A leisurely stroll along Kensington Gardens brings him to the antique shop. *Restorations a Speciality.* He presses his nose to the smeared glass. We Are Closed, says the sign. And not likely to be opening soon, neither, thinks Ray. No, not in a month of Sundays.

Ray's never been the fanciful sort. Superstitious fears about black cats and unlucky thirteens don't trouble him at all, as a rule. But he has to admit it doesn't half give him the willies, pushing open that door and stepping inside. Maybe it's the smell. Old furniture and dust, with a suspicion of something decaying. The smell a room gets when it's been closed up too long. On the mat is a slew of brown envelopes. Bills. He bends to pick them up, recalling his promise to Auntie. As he does so, he sees something move out of the corner of his eye. *There's somebody there.* He feels the hairs start to rise on the back of his neck. But when he looks again, there's nothing to be seen. Old books. A cracked mirror. Junk. 'Getting the horrors,' mutters Ray. ''S only natural . . .' The moose's head on the far wall regards him glassily.

The flat is reached through the shop; he lets himself in.

Here, the feeling of abandonment is stronger still. The very neatness of the place adds to the sense of forlornness. The row of clean milk bottles, lined up on the draining board, ready to be put out on a Monday morning. The single cup and saucer, washed up and left to dry on the rack. The ranks of carefully polished shoes, each with their shoe-trees in place, marching along the wall beside the bed.

Idly, Ray slips his foot out of its down-at-heel loafer and into one of Sandy's well-cared-for brogues. Too small. Though it's not really his style. A bit too conservative, like most of Sandy's things . . . This reminds him of one of the reasons he's come. He opens the wardrobe. A nice dark suit's what he needs. Black – or navy, at a pinch. No sense in spending good money (the twenty nicker Auntie's given him) on something he'll wear only once. Here we go, thinks Ray. Slipping on the jacket (a trifle snug across the chest, but no matter); trying the trousers up against himself (a bit on the long side, but they'll do). Now all he needs is a shirt (white) and a tie (black). And in fact, once on, the black suit doesn't look half bad. Kind of a lean, mean, Italian-tailored look. Sharp, thinks Ray. Very sharp.

After his hard morning's work, he feels in need of a break. He looks at his watch. Just gone midday. They'll be getting them in at the Hope and Anchor – Candy and Lulu and the rest of the girls. He might take a little stroll down there. See what's cooking. He can't wait to see their faces when he walks in, looking like this. 'Get you!' he can hear Candy say, with her laugh that sounds like cigarettes and gin. 'Who's a pretty boy, then?'

Alone in the big, deserted house, with the wreckage of her life all around her, Connie invokes her familiar ghosts: Hugh, Julian, Wilfred, Strickland and now Sandy. Her dear, dead boys. How she misses them all. Already the memory of Sandy's face, which had so recalled that of her lover, is blurring into that of its earlier incarnation. What a lot of damage you've done, she tells Strickland severely. I was wrong to have had anything to do with you . . . Yet how sweet it had been. And how sad she is that everything is over. 'Soon, it'll be over for me, too,' she murmurs aloud to the empty room.

She wondered what had possessed him to get in touch with her again. Sentimentality, perhaps? Or some atavistic sense of doing the right thing. She knew there'd been no children – or none he could acknowledge. Perhaps it was simply loneliness – who could say? He'd survived the war, she knew that much. Had made quite a name for himself. She remembers the last news she'd had of him, not long after she got married – 1920 or so. She'd picked up a parcel of chops from the butcher's, the blood soaking through the white paper on to the sheet of newspaper in which he'd wrapped the meat. *The Daily Express*, she recalls (not a paper Wilfred liked, as a rule; he preferred the *Telegraph* or, occasionally, *The Times*, for the crosswords). In any case, there it was, large as life: DISTINGUISHED WAR ARTIST MR GUY STRICKLAND HANGS HIS FIRST CORK STREET SHOW; and underneath, a photograph of the artist in a white silk muffler and broad-brimmed felt hat, standing in front of one of his pictures. *Cubist Self-Portrait*. One of his better efforts, she rather thinks. It hung in the morning room now.

Her first thought, spreading the bloodstained page flat on the kitchen table, was how thin he looked, his eyes owlish behind round hornrims, his stringy neck poking out from his fashionable soft-collared shirt like that of an old man. But of course, she'd told herself, he must be over forty. Incredible to think almost ten years had passed since their last, brief, passionate encounter. His lips on her neck. *My darling, oh, my darling*. She'd read the thing through once more and then thrust it into the fire.

She still doesn't know what impelled her to do it, but a day or so after, she'd looked out the photograph of her and Sandy and the others at Bexhill. A beach photographer had snapped them as they stood there; they'd had several prints made – one for each of the three sisters, and a couple over. It was one of these she'd put in an envelope addressed to Guy Strickland, care of the Cork Street gallery, and dropped in the pillar box at the end of the lane. She'd heard nothing for a week or two, then a cheque (quite a sizeable sum) had come, made out to her in her maiden name. She'd torn it in two and sent it back. After that, there'd been nothing – until the solicitor's letter last year, with its legacy of misfortune.

Perhaps the worst thought, of all the terrible thoughts she's had since Sandy died, is the knowledge that, if she'd been less proud about taking Strickland's money in the first place, what happened might not have happened. She has to live with that. She'll make amends, though – it's the least she can do. It's not too late for the money to do some good . . .

Wilfred would have known what to do (he was always long-headed about such things), but Wilfred isn't here. In the days since the shooting, he seems to have made himself scarce. There've been no further manifestations – and when she walks into a room, it no longer feels as if he's just left it. If there are unquiet spirits about, his isn't one of them.

Looking back, she supposes he must have known the true state of affairs – but if he did, it was never discussed. His manner towards Sandy had been what it was with everyone else he'd allowed into his circle of intimates. Not affectionate, exactly – because that would have required a greater degree of physical closeness than Wilfred was able to show. Though you wouldn't call him cold. Shy was nearer the mark. But a crippling kind of shyness that permitted only the barest contact.

And yet, in spite of this, she knew him to be capable of feeling. The proof of this was that he'd accepted Sandy for her sake. Knowing how much she loved the boy – and that there'd never be other children, to take his place.

A *mariage blanc* – wasn't that the term for what they had? A white marriage, instead of the white wedding she'd never had. It wouldn't have been suitable, Mama said – not with the family so recently out of mourning. (Although in China white was the colour of mourning, thinks Connie.) That wasn't the real reason, of course. But naturally no one breathed a word about *that*. So she'd worn grey: a two-piece costume, quite becoming. After the ceremony, they'd driven back to the house, where Mama and the others were already waiting. She'd have liked a few days somewhere quiet, just the two of them – but there'd been no money for that. And in any case, Wilfred's nerves wouldn't stand it. Even the out-of-season crowds at Bournemouth or Hastings would have been too much for him.

The plan was that they were to live with Mama for a month or so, until they got themselves settled – but it didn't turn out quite like that. Because there was always some reason (Wilfred's health wasn't up to it, or there was a war on) why the move had to be put off. So the months stretched into years. And then Mama died and they were left with the house. Funny, thinks Connie, how temporary measures can end up lasting a lifetime.

He sees now that it wasn't a very good idea, having that last vodka. Because until then he'd been getting along just fine, thank you very much. They'd left the Hope at chucking-out time, him and Candy and the rest of the girls, and then they'd gone to Ethel's for a cup of tea and a bun. She was a good sort, Ethel – letting them sit for as long as they liked over the one cup (a godsend when the weather was bad); had even been known to rent out a room on occasion. 'Customers is customers,' she was wont to say, her fat jowls wobbling. 'What's it to me what they gets up to in their own time? It's a free country.' But this time she'd got the hump. The boys from the station had been breathing down her neck again, it seemed. 'No more than two of you at a time. No hairspray, no make-up and no soliciting. You know the rules as well as I do, girls. You –' jerking her thumb at Ray – 'sight for sore eyes, you are. You can come in. The rest of you can hop it . . .'

The sensible thing, he sees now, would have been to have accepted Ethel's offer. A nice cup of tea and one of her famous fried-egg sandwiches would have sorted him out good and proper. For a minute he'd been torn – but then the thought of the bollocking he'd get next time he showed his face in the Hope decided him. 'Sorry, luv,' he says to Ethel. 'I'm fully booked this afternoon.'

'*Such* a popular girl, our Ray-lene,' says Lulu, snidey bitch. A bit too clever for her own good, that one.

Then they'd drifted down to the front and had a good laugh at the townies in their open-necked shirts and their Sta-Prest Trevira. 'Cortinas' was Candy's name for them, because ten to one that was what they'd be driving. You could tell when a Cortina was going steady, Candy says, because they had their names stuck up on the windscreen. STAN – MAUREEN, or COLIN – DAWN. Cortina names, said Candy.

Then they'd gone to the Metropole, because one of the waiters was a friend of Ricky's, and he was always good for a drink or two if you played your cards right. But it was his day off, as it happened, so they'd kicked around on the front some more until opening time, and then looked in at the Prince Regent to see if there was anything doing – or anyone *worth* doing, says Lulu. She'd got her eye on a *very* nice gentleman, she said. Nice little flat in Devonshire Gardens. Independent means. Well, by then Ray'd had a couple, so it didn't take much more of this sort of bragging to make him start dropping a few hints about his own good fortune. 'Coming into some money, are we?' says Candy (always quick on the uptake, that girl). '*Very* nice. Don't forget your old friends when you're rich and famous, will you, doll?' Which of course meant he had to stand the next round, on the strength of all the money he was supposed to be getting – which took care of a fair old chunk of Auntie's twenty quid. And then Lulu (who was sore because her 'nice gentleman' hadn't showed after all) kept introducing him as 'Ray-lene, who's ever so rich' – which wasn't something he wanted spread around at all, the silly mare. So they'd ended up at the Pussycat, where a flash type in a suit was buying him vodka-martinis all night. He remembers going back to the trick's place and passing out on the bed. To judge from the head he'd got this morning, it'd been a good night.

It wasn't until he was having his tea and a fag at Ethel's, after polishing off one of her slap-up fried breakfasts (the best hangover cure he'd ever come across), that he remembered that today was the day of the funeral. It quite spoilt the taste of his cigarette.

' "Then I saw her face",' sings Iseult softly, her cheek close to the rough, earth-smelling flank of Buttercup, whom she is endeavouring to milk. ' "Now I'm a believer . . ." Don't fidget,' she says sternly to the beast. Skittish, this morning. Daisy, from the next stall, regards her sorrowfully, her jaw working steadily, like a dowager whose false teeth are giving her trouble. 'Nearly done,' says Iseult, patting the cow's rump affectionately. 'Good girl,' she adds, feeling that perhaps she's been a little harsh. It isn't their fault they're upset. Sensitive creatures, cows. If there was an atmosphere, they picked it up.

She finishes Buttercup, moves on to Daisy. The sweet smell of warm milk fills the byre. *Splish* goes the milk into the bucket – and *splash* go Iseult's tears, running suddenly down her face to sour the milk with their salt, as she thinks of what the day ahead will bring.

Iseult wipes her eyes. Brusquely, with hard little strokes. She blows her nose. Lingers there for a moment or two longer, her head resting against Daisy's angular hip, because Fred, the odd-job man, is in today, and it wouldn't do to let him see her in such a state. When she is calm again, she picks up the buckets and sets off back towards the house, stopping off at the dairy on the way to leave the milk and to collect a fresh pat of butter for breakfast. Not that she feels much like eating, but Mummy will be expecting her rations as usual. Funerals were such enervating affairs, said Leonora. All that waiting around in a draughty church, and then the damp churchyard. It was enough to make one catch one's death. And there was never much to eat afterwards, even in the best of circumstances – which these definitely weren't. Shocking business. She'd always had her doubts about Sandy. Emotionally unstable, like all his kind. She'd tried to warn Constance what he was like – but of course she wouldn't listen. Now she was paying the price, Leonora opined, tucking into her eggs and bacon with evident relish.

It had taken an effort of will not to say something very rude indeed. Iseult had contented herself with banging the saucepans around while she was washing up. With the washing-up done, there'd be just the dogs to walk, and the sandwiches to make for later on. Then it'd be time for Mummy's bath. She'd need help getting dressed, of course. Once she was ready, with her hat and gloves on, it'd be time for Iseult herself to change. She wonders if Aunt will manage all right on her own . . .

Aunt hadn't wanted hymns. Or a sermon. It didn't seem appropriate, somehow, she said. 'Just some prayers, I think, don't you? And that nice passage from Isaiah: "though your sins be as scarlet, they shall be as white as snow; though they be red like crimson, they shall be as wool . . ." Rather pastoral, don't you think? Colourful, too. All those reds . . .'

Quite how much Aunt had told the vicar, Iseult never dared ask. The very fact that he'd agreed to cut short the obsequies was a clear enough indication that he must have known *something*. Violent death wasn't so common an occurrence in a community like theirs that it could pass unremarked. The rumours she knew to be circulating in the village about what had happened at Dunsinane that night were enough, in any case, to have kept bystanders away. Apart from Aunt herself, she and Mummy are the only mourners. She'd never been to a service so poorly attended.

'We brought nothing into this world and it is certain we can carry nothing out . . .'

The Reverend Allbright's voice – high and rather nasal – carries on over her head as Iseult sits bolt upright on the uncushioned pew, reflecting on her own sins of commission and omission. She *should* have made more effort to get through to him that day; if he'd been able to confide in her it might have eased his mind of its terrible burden. She *shouldn't have* gone to bed with that boy. If she'd made a point of seeking out Sandy instead, he might have been deflected from his dreadful purpose. Round and round they go in her head, these and other, no less futile, regrets. If circumstances had been otherwise. If one thing had not led to another. If Fate had dealt them all a different hand . . .

How lonely he must have been, thinks Iseult. How lonely and how afraid.

Dry-eyed, she watches as the undertaker's men raise the coffin to their shoulders and proceed, with slow and halting steps, along the aisle towards the chancel door. Iseult gets up, helping first Aunt, then Mummy to their feet in turn. Mummy is crying; Aunt is not. Iseult gives an arm to each. Then, arm in arm, they fall in behind the cortège. A strange, three-headed, mourning sisterhood.

By the time he's stopped for petrol and lost his way and had to stop again to ask directions, it's getting on for half past eleven, and he starts to think he might have missed the whole thing. He almost misses the turning for the church, as it is. But once there, at the end of a bumpy little track which nearly does for the Morris's suspension, there's no mistaking that he's come to the right place. Because bang in front of the church itself is a dirty great black Daimler. In front of that is the hearse. No flowers, he notices. A bit stingy, that. Himself, he likes a funeral to have flowers.

It looks like he's too late for the church bit, which is a relief. The priest is just winding up his spiel as Ray approaches. It's the usual bollocks about earth to earth, dust to ashes and all that rubbish. Mumbo-jumbo, thinks Ray scornfully. Witch-doctor stuff. For a minute, he isn't even sure that he's got the right funeral, because they all look so different, the three of them. The two old girls in their black get-up seem completely out of this world. *Very* Dracula is Risen from the Grave. As for Horse-Face – she's a revelation. Unrecognizable in a tailored two-piece that actually *fits* her for once, her hair up and a bit of lipstick on. On a dark night you'd almost consider giving her one. *If* you were so inclined . . .

The dirty look she throws him is just as he remembers, however.

'Sorry I'm late,' he whispers to Auntie. 'Puncture.'

Her face lights up. 'Julian, dear,' she murmurs. 'You made it . . .'

On the drive up from Brighton it'd looked as if it was going to tip down any minute. Black skies and that dull, heavy feeling of thunder in the air. Now it starts in earnest: spitting turns to big, fat drops, growing steadily bigger and wetter until it's raining cats and dogs. You'd have thought the vicar – mincing prat – would've speeded things up, seeing as how they were all standing there getting soaked, and the open grave filling up with water, so that poor old Sandy-poos would soon be as drenched as the rest of them, coffin or no coffin (though he'd be warm enough soon, thinks Ray), but not a bit of it. Silly tosser with his *Lord, have mercy upon us* and his *Deliver us from evil*. In fact he seemed, if anything, to be taking his time, as though making them stand there with the water running down their necks while he rambled on about the *miseries of this sinful world* gave him some kind of pleasure. Power-mad, thinks Ray disgustedly. I know *your* sort. Not averse to a bit of slap-and-tickle with a pretty choirboy over the communion wine, oh no. Lift up the – what was that dress thing they wore? Hassock or some such – and Bob's your uncle. Dirty old man.

Then just as he's thinking he can't stick it a moment longer, the tedious droning ceases. Leaving Sandy to his watery grave, they squelch back through the long grass towards the lych-gate, skirting tumbled gravestones and the mounds of rotting flowers which mark a recent interment. For a minute Ray's afraid that the vicar is going to invite himself back for a glass or three of sherry – but it turns out he's got another engagement. So it's just the four of them. Nice and cosy. Soon it'll be just two. And – once Auntie's done the right thing and made him her beneficiary – it'll only be a matter of time before there's just the one of us, thinks Ray. He's got a feeling it's not going to be Auntie.

Ray's on his third or is it fourth sherry, and has just finished giving them a (suitably edited) account of his trip to Brighton, when they hear the car. Who the hell's this? he wonders, thinking maybe the vicar's changed his mind, but Auntie, looking up from her frowning perusal of the bills Ray's brought from Sandy's flat, only murmurs, 'Here's Mr Cowper. Do let him in, would you, dear?' And Ray, getting up to obey this injunction, almost collides with Iseult, who's got up for the same purpose, it seems – so that for a minute neither of them moves, rooted to the spot by their mutual mistrust.

Then Auntie says, 'Iseult, dear, might I have a word?'

Leaving it to Muggins to let the visitor in.

It's the lawyer, of course. Silver-haired old geezer in a camel-hair overcoat. Worth a bob or two, Ray guesses. Lawyers always dressed expensive. Coining it, no doubt, the artful old codger.

He gives Ray a look as if he's got a bad smell under his nose. 'Is Mrs Reason in?'

'When I last looked,' says Ray. Snobby old git. *You'll* change your tune when you find out who I am, he thinks gleefully, ushering the old boy towards the study. It'll be Yes, sir, No, sir, Three bags full, sir, *then*.

'Ah, Mr Cowper,' says Auntie. 'So good of you to come out on such a dreadful day. Ray, dear,' she adds, seeing him still standing there, 'would you leave us for a moment? Mr Cowper and I have some business to discuss . . .'

Ray doesn't have much choice, does he? He goes, but as slowly as he dares, copping an eyeful of the documents old Cowper's pulling out of his briefcase, but learning nothing significant. He lingers for a minute or two in the passage, with his ear to the door, but only tantalizing phrases – 'in respect of the aforementioned'; 'with a view to augmenting the said capital' – can be discerned. Iseult, emerging from the kitchen with a tray of tea things, gives him a hard stare.

'Waiting for someone?' she says, and he says, 'Only you, darling . . .'

So there's nothing for it but to mooch around the house, with only Horse-Face and the old boot for company. The latter, having woken refreshed from one of her frequent cat-naps, is now demanding tea and biscuits. What a bleeding shower. The rain lashes down over the wet green garden, hammering against the panes of the French windows in the drawing room. It's here they end up sitting, in an atmosphere made oppressive by the ticking of a clock – for all the world as if they were at a wake, thinks Ray. Bored with staring out of the window at the sodden grass, he prowls around the room for a while, picking up objects and putting them down again. Mine soon, he tells himself. Get shot of the lot, I will. Ship it all down to Sammy the Greek's. Fetch a nice price, this old rubbish. He fingers a Meissen shepherdess – once part of a pair, now separated from her rustic swain. Bit fussy for his taste, but some people liked it . . .

'Oh, for heaven's sake – sit down, can't you?' cries Iseult suddenly. Temper, temper, thinks Ray. 'You're making me nervous, creeping about like that . . .'

'Guilty conscience, have we?' grins Ray wolfishly. 'P'raps you're thinking about that handsome *friend* of yours. That Nick. Heard from him lately?'

She doesn't bother to reply, but Leonora – a fantastic apparition in black crêpe, with a towering turban of inky satin, her wrinkled neck and earlobes glittering with jet – pipes up from the sofa, 'Cradle-snatching, *I* call it . . .'

Ray, very pleased with the success of his sally, wanders over to the piano, where the photograph of Sandy, aged eight, with his mum – his two mums – and one remaining aunt, smiles back across the yawning gulf of years.

'Who's this, then?' he says, although he knows very well. 'Auntie I recognize. And this must be Sandy's mum. Or should that be the other way round? But who's this other one? Cracker, *she* is, an' no mistake. Don't tell me it's *you*, Leonora? Blimey. I'd never have guessed it . . .'

He replaces the photo. Runs his hands lightly over the yellowing keys, releasing a tremor of sound. Mum (Gran, that is) liked to tickle the ivories, when she'd had a few. 'Pale hands I loved, beside the Shalimar . . .' he remembers her warbling, in her fruity Guinness contralto. 'Roses are smiling in Picardy . . .' She knew all the old ones, did Mum. Not bad on the old joanna, neither. He's never had the knack. 'Chopsticks'. That's all he knows. He tries a bar or two of the jerky little tune.

'Do you *mind*?' snaps Iseult. 'This is a house of mourning . . .'

He's on the point of telling her what he thinks of *that* one, when the door of the drawing room opens. It's old Cowper, the lawyer, very full of himself in his snazzy pinstripes. 'Would you all mind stepping this way?' he says, pompous old fool. 'Mrs Reason has something particular she wishes to say . . .'

To tell the truth, she's been rather worried about what the old girl might do, because she'd been getting a bit strange of late (Aunt, that is) – and not only since the dreadful events of last week. Iseult knows it isn't fair to blame her for what happened (heaven knows, the poor old thing's been punished enough), but it did occur to her (Iseult) that the whole thing might have been avoided if Aunt had only made her intentions clearer in the first place. Iseult's the first to admit she was in favour of Aunt's drawing up a new will – if only because it would do away with the uncertainty about this wretched money. Even if she ended up leaving the whole lot to the local dogs' home, it would be better than having things up in the air, with all the headache of sorting out what's what when she (Aunt) was no longer around. Although it does seem a bit like shutting the stable door after the horse has bolted, thinks Iseult. Because what good was the money to anyone now?

So here they all are: herself and Mummy and Aunt and old Mr Cowper – looking for all the world like a – what was it? – *murder* of crows, in their black finery. Although Mr Cowper was more a secretary bird, with his gold-rimmed glasses and his watch chain and that funny stiff way of walking . . . As for that horrid, conniving youth, who's sitting over there in the corner smirking to himself, he's a magpie if ever there was one. A carrion crow. Or a . . . (what was that Scotch word for crow?) . . . *corbie*. 'Twa corbies'. She remembers learning it at school:

Ye'll sit on his white breast-bane,
And I'll pluck out his bonny blue e'en
O'er his white bones, when they are bare,
The wind shall blow for evermair . . .

You nasty *corbie*, she hisses silently at Ray.

The room where they are gathered together – a fusty-smelling chamber furnished with worn leather armchairs and shelves full of unread books – used at one time to be Uncle Wilfred's study. Iseult remembers hiding in here from Sandy once, long ago, when she was a child. She recalls the moment now. Crawling under the desk and crouching there, quivering with fright. *Coming to get you* . . . Then the door opening and someone coming in. Her heart beating faster and faster. Heavy footsteps. The realization that it wasn't Sandy, come to find her, but one of the grown-ups. The sudden shock of knowing that it must be Uncle Wilfred. His mild-eyed gaze, as he caught sight of her, cowering there. *Hello! It's little Izzie* . . .

With something of an effort, Iseult drags her thoughts back to the here and now. Mr Cowper's voice droning on. Clause this and clause that. Mummy dabbing her eyes. Aunt gazing off into space. That ghastly boy licking his lips in the corner. Although what *he's* doing here she can't imagine. Not even a member of the family . . . All of a sudden, Iseult is seized by the horrible fear that Aunt is about to do something very silly indeed. Surely she can't be going to leave it all to *him*? She can't suppress a shudder. Rather the dogs' home than *that* . . .

Well, of all the bleeding nerve. I mean, would you fucking credit it? Did you ever in all your born days? The sheer gall of the old woman. Sitting there as meek as you please while that old fart waffled on, pausing every now and then to peer over his bifocals at them as if to say, Aren't *I* the clever one? It wasn't until he'd got to the part about providing an income commensurate with his duties for Raymond Anthony Brown of no fixed address, to wit: one thousand pounds per annum payable in monthly instalments for services rendered viz. domestic help and general factotum to the aforementioned client Constance Alice Reason (née Joliffe) of Dunsinane House Pottersfield Sussex payment of the aforesaid monies to cease on the death of the said client that he'd smelt a rat.

'Say that again,' he'd said.

And the lawyer – after giving him another of those oh-so-superior looks over the rims of his grandad specs – had read it all again, this time much slower, as if Ray were retarded or something, the sneering old stiff. But there it was in black and white: *one thousand pounds per annum*. He'd have to work a hundred years to get what was owed him.

What was a *real* laugh was the way the rest of them acted when they heard the news. As if it was more than he'd any right to expect under the circumstances. As if he ought to be *grateful* or something.

'My word. That's awfully generous, Aunt,' Horse-Face had said, when she'd got the gist of what the arrangement was. 'An annuity. Well, well. I only hope –' condescending sniff – 'your generosity's repaid in kind . . .'

By which she meant working his balls off, of course. Fetching and carrying and generally skivvying for that horrible old woman for the rest of his natural life – or hers. The worst of it was he wouldn't be doing himself any favours by bumping the old girl off. Because then the payments would stop. It was diabolical, that's what it was.

It had all begun so well. When the lawyer had called them into the next room to hear the upshot of his confab with

Auntie, he hadn't suspected a thing. 'Reward,' she'd said. 'You'll get what you deserve,' she'd said. When all the time she'd been intending to diddle him. Oh, he wasn't such a fool as to think he'd get the whole bloody lot (although stranger things had happened). Why else were Horse-Face and her mum hanging around like a pair of vultures if not to make sure they got *their* cut of the loot? But after all he'd done for the old bag he'd expected at least fifty grand. Because if it hadn't been for *him*, she wouldn't be sitting pretty now. She'd be where Sandy was. Pushing up daisies. (With each day that passes, Ray's version of the events surrounding Sandy's death grows less precise; his own part in that unhappy episode more heroic.)

He had summoned them together, the lawyer said, at Mrs Reason's especial request. She was taking the highly unusual but by no means unheard-of step of making the contents of her last will and testament known to those it would in due course concern in order to avoid the conflict of interests which had, it appeared, been a contributory factor in bringing about the sad events of a week ago . . .

'I felt responsible, you know,' the old girl had interrupted at that point. 'Because if poor Sandy hadn't been swayed by the thought of the bequest, he wouldn't have done what he did. It was too much money all at once, you see. A temptation to someone in his position . . .'

With a dear-dear-what-is-the-world-coming-to shake of the head, the lawyer had picked up from where he left off. And Ray was getting his face all ready for the look of pleased and grateful surprise it was going to wear when the announcement came – the one saying that as a reward for his selfless action in preserving the life of the aforementioned etc., etc. he was designated the sole (or at least the major) beneficiary of her will – when the real truth hit him. She'd outfoxed him, the evil old crone. Stitched him up good and proper. Because if he turned it down now, it was going to look bad – as if he'd been planning on getting the money all along. It might even raise unpleasant suspicions about his part in the attempted murder which had hitherto remained dormant. He'd be cutting off his nose to spite his face. And (even if it was measly compared to what he'd bargained for) a thousand smackers a year was better than a kick in the teeth. It was a regular income – something he'd never had before. And there were other perks. His board and lodging for starters. The car. He might even persuade Auntie to keep the flat in Brighton on for weekending purposes. On twenty quid a week he could live like a lord . . .

Even though it hurt worse than poison, he'd managed to pull himself together. Pasted a smirk on his face. Stammered out his surprise (that part at least he didn't have to fake). His delight (that was stretching it a bit). His unworthiness. Blah blah blah. And all the time what he'd really wanted to know was, 'Who's got it? Who's got the money?' Because unless she was planning to live for another hundred years (and he wouldn't put it past her), there'd surely be *some* of it left over when the old woman snuffed it.

It wasn't exactly a surprise to learn that the lucky one was Iseult. Because even after all she'd suffered at the hands of her offspring, the old fool still thought blood was thicker than water. Some people never learned.

The only bright spot was that the longer the old woman lived the less Iseult got in the end. Because his thousand a year had to come off the top, didn't it? So every year is a thousand less in old Iseult's pocket. And that, thinks Ray, is incentive enough as far as he's concerned. Just knowing he's burning a hole in that tidy little fortune is its own reward. Oh, he'll make her pay. He'll have the last laugh yet. If Ray has anything to do with it, Auntie's going to live to be ninety-nine.

II

One Rose That Dies Not

Being dead, he doesn't feel things the way the living do. Such ranting and storms of tears, you'd think it would never end. *His* passions are quieter; more attenuated. A fading out, a dying away. A not quite letting go.

He can't let go. Not yet.

Although in all the long years that came after his first death (that shutting down of all that gave life meaning) he'd thought about it often enough. Because the body was nothing, after the spirit was dead. How glad he'd be to leave his poor carcass behind – to leave it all behind. His memories most of all. It wouldn't take much. One shot, through the roof of the mouth. He'd seen a man finished off like that. A merciful release from a living hell.

It was she who'd held him back. Not knowing it, half the time. (Though once when he was bad, he'd noticed she'd put away the gun.) She'd stood between him and his nightmares. Calmed him with her voice, her touch. Like gentling a frightened horse, the way he'd seen men do out in France with the beasts that pulled the gun-carriages. *Their* terror – poor creatures – had been worse than anything human. Screams. He hadn't known till then how beasts could scream. Men, too.

She'd kept him from all that. The faces in his dreams. She'd brought him out of the tomb where he'd lain confined. Neurasthenia, the doctors said. Morbid imaginings. All he knew was he'd been in darkness (a restless darkness, full of cries and groans) and then Constance had come and rolled away the stone . . .

He'd known the minute he saw her that she was the one. 'Too old,' his mother had said, with a disparaging sniff, because of the five years' difference in their ages, but it hadn't been a serious objection. They both knew by then that what he needed was a nurse, not a wife. And Mother had Father to care for. The girl seemed quiet enough. Marriage was a bargain, his mother said. His was no worse than most. So it was settled. His life – the forty-odd years that remained of it – had been placed in Constance's safekeeping. A poor bargain for her, he sometimes thought.

He'd known about the child, of course. He can't recall exactly when the situation became clear to him. Had Constance told him herself? He rather thinks not. Perhaps he'd gleaned the information indirectly, from sidelong looks and whispered conversations. An indiscreet remark let slip by one of the sisters . . . It doesn't matter now.

He remembers the way her voice changed when she spoke to the boy. The light in her eyes. For days before Alexander was expected on one of his visits (increasingly few and far between as the years went by), she'd be distracted. Moving from room to room in a fruitless attempt to set the house to rights. Bursting into fits of tears or freakish laughter. Sometimes he'd wondered if it wouldn't have been better for them all if the boy had been sent away: somewhere far off – Canada or Australia – to make his way. He'd never ventured such an opinion, of course. He had no children. It wasn't his place to speak.

But this latest visit was different. Even before they'd set foot in the house, he'd known it would come to no good. Being dead, he's sensitive to atmosphere. And this was evil. A stench of death had filled every room in the house. Against his will, he'd been drawn by the smell – which was the smell of the fearful passions they'd brought with them. Interlopers.

All he'd meant to do was warn her. Make her see what sort of viper she'd nursed in her bosom all those years. But she'd been deaf to his warnings. Perhaps the truth had been too much for her to bear . . .

He regrets what happened that night, but it isn't his fault. The living make their own catastrophes. All he could do, he'd done.

Now Alexander is dead. His bloody, reproachful ghost hangs about the hall, awaiting its ticket of leave. One thing remains to do, before either of them can depart. A usurper sits at the head of the table now. A boy with a black heart and the face of a long-dead child. It won't be easy to persuade him to go, but it must be done, for Constance's sake.

If dreams won't shake him, then other things might. Footsteps outside his door. A shape brushing past on the stairs. Objects disarranged on a dressing table. Clothes scattered around a room . . . All these, given time, will do their work – even for one without remorse or imagination. He'll not stay long, the boy. Soon, the house will be empty of all but its rightful tenants.

12

Honourable Ladies

Connie sits, as she has sat many times in the four months since the funeral, on a bench in the churchyard, overlooking a row of gravestones, one of which is new. Sheltered by the church wall from the underlying chill of a fine October afternoon, she narrows her eyes against the bright sunshine and allows her thoughts to dwell on him: her poor Sandy. How much she misses him. How clearly she can picture him in her mind's eye. The dearest little boy. Bright as a button. She can see him now, at seven or eight, with those round blue eyes looking up at her from under his silky fringe. ('Look, Auntie. My new knife. Isn't it wizard? It's got six blades *and* a corkscrew . . .') And then, a few years later, when he'd got the Latin prize for his translation of Catullus, and she'd taken him to lunch at the George to celebrate: 'I say, Auntie, this is most frightfully good of you. I feel as if I haven't eaten for at least a week. School food is so unutterably vile . . .' Such a tall chap he was then – and getting so handsome. Already the image of his father. She remembers thinking (helping him to more roast potatoes) that he might break a few hearts, in a year or so. Well, she hadn't been wrong about that . . .

Her gaze lights on Iseult, who is kneeling on the grass a few feet away, tending a grave. It is Sandy's grave. My only child, thinks Connie, feeling once more the sharp pang – like a sword through the heart – that accompanies the thought. She watches as her niece carefully tips out the stale water from a stone vase of chrysanthemums and pulls out a stray weed. From a large canvas bag lying on the ground at her side, Iseult takes out a trowel and something wrapped in brown paper, which, unwrapped, turns out to be a small rose bush (a crimson Tuscany Superb – they'd chosen it together). This she holds out over the grave's uneven turf so that Connie can see the effect.

'What do you think, Aunt?'

'Lovely, dear,' says Connie.

'I think in the middle, don't you? Rather than at the foot? Because it'll need a bit of space to grow . . .'

'Whatever you say, dear.'

Iseult nods as if satisfied, and sets to work, cutting away the turf over the centre of the grave where the rose is to stand, and then starting to dig. She sings under her breath as she works, in a light, tuneless voice. Connie catches a word now and then. *I'm a believer*. One of those new-fangled hymns, evidently. It isn't one she knows. She thinks to herself how well Iseult is looking. Quite full in the face, dear thing. Having her hair cut short rather suits her. She'd had it done one day a month or so ago, after the funeral . . .

Oh, where did I go wrong? thinks Connie. How did it come to this?

Of course, after Oxford he was never really happy. Peggy'd blamed the 'set' he'd got into – a fast lot, apparently. They'd led her boy astray, according to Peggy. Given him a taste for expensive things. Encouraged him to live beyond his means . . . Connie doesn't entirely accept this account of things. She wonders now if perhaps there'd been a love affair which hadn't worked out. That was enough to send anybody off the rails. Certainly, Sandy's character had changed in those years – from that of the sweet-natured boy she'd known to that of the cool, rather cynical young man he was to remain. As much a puzzle to her as his father had been. Bad blood, Leonora said, but that was all rot . . .

She gazes – with what to a casual observer might appear vacancy – over the churchyard, whose humped mounds and leaning tombstones are interspersed by an occasional, grander edifice. When she was a child she'd thought they were beds – a confusion not helped by the tendency, in literature as in the liturgy of the Christian Church, to treat sleep and death as synonymous states:

> Sleep on my Love in thy cold bed
> Never to be disquieted!

Another of Wilfred's favourites. She'd always thought it rather morbid – a love poem to a dead wife – but then, death was more a fact of life in the seventeenth century, she supposes. And there was, after all, something rather splendid in the idea of a love that outlasted death – although it was a bit unfortunate for the poet's second wife . . .

It occurs to Connie, shifting a little on her bench to dispel the stiffness in her joints, that there are already more of the family in the churchyard than out of it. Soon, she'll join them. Father and Mother (united in death after a hiatus of thirty years) and Cyril (but not yet Leonora) and Peggy (a bare year after Harold) and Hugh (who was present in name only; his body lay somewhere in Belgium) and Julian (full fathom five) and Poppy (the mother outliving the son by as many years as the latter had been alive) and Wilfred (can it really be three years?) and now Sandy. One death too many, in a lifetime filled with death.

'There.' Iseult has finished her planting and now surveys her handiwork with some satisfaction. 'Doesn't look too bad, does it?' she says, brushing the earth from her hands.

'It's splendid.' Connie gets up. Slowly, with the tottering steps that have become habitual (like having bound feet, she sometimes feels), she walks towards the grave. 'He'd have been so pleased,' she says.

'Hope so,' says Iseult gruffly. She makes as if to rise.

'Let me help you, dear,' says Connie.

'Thanks, Aunt. I can manage.' But it is with a visible effort that she heaves herself back on to her feet. 'Getting fat,' she says, panting a little.

'Mmm,' says the old woman.

They stand side by side for a few minutes longer, contemplating the newly appointed grave. Its clean white stone and sharply incised inscription are pleasing to the eye. *I am the Resurrection and the Life.*

'I like the way he's done the lettering, old Mr Cardew. Roman, isn't it?' says Iseult.

'I believe so. It generally is, unless one asks for Gothic.'

'Rather bold and masculine. *Dear* Sandy,' says Iseult, with a rush of feeling. 'I do miss him so.'

'Dearest Iseult. You two were always such chums. I believe he loved you . . .' Connie hesitates a second. 'In his own way.'

'I know. I mean . . . I . . . I was awfully fond of him, too.'

There is a brief silence, which is broken at last by Iseult.

'The thing is, Aunt Con,' she says. 'I've started a child.'

'I rather thought you had,' her aunt replies, with a quick sideways glance.

Iseult pulls a face. 'It's getting obvious, isn't it? Although Mummy hasn't noticed yet. She merely thinks I've been eating my head off. I dread telling her,' she says. 'Mummy can be so . . . well, *stuffy* about things like that . . .'

'Oh, I shouldn't worry about your mother. Mothers usually come round in the end.'

Another pause; this time it is broken by Connie.

'Does the father know?'

'No.'

'I should keep it that way,' says Connie lightly. 'That is, unless you've a particular reason not to.'

'I can't imagine why I'd want to tell him. He's hardly likely to welcome the news, is he?'

'I wouldn't have thought so. Best to leave things as they are.'

Which is only what she's told herself all along, Iseult reminds herself, conscious nonetheless of a momentary pang of disappointment. Anything else would be ridiculous. Entirely impractical. And yet there have been moments, daydreaming over her first cigarette of the day or mucking out the cowshed, when she's allowed her thoughts to stray in a different direction. Permitting herself to think the unthinkable. Because it *is* unthinkable – the idea that she might get in touch with Nick de Vil again. Out of the question, Iseult tells herself sternly.

All the same, it was rather a shock to turn on the television the other day, expecting Hughie Green, and see instead *his* face staring back at her, in sharp black and white. Looking paler than ever under the harsh studio lights, and with his hair tied back with a velvet bow, like a rather effete Dick Turpin. As she'd watched him sleepwalk his way through the verses of the song, while a trio of girls in preposterously short skirts gyrated in the background ('Ooh, Ooh, Vampire Love . . .'), she'd thought of their stolen hour together in the topsy-turvy bedroom. How sweet he'd been. After all that's happened, it's no small consolation to know that someone, for however brief a time, once wanted her. Although in all probability it meant rather less to him . . .

'You'll be well looked after here,' Aunt Con is saying. 'After all, it's not as if you're going to be short of money, when I die . . .'

'Don't say such things,' says Iseult. 'You're going to live for ever, Aunt. Why, if it comes to that, I've quite enough money of my own. When the baby comes –' how strange it felt to hear the words spoken aloud! – 'I shall just jog along as I always have.'

'I'm very glad to hear it,' says Connie.

'Enough about me,' says Iseult. 'How are you getting along, Aunt? You know, I meant what I said about doing out the spare room for you . . .'

'Thank you, dear. But I shall manage for a while yet, I think. Although admittedly the house is rather too large for one person . . .'

'That *wretched* boy,' says Iseult.

'My dear,' objects Connie mildly.

'Well, I ask you!' cries Iseult indignantly. 'Leaving you in the lurch like that. Without a word of warning. Disgraceful, *I* call it.'

'Now, now,' says Connie. 'One really mustn't jump to conclusions. There was probably a very good reason why Julian . . .'

'Ray, you mean.'

'Ray. Of course. Why *Ray* decided to go. Perhaps he was called away on urgent family business . . .'

'But you said yourself he didn't have a family . . .'

'. . . or maybe he simply got tired of living with an old woman. The young have different preoccupations, you know.'

Iseult gives a contemptuous snort.

'At any rate, he's gone,' says Connie. 'No sense in worrying about it unduly.'

'Good riddance, say I . . .'

'Sometimes I think you were a little hard on poor Ray,' says Connie. 'He was of *some* use, after all. Look at the way he took charge of clearing up the house. Getting rid of all that dreadful, old-fashioned stuff. It's so much less cluttered now . . .'

'I just hope you didn't let him take away anything of value,' says Iseult.

'Oh, I don't think so,' murmurs Connie. 'It's rather hard to say. But, you know, I think one tends to attach too much importance to things.'

Iseult's only response is a sniff.

Dear thing. She means so well, thinks Connie. And perhaps she'd been right about Ray. He *had* been a bit unreliable. Going off like that a month ago, without a bit of notice. He'd taken the car, too (not that she needed it back). Since then – not so much as a postcard to say where he'd gone. Rather odd. But then, she'd always been drawn to unsuitable men. Men like Strickland – a thoroughly bad lot, she has to admit (but charming with it). Men like her poor, dear Sandy. Wilfred was the exception – but really, it was he who'd chosen her, not the other way about. She'd never expected – or deserved – such devotion.

Arm in arm, the two ladies have been walking slowly back along the gravel pathway towards the church, on the spire of which (a mid-Victorian addition to the Norman tower) a brazen weathercock flashes in the light. It really is a lovely day, thinks Iseult, her heart lifting. Yellow leaves against a blue sky; a warm, golden light over everything. Season of mists and all that. Iseult isn't much of a one for poetry, but some things hit the nail on the head. Mellow fruitfulness. She'd always rather liked that bit . . .

Reaching the lych-gate, they stand, face to face, among drifts of fallen leaves.

'Well, my dear,' says Connie, 'are you coming back for a spot of lunch?'

'Thanks, Aunt. Better not,' says Iseult. 'You know Mummy can't bear to be left for very long. By the by,' she adds. 'I did think that when the time comes I might hire a nurse. For Mummy, you know . . .'

'What a very good idea,' says Connie.

'Because I shall have my hands full – what with the farm, and the young 'un, and so on . . .'

'You will, rather,' says Connie. 'But I'm sure you'll manage splendidly.'

'Oh, I know some people will object, but let them,' Iseult says stoutly. 'I've gone my own way too long to care much what people think . . .'

Because life would go on as it always had, she thinks contentedly. She'd get by. More than that, she'd get by on her own. If it meant selling off another field or two to cover the expense of bringing up a child, well, she'd have to do it, that's all. Father wouldn't have minded. He'd have understood. She'd never say as much to Aunt, but she hadn't the smallest intention of touching the money. She'd rather die. The memory of Sandy's face, as she'd seen it, that last day, was enough to keep her from avaricious desires. Even so, it was nice to think of what would be by then a considerable fortune sitting nice and safe in the bank, gathering interest for years and years, until that distant, hitherto undreamt of day when (the vicissitudes of his mother's life and the irregular nature of his conception notwithstanding) her son – *her* Alexander – would turn twenty-one and come into his inheritance at last.